This major novel offers a vision of hope for the future: Citation of Alexander Blackburn's *The Voice of the Children in the Apple Tree* for the International Peace Writing Award.

Cover illustration image: *Trinity Test,*
July 16, 1945, Alamogordo Air Base, New Mexico
Image Courtesy: U.S. Department of Energy

Books by Alexander Blackburn

Author

Novels

The Voice of the Children in the Apple Tree
The Door of the Sad People
Suddenly a Mortal Splendor
The Cry of Every Human Heart *

Literary Criticism

The Myth of the Picaro

A Sunrise Brighter Still: The Visionary Novels of Frank Waters

Autobiography/Biography

Meeting the Professor: Growing up in the William Blackburn Family

Essays

Creative Spirit: Toward a Better World

Editor

Anthologies & a Collection

The Interior Country: Stories of the Modern West (with Craig Lesley)

Higher Elevations: Stories from the West

Gifts from the Heart: Stories, Memories, & Chronicles of Lucille Gonzales Oller

Literary Magazine

Writers' Forum, 21 vols. (with Craig Lesley, Bret Lott, and Victoria McCabe)

*published originally as *The Cold War of Kitty Pentecost*

THE VOICE
OF THE CHILDREN
IN THE APPLE TREE

A Novel

by

Alexander Blackburn

EAST OF THE MOUNTAINS

AND WEST OF THE SUN

RHYOLITE PRESS LLC
Colorado Springs, Colorado

Published in the United States of America by
Rhyolite Press, LLC
P.O. Box 2406
Colorado Springs, Colorado 80901

www.rhyolitepress.com

Blackburn, Alexander
The Voice of the Children in the Apple Tree / Alexander Blackburn
1st ed. January 2015

Library of Congress Control Number: 2014956913

ISBN 978-0-9896763-2-8

PRINTED AND BOUND IN THE UNITED STATES OF AMERICA

Cover design, book design, illustrations & typographical layout by Donald R. Kallaus

Inés, always

CONTENTS

Part I: The Rich Girl

Part II: The Physicist

Part III: The Planetary Imperative

I alone, in one sense, support the common dignity that I cannot allow myself or others to debase. This individualism is in no sense pleasure, it is a perpetual struggle and, sometimes, unparalleled joy when it reaches the heights of *intrepid compassion*. We shall choose Ithaca, the faithful land, frugal and audacious thought, lucid action, the generosity of the man who understands. Our brothers are breathing under the same sky; justice is a living thing. Now is born that strange joy which helps one live and die, and which we shall never again renounce to a later time. On the sorrowing earth it is the unresting thorn, the bitter food, the harsh wind off the sea, the ancient dawn forever renewed. With this joy, through long struggle, we shall remake the soul of our time . . . [emphasis added]

Albert Camus, *The Rebel*

During his [Secretary of War Henry L. Stimson's] recitation of the relevant facts, I had been conscious of a feeling of depression and so I voiced to him my grave misgivings, first on the basis of my belief that Japan was already defeated and that dropping the bomb was completely unnecessary, and secondly because I thought our country should avoid shocking world opinion by the use of a weapon whose employment was, I thought, no longer mandatory as a measure to save lives.

General Dwight D. Eisenhower

Supreme Commander of the Allied Expeditionary Force who directed British and American operations against Germany and who subsequently became President of the United States of America

PART I

The Rich Girl

1

TRINC

UNCONFINED AND VIRGIN AND WILD the land lies open to the Riders. Motionless waves of a boundless sea of prairie bear the transmogrifying imprints of dark scudding clouds. There are no Indian trails to be seen, no wagon tracks, no telegraph poles. Tumbleweeds snag on no fences. A herd of antelope flows over the shimmering wind-rippled grass as if never touching it. The sun blossoms poppy-strange through heat haze even while lightning silently spiderwebs the horizon with a radiance like violently shaken tin foil.

Hoof-thunder accompanied by whoops and yelps and whistlings breaks silence. A jack-rabbit twitches his ears above a clump of greasewood and sagebrush. A rattlesnake coils. A covey of quail bursts fluttering from the land and leaves long streaks of grief in the air. The Riders appear, first their heads with the high-crowned wide-brimmed hats blown back, then their leaning bodies, bandannas, blue or maroon shirts, gloves, chaps, boots. Their rifles and revolvers are gripped. Momentarily the Riders seem to disappear, gulped down into earth. All is silent again. Suddenly the Riders, undwarfed against the sky, come galloping out of the arroyos and cutbanks that hid them. Ear-splitting cries mingle with nostril-snortings and the strains of horsebreath against looped-up reins.

"Hee-yah! Yippee!"

A mixed pack of wolves and coyotes runs zigzagedly just in front of the onrushing strangers. One great gray wolf looms, leaps, glides, swerves, and finally stops running and heavily pants. The pack is encircled.

When shots ring out, first in isolated pops, then in withering volleys, there is a roiling, writhing mass of screaming animals. After a while the wolves and coyotes lie still, limbs stiffening, eyes rolled up in sockets.

The great gray wolf remains alive, unscathed. He besieges with hate the stinking strangers who blot out his sky. A lasso loops down and catches him around the throat.

The person who has thrown the lasso is a tall, broad-shouldered man in his mid-forties. His blond Van Dyke beard and handlebar mustache give him a vague resemblance to Buffalo Bill. There is also something Roman encoded in the long nose, the straight mouth, the dark, level-shadowed eyes. He leaps from his mount, having tied the rope to his saddle. With practiced hand he loosens a Colt .44-caliber revolver in the holster at his hip. There is a quietening among the Riders as the man moves one cautious step at a time toward the wolf who bristles, upper lip flayed back from the teeth. With one swoop the man yanks the rope and lunges. Before the wolf can bite, the man thrusts a gloved hand deep down the slavering maw. Presently the wolf is bound tightly with rope. The man flashes a grin to a Rider, hammers fist toward sky.

"Yah!"

The Rider is a plump man with spectacles and jutting teeth that gleam behind a mustache shaped like an inverted "V." He raises his rifle. "Bully!" he cries. The Riders cheer and discharge their weapons. The sound reverberates across the land until silence returns, falling like a shroud.

"UNCLE DOC?"

The man known to the medical world as Dr. William Nathaniel Knight, personal physician to President Theodore Roosevelt but to his family as "Uncle Doc," finished swallowing a cucumber sandwich and smiled at his guest, the little six-year-old girl dressed in a pinafore and wearing two blue ribbons in her long auburn-colored hair. She was seated across a small tea-table from him and next to his wife, Emma, or "Auntie Em" in the language of the tribe.

"What is it, Trinc?" Uncle Doc's tone was solicitous. He had noticed during tea that she had been reserved, a sadness in her usually laughing eyes.

Trinc bit her lip. "You know that big bad wolf you captured?"

Uncle Doc nodded slowly. "Your father read to you my wolf story, did he? In my letter to him I never said the wolf was bad. He was majestic, he was magnificent, neither good nor bad. It is my nonscientific opinion he had a soul, the soul of a brave warrior . . . Go on, princess. What do you want to know?"

"Did he die?"

"Not to my knowledge."

"Did you put him in a zoo?"

"Why would I put him in a zoo?"

"Father said. He said you captured him for the zoo."

After glancing quickly at Em, Uncle Doc masked—and not for the first time that day—his annoyance with Gayle DeRoman, Trinc's father and husband to Em's niece, Hen. "Well," he said, "I don't know where your daddy gets his information. You can tell him from me that Uncle Doc would never, ever, put behind a fence a wild animal born to be free."

Trinc stared at him with large brown eyes from which the sadness now seemed to disappear. "Good," she said.

For a moment there swam behind Uncle Doc's eyes a vision of Rough Riders gathered in Oklahoma for the hunt and in San Antonio for the reunion with Roosevelt. They were good, simple cowboys who would have followed their leader to the ends of the earth. Teddy loved the Riders as if they were his own children.

Passing, the moment kindled Uncle Doc's feelings of devotion. He was back home again in New York, celebrating a reunion with his own devotees, Emma ever the rosy-cheeked New Englander, ever the bred-in-the-bone lady dressed in a taffeta ballgown, and Trinc, ever the child he would never have, ever the princess who wore, as he knew, those blue ribbons just for him. He shifted in his chair. "Well," he drawled, "I'll tell you . . . Some folks figure wolves and coyotes are just varmints. From their point of view it's necessary and proper to have a shoot-up party once in a while to thin out the ranks of predators. Can't say I agree with them, but Teddy likes his trophies, you know . . . Anyway, when I saw that wolf, I decided to lay a rope on him before any of the cowboys got more bloodthirsty than they already were. The upshot of it was, I took that wolf with me to San Antone. When I arrived there, I paid an honest-lookin' fella who was heading up for some gold-prospecting in the San Juans, in the wildest part of New Mexico Territory, to turn the wolf a-loose up there. Too many buzzard-pissin' people moving into the land nowadays, fencing things in . . . Look-a-here, princess," Uncle Doc went on in another voice. "Maybe you wanted that wolf for a pet?"

He had fired this shot across Trinc's bow in order to make her feel a tickle in her funnybone. He saw that he had succeeded. Her mouth had dropped open. The impish sense of humor which was part of their secret bond lit up her face. She burst into a fit of giggles. Her Auntie Em, sensing a game, took her side. "Billy Knight, as I live and breathe," she exclaimed with a roll of eyes, "if I didn't know you so well, I'd think you were serious about giving her a wolf for a pet! Isn't he silly, Trinc? Can you imagine what Daddy and Mummy would do if you had a wolf for a pet? Shame on you, Uncle Doc." Em moved a finger atop another finger in the shaming sign. Trinc did the same, tease-laughter erupting: "Shame on Uncle Doc! Shame on Uncle Doc!"

"Goodness!" He ducked head and waved hands as if surrounded by a mob of villagers throwing stones. "Come now, no fair. Don't you think, princess, your parents would want you to have a pet?"

A look of wild disdain came over Trinc's face. "They don't even want *me!*" The spontaneous, bleak, and incontestably honest verdict of the child sent Uncle Doc's emotions sprawling. He heard a far-off, deep-down rumbling of a subway train as if it were a reminder of old hollowness in his life and Em's, the one they had filled with fidelity in love. Was he overstepping the boundaries between the Knights and the DeRomans, enticing their child away from them? Surely there was no harm in expressing to a child one's warmth and affection. This was especially an entitlement of families. He snapped fingers in the air.

Mary Mulligan, cook and parlor maid, had been hovering near the tea-table, awaiting precisely this signal. She glided out of the room. He watched her long, braided red hair with bow-knot ribbons catch fire in a shaft of afternoon sun slanting in from the East Seventy-Second Street window. Then he leaned across the table, took Trinc's hands in his. "Of course they want you," he said. "Some people just don't show their true feelings as readily as others." He squeezed Trinc's hands before releasing them, sat back and again snapped fingers.

Mary Mulligan came gliding back into the room. The shaft of sunlight illuminated the little cage she was carrying. A furry white guinea pig inside the cage made a sound like *queek*. "And now, ladies," Uncle Doc intoned magisterially, "it gives me great pleasure to present to Miss Susan Heartwell DeRoman, also known as Trinc, the one and only Puff Ball, henceforth and forever her very own Mr. Puff Ball DeRoman!"

"And very well indade is Mr. Puff Ball," said Mary Mulligan. She set the cage on the table in front of Trinc. "It has plased himself to have a foine tay of carrots. So, noo, we open his lordship's cage—so . . . We lift him oot gently. So. He's light as a feather. We stroke his fur—so. And aren't we grand this day with our pink eyes and quiverin' nose? Here's the missus, and no shenanigans noo."

He had hoped that Trinc would not flinch from the animal, that she would take him in her spiky arms and lift him up to her face and let him lick it, and that there would be laughter from the young heart and some proper moistening of the eyes. So it came to pass. When Trinc exclaimed, "He loves me all over!," Uncle Doc felt so touched that, without thinking of what he was doing, he spread marmalade on a cucumber sandwich and ate the stuff in a kind of rapture.

Some while later the DeRoman governess, Miss Bridgit, came to fetch Trinc home. Uncle Doc accompanied them downstairs to the front door. He bent down and brushed his pointy beard across Trinc's chin. "Goodbye, princess," he said. "Take good care of Puff Ball."

Miss Bridgit, who was holding the cage away from her starched uniform, met his glance with a frosty disapproval.

"I will," said Trinc. "Thank you, Uncle Doc." She came and threw her arms around his neck and kissed him on the cheek.

"Buzzard-pissin' hell!" he roared a few minutes later as he returned to Em's companionship in the upstairs parlor. "What's wrong with Gayle DeRoman?" He paced the floor with hands thrust into trouser pockets in order to control his itch to pick up a piece of Victorian bric-a-brac and smash it against a wall.

Em, who was seated on a sofa, quoted matter-of-factly, "'Happy homes are all alike. Unhappy homes'—" The misquotation did not improve his mood.

"Damn Tolstoy . . . Excuse me," he said. From his coat pocket he extracted an envelope and waved it in the air. "See this letter? The other day I wrote to Gayle, telling him about the trip with Teddy, and I happened to introduce the subject of Trinc's nickname. I was just giving him a cue so that he would feel at ease and exhibit his talent for telling a charming story . . . Well, he did reply in that manner, to some extent. But the fella has taken offense."

"He's an exhibitionist," Em said. "You've often said so."

"Exactly. But his egotism never got me good and sore before.

It's all very well for Hen, I suppose. She copes by pretending to be deaf, sticking that trumpet of hers in her ear where it sprouts like a metallic lily whenever he blusters. He's really a pussycat, really, in his way, an amiable soul. He evidently cannot forgive Hen for bearing him a daughter instead of a son. If I were Trinc's father . . ."

Uncle Doc cut the phrase off. He slumped on the sofa, took Em's hands in his. "Forgive me, darling," he sighed. "I'm not angry with the DeRomans or anybody else. I can't save the world."

With this awkward speech to his adored, barren wife, his anger did in fact melt. In its place what he felt for all the parents and all the children in the world was indeed compassion, perhaps a compassion which seemed to him paltry in proportion to the need for it, but none the less compassion.

Letter from Gayle DeRoman, dated June 3, 1905, from New York, New York, to Dr. William Nathaniel Knight, the same:

Bacbuc throw'd I don't know what into the Fountain, and strait its Water began to boil in good earnest, just for the world as doth the great Monastical Pot at Bourgueil, when 'tis High Holiday there. Friend Panurge was list'ning with one Ear, and Bacbuc kneeled by him, when such a kind of Humming was heard out of the Bottle, as is made by a Swarm of Bees . . . Immediately after this was heard the word TRINC.

Bacbuc arose, and gently taking Panurge under the Arms, said, Friend, Offer your Thanks to Indulgent Heaven, as Reason requires, you have soon had the Word of the Goddess Bottle; and the kindest, most favourable and certain Word of Answer that I ever yet heard her give since I officiate here at her most Sacred Oracle: Rise, let us go to the Chapter, in whose gloss that fine Word is explain'd. With all my Heart, quoth Panurge; by Jingo, I am just as wise as I was last Year: Light, where's the Book. Turn it over, where's that Chapter; Let's see this merry Gloss.

The Works of Mr. Francis Rabelais

My dear Uncle Doc,

I have taken the liberty to copy out for you the passage from Monsieur Rabelais wherein the Oracle of the Bottle utters the Word—TRINC. If we could but agree that the Oracle does not encourage alcoholism as a substitute for Divine Revelation— but, rather, to celebrate that Joy of Life for which TRINC must needs serve as a metaphor—then, sir, we have no quarrel. Would I so name my daughter as to give offense to the very physician who is famed far and wide for treating alcoholism as a disease instead of as a deficiency in moral virtue? To my own Rabelaisian propensities, I enter a plea of guilty. Construe them as weakness of character if you will. I had hoped for better from my wife Hen's uncle-in-law, from our little Susan's beloved "Uncle Doc". I must trust your judgment absolutely. I shall not presume upon it to the extent of believing that Uncle Doc and Auntie Em—if not the Heartwell clan as a whole—no longer accept me the way I am.

Therefore, Sir, your recent inquiry leaves me puzzled as to where I stand. I refer to your letter of Wednesday instant. Your question comes out of a whirlwind of criticalness, to wit: "How, Gayle, did you find a nickname like Trinc for your only child, Susan Heartwell DeRoman?"

I shall reply to your implied allegations presently.

First, let me congratulate you upon your adventures with the President in the West. O to be Teddy's close friend and physician! Now that we are united in the same family, your Em and my Hen being treasures rescued from spinsterhood in Connecticut, my esteem for you swells into justifiable pride. *Trinc* adores you. Because, sadly, you and Em have no children of your own, permit me to boast of the pleasures a father receives in reading aloud to his six-year-old clown. I read to her the "western" portion of your letter. Her eyes, already so Heartwellian brown and large, were rounded in wonder. She became your phantom partner in the saddle nine hours a day when you and Teddy went wolf hunting in Oklahoma, galloping over the cutbanks, prairie dog towns, and flats and creek bottoms, whooping like savages, and shooting dozens of wolves and coyotes and rattlesnakes with your rifles and revolvers! How *Trinc* squealed in delight when I gave your description of the wolf whom you captured by thrusting your gloved hand down between its jaws, that he might not bite you while you tied him up!

Verily, I believe she would give heart and soul to become a Rough Rider and a professional wolf hunter—or just a boy. Were it in my power to transform the destiny to which Nature has confined her, I would gladly encourage the sexual metamorphosis. Alas, she is but a girl. At least she's a good little Stoic. Unlike her Yankee mother, she does not have to read *The Meditations of Marcus Aurelius* in order to learn that there is naught of comfort in this vale of tears. *Trinc*, unlike Hen, does not retire to bed whenever there is the slightest pain, real or imagined.

I myself am named after an ancestor, John Gayle, the Governor of Alabama. His beloved wife was Susan. My Susan was named after her. I should be quite content were my Susan to remain a Susan, but my Susan prefers the name from the Goddess Oracle — *Trinc*. Although it is perhaps an insult to the memory of Susan Gayle, to suppose that her name could ever be filled by anything so good, *Trinc* will stamp her foot and scream if Hen or I or the governess or the servants dare try to instill in her a proper sense of her forebears.

Trinc, I verily believe, repudiates all of us. Except, of course, "Uncle Doc". The union of the Heartwells of Connecticut and the DeRomans of Louisiana moves her not a jot . . .

Now I shall specifically address your question, "How, Gayle, did you find a nickname like *Trinc* for your only child, Susan Heartwell DeRoman?"

The answer is, I didn't. *Trinc* herself was both Muse and Oracle.

She was not yet three years old when we were living in New Orleans, just before I resigned my law practice there to take up my present position in the law firm on Wall Street.

We always had a bottle of French claret on the table at dinner. Every two or three years a great hogshead of it would arrive from Bordeaux, and I as a child would watch with interest the operations of the bottlers as they washed the old bottles, then filled and corked them. The wine was stored in the round brick closet which constituted the foundation of the big cistern that supplied our drinking and washing water.

Well, one evening Hen and I were to entertain a few friends to dinner. Not many years earlier I had graduated from Tulane University Law School. I played foot-ball for Tulane in 1893; I scored a touchdown, from my position as tackle, in a match with L.S.U.; and our friends were from the foot-ball crowd at Tulane . . . Two hours before the party I set out to make an inspection of preparations. Hen was upstairs suffering from one of her attacks of nervous colitis. I assumed that little Susan was also upstairs and that Nanette, her sixteen-year-old Negro nanny, had tucked her into bed.

Therefore I limited my inspection to the downstairs.

Everything seemed to be *comme il faut*. The candelabras were lit. The oval mirrors reflected the portrait of Susan Gayle, wearing a rose-colored dress with low square neck trimmed with appliquée lace, topaz necklace, diamond pendants, and pink and white plumes. The Hepplewhite mahogany furniture gleamed. A freshly ironed damask cloth was spread over the dining table; it cascaded to the parquet floor. The table was set with pieces inherited from my father, Colonel Tom DeRoman. The English silver was polished. The Louis Quatorze plates were spotless. The Venetian finger bowls, the crystal wine goblets—all—all was in order except one thing: the bottle of claret. This wine was not on the table as it should have been. When I went to the round brick closet, I found that the bottle had disappeared. I came to the conclusion that someone in my own household had removed the precious liquor!

Hen? I asked myself. Although abstinence does not contribute to connubial bliss, Henrietta does not drink. Ever since we were married she has campaigned against what she is privileged to call my vulgarity—i.e., consuming alcoholic beverages, smoking Havana cigars, and sprinkling Tabasco sauce on my food. But her methods have never been underhanded. I eliminated Hen from suspicion.

That left Mammy Victoire.

Mammy Victoire, my cook, was a mulatress who wore a bright plaid chignon tied around her head. She was reputed to be a "lowdown Voo-doo mama," a powerful personage presiding over incantations at moonlight in the swamps. Powerful or not, Mammy Victoire had a temper which flared into a blaze upon the slightest provocation. I had no desire to risk an undignified confrontation with a low-down Voo-doo mama.

Yet in the circumstances I had no choice but to march into the kitchen. Finding neither the bottle nor Mammy Victoire there, I peeped into the back yard. There she was, busily chopping heads off of chickens and crooning, "Ah, mes bébés, lay still, you-all, lay still. Mais oui! Mais oui! Mammy Victoire takes youall to Heaven. Youall quine to de gate ob Heaven. Dey's room an' to spare in de golden house ob Heaven . . . Jois petits. I puts youall on de block an' I—axes you *dade!*" With this, she swung the axe in her right hand from on high—*thunk!* Bright blood squirted upon her face. She dropped a headless chicken into swamp grass. It went flip-flop, flip-flop. I tell you, I could feel the keen edge of her axe tickling the back of my neck. The subject of missing wine was to be approached most delicately.

I cleared my throat and essayed quietly, "Mammy Victoire, those chickens will taste mighty fine tonight."

She glared at me as if I were beneath contempt, then nodded, "Uh-huh." Returning to her work, she pounced upon another chicken and threw her hapless victim upon the block with the efficiency of a Robespierrist. Feathers soon see-sawed in wet air.

"Especially," I continued, "when we drink our toast to the cook. With claret from France."

She went and got another squawking victim before she paused and cracked her toothless grin. "Parbleu, Mistuh Dare-o-man, I ain't studyin' no wine." She raised her axe.

"I have a small problem," I said. "The problem is, this house has the haunts."

I had measured my words carefully. Mammy Victoire lowered the axe and peered at me a-squint as if she were threading a needle. The chicken blood on her face was like mud from volcanic springs. "Haunts?" she repeated in a whisper.

"Why, surely it's haunts, Mammy Victoire. Don't you recollect seeing a wine bottle rise from the dining table all by itself? Didn't you see the bottle floating on the air, like a cork in a cistern, leaving the dining room, and entering the kitchen, all by itself? There are haunts drinking my wine!"

Her lips rolled back from pink gums. She began to roar with laughter. "Hee hee hee! Parbleu! Parbleu!" Dropping chicken and axe into grass, she bent forwards and backwards several times. Finally, she stopped laughing. "Lor', Mistuh Dare-o-man," she declared, "dat ain't no haunts . . . Seem like, though, I *did* done see dat bottle floatin' in the air. Hit done gone upstair."

"Upstairs?"

She nodded, meaningfully. "Yo petite chat unnerneath dat bottle."

"My little cat?"

"Miss Susan done take hit."

I thanked Mammy Victoire and ran to the house and upstairs to the nursery.

What a sight met me there! Nanette swaying her hips, clapping her hands, and singing, eyes closed, *my* song!

> *Auprés de ma blonde*
> *Qu'il fait bon, fait bon dormir . . .*

As for Miss Susan Heartwell DeRoman, she was naked as the day she was born, dancing and spinning around the room to beat the band, like a little Whirling Dervish!

Her spiky hand clutched a green bottle. From her mouth drooled a reddish liquor like chicken blood. It dribbled over her boy-chest.

What to do? If I made a scene about petty thievery, poor Nanette would have to be discharged and poor Susan would have to be spanked. Hen, moreover, would everlastingly blame the episode upon my "vulgar" influence. On the other hand an argument could be found in favor of wine, as in the Nightingale Ode:

> *O for a beaker full of the warm South,*
> *Full of the true, the blushful Hippocrene.*

All singing and dancing, of course, had stopped. Nanette's hand was clamped over her mouth. Susan watched me warily like a mischievous little puppy. Down on my knees I went to her. In a coaxing voice, softened so as not to disturb Hen in the bedroom on the floor below, I held out my hand and told Susan to give me the bottle. She extended it to me. Just as I reached to grab it, she snatched it back and tilted it to her lips. She took a hearty gulp of wine. The blushful Hippocrene dribbled over her flushed and merry face.

"Moi, je *trinc*, Papa! Moi, je *trinc*!" she exclaimed with giggles.

I found her most charming. Much I would prefer to have a son, but on this occasion my daughter displayed the DeRoman spirit. "*Trinc*!" I said.

"*Trinc*," she giggled. "*Trinc, Trinc, Trinc.*"

The Goddess of the Bottle had spoken.

I grabbed the bottle at last. I placed it on the floor next to a porcelain doll. I took my girl's wee hands in mine. We stood up and began to dance and sing:

> *Auprés de ma blonde*
> *Qu'il fait bon dormir . . . etc.*

Lest my devotion to family matters be called into question, I now reveal the secret, immutable, abysmal grief of my heart: my mother, Anna Maria, born in Tuscaloosa in 1835 during her father's second term as Governor of Alabama, died in 1879 at the age of forty-four years. I was but six at the time.

I will always remember her lovely smile. It used to lift me up as it beamed upon me. I loved to watch her arranging the flowers spread out on the dining room table and to hear her singing while she fixed them. She loved her husband, and Tom loved her. She always followed him to the front door when he left the house for his office—or for Washington where he frequently argued cases before the Supreme Court. She always gave the collar of his black broadcloth coat a farewell brushing to remove the dandruff.

In 1879 when my mother took ill, our family physician believed that the climate of Colorado might do her good. Mother, Father, and I went to St. Louis by steamboat, thence to Denver by train. Denver was a pioneer town with one-story stores and bar rooms with wooden false fronts. Only the snow-capped Rocky Mountains beckoned to our souls in this barbarous land. The mountains signified that Transcendent Mystery that surpasses, though it may not assuage, all human weal and woe. There in the Rockies—not the quiet landscape of New England but an untamed wilderness—Mother died.

This is the greatest horror I have ever endured. Time has not healed the wound. If only such another smile as Mother's would beam upon me! If only *Trinc* would smile at me and love me as she did on that single occasion when she was baptized by the Oracle of the Bottle, I would consider leaving to her in my Will my entire fortune.

I will no longer tolerate being abused by Yankees who mistake a Rebel for their moral inferior. Rumor has it that Grandpa H. Dexter Heartwell has sowed many wild oats—and that your father kept a mistress on Murray Hill.

I must close. As legal counsel to my Italian friend, the Conte da Braga, I am frequently called upon to leave my dear family in New York and to spend time in Philadelphia.

I have decided to pay more attention to Trinc. I have, accordingly, directed Lazard Frères, my bankers, to set aside a capital sum of $50,000 (Fifty Thousand Dollars) to be invested solely for the benefit of Susan Heartwell DeRoman. Commencing with her sixteenth birthday she is to draw income from the capital for the rest of her life. Furthermore, it is stipulated that she is entitled to invade the capital, in part or in whole, at any time thereafter should she so desire. But should the capital be depleted or exhausted, she is not to apply to me for recapitalization or for further funds of any kind, nor to expect an inheritance under provisions of my Will.

Far from banishing Cordelia, I protect her until such time as her genius and beauty attract a husband to support her.

Sincerely,

GAYLE THOMAS DEROMAN

2

THE DISAPPEARANCE OF CHILDHOOD

NEW YORK'S WINTER BEGAN with a freezing Jack-the-Ripper fog. Confined to her small fourth-story room, Trinc watched the fog as it swirled past curtainedoff window lights of brownstones. It wrapped itself around blurred gas lamps on East Seventy-First Street. By day she could see only as far as Central Park. The trees there were dark and billowing, the sky behind them slate-gray tinged with a subdued orange glow. When she lay in bed at night she could hear the howl of the wind at the cracks between doors and up the five stories of the switchback staircase. She liked fog and wind and rain. Sometimes she wished she were the water-fairy who dragged obnoxious people out to sea.

For a week Miss Bridgit had not taken her for a walk in the park. This was because Mother had warned Trinc for perhaps the millionth time about catching cold, influenza, scarlet fever, TB, and pneumonia. "Your Heartwell weak chest," Mother always said, diamondy hand on bosom.

One night a freezing rain fell, followed by snow. When Trinc rose from bed at six-thirty, shivering with cold, teeth chattering, she clamped her jaw tight and found that, with a little practice, she produced a sound somewhere between a stalled motor car and a runaway subway train. She threw open the sash, poked head into a vast, magical ice-box.

She was the healthiest girl in New York.

The city lay under an enchantment. The far-off muffled *hooguh hooguh* of motor cars. Shoveling noises in the snow-drifted street, the rasping, grating noise like a giant's sucks of breath. Blinkered and stooped, a carriage horse stamped hooves on stone, blew steamy balloons out of its snort and whinny. Trinc had the feeling of not really being confined at all. The thought went through her like something wild and warm that trickled between her thighs when she was excited. She would go to the park today with or without the Heartwell chest.

But not, of course, without Miss Bridgit. She was the last in that year's starched procession through the DeRoman establishment of the chronically feeble-minded—a ghost-like, round-headed creature with a blob for a face, an ellipse for a body, and sticklike appendages for arms and legs. Miss Bridgit was in fact much like the Stone Age statuettes that Trinc drew with the colored crayons Uncle Doc had given her. To her credit, Miss Bridgit, who came from London, had told Trinc about the Ripper. You needed to know things like that when you contemplated running away from home in the fog. As for Miss Bridgit's lessons in reading, arithmetic, piano and needlepoint, you just had to listen to them and pretend she was really invisible.

By ten o'clock she and Miss Bridgit were bundled into sweaters and knitted caps and mittens and buckled galoshes. They were walking to Central Park. When they reached it, Trinc ran around and gulped frigid air, about a ton of it at a time. She watched be-scarfed skaters out on the frozen pond. She made a fat snowman as a complement to her portraiture of Miss Bridgit's ephemerality. Then it was time to go home for lunch.

Where she and Miss Bridgit usually crossed Fifth Avenue, there was a slight rise of ground. Now it was slick with hard ice. Four dray horses, who were pulling a coal cart, were scrambling to keep their footing on the ice. The driver, a redfaced, squat-bodied little man with bowed legs, stood up to crack his whip. The horses frantically neighed. Suddenly one horse fell down, and the driver was beating him to make him struggle up before the harness got tangled.

Miss Bridgit tugged Trinc's arm. "Come along now," she said sharply, "we'll be late for lunch. We can play some more at home." She began to pull Trinc across the avenue.

"No. I want to play here."

Just then the other horses went sprawling, the coal cart toppled on top of them. Trinc yanked her arm loose and ran to join the crowd gathering to observe the scene. Although she could hear Miss Bridgit's "Don't look, you little fool! Come here this instant!," the piercing screams of the horses created, for Trinc, the more necessary imperative.

The horses kicked each other in the belly, thrashed and strained their necks up, all caught in the harness, their nostrils dilated and bloodred, their eyes rolling in terror. The driver had been thrown from the cart. He staggered to his feet amidst a volley of violent oaths and curses, flung his whip away, and went and fetched from the cart a heavy-looking shotgun. Although Trinc had seen one at Uncle Doc's home, the first blast from it was louder than anything she had ever heard. The head of one of the horses looked funny for an instant and seemed to look directly at Trinc as if he had something to tell her. The head was twisted and stretched tight before it relaxed onto ice.

"You're not to look at this! You naughty girl! Their legs are broken!"

Even while Miss Bridgit was tugging her across the avenue, Trinc heard the driver's gun click as he pumped another shell in, heard a resonating blast that made her hair stand on end.

When they got home, Trinc went straight upstairs to her room and bolted the door. She felt sure that the shot-up horse had spoken to her,

Unwanted! Unloved! Give me your childhood, Trinc,
and I will eat it, and it will disappear!

She burst into tears.

It was never all right to cry for yourself. It was all right to cry for the suffering of horses.

UNCLE DOC AND AUNTIE EM lived just around the block. Trinc had an open invitation to visit them at any time, but she was seldom allowed out of the house except to walk with Miss Bridgit. Occasionally Mother took her downtown for a matinee theatre to see a play or a masque or a touring troupe of ballet dancers. Once Father himself had taken her to the Bronx Zoo and called her Monkey Face. When Trinc was allowed to visit the Knights, such a feeling of delight came over her that afterwards she would lie in bed musing, "I wish I was their little girl and lived in their house with them all the time."

It was, she knew, a dreadfully disloyal thing to say to herself. How could she help herself for contrasting a deaf, querulous mother with a jolly aunt, or a father who treated her like a little monkey with an uncle who treated her as a princess? The Knights employed a wonderful cook, Mary Mulligan, whereas the DeRomans employed, in addition to Blob Face Bridgit, old Annie, the maid whose swollen ankles bulged over her shoes, and Cook—another blob.

Besides, Uncle Doc had given her Puff Ball, the guinea pig, whose pink-rimmed, pellucid eyes, quivering white fur, and extraordinary ability to say "queek queek" qualified him as the most appreciative audience an actress was apt to find north of Broadway. Alone in her room Trinc often would wrap Puff Ball in his blanket and tiptoe into the dark hallway. There, the bannisters went coiling down four stories. The stairwell made her feel dizzy. She let her braids dangle between slats and down, down as from a great tower. A prince was waiting for her, below.

UP ON THE FIFTH FLOOR was the Throne Room, a lofty closet next to the bathroom and separated from it by a stained glass window. The toilet in the Throne Room was on a dais about a foot above the level of the floor; above the toilet was a linked metal chain attached to a water tank near the ceiling. Trinc always enjoyed pulling the chain. The roar and hiss that followed, like that of a steam engine toppling over Niagara Falls, shook the entire house and infuriated Father. She pulled the chain whenever an important visitor was announced by Annie downstairs. The Throne Room was also an excellent hiding place. If she stood on top of the toilet cover, she could hear her parents talking in the bathroom.

It was a very strange thing, but when Mother was in the bathroom she seemed to be able to hear everything that was said to her as water tumbled into the tub. Mornings, as Mother drew a deep bath and Father shaved, Trinc overheard normal conversation. Because Father was an inspired and dramatic talker at any time, when it was necessary for him to win his point before the tub filled up and Mother retreated into deafness, he ranted like someone selling newspapers on a street corner. If on the other hand Mother wanted the last word, all she had to do was turn off the faucet, wait until Father's declamation had spent itself, then open the faucet suddenly.

Usually when Trinc was listening, her parents said little that interested her. What, after all, was a High Tariff? It sounded awfully important, but all a High Tariff made her think of was the sheik at the ballet, scimitar brandished above the cowering figure of Scheherazade. One morning, however, her parents were talking about *her*. She discovered later that she had memorized the dialogue.

At first Father was singing "Auprès de ma blonde" in his softly muted baritone. Then the *plush dush whump* of falling water lured from its exile the catarrhal whine and harsh vowels of the Connecticut Yankee.

". . . not satisfied with Trinc?" Mother was saying on a rising inflection.

"Irrelevant and immaterial," Father intoned. "The point is that you refuse to bear me a son. I have a right to demand issue to carry on the DeRoman tradition. A son."

"Pish tash," Mother retorted. "You'd spoil him to beat the band . . . I'll give you a divorce, if that's what you want."

FATHER: Have I said anything about a divorce? Will you have the sand to stick to the subject?

MOTHER: Divorce, divorce. All you talk about is divorce. The divorce of Mrs. da Braga, for example.

FATHER: Contessa. The Contessa da Braga. I do not represent her. I represent her husband, Umberto.

MOTHER: I am sorry that your profession forces you to mix with people like Mr. and Mrs. da Braga.

FATHER: Conte and Contessa!

MOTHER: The Count and Countess Spaghetti, then. He married her. Let him take the consequences.

FATHER: Why not set aside your provincial standards of morality? Marriage customs in Europe are altogether different from those in Connecticut.

MOTHER: More like those in New Orleans, I dare say.

FATHER: There is only one verdict to be reached in a case of broken hearts.

MOTHER: Sin.

FATHER: Poor Umberto owed allegiance to his family estate.

He never questioned his father's command to give up his mistress, Maria, and come to America to marry money. I thought that he and Maria would commit suicide together. Instead—

MOTHER: —He married a moron.

FATHER: Your tone implies no sympathy on that score either. He went through agony. So did his lovely, pathetic Maria. The estate was saved, but, oh, the wreck of those fine lives! The divorce is inevitable. Yet the Contessa is stubbornly hanging on to the da Braga jewels.
   . . . Accordingly, and I admit it without shame, I have buttered her up for many years, in hopes of persuading her to surrender the jewels.

MOTHER: Which side do you butter her on, her bosom or her buttocks?

FATHER: Don't be vulgar!

MOTHER: The pot calls the kettle black . . . How's your whore in Philadelphia?

FATHER: Hold your tongue! You have no idea what you're talking about!

MOTHER: Oh, don't think that I give a darn about your lies. . . . Why not ask Mrs. da Braga's friend in Chestnut Hill to provide you with a son and heir? You can call him Umberto Spaghetti DeRoman. Not exactly traditional in your family, but you had no objection to naming our child Trinc . . . It doesn't matter what she's called. God knows, I never wanted her.

FATHER: Have you finished? It's Contessa da Braga. The least you could offer to do to help me with this case is to invite the

Contessa to tea next time she's in town . . . Are you listening, Hen? . . . Oh . . .

Father had resumed singing, "Tous les oiseaux du monde vienent y faire le nis . . ." because Mother had turned off the faucet.

Trinc covered her ears with her hands. It was terrible what the Contessa was doing! Trinc hated the Contessa for making Mother say things! In her imagination Trinc drew a picture of the Contessa—a creature with a mass of diamonds and with a chin pock-marked, like a rotten mushroom, from the effects of "moron." Father had once called Puff Ball a moron when Puff Ball said from his basket on the floor, "Queek, queek." She would have to ask Miss Bridgit what the word "moron" meant.

THE LIVING ROOM WAS THE ONLY ROOM on the second floor where Trinc could play post-office before Father came home in the evening. She kept the post-office between the velvet sofa and the shelves of Father's leatherbound books. The post-office itself was a large law book stuffed with verses and drawings which Trinc made and pretended to mail to Puff Ball.

She was in the living room on the occasion of the visit of the Contessa da Braga.

What a handsome, clever family Trinc had! People called Father things like Spellbinder and Life of the Party. Even though Trinc suffered when Father was showing off, everyone else enjoyed his—what did Mary Mulligan say?—shenanigans. As for Mother, she was a great portrait painter in oils even though she had ceased to paint when she left art school in Boston and married Father. Why, Uncle Doc said Mother could have been an American Rembrandt! Trinc had seen a real Rembrandt at the Metropolitan Museum and agreed with Uncle Doc. Everything about Mother was so secretive. Only to members of the family did she show her old paintings and her witty verses—and these were so much, much better than Trinc's own, and Mother herself so much, much more beautiful than Trinc, that there seemed little purpose in having to grow up.

When she wasn't playing post-office, she danced on the oriental rug. She pretended that, if she could step out a perfectly graceful dance, following the pattern on the rug and matching the rhythm with poetry, her dream of becoming as beautiful as Mother would come true.

On the afternoon of the Contessa's visit Trinc had slipped off her shoes, assumed dancing position on the main figure on the rug, and, dancing, murmured:

> "Magic rug, magic rug, dancing on you,
> Magic rug, magic rug, dreams shall come true . . ."

The doorbell went *gring-a-ling, gring-a-lang.*

After running to put on her shoes, Trinc snatched a law book from the shelf, sat on the sofa and pretended to read. Old Annie had already clumped up from the basement and opened the front door. That meant that Annie would show the visitor into the reception room downstairs and then come to the living room, looking for Mother. Presently Annie waddled in with a card on a silver tray. Trinc knew exactly what was going to happen: Annie, to save herself the trouble of climbing another flight of stairs, would give the card to her. Trinc closed the book with a thud and glared. "What is it, Annie?"

"Miss Trinc," Annie gasped and theatrically patted her heart, so greatly had she sacrificed herself in the performance of duty. "There be a Countess in reception to see Mrs. DeRoman . . . Ah, me bones is achin' somethin' terrible, child . . . Take pity on old Annie and deliver the card, there's a proper girl." She leaned forward with a groan. Trinc took the card, read aloud: "The Contessa da Braga." A shiver ran up her spine, but you didn't show excitement to servants. "Is she wearing the jewels?"

"To be sure. And a sealskin muff."

"Good. She's not divorced."

When she bounded upstairs to Mother's bedroom, she expected to find her in an old flannel wrapper, lying on the chaise longue with a cloth across her eyes. Mother, however, was standing before the long gilt mirror and putting gold combs in her coiffured hair. A wired lace collar was fitted high behind the ears. Mother's figure looked like a pale flower on a stiff stalk of green taffeta.

Card tray in hand, Trinc waited. You were not to speak until spoken to. You were never, ever, to touch. It was this very aloofness of Mother that made her so different from other girls' mothers. Beautiful Mother! Greateyed Mother! When Mother turned from the mirror and saw Trinc, she took the card from the tray. She gave one of her bitter little laughs but smiled as she said, "You may come to tea if you wash your face."

Trinc ran and, upstairs in the bathroom, studied her face in Father's shaving mirror. Oh, she was the ugly duckling in a radiant family! Mother could sweep downstairs in rustling taffeta, chin up because she had something finer than jewels— the Heartwell eyes! Trinc washed and dried her face. As she dashed for the staircase, she realized that she had forgotten something, so she ran back to the Throne Room and pulled the lavatory chain. As she began to descend the stairs, she had the immense satisfaction of feeling the whole house shake and shudder as if from an earthquake.

In imagination she rehearsed her entrance into the reception room, the curtsy she would make even though the room was hideously ugly, thanks to clever Mother. When callers spoke of the room as the only really fashionable room in the house, they did not understand Mother's sense of humor. The room had been hung with mulberry brocade draperies and cluttered with tasteless plaster statues and a marble clock with gilt Cupids on top—Mother's unwelcome wedding presents. There were ornate French chairs from New Orleans and Navajo Indian rugs that shut off the view of the truly elegant room, the Sheraton dining room. And there were ottomans covered with prickly black horsehair, relics from the DeRoman plantation in the South. Visitors for tea had to sit bolt upright on the ottomans. They made you itch all over. Clever, clever Mother! Ladies too polite to scratch their legs endured agony while they spread butter balls and mince jelly on toast.

Trinc paused at the entrance to the reception room, took a deep breath, and peeped in. The Contessa was seated on an ottoman, a seal-skin muff on the floor beside it. She glittered all over and was wearing a velvet hat with curled ostrich feathers. "At Nice," she was barking into Mother's outstretched ear trumpet, "they play for even higher stakes—"

Trinc entered the room and curtsied.

"This is my daughter," Mother said. "Susan Heartwell DeRoman."

The Contessa let a fluttering hand settle to her bosom before the watery eyes in the plump blob of her face came to rest upon Trinc.

"Enraptured!" the Contessa exclaimed through painted lips. "The Contessina Francesca is your age precisely. You must play together!"

Trinc thought and said, "Does she have a guinea pig?"

The Contessa frowned, turned, and shouted to Mother, "What did she say? Guinea pig?"

"Yes," Mother replied in sugary voice. "Susan has a little pet rat. You must have your Francesca over to play with it."

"Alas!" sighed the Contessa with so much anguish that Trinc thought she would burst into tears. "Francesca is in *bella* Roma . . . But, dear Susan," she went on, clasping hands together in a kind of ecstasy, "what beautiful eyes you have!"

"Nonsense," Mother cut in. "We do not say such things."

"Why not, Mrs. DeRoman? She has beautiful eyes. Like your own."

"Vanity is not to be encouraged," Mother said. "You may go," she said to Trinc.

She was glad to leave the room. The tea and the toast and the pink iced cakes that usually made her greedy would have choked her now. She wanted to look at the Contessa's compliment in all its wonderful lights. Beautiful eyes like Mother's! She went to the living room and removed her shoes. She began to dance and murmured,

> "Magic rug, magic rug, dancing on you,
> Magic rug, magic rug,
> Dreams shall come true,"

over and over, her stockinged feet seeming to glide like a water fairy's.

After a while she stopped and bowed, deep and low, to an imaginary Contessa da Braga. "Enraptured," she said. She squeezed her Heartwell eyes as tightly shut as she could and opened them suddenly.

"Enraptured!"

HORSES SCREAM AND THRASH ABOUT and strain their necks up, nostrils dilated and eyes rolling in terror, and a gunshot rings out . . .

She stifled a scream as she woke. Puff Ball still slept in his soiled blanket at the foot of her bed. A pale light filtered through the window. The door was open. Although she had commanded Miss Bridgit to leave it open last night, you could never be sure whether Miss Bridgit would betray you. Trinc rose and went to the door and sniffed. An acrid odor of carbolic acid still rose up the stairwell, the odor that came from behind the sheet hung over Mother's bedroom door.

She ran and opened the sash, hoping to see the arrival of Uncle Doc's Rolls-Royce. A milk wagon rattled and clip-clopped. Here and there little birds swooped and canted in a small sky. She went and picked up Puff Ball. He *queeked*.

She had knitted his blanket and embroidered his initials in it in gold thread: P.B. DeR. Lately she couldn't look at the initials without remembering how she had shown them as a secret to Father and how Father had told the secret at a dinner party in order to make everybody laugh about "rats" in the family. She hated laughing people—except Uncle Doc. For Uncle Doc could laugh louder and longer and more often than anybody else in the world, but with a laughter that never wounded. You could tell a secret to Uncle Doc, too, and it was like tossing a stone into the pond in Central Park, knowing it would never rise again.

Something was wrong with Puff Ball. He flopped in her hands, listlessly, like a shoe-last. His nose was hot.

Gring-a-ling, gring-a-lang, rang the doorbell.

She placed Puff Ball in his blanket on the floor, ran to the stairwell, leaned over. *Clump, clump, clump.* Annie was coming up from the basement. *Crrr-eak, foomp.* The front door was opened, shut. *Wham, thump.* That was Uncle Doc knocking mud off of his galoshes. "Hell-O there, Annie! How's the rheumatism?" he boomed.

Usually on his recent, daily visits he would look up the stairwell and blow a kiss through his beard and she would catch it and blow it back to him. Today he seemed to forget. She heard him mounting the stairs to Mother's room. Afterwards she heard nothing distinct until he was apparently splashing his hands in the basin of disinfectant on Mother's dressing table; after that, some soft laughter and mumbles. She would have to act swiftly before he went away. She ran downstairs in her nightie and stood outside Mother's room near the reeking sheet of carbolic acid.

Uncle Doc emerged from the room and brushed past her in a hurry, his stethoscope still swinging from his neck.

"Uncle Doc!"

He stopped at the head of the stairs and drew a package from a vest pocket. He looked at the package as if he were reading a thermometer. Throwing the package to Trinc, "Catch!" he roared. "Time you went outdoors, young lady."

It was a bag of marbles. "Uncle Doc?"

Uncle Doc had one hand on the bannister, in the other hand a medicine bag. "Something wrong, Trinc?"

"It's Puff Ball. He has pneumonia. He caught it from Mother."

Uncle Doc stroked his beard. "Where's the patient?" he finally asked. Soon he was in Trinc's bedroom, examining Puff Ball with stethoscope, listening to fur on the floor.

After a while he stood up. "You've been worrying about your mother, haven't you? Well, she's going to be all right, and you're going to have to remember when it's feeding time." He fetched a quarter out of his trousers and threw it to Trinc. "Patient needs some carrots. You must go at once to the market on Sixty-Ninth and Lexington. Buy Mr. P.B. DeRoman a bunch of carrots and a head of lettuce."

Trinc was thunderstruck. Surely, she thought, Uncle Doc is laughing at me for the very first time. The idea of going alone as far as Sixty-Ninth Street and Lexington was ridiculous! She bit her lip. "What if Jack the Ripper gets me?"

Uncle Doc took her shoulders in his big hands, pondered a moment, said, "Just run as fast as you can . . . Look'ee here. The patient needs medicine. Are you going to get it or are you going to stand there till the cow jumps over the moon?"

"Go with me, please, Uncle Doc?"

He shook his head. His smile brightened as he said gently, "No . . . Auntie Em and I are having a tea party for you when you stop by our house at four o'clock . . . What say?" He turned quickly and started downstairs, a step ahead of her. Her feelings were too big for explanation. As she followed him she leaned over and patted him on the back all the way to the front door. After he struggled into his galoshes, he bowed low, lifted her hand, and stroked the back of it with his beard.

Half an hour later, after she had dressed, she opened the front door all by herself and reached the sidewalk without being seen by anyone. The sun was steaming rain puddles off the sidewalk and street. At the corner of the street some children were squatting, playing marbles. Slowly, as if she were walking on ice, Trinc started in the direction of Lexington Avenue.

She ran as fast as she could.

3

HAMLET IN BLOOMERS

UP IN HER ROOM ON THE FOURTH STORY Trinc conjured up the bacchante. Dressed only in her new camisole and bloomers and having only a silk ribbon to suggest the sweep and flow of the Free Spirit, she raised her face skyward, hands uplifted. She made little jumps with the leg extended in an arc toward the back, head tilted over one shoulder, hands pressed against sudden breasts or extended in a sort of benediction. After a back-arch, she practiced turns ending with an open-legged stance, the body held high, the head proudly erect.

Up in her room she played all the major parts in *Hamlet* except those of Claudius and Polonius, both of whom reminded her of Father. Dying of love for Hamlet, she was Ophelia saying to Gertrude, "He is so lonely that he sees ghosts and fears my love, and yet he fights over my grave." She was Gertrude, ear trumpet lifted, saying to Ophelia, "Who is this madman you are talking about?"

It was on the rooftop that Trinc found her true Century Theater. Evenings in summer she climbed the narrow staircase next to the Throne Room, opened the skylight, and had to herself a stage of tar and chimneys, an audience of Puff Ball and pigeons. Gazing off toward flat roofs of other brick buildings, she would repeat the suicide soliloquy. She imagined the shuffling off of her mortal coils by means of a leap to Seventy-First Street over one hundred feet below. *There* she was Horatio saying "good-night, sweet prince" over her body as that young, calm face, perfect in profile and white as marble, fell back into the undiscovered country from whose bourn no traveler returns. A traffic cop sometimes intruded on the text. Alighting from his white horse and twirling a brass button on his uniform, he would say with a sigh, "Alas, poor girl! Like our Prince Hamlet, she understood life in all its immensity and duplicity. Now she has been taken up in its stream of sorrow and swept away like a rose petal on the Hudson River."

Hamlet in bloomers, she wrote, directed, and acted in fairy tales and masques, and performed them on the rooftop.

A MASQUE OF DARKNESS AND LIGHT
by
Trinc DeRoman

Act I

(The stage is dark. Lithe figures in gray, the Hours, move slowly past with hands joined, making an unbroken and unending chain).

THE HOURS:

Forward forever, forward and forward,
Time is unending, before and behind us.
Hail to the future, brilliant and glorious,
Farewell, sad memories, fading, forgotten.

Act II

(An open space is disclosed by dim green light. A throne is in the center toward back stage. Weird music plays, and grotesque figures dance. Darkness enters in a haze of red light).

DARKNESS:

Out by the lake where serpents writhe in ooze
There came a voice that whispered in my ear;
Its icy breath, its tone of dire dread
I did mistrust and fear. I drew away.
But when the whining wind was hushed and still,
And plashing waters lapped to measured beat,
I heard again the voice and turned to see—
A monster spouting flame!
His syllables hissed
Like hideous snakes. In him I recognized
A power superior to mine.
    He spoke:
"Vile serpent, doer of my will,
Bow low and listen, for I bid you be
Lord and Sovereign King of Evil Things.
Arise and rule the Hours with thy sword!"
So saying, vanished. Now I forever rule.

Act III

(A yellow light appears, gradually brightening. Light dances center stage, holding a torch).

LIGHT:

Born of the rhythm of Hours I come
Bearing a torch for the world.
Emperor Darkness, the battle is on,
The banner of Light is unfurled.
Come now, all happy moods and noble thoughts,
Dance out the Darkness with living flame!

(After a fierce battle, Light conquers Darkness).

The battle of the Universe is won,
The victory is ours,
Light defies stupendous powers,
Forward forever, Oh endless Hours!

Trinc was reasonably pleased with the rhyming of "stupendous powers" with "endless Hours," but making a rhyming couplet out of "noble thoughts" and "living flame" had her stumped during the heat of the summer of 1912. One evening while Trinc was rehearsing, Father pushed up the skylight, came and stood by the brick wall. He puffed on a cigar, his smooth-shaven cheeks and prominent, freckled brow reflected in its glow. He was wearing his white turtleneck sweater, a blue flannel "Y" stretched over the footballer's chest. She tried not to look surprised by this unexpected intrusion of a man she seldom saw. She struck a pose, leaning backwards, lifting rounded arms skyward only to sweep them forward in order to scatter imaginary beams of light. "Come now, all happy moods and noble thoughts, dance out the Darkness with living flame!" She relaxed the pose. "Hellow, Father," she sighed with her idea of bored sophistication. "Silly me. I can't find a rhyme for 'thoughts'."

"Repeat the lines," Father said.

She repeated them. Cigar light revealed a gleeful expression on his face. "Change 'thoughts' to 'ideas'," he said. "Thus: 'All happy moods and noble ideas', tiddle-de-pum, tiddle-de-pum. Repeat."

She repeated the lines, changing 'thoughts' to 'ideas'.

Father cleared his throat and flourished the cigar against the backdrop of night sky, keeping time. "'All happy moods and noble ideas' 'dance out the Darkness with lots of beers'! That's got it. *Je tiens l'affaire.*"

"You're always making fun of me," Trinc said. Acute sadness of soul came over her. Something within it was letting in an almost unbearable yearning.

"Try this one," Father went on. "'Come now, all happy moods and noble hokum, ladies will dance if you know where to poke 'um' . . . Mademoiselle," he bowed to Trinc's silence. He flipped his cigar over the wall. "Come," he resumed in another voice, "we have good news for you, and your mother has a surprise. In your room."

The bonhomie of parental unction alerted Trinc to the presence of treachery. Strange, though, how her heart rose to the bait. She waited for Father to explain himself.

"You're going away to school. Starting tomorrow. What do you say, *petite chat?* Are you happy?" He approached her so closely that she felt almost faint from the mingled odors of tobacco, whiskey, and sweat.

"Yes," she said. "I am happy."

"Do you love me?"

Trinc's feelings for her parents had been pushed long ago to a dark corner of her mind. She didn't want her conscience to be burdened with responsibility for feelings of love. Although she didn't like her parents, she probably loved them in spite of herself. She wondered if her soul's almost unbearable yearning for love would ever find release. She leaned into Father's opening arms, pecked him on the cheek, and stepped back quickly, aware of her body's new sensitivity to touch.

"School will do you good," Father said. "You'll make friends and go horseback riding and play patty-cake tennis."

As she followed Father downstairs, closing the skylight after her, she noticed that the back of his head had turned bald. Tufts of red hair encircled a shiny pate, lending him the appearance of a king in a play. When they reached her room, Father pointed to a box on her bed. "Put on your new school uniform and come down to the living room. Hen and I will be waiting for you there . . . One more thing." He went and scooped up Puff Ball in one hand. "You'll have to get rid of this rat. You can't leave him here. You can't take him to school. Do you want Annie to dispose of him? If you were my son, you'd wring his neck and have done with the nuisance."

When she understood what he was saying, and that, for once, he was in earnest, she took Puff Ball into her hands. She fixed Father's eyes with her gaze while at the level of her waist her hands made hard, twisting motions. Puff Ball *queeked* once. While she was thus pretending to wring Puff Ball's neck, Father stared at her in undisguised disbelief. Color drained from his face. He backed away, fled the room. She relaxed her strangle hold on the guinea pig.

TRINC LISTENED TO HER BLOOD as she descended the stairs. When she had been dressing, she had felt a hot rush between her legs. Perhaps the new uniform would be soiled. The thought was not without its humor. The ermine muff was pleasant enough. You could get used to wearing high, patent-leather shoes. Even the blue and white striped blouse had its charm. But who would want to wear baggy, black silk bloomers except a Cossack?

Father, seated cross-legged on the sofa, was reading the *Times* that Annie had ironed for him. Mother was reclining in the leather Morris chair, wrapped in a steamer rug even though the unventilated living room had retained the heat of the day. Seeing Trinc, Father folded the paper, stood up and began talking at once:

"St. Benet's School is about ten miles from Poughkeepsie.

The chairman of the Board of Directors is Grandpa Deck, an atheist, so you needn't worry yourself about the saintly name. No Heartwell would permit the minds of young ladies to be seduced by religion.'

"You'll have all expenses paid—room, board, tuition—until you are sixteen, at which age you will pay for them yourself. You'll have a clothing allowance so that you may be suitably attired for your lessons in riding, tea-service etiquette, and so on. You'll have a weekly allowance of ten dollars which you may draw upon application to the Bursar. This will enable you to purchase candy, comestibles, and articles peculiar to your sex. No chewing gum is allowed. No cosmetics are allowed . . . Grandpa Deck is sending his chauffeur here at eleven o'clock tomorrow morning to drive you to Poughkeepsie and the school. Any questions?"

"Vacations!" Mother shouted, extending her ear trumpet. "Have you told her about the vacations?"

"Will you please shut up, please?" Father's face was red from liquor and heat. Trinc wondered why he didn't take off his motheaten Yale sweater. "Vacations . . . You will be spending vacations in Orford Parish. You and Hen will heretofore be living permanently at Grandpa Deck's house . . . It is my duty to inform you . . . Darnit, Hen, I told you to do this!"

"Stop beating around the bush!" Mother said. Father began to pace up and down on the oriental rug. "Your mother and I," he said without looking at Trinc, "have decided, in the best interest of all parties concerned, to get a divorce . . . Understand that we shall maintain cordial relations in all affairs."

"Affairs!" Mother hooted. "He's been having an affair with a graduate of Vassar College who has consumption. Your father is irresistibly attracted to intelligent, sick women who remind him of his mother."

"Very well," Father said, "I'll not deny that I'm in love with Amelia Jay Ford. She's a darn sight better educated than you are, and her family is a darn sight more respectable than yours. She understands me—something you never tried to do!"

It's blood, Trinc thought. *As if your body has been waiting all this time to belong to everything.*

Father had stopped talking and was standing in front of her. His sweater and brick-red face, his mustache and thick neck and liver-spotted hands—all the assembled parts of him—gave her the impression of someone much younger and weaker than she, a king on stage, perhaps, but in reality a little lost boy.

"Trinc," he said in a solicitous tone that he probably employed with clients, "all this must be very painful for you."

"Oh," said Trinc, "I have moral reservations about really enjoying myself. I shall be very happy to do whatever's best."

Father half smiled. "I want what is best for us all. In that connection I am pleased to inform you that, commencing on your sixteenth birthday, you will be rich."

"Oh," said Trinc, "ten dollars a week upon application to the Bursar, I believe you said. What is a Bursar, anyway?"

"Listen," Father said.

Later, she would reflect, it certainly sounded all right, all the lawyerly fuss about having $50,000 in her own investment account. It seemed best not to think about such things. She was quite sure that she didn't want to become a Social Parasite.

Her first blood made a difference. Uncle Doc had once told her what would one day happen to her body, and why. She was part of a pattern of primal mystery, he had said, one that related her to a living universe, even to the elements in stars. So, later, she knew she was feeling self-conscious in an entirely new way. It was as if she were not just here and alive but saw herself here and alive, exposed and ashamed, fearful of what others would think of her yet glad to be accepted into the scheme of things.

When she finally was excused to go upstairs, she went to the bathroom, tidied herself up, and exchanged the horrid black bloomers for a summer skirt suitable to her new estate of womanhood.

It had been fun, deceiving Father into thinking her willing to kill for his love. She had turned the tables on him, as Hamlet had done to Rosencrantz and Guildenstern. Now that she was back in her room she noticed that Puff Ball showed little more animation than the quivering palpitation of pink nose. "Goodnight, sweet prince. Uncle Doc will find you a new home."

She stuffed him inside her ermine muff and walked with him, in a lady-like manner, downstairs and outdoors without telling anyone where she was going. She ran for a block, mounted the steps of the Knights' brownstone, and pulled the doorbell—*gring grang a-ling, grang a-ling* . . .

Mary Mulligan opened the door. "Well noo, Trinc," she exclaimed, "it's a grand night for visitors! And what might we be doing for you?"

"O Mary Mulligan! Puff Ball's sick and I've got to see Uncle Doc and I'm going away to school tomorrow and Father wants to kill Puff Ball and I have to find him a new home!"

Mary Mulligan studied her quizzically, held out hands. "Give us the patient . . . Pore fella is lookin' peaky . . . Well noo, I ask the dorktor to consider this mahter while you make yourself comfy in the reception . . . There's a gentleman there as you'll be glahd to make acquaintance of." Mary Mulligan took Puff Ball and whisked herself out of sight.

In the reception room a beefy-looking old man in a tuxedo stood up and looked at her through a pince-nez perched above an upside-down "V" mustache. She recognized ex-President Roosevelt before he bowed his head, sat stiffly down, and patted his knee. "Come here, young lady," he beckoned hoarsely. "I've something to show you."

Trinc went and sat on Mr. Roosevelt's knee. A curious sensation of its hardness wriggled up her spine while his thick arms encircled her waist. Then with a wheeze he extracted something from a pocket and held it up.

"See this bullet? Took it from my body. Yes. Took it from my body."

"Keen!" Trinc had never seen a bullet before. The sight of this one reminded her that Uncle Doc and Mr. Roosevelt had gone wolf-hunting together. "I wish I had a gun."

Mr. Roosevelt laughed. "Bully! I'll tell Dr. Knight to get you a gun!"

"Excuse me, Mr. Roosevelt." Mary Mulligan motioned from the door. "Dorktor will see Miss DeRoman in his office."

After thanking Mr. Roosevelt for showing her the bullet, Trinc went to Uncle Doc's office. He was wearing a starched white dress shirt with the sleeves rolled up. "Hell-O!" he roared. She flew to his arms and kissed him.

"Trinc," he began and stopped until Mary Mulligan had closed the door. "Trinc," he sighed, "we've always spoken frankly together, you and I. I won't try to pull the wool over your eyes . . . Your little guinea pig has got a punctured lung. He'll recover. With your permission, I'd like to take him to the lab at the hospital. We'll look after him there . . . My," he went on, face beaming, "I'm so glad you came over tonight, to say good-bye. You see, I've known for some while that they're packing you off to school, and that you'll be living with the Heartwells . . . I'll miss you. We'll be meeting again before the cow jumps over the moon . . . Mary Mulligan will see you home. I'd go myself, but Em and I are tied up for dinner with Mr. Roosevelt . . . Give us a hug."

It was raining as she and Mary Mulligan were walking home. Suddenly as they turned a corner she stopped and pulled herself into Mary's arms. Father had just descended the brownstone steps. He paused to flip up the collar of his raincoat, then walked quickly in the direction of Central Park. She was glad he hadn't seen her.

Next morning, after Annie had packed her belongings and while Trinc and Mother were waiting in the living room for the arrival of Grandpa Deck's chauffeur, Mother tightened white Parisian gloves and shouted, "What happened to your little rat?"

Trinc drew up her head, like a royal dancer. "He's dead," she lied.

THE NEXT FOUR YEARS SEEMED TO GLIDE BY, but there was a

dramatic start to them that very morning as Bruno Rancis, Grandpa Deck's chauffeur, was getting Mother settled with a steamer rug in the back seat of the Rolls. Another chauffeured Rolls—Uncle Doc's—sped around the corner of the block and was pulled to a throbbing, sputtering halt by the curb. Uncle Doc leapt out with a war-whoop, waving something shiny in the air. When Trinc saw what it was, her heart stopped.

A gun!

"Why, Billy Knight," Mother cried, "what in the world are you doing with that thing in the middle of the street! Are you out of your mind? Put that thing away this instant!" Mother was almost smiling as she spoke. She had a soft spot for Uncle Doc, Trinc knew. Uncle Doc could do anything he pleased, whatever Mother said, because he was a Magical Uncle and had a boyish streak in him that could charm the crown off the Statue of Liberty.

"Hell-O, everybody," he bowed with a mischievous gleam in his eyes. His Van Dyke beard and handlebar mustache always gave him a certain resemblance to Buffalo Bill. The gun confirmed the impression. He straightened and said, twirling the gun with a forefinger, "A friend of mine just happened to mention that a certain young lady is heading west of the Hudson River into Indian country and needs to protect herself against attack. . ."

"Mr. Roosevelt!"

"Mr. Roosevelt, no other . . . This 'Frontier' six-shooter revolver's for you, Trinc. It's the Colt's .44-caliber that I used to carry when I was riding with Teddy and hunting wolves. I don't need it any more. It's yours. Go on. Take it. It won't go off unless you cock the hammer and pull the trigger. Watch out, though. It's heavy."

As he passed the butt of the revolver over to Trinc's hand, Mother shrank back as if she were seeing the Prince of Darkness. She grimaced, moaned, shielded her face. "Take that thing away, Billy! I won't stand for another minute of this ridiculous farce! You can't give a gun to a little girl . . . Can you? Is it loaded?"

Trinc's hand, with the revolver in it, sank to her lap. She

simply stared at the revolver in amazement.

"No, Hen," Uncle Doc was saying, "it *ain't* loaded, but if anybody *aims* to give my sweetheart here a hard time, you can bet they'll have second thoughts when she pulls that Colt's .44 on 'em. . . . Besides, come Christmas, I'll be up in Orford Parish to teach Trinc how to use that little equalizer . . .

What d'ya say, Trinc? Strap on that dandy . . . Hold it. Forgot the belt and holster." He went to his Rolls, fetched these items, and tossed them into the seat beside Trinc. "There. The whole shootin' match. Like I said, strap on that dandy when you go horseback riding at that buzzard-pissin' school of yours, and you'll get some respect out of those prissy little rich girls. What's a finishing school for if you can't finish first?" He winked his eye.

"Billy—!" Mother started to remonstrate with him but burst out laughing until she had tears in her eyes. "Billy Knight," she blurted, "you're a wicked man. And I love you."

Trinc stared at Mother. If there was anything more astonishing than the gift of the revolver, it was Mother's saying she loved somebody.

True to his promise, Uncle Doc did come to Orford Parish that Christmas; did take her out to a remote, enchanted, snow-driven forest that was part of the Heartwell estates; and did teach her locking and loading, positioning, aiming, trigger-squeezing and other mysteries of the art. She became a competent marksman.

Such an accomplishment apart, she was reared to play a role in a world that no longer existed, not even, after the Bolshevik Revolution of 1917, in Czarist Russia. She was not unintelligent, or so she judged; not bright but not unintelligent either. She was a reader and a thinker. She knew that family and schoolfriends considered her to be rather odd, but she was not unpopular and was no longer an ugly duckling. She had a slender figure and a rounded bust. She wore her long, dark, auburn hair braided or tied into a bun. She hid her striking brown eyes behind a pair of owlish glasses, but she could see perfectly well without them.

Such was her life at St. Benet's and in the Cloud-Cuckoo-

Land of the Heartwell's feudal aristocracy, her sympathies for humanity at large remained mainly in the abstract. She heard from a distance the thunderous machinery of Heartwell Bros. Mills and saw the smokestacks belching soot, but the workers who toiled and their families who lived on beans and fatback—as she later learned—were hidden from sight.

The Heartwells proved kind. Having taken in Hen and Trinc and given them a private suite of rooms on the second floor of the mansionhouse in Orford Parish, Grandpa Deck and Granny Ah treated them as part of the family even though Hen had money of her own in addition to that from her divorce settlement in 1916 and could have purchased a house and moved out. Life as part of the Heartwell clan was irresistibly privileged.

During the Revolution, Heartwells had fought against the English. When members of the family referred to themselves as a "feudal aristocracy," they did so lightheartedly. Although they retained some admiration for European manners at their best—sang-froid in the midst of chaos, decency in the midst of vulgarity—they abhorred treachery and violence and believed that their devotion to themselves as a more or less exemplary family sufficed to elevate them above such a European vice as avarice. Generation after generation of this Yankee dynasty produced brothers who were genuinely fond of one another, who settled down with their wives and children in the same place together, who managed the mills together with some personal regard for the Rights of Man, and who engaged in philanthropic enterprises not because they needed to adjust their relations to an Almighty in whom they didn't believe but because a natural goodness of heart impelled them. While on the one hand the Heartwells had fixed, Puritanical prejudices about sex and race and were distrustful of those who possessed intellectual and artistic depth, on the other hand they had and expressed Conscience. It told them that they were right, and that it was their duty to be right. This Conscience, moreover, had nothing to do with religion. The Heartwells were Free Thinkers, not because they had read Renan, Darwin, and Huxley—as Trinc had—but because Conscience incapacitated them for any passion that was impractical or socially inconvenient. Like the personae in Ibsen's Rosmersholm, they kept their voices and their passions subdued, and their children, who were encouraged never to cry, upon attainment of maturity were seldom able to laugh.

Travelers to Orford Parish frequently remarked upon the Old World charm of the Heartwell estates. The dozen and more mansions were spaced well apart amidst the acres of gently undulating lawns bordered by great oaks and elms. This quiet beauty of landscape seemed to exemplify an ideal order for life in the New World.

Trinc's favorite house was the Heartwell Homestead. "Built 1780," the sign said that pointed her to the white clapboard structure nestled in the gloom of an old forest. Here she felt a holy hush as small birds streaked through pencilled beams of sunlight. Blossoms from a giant magnolia tree perfumed the air. A little brook sang, crystal clear, playing on mossy rocks, drumming in hollows. The house itself reminded her that the Heartwells had not always been rich, nor were their tastes originally other than simple and unpretentious. The keeping room and the buttery downstairs, with the great fireplace and Dutch oven, were especially charming; the upstairs dining room was furnished with Chippendale chairs; there were sundry bedrooms, a nursery with old pine cradle, a spindle crib, and a doll's house. In the pine-paneled parlor, she learned, eight brothers had been born in the eighteenth century; six became tycoons of industry, two became artists, their easels and palettes, portraits, engravings, and marble busts being everywhere displayed.

Most nights, after an afternoon of lawn tennis and a formal tea with Granny Ah, Trinc dressed in a starched costume with a high-necked gamp and a sash of blue taffeta. She also wore white silk stockings and patent leather slippers. Mother and the aunts—Edith and Dodo—dressed in what they called "little dresses."

These were actually long, silk evening gowns, distinguished from ball gowns because they had sleeves and no train and were made by New York dressmakers instead of Parisian ones. Grandpa Deck and the older men wore old-fashioned Prince Alberts, while the younger men and the uncles—Henry, Charles, Clifford and Robin—wore tuxedos. The usual evening meal would be set for about seventeen, though a service for a hundred persons was not unusual for family reunions.

The dining room was nothing if not ostentatious. It was decorated with sprays of yellow butterfly orchids in a crystal vase that was connected to smaller vases of orchids by chains of crystal links which shimmered under the lights of silver candelabras. The table itself was set with an Irish linen cloth of the delicate fern pattern, the center-piece being cloth-of-gold brought home from Egypt by Grandpa Deck before the turn of the century. The goblets for wine and for water were of Bohemian glass, and the dishes were Chinese.

Here at the table Trinc sat and said nothing. She was actually forbidden to speak. She was supposed to listen to the men as they talked of business or of moral and political philosophy. If she were "good" all through the dinner hour and always remembered to use the correct fork, she was given permission to dance in the Big Room. Rugs were rolled back in half. Uncle Robin sat at the Steinway piano. Those of the "children" who were under the age of twenty-five danced polkas and waltzes while the "grown-ups" sipped demi-tasses and liqueurs before the colossal, blazing fireplace. Rex, the old shepherd dog, slept through the proceedings. At the entrance to the Big Room the servants were allowed to watch the dancing—old Augustus, the butler, the cooks and the waitresses and all the upstairs-downstairs maids. The servants were regarded as being artists in their specialties and genuinely indispensable to one another and to the family.

Open-mindedness and frank, honest talk were considered to be the essence of the Heartwell tradition. No topic, not even religion, was forbidden. The Heartwells in fact prided themselves on their atheism. Grandpa Deck called the God of the Old Testament "an all-knowing, all-invading, shameless impostor." Mother kept by her bedside a copy of the *Meditations of Marcus Aurelius*. Readings in Stoic philosophy did not seem, however, to improve her nagging, querulous disposition.

Then there was the school. A hundred "poor little rich girls" were obliged to ride horses with Mexican saddles; to act in plays deemed suitable for genteel Lilliputians; and to serve tea without exposing an ankle or the curvature of a breast. If the world outside the high brick walls of St. Benet's largely consisted of dirty old men who paid dimes to little girls to turn somersaults, no one directly conveyed the information to Trinc's schoolmates—but they seemed to know it was so. They were taught to uphold the most wholesome ideals but also through the power of implication to prepare themselves to become acrobats in a future circus of marriage and materialism.

At school Trinc dreamed of going home to the Heartwells. She could hardly restrain her excitement come time for a vacation. It was glorious to find Bruno Rancis—whom the family called "the coachman"—waiting for her in the Rolls parked in front of the girlish gush of the dormitory. But when she came home, she dreamed of running away to New York to live with Uncle Doc and Auntie Em. They represented inviolate space. The strange thing was, after Trinc received $50,000 of Father's capital in the form of a Trust Fund on her sixteenth birthday in November, 1914, the income from which amounted to more than $2,500 a year, she had means to do almost anything she wanted. She didn't, however, have the foggiest idea what she really wanted. Apparently in the grip of an inexorable force, she seemed doomed to be a poor little rich girl for the rest of her life.

She also dreamed a lot about Father, whom she never saw during all these years. After his divorce, he married Amelia Jay Ford. She gave him a son, inevitably named Gayle DeRoman, Jr., and the same year—1917—he went to Plattsburg for officer's training and then to France as a judge advocate on General Pershing's staff. To Trinc, Father was as remote to her real needs as a nervous breakdown. Even though he now wrote her affectionate letters, why he loomed in her imagination as a man who needed her, she couldn't say. She dreamed that Father would take her on round-the-world cruises where ladies and gentlemen would dance during infinite ports of call.

At seventeen, although she had never had a "date," she did not lack for notions about the man whom she would consider a suitable partner. He would have to need her quite desperately, and she certainly hoped that he would be handsome. If he were gentle and of good heart with a tolerable sense of humor, she might be satisfied. He had to have intelligence, and, above all, compassion.

TABITHA VAN DYKE CAME FROM A RICH FAMILY in Oyster Bay. Everyone at the school called her Tubby. The "manners" teacher made fun of her plump figure, calling her a washer-woman, and, it was true, Tubby had a waddling gait and was fond of free gestures. But it was unfair. Although Trinc disliked Tubby's affected cynicism, she recognized that Tubby had her own kind of beauty. She had violet eyes in a face like a flower turned petal outwards; she had slender fingers with almond-shaped nails. Tubby was just another sad, horribly lonely girl.

In the spring of their senior year Trinc discovered just how lonely Tubby had been. It was a cold, rainy afternoon. Happening to be seated with Tubby at the Beanery, and feeling sorry for her, Trinc proposed that they go out riding. Cheerless as the weather was, with fog rolling in from the Hudson, there was in the air a scent of new grass. They decided to go. Clad in jodhpurs and turtleneck sweaters, they found their favorite horses in the stables, saddled and bridled them.

"Let's go bareback," Trinc suggested as she removed the saddle from Lucky, her white horse. Local folklore had it that if you looked into a well on the first day of May with the sun shining, you would see a white horse, and this was a prelude to meeting one's future intended! Trinc liked the feeling of grasping Lucky's mane, of gripping him with the muscles on the inside of her thighs, letting her legs dangle and giving herself from the waist down to every motion.

"You ride bareback," Tubby smirked, wriggling her eyebrows obscenely. "An orgasm would do you good."

Trinc wondered if befriending Tubby had been a wise idea. Trinc let the remark pass as humorous, walked Lucky away from the stable, then broke him into a canter, taking care not to lean back on the reins. Then she slowed him to a trot, stopped and looked back. Tubby was just getting mounted. She was jerking the reins, and then, suddenly, her horse had bucked her off and sent her sprawling to the ground hard, not in the limp, ragdoll flop that all the girls had been taught to execute.

Trinc galloped to where Tubby lay, dismounted, and took care to secure the reins of both horses before she dared look closely at Tubby. Who lay on her side, body curled up in a fetal position. Whose mouth had an ugly twist.

Trinc asked Tubby if she were all right.

"Go to hell," Tubby moaned. "Just leave me alone."

"Well," Trinc said, "don't just lie there. You're supposed to re-mount after a fall."

"Who says?"

"They say."

"They can go to hell." Tubby crawled to her knees, stood up, brushed herself off. Her mouth flickered into a nervous smile. "I don't mean you, Trinc. You're the only decent guy in this morgue. . . . You're the only friend I've got."

It was probably, Trinc thought, true. Unlike the other girls, Tubby didn't gush or hold hands or share forbidden chewing gum. Her highest praise was an abrupt "good work."

Tubby came and threw her arms around Trinc's neck and hugged her, backed off and said, "I'm sorry to get you mixed up with a tramp like me."

Mother of god, Trinc thought. It exasperated her when girls expressed bad feelings about themselves. Still, it seemed, Tubby wasn't making an appeal for pity. "Tramp?"

"Forget it," Tubby replied. "Just unsaddle that bastard and put him back in the stable. Do that for me, pal?"

Trinc returned the horses to the stable. When she came back, she found Tubby crumpled in a heap, sniffling forlornly between gasps for air.

A dark stain was spreading across Tubby's jodhpurs from the crotch.

The last time one of the girls had gotten herself pregnant, she had been kicked out of school and disowned by her family. Trinc had never learned what had happened to the girl, whether she had an abortion or got married or committed suicide or murdered her parents as Lizzie Borden did—the choices she imagined as available for women. So, now, she tried to think of what Uncle Doc would do in the circumstances. She formed a plan at once: get Tubby to the bathroom in the dormitory, avoiding the prying eyes of anyone who might call for an ambulance from Poughkeepsie or, worse, notify the police. After cleaning Tubby up and putting her to bed with a hot water bottle, she would have to decide about the risks of miscarriage. Poisoned blood? Bleeding to death?

She breathed deeply, went and kneeled by Tubby, and explained what she was going to do. She stripped off her sweater and tied it around Tubby's waist in order to cover the melon-shaped stain. Tubby rose to her feet. "Good work," she said.

They walked with pretended nonchalance to the dormitory. When Tubby had stripped off her clothing in the bathroom, Trinc saw in the panties little liverish gobs of flesh such as she had never seen before except on a tour of the Fulton Street fish market in New York.

When Tubby was finally settled under the covers of Trinc's own bed, Trinc had formed a plan. She would saddle Lucky and gallop about two miles from school to a general merchandise store on the Poughkeepsie Turnpike. She had taken note of the store when Bruno Rancis was driving her to and from home. If memory served her correctly, the store had wires leading to a telephone pole. She would call a taxi. Tubby would be taken to a hospital, would register under a false name, and would have all bills sent to Trinc's bankers in New York. When Miss Bates, headmistress of St. Benet's, made inquiries, Trinc would invent a story that Tubby had gone to New York due to a death in the family.

"Good work," Tubby nodded when Trinc had explained the plan, "but old 'Master' Bates won't swallow it. I have another plan."

A cousin of hers was teaching at Vassar College in Poughkeepsie and living on Fulton Avenue. Trinc was to call him. He would know what to do.

His name was Aeneas Caldwell.

4

Passion in Poughkeepsie

AT THE LAST MINUTE SHE REMEMBERED the Colt's .44 and belted the contraption around her raccoon coat. She had no ammunition, but fear put in a word for common sense and persuaded her that an unarmed device, once she reached the Poughkeepsie Turnpike, was better protection than nothing at all. As she cantered Lucky down the turnpike in the direction of the general merchandise store, she was glad to have the belt itself: it kept the coat tightened against her body. Cheeks and hands were already numb with cold. A freezing drizzle of misty rain slanted in windy gusts across the road. The occasional touring car, overtaking her with a dangerous speed in excess of forty miles an hour, its tires sounding like a long rip of adhesive, seemed a far less formidable adversary than the weather—and perhaps her own folly.

She did not want to pick a quarrel with Nature when Nature stood a good chance of winning. She had to admit that she must be a little in love with the idea of sacrifice, allowing herself to behave recklessly. After all, she was perhaps less interested in Tubby's welfare than she was in talking over the telephone to Aeneas Caldwell. From Tubby's description of him, he might turn out to be the one man in whom she could anticipate feeling the slightest interest.

He was said to be tall, dark, and handsome. He was said to be brilliant, a genius. He was honest, sympathetic, of good heart; he was poor. Tubby made no bones about the fact that Caldwell was not *really* someone out for the main chance but a choosy bachelor interested primarily in women who shared his values and refrained from judging his behavior. He tended to be a romantic, had a sweet disposition, and was not conceited about himself even though he was an intellectual with a habit of talking rot enthusiastically but, for most women, boringly. Trinc recalled some of the other details: twenty-six-years old, the son of Tubby's Aunt Betty from Long Island and of a potter from North Carolina; who had moved with his family to New Mexico and briefly lived with his mother there before returning east to Harvard, from which he had recently graduated with a Doctor of Philosophy degree in physics; who taught at Vassar College; who was accepted in Mabel Dodge's Washington Square salon, where only those willing to shatter themselves for the sake of ideas were respected; and who had "dark, penetrating green eyes."

"When you call Aeneas," Tubby had said with creamy chin jutting defiantly, "tell him it was the old Freudian creep from Greenwich Village who got me plastered so he could knock me up."

Soaked with rain, the raccoon coat which Trinc had purchased for herself as a present for her seventeenth birthday weighed heavily on her shoulders. She began to worry that she had passed the store without seeing it. When she jerked her head up, she could see telephone poles set back from the turnpike, wires strung beneath small inkblots of angry birds. After a while the store materialized in the mist up ahead, a dingy, ramshackle building with weather-beaten boards and with rusty tin signs for Campbell's soup, Bull Durham, and Singer sewing machines. A telephone wire sagged from a tilted roadside pole to the store.

She wondered if the storekeeper could sell her some brown sugar and turpentine to staunch the flow of Tubby's blood.

She dismounted when she got to the store. After tying Lucky to a hitching post, she went to the paned-glass door and peered inside. All she could see were a few silvery strands of cobwebs connecting a coal-oil lamp to a cash register. When she tried the door, she found it locked. There was a handwritten notice tacked to the inside of a door-pane. It read:

FED UP GONE

TO TEXUS

TO FITE

PANCHO VILLA

Rain pounded on the corrugated tin roof. The mewling of a buzzard arose nearby from a darkening forest. *Fed up gone to Texus.* The owner had apparently abandoned his store in order to fight a bandit on the Mexican border a couple of thousand miles away. She didn't blame him for trying to escape the dreary Hudson Valley. The sad thing was, he was bound to be disappointed. She remembered a good line from Horace to the effect that he who changes climate changes nothing else but the climate. Better the Roman motto about seizing the day, but how many people could even do that? She realized with her old, acute sadness of soul just how lonely and enclosed were the lives of the people. She had seen women stringing washlines over alleyways and old men leaning out of windows as a subway train on the El clattered past. Once, strolling near the family's mills, she had caught a glimpse of hundreds of uniformed workers moving arms in automatized motions attuned to a deafening *clackitty-ack, clickitty-ack* of machinery.

Lucky stirred, tossing his head as if he reproached her.

Why did she want to intervene in other people's lives? Why shouldn't they take responsibility for themselves? Was empathy unwelcome? Did she expect gratitude?

No, she didn't expect gratitude. She wanted to be needed. If she felt needed, she formed part of a pattern, part of a stable condition.

She would have to go, she decided, all the way to Poughkeepsie.

She mounted Lucky. His flanks were slick and steamy. Her mood of sadness fell away. A thrilling sense that all things were possible rushed to her head. She whipped Lucky.

"Giddap," she whooped, "we're going to Texas!"

HOURS LATER IN POUGHKEEPSIE she had added accomplishment to an inventory of small worth. Wrapped in a steamer rug, she sat cozy and warm on the sofa in front of Aeneas's crackling fireplace. Her shamefully large appetite had been satisfied with cups of hot cider just a wee bit laced with rum and with second helpings of his remarkable chocolate cake fresh from the oven. The man liked to cook. Extraordinary!

Less than an hour ago she had appeared at his front door as unannounced and unexpected as a fugitive in a dime novel. Now the raccoon coat was drying on a hanger by the fire, above the riding boots. The belt with the holstered revolver was slung over a rocking chair. Less than an hour ago: for so many years Time stood still, and now it seemed to be sweeping her pellmell toward a destiny for which she was ripe and aware. In what former existence, more than an hour ago, would she have tied a white horse to a white picket fence on Fulton Avenue in Poughkeepsie, approached a cheerless white clapboard cottage in a freezing rainstorm in the dark, rung the doorbell, announced her business to a man in a cowboy hat, entered his den, stripped off her coat, taken off her shoes and eaten his chocolate cake? Mother, had she suspected what Trinc was up to, would retire permanently to bed with a migraine for a good, healthy reading in Stoic philosophy. Father, who believed in the expediency of killing pet pigs, would, if satisfied with Aeneas's pedigree, have marched him off for a shotgun wedding. The improprieties of the present occasion had already tilted Trinc in favor of intimacy.

She was in love. She didn't want Aeneas to guess about her

feelings, but, darn it all, she was in love.

Probably she had fallen in love at first sight!

Mother of god. How trite!

There he was, opening the door, the porchlight revealing this big, square-jawed man who wore boots, denim shirt, galluses, and a low crowned hat with a four-inch brim pulled down tight. His deep-set eyes under heavy brows were bright and intense. After motioning for her to come in, he left the door slightly open. Perhaps he thought the revolver was loaded and he would need to escape. Perhaps out of courtesy he understood her apprehension and was leaving her space for retreat. Perhaps he didn't want a visitor. Or perhaps, as seemed likely, he didn't reason about doors at all and left them open instinctively.

He had already opened doors for her, inspiring her, even crediting her with a mind. No one in the family had done that except Uncle Doc. Men, Aeneas had explained, believed they were the rational sex, whereas women, who were supposed to be merely intuitive and creative, were irrational. These were catastrophic misunderstandings based upon false "scientific" assumptions. Not only was "mind" not restricted to reason, but also reason itself was inferior to intuition in the biological evolution of mankind. What a novel idea!

He was a big, rough-hewn man—true—and as tall and broad-shouldered as Uncle Doc. His movements were graceful, not cumbersome, and his hands were delicately expressive. He was handsome—true—but not conventionally so, for he had no beard or mustache, and his hair, instead of being slicked back, was— once she had made him take off the hat he absentmindedly wore indoors—such a rumpled mass of dark curls that she wanted to dance bare-foot upon them. He smoked a Sherlock Holmes pipe which gave his mouth a pursed, ascetic shape— true—but he had a shy, gentle smile and when he talked—and, true, he was a paralyzingly windy talker—the ravishing beauty of mockery of himself lingered at the corners of that mouth. As for the eyes, true, they were green, like turquoise aged, and nice girls might be lured to their depths, but these eyes smouldered with an intensity that probably warned everybody to keep their distance—everybody except Trinc. He had already declared, after less than an hour's acquaintance, that he loved her!

I'll sleep with him if he asks. The thought surfaced to her consciousness from the depths of the recognized world of instinctive knowledge. Sitting up, she removed the pins from her hair. It tumbled warmly to her shoulders.

She closed her eyes . . .

THE RAIN WAS BEING SWEPT IN A TORRENT into gutters. It pattered and glistened on leaves of the elms of the street. A Ford was parked by the cottage. From a chimney there was curling a frayed, misty scarf of smoke. She tied Lucky to a picket fence, felt the soggy weight of her coat, felt, too, the suck of boots poking holes in mud, and then she stood at the white door and *thock-thocked* its knocker, and the porchlight was turned on and the door was opened and there he was.

"Professor Caldwell?"

He seemed to take in everything on a swift appraisal—her, the revolver, Lucky steaming by the fence. "Come in, come in. I'm baking a cake. I'm Aeneas Caldwell. I don't suppose you have your calling cards abroad with you—?"

"I'm Trinc DeRoman. From St. Benet's. Your Cousin Tubby has had a miscarriage. She needs your help."

"You rode all the way from the school?"

"I tried to phone you first, then decided to come all the way."

"I'll be damned. You look chilled to the marrow-bone, Miss—?"

"DeRoman." She pronounced the Dare-oh-mahn slowly as she met the gaze of his eyes. She dropped it. "Trinc."

"I'm fixing chocolate cake, Miss DeRoman. You look like a chocolate cake person to me. And a hot-cider-with-rum sort of person . . . Cousin Tubby, you might be interested to learn, is hysterical."

He did not close the door. He helped her remove her coat. Lightened, she went to the fireplace, rubbed arms and shoulders and asked, "Hysterical funny or hysterical sick?"

"Cider and cake first. Explanations later. Take your boots off. Sit by the fire. I must say, it was a good idea to bring a gun. Can you shoot that thing?"

"Of course."

"I never doubted it, Trinc. Trinc?"

"Trinc."

"Well, Trinc," he half laughed, "we're not to worry about Tubby's problem. We have a problem. We have to get you and your horse safely back to school. . . I hope you're not in a hurry. Why, you're half frozen to death! And a ten-mile ride in any weather can be exhausting . . . I'd be pleasured if you'd make yourself at home . . . I'll be back right smart." He paused at an inner door and grinned shyly, nodding over his shoulder. "Cake's in the oven. Back . . . right . . . smart." His voice trailed off. He was staring at her, his head cocked sideways as if he were puzzled as to whether she manifested someone real. He spun away.

He was right about her exhaustion. Boots off, she sat by the fire, feeling the effects of long exposure to cold wind and rain flaming through face and limbs until drowsiness suffused them. Firelight danced on the plaster walls. She heard the neighing of a horse: Lucky. A steamer trunk in a corner of the room caught her eye. Was he going somewhere, this man who baked chocolate cakes for himself?

He returned from the kitchen and placed before her a plate with a thick slice of cake and a steaming mug of hot cider and rum. He sat in the rocking chair, took a Sherlock Holmes pipe out of the breast pocket of his denim shirt, struck a match on the hearth and lit the pipe. A pleasant aroma immediately began to permeate the room.

"May I?" Trinc said, lifting her fork.

"Of course!" he cried. "That's the idea. Second helpings to follow."

"Aren't you having anything?"

"I had just finished eating when you bearded the lion in his den. I'd like to watch you, though, if you don't mind."

"You teach physics, I believe?" Trinc asked between mouthfuls. He was studying her so intently that she was afraid she would do something awkward and displease him. She had evidently touched the right chord. He leapt to his feet, moved from the fire as if to give himself room to expand, and began to talk rapidly, engrossed in his world without apparent self-consciousness:

"Physics? I teach a new world of knowledge upon which to base a new awareness! Science, you see, has the worthy aim of understanding the nature of things. If you want to understand the fundamental nature of the physical universe, it is to small-scale phenomena that we must turn our attention. ... Where to begin? ... Near the end of the last century Sir J.J. Thomson broke up the atom, detaching small fragments charged with negative electricity, accordingly called electrons. These electrons are intensely electrified. Take, for instance, a gram of gold, and beat it as thin as it will go into a gold leaf a yard square. This gold leaf can with luck be made to hold a charge of about 60,000 electrostatic units of electricity. But a gram of electrons carries a permanent charge which is about nine million million times greater. What then is matter? Why, matter proves to be nothing but a collection of particles charged with electricity! Do you realize the significance of that?'

He's cute when he waves his arms like a conductor.

"Well, you are eating cake, Trinc, and a more lovely sight I could not imagine, and yet, I'm sorry to tell you, you are only a speck in the insubstantial pageant of space, time, and matter! Five years ago Rutherford introduced the greatest change in our idea of matter since the time of Democritus. The most revolutionary change in our conception of the universe is the dissolution of all that we regard as most solid into tiny specks floating in a void. The energy of the universe, you see, is contained in a nucleus that is minute in comparison with the dimensions of an atom.

What Rutherford found was that atoms are like infinitesimal little solar systems with the atomic nucleus as the sun and with electrons, like planets, circling around it. Such systems should be extremely sensitive to collisions . . .'

Insubstantial pageant of space, time and matter. How beautiful he is!

"Which brings me to cosmic radiation. Rutherford and others detected in the earth's atmosphere a new type of radiation, distinguished by its extremely high powers of penetrating solid matter. This is cosmic radiation. Every second it breaks up about twenty atoms in every cubic inch of our atmosphere, and millions of atoms in each of our bodies . . . Now, space is drenched with almost all the cosmic radiation since the universe began. The rays come to us from the farthest depths of space and from the farthest depths of time. It is clear, somewhere in the history of the universe matter has been annihilated in stupendous amounts!'

"That means that if we split a single atom we can release the stored-up energy of the universe. Who knows? Perhaps we can discover permanence in the universe—a natural order like the Greek idea of fate! I tell you, all through the world runs a mysterious content. Perhaps it is the stuff of our consciousness. If so, we human beings are not only related to every living thing— bird, leaf, rock, and the stars of the Milky Way—through matter that is energy, but also we are part of a universal mind!"

He paused.

And suddenly lunged toward the rocking chair, drew the revolver from its holster, turned it deftly in his hand and presented the handle to Trinc.

"Here! Take the revolver! Shoot me!" he cried in a theatrical voice. Trinc believed he might just be a little daft except for the self-mockery that twitched at the corners of his mouth. "How can I die when my body is constantly interchanged with the entire universe? Right now, almost all the almost infinite number of cells in my body is but replacement for what my body was a year ago . . . Here! Take the revolver!"

Although Trinc felt dazed by the most bewildering discourse she had ever heard, and had understood some of it only because Uncle Doc had also spoken of relation to a living universe, she took the revolver and playfully pointed it at Aeneas. "Take off your hat," she said with a deep-throated intonation.

"My hat?" He put hand to hat, removed it with a flourish, and held it over heart. "Excuse me," he said with a self-minimizing shrug, "I've been so excited ever since you arrived that I forgot to take it off. I deserve to be shot for discourtesy. And for talking physics, too."

"Excited, Professor Caldwell?"

"Yes. . . . Aeneas. Please call me Aeneas. And please don't shoot. I'm beginning to live for the first time. . . . I hope you won't be alarmed. My good spirits are positively unnatural and immoral. My intentions are most praiseworthy, but I cannot praise my wisdom in carrying them out. I get a peculiar pleasure in seeing myself abashed by my own tongue. . . . Trinc? I think I've fallen in love with you!"

Her retort came quickly. "You're extremely sensitive to collisions." Her heart skipped a beat. What could this man see in a dumbbell like her? Firelight danced on the walls behind his dark, curly hair. "Perhaps you should make a phone call about getting me back to school? And were'n't we going to discuss Tubby's hysteria?"

She had thought for a moment that Aeneas was going to fling himself at her feet. She was very relieved when he made a courteous bow, said, "Everything you tell me goes straight to my heart," and left the room carrying her empty plate. He returned with more cake and sat on the sofa beside her. He gave off a faintly spicy odor. "You're right," he said with a sigh. "We have business."

She could not resist a smile. At Grandpa Deck's dinner parties her principal role was to eat without vomiting and to listen without speaking. "We?"

He opened his hairy hands before him and made a tee-pee

with them. "Forgive me. It must have seemed callous of me to dismiss your concerns about Tubby as if I were not taking them seriously enough. Believe me"—he closed his hands for emphasis—"I am in awe of the power of your loyalty to a friend, one, moreover, whose mental balance is of extreme concern to me as the only member of her family in whom she dares confide. Tell me what happened."

Trinc told the story of Tubby at the stables and afterwards. "Tubby is scared," she concluded.

"You've done splendidly," Aeneas said, rising. He had, some while back, put his pipe down and forgotten it. Finding it on the mantelpiece, he clamped it in his teeth, struck a match and lit the pipe. He returned, puffing smoke, to her side, then leaned forward, elbows on knees, one hand cradling the pipebowl. Trinc had grown used to his odor. "Let's put it this way," he began. "Consider our ability to see stars in daytime. The sun is so bright that the stars are invisible, and yet they are just as present in our daytime sky as they are at night. Now consider the human mind. The brilliance of our reasoning ability obscures our awareness of other kinds of perception." He paused to puff on his pipe. "How did we get into our daytime blindness? Simple. We identified 'mind' with reason and relegated all the other processes to a little black box . . . Nowadays it is coming to be called the "unconscious". And there in the unconscious—in the black box, so to say—lies the source of instincts, emotions, passions, dreams. Out of the black box comes art. Out of it comes the principal means of perceiving the world for many a human being, women, children, so-called primitive people, and so on. And yet the black box is denied authority due to the tyranny of reason. Let us not complacently assume that natural phenomena that appear mysterious are nonsense and only reason is sense. In science such an assumption would be laughed out of court! Does passion in Poughkeepsie, for instance, make sense or nonsense? I'm not saying that reason is the only tyrant. The instinctive life, bereft of reason, is also a tyrant. We remain at its mercy unless we open the black box . . . Bear with me. I'm coming around to poor Tubby."

Passion in Poughkeepsie? I'm yours.

"Go on," said Trinc, mouth full of cake. "I like the stars in daytime and the black box."

He met her gaze, smiled, resumed. "Okay . . . Back a quarter of a century ago William James argued that phenomena of consciousness have direct bearing on behavior. Each act of consciousness, he suggested, has biologically significant purposes to accomplish. So, you see, the black box that prompts behavior does so in a meaningful way, and, if we open the black box, we will begin to find out how the whole mind exercises control. In fact, scientists are learning that intuitional and emotional knowledge is as primary and hence as justified a criterion of trustworthy knowledge and of the good and divine in culture, as rational knowledge . . . We become, as it were, children again. We re-gain the innocence of insight. We open ourselves to the instinctive. We become receptive to a sense of being related to all peoples, past, present, and to come. Are dreams not real experience? Is breathing not real, even though we have better evolutionary things to do than to pay attention to it all of the time?'

"Let us peer into the black box. As our eyes become accustomed to the dark, and as we train a metaphorical telescope on the interstellar spaces of the brain, we discern a marvellous constellation of stars: memory, imagination, music, mathematics, dance. These are but a few of them."

"Dance," Trinc interjected. She swallowed the cake down with cider. "I like that."

"It's *all* a dance in another sense. No line can be drawn between conscious and unconscious brain functions, because all are involved in directing our behavior and in allowing us to select appropriate actions. Now, to us—to the two of us here who are mysteriously attuned to one another—this makes sense. But no matter how true a thing may be—and my feelings, Trinc, are true—the world at large at first refuses to believe it. It's too radical, too revolutionary. Do you believe in love at first sight? I've only begun to believe in it myself.'

"In New York I've listened to lectures on sexual behavior and the interpretation of dreams. Well, let me tell you, we who conduct our lives as if we are perfectly normal, are, in fact, neurotics. Our instinctive life is partially blotted out except when it reveals itself in dreams . . . Have you guessed, now, what I'm going to say about Tubby?"

Trinc had finished the cake and was licking her fingers, something, she realized, she had never done before in another person's presence. But, then, she thought, you've never before been in the presence of someone who lets you be yourself, not even Uncle Doc. She screwed up her face to show that she was thinking, then let it relax to show there was nothing to it. "Since you said, before, that she is hysterical, what you're going to say now is that she didn't have a miscarriage, though she produced the symptoms . . . I have a question. Why does she accuse an old man in Greenwich Village, a "Freudian" someone you apparently know, of getting her drunk and seducing her?"

"I was coming to that," Aeneas said. "But, first, I have a question. Was the gun loaded?"

"No."

"I thought not," he sighed with comic exaggeration and, turning to her, searched her eyes deeply with his own. It seemed to her that she would be surrendering her lips, her body, at almost any moment. Her drowsy sensations, the fatigue mixed with food and warm drink, had her leaning closely enough to him to surrender her chastity, upon request, without a scruple.

He withdrew his gaze. "I have a friend," she heard him say, "one of Dr. Brill's crowd, a German Freudian psychoanalyst. He's in his fifties, not old. Tubby has been his patient for some time so he wouldn't seduce her. Besides, he's married. I'd bet my bottom dollar that Tubby is as pure as the driven cliché." Aeneas groaned in exasperation, waking Trinc up just as she was toppling. "The thing I don't understand is why she would let you risk your life for her out on the turnpike!" He pounded his fist into the palm of his hand, hard.

Trinc liked his protectiveness. "Now that we've met," she prompted sleepily, thinking Now.

He didn't seem to notice her unfinished remark. "Tubby told me about her diagnosis, last summer. It sounds bizarre—something about the fulfillment of an unconscious desire. She wants to bear her father's child. Having repressed this desire from consciousness, she expresses it in symptoms of a miscarriage and projects her guilt onto the old doctor. Of course in Greenwich Village the intellectuals are turning psychoanalysis into a parlor game, pretending that we must all cast off inhibitions like a suit of Puritan clothes. It's rot, don't you think?"

"It depends on the inhibitions," Trinc said. "Why pretend to cast off clothes when all you need to do, as you say, is to be like children?"

Aeneas rose. "I'm going upstairs to the bedroom to telephone a friend of mine with a horse trailer. Mr. Toomey can take your horse to the school gates. We can follow in my car. When we get near the school, you can ride to the stable. When you speak to Tubby, tell her there's no parting from one's own shadow. As for us, now that we've met—" he paused to smile gently and caress her with his eyes—"our need is to admire magnificence and rejoice in the beauty of things, to remember that there are swirls of galaxies flashing with fire, and to reflect that two people like us can be a divining rod to find a path to the stars. I'll be back, right—"

"—smart!" Trinc completed his idiom for him. She was glad to discover that he could chuckle in his throat . . .

SHE HAD HALF-LISTENED TO THE MUFFLED SOUND of his voice from upstairs, talking over the telephone to an operator, then to a friend, the voice see-sawing in and out of other sounds, the water-fairy wail of the wind through the crack of the door, the slap and patter of rain ejaculated on window panes. She felt an irresistible urge to dance. She tossed aside the steamer rug, stripped off her stockings and sweater. She placed a screen in front of the fire and went and closed and locked the door.

With her eyes half closed and her hands pressed to the warmth of silk blouse, she began to sway and turn, sway and turn, letting her arms sweep darkness back to the farthest depths of space and time, then bringing them back so that slowly, rapturously, they opened like the petals of a rose.

After a while she knew he was watching her. She didn't want to open her eyes fully, all at once. She hoped he would come to her as in a dream. Then he was near, holding her hands in his—releasing them, holding them—and, dancing to her rhythm, pulling her, little by little, into his arms. In quiet voice he spoke to her. His friend, Mr. Toomey, would be ready any time. There was no hurry. "Peter Rabbit's a-cold," Aeneas whispered, "but, if you wish to leave at once, I'm a gentleman. As the saying goes, 'a gentleman is too indolent to harbor malice'."

She knew what the words meant. She opened her eyes, met his gaze, and nodded to his beseeching. "Don't talk now," she murmured as she leaned into his arms. "We don't want to blot out the instinctive life."

"I love you, Trinc."

She knew as he kissed her on the lips that she loved him, too, and she knew that when he was lying naked in bed she would undress herself by window-light so that he could see the moons of her breasts, the Milky Way of her belly and thighs. Even before he took her hand and led her upstairs to bed, a constellation of her inner stars had become exquisitely bright. Later, in bed, she felt him deep inside her. The stars exploded again and again, and words came too, tender and ecstasy-blurred, of love and belonging.

5

THE WOUND

(Letter one)

Letter from Aeneas Caldwell, dated April 21, 1916, from Poughkeepsie, New York, SPECIAL DELIVERY to Miss Trinc DeRoman, St. Benet's School:

O MISTRESS MINE,

Where are you roaming?—or rather, just where do you want me to roam? Into the paths of sin? Apparently. I haven't heard from you since we parted three hours ago.

I'm not surprised. But the law of supply and demand in these matters is potent as well as in economics: if there is free love going a-begging, I was, before last night, but virginally hopeful of the fact. As I view the nature of my wants quite calmly, you may tolerably expect a continent lover to return to your arms. I won't count it a particular virtue, if such turns out to be the case; for I don't like smugness. Besides, it seems finer to wait for your sweet, wild passion.

I'm a romanticist. I still protest in behalf of useless words like *soul, spirit.* I cling to you because my memory of our love remains terribly spiritual, and because it seems more beautiful to wait. I hand you the palm for courage, but should we not fear for our love?

Is the cabbage season over so soon? Have Mr. and Mrs. Macgregor gone into winter-quarters when it is spring? I miss your company—which warms my rabbit heart—and I do sorely miss your nice soft fur. After we parted, I needed your fur especially, for the wind blew and the patch was desolate. I reflect on how miserable the cold barrow is without you. I am all a-cold without you. I love you, and you love me—at least, you say you do—and under the wise moon I hope I shall some night find you safely tucked away by a hay-rick, where I shall always thereafter find you.

> *I do not think that Time should find us late,*
> *The prophet of eternities of parting;*
> *I did not speak farewell as if our fate*
> *Were yesterday without tomorrow starting.*
> *To Time we leave one April night behind,*
> *Seizing the hours before they plague the mind.*

If spiritual oneness is the achievement of only the dull and happily unconscious, I can't say I'm all for it. Toward love, until we met, I went to scoff, but now I remain to pray. I should never have let you go. As it is, I have not only let you go but neglected to let you know that I am pledged to your happiness forever.

When you galloped back to school at three o'clock this morning, leaving me and Mr. Toomey out in the fog of the turnpike, did you know that I was overwhelmed by a sense of despair? The plain, unvarnished fact of the matter is, I am supposed to leave Poughkeepsie the day after tomorrow. I resigned my temporary position at Vassar a week ago. I am driving west to attend my mother's remarriage in northern New Mexico. Until last night I was planning to see Mother happily married and then to join the Army in El Paso where it is currently chasing Pancho Villa. We are certain to be drawn into the war in Europe. I realize it's thumbs down on patriotism among intelligent people, but I have been so lonely for so long, and relatively poor (though I shan't urge any sympathy on that score), that I've had a curious desire to throw my talents away, like a bundle down an elevator shaft, and a plaguey guilt about letting lads with wives and sweethearts and families do all the dirty work for our country.

Marry me, my darling!

Please telephone me at once to say Yes! This afternoon will not be soon enough, but this afternoon and all day tomorrow I shall be waiting for you in my car by the school gates. Come with me. We can be married tonight, or whenever you say. We can live at my mother's home in New Mexico until I find employment at a university here or abroad. If your answer is Yes, but you cannot come with me, I will return for you as soon as possible. Wait for me! I will always wait for you.

If your answer is *No*, I join the Army. I shall write to you if it is permitted. I love you, I love you.

That school of yours is no good. If you should choose to prepare for college education, I shall do all in my power to encourage a person of your exceptional character and mind, irrespective of the feelings that I have declared to you, and for which I shall always remain, wherever I shall be and in whatever circumstances,

Your devoted friend,
PETER RABBIT

Your adoring and hopeful,
AENEAS CALDWELL

P.S. Among country folk in North Carolina, there is a superstition that, if the first child is a boy, all his father's hats must be burned, else he'll be "a no 'count, dirt-eatin', yeller coward." I have the hat ready—and the matches.

(letter two)

Letter from H. Dexter Heartwell, Office of the President, Heartwell Brothers Mills, Orford Parish, Connecticut, dated April 28, 1916, marked PLEASE FORWARD, to Aeneas Caldwell, Esq., Vassar College, Poughkeepsie, New York:

Dear Mr. Caldwell:

Your letter of April 21st, addressed to my granddaughter, Miss Susan Heartwell DeRoman, has been brought to my attention by the Headmistress of St. Benet's School. Fortunately the letter was intercepted before it could be delivered. Since you choose to have a low opinion of the school, you'll be interested to know that I am its principal benefactor and President of its Board of Directors.

Enclosed with this letter of mine you will find a letter from my daughter, Henrietta, Mrs. Gayle DeRoman, Susan's mother and legal guardian.

It is her wish that you cease and desist at once from further communication of any kind with Susan.

If you are a gentleman, as I seriously doubt, you will withdraw honorably from the field. If you are a scoundrel, as I seriously believe, I am obliged to warn you that you will be exposed and that painful consequences will follow for you, and for the rest of your life.

I have spoken with your former employers at Vassar College and am given to understand that your behavior there has been exemplary and that you have a "brilliant" academic career ahead of you. In future, I trust, you will devote yourself to that career and not insinuate yourself into the affections of young ladies beyond your station.

Sincerely,

H. Dexter Heartwell
President

(Letter three)

Letter from Mrs. Gayle DeRoman, dated April 27, 1916, to Mr. Aeneas Caldwell:

Sir:

Who do you think you are? With whom do you think you are dealing? Do you believe that an intellectual of your class and pretensions is going to get away with an elopement with my child? If so, you are very much mistaken.

We are not going to tolerate your under-handed conduct. If there is further communication of any kind between you and my daughter, or between you and other members of our family, you will answer for the consequences. As it is, we could have you tried and convicted on a charge of statutory rape.

Your conspiracy has been nipped in the bud. Before Miss Tabitha Van Dyke was expelled from school, she confessed everything to Headmistress Bates. We know how you coerced Miss Van Dyke into procuring for you, quote, "a rich, naive young girl," end-quote, that she would support you for life. Not only is your opportunism evident, but also your cowardice. It is perfectly clear that you intended to marry into our family in order to avoid military service. We also know that you conspired to have Miss Van Dyke pretend to have a "miscarriage," that my daughter's decent feelings would be aroused on behalf of a troubled friend; and that thus she would be lured into your trap. You have succeeded in ruining Miss Van Dyke's life. Had Miss Bates not been performing her duty to read all in-coming mail, as she also reads all outbound mail, you might have succeeded in the ruin of my daughter also.

My daughter knows nothing of your preposterous scheme. She is strictly confined to the school's premises until she graduates. At that time she will remain under my custody at Orford Parish. Do not trouble yourself to write her further "love" letters. Do not attempt to reach her via telephone. Do not employ third parties in an effort to lure her away.

We have methods to stop you. We shall use them.

As for kidnapping, be assured that the constabulary is already in possession of a description of you and will arrest you on sight.

Do I make myself perfectly clear?

Peter Rabbit? How repulsive!

Mrs. GAYLE DEROMAN

(Letter four)

Letter from Aeneas Caldwell, dated May 15, 1916, from Los Remedios, New Mexico, to Mr. H. Dexter Heartwell:

Dear Mr. Heartwell and Mrs. DeRoman,

Your letters were forwarded to me by my former "employers" in Poughkeepsie. I am grateful for your candor, for I was under the impression that Trinc had rejected me. Now I know that is not the case. There has been no "under-handed conduct." You've thought of everything except Trinc's happiness.

Since her happiness, and not your "method" of intimidation, comes uppermost with me, I shall not purge myself of concern for her welfare. I refuse to bind myself to your quaint notions of class and caste.

I extend to you due respect for authority. Where Trinc's happiness is concerned, however, she should be informed about your rules, given a chance to refute this nonsense about a conspiracy, and be respected for making her own decisions. If she does injury to herself, you "will answer for the consequences," etc.

Felix qui potuit rerum cognoscere causas.

AENEAS CALDWELL

(Letter five)

Letter from Major Gayle DeRoman, dated June 4, 1917, from the S.S. "Baltic" to Trinc DeRoman, Orford Parish, Connecticut:

Dear Trinc:

When I was six-years-old my mother took me to the old French opera house on Bourbon Street in New Orleans to hear Lecoc's delightful *"La Fille de Madame Angot."* I came to know by heart every one of its catchy songs. At Yale my most popular stunt was to represent the market woman who sings a song from *Madame Angot.* I'd don a skirt, if one was handy, or, if not, tuck a towel in my belt, stuff a cushion inside of the breast of my coat, roll up my trousers, and with appropriate gestures sing, "Marchande de marais, pour cent mille raisons," etc.

Now for my story.

In April, after President Wilson finally declared war on Germany, I immediately filed my application with the War Department for a commission in the Judge Advocate's Corps. I'd attended the Officer's Training Camp at Plattsburg and yearned to be appointed a lieutenant of Infantry. But General Leonard Wood told me that the War Department had decided not to appoint anyone over forty-four years of age as a lieutenant or a captain in the Infantry. With regret, therefore, I applied for that commission in the Judge Advocate's Corps. Then on May 16, 1917, a telegram arrived from Washington signed by General Crowder, the Judge Advocate General of the Army, asking whether I could absent myself from dear Amelia and Gayle, Jr., and from the United States for an indefinite period; if so, to come at once to see him. In a state of suppressed excitement I took the first train to Washington, presented myself at General Crowder's office, and was ushered in. He asked if I could wind up my affairs in the course of the next twelve days so as to be ready for an absence for the period of the War. I said I could.

"Very well," he said. "I have recommended to General Pershing that you be appointed the Assistant Judge Advocate of his Staff of about fifty-four officers who will accompany him to France in the course of the next two or three weeks."

My heart beat with joy. Recommended to the Staff of the Commanding General of the American Expeditionary Force! General Crowder then took me to General Pershing's office and presented me. The General was standing. "Gen'l Crowder says you speak French fluently, is that so?" he asked.

"My mother taught it to me, General, as a child," I replied. "I believe that I speak it fluently."

"Good," he said. "Report to my Chief of Staff."

When I reported to Colonel Harbord, I was told we could be sailing for France in the course of several weeks. I was to mention the fact to no one, for the Germans must not know when General Pershing sailed, else submarines would swarm to attack his ship.

One day, I packed my uniform, boots, and belts in a suitcase, donned citizen's clothes, and drove in a taxicab all the way from Philadelphia to New York, so as not to be seen by a German spy; early next morning I reported at Governors Island. But instead of embarking at the White Star dock we were taken from Governors Island in a ferry boat far down the bay, where the "Baltic" awaited us. It was foggy and raining. Crossing the slippery gang plank from the ferry boat to the liner was ticklish work.

Today we are approaching the zone of German submarine operations. We have already received S. O. S. radio calls of distress from eleven vessels which have been torpedoed, but the War Department has ordered that we should not respond to such calls, the safety of the Commanding General of the A. E. F. being too important to warrant our taking risks.

I met an old college mate, General Billy Sherrill. Says Billy, "You didn't know, I suppose, that Cornelius Vanderbilt and I were responsible for your appointment on General Pershing's Staff."

"Why," I asked, "how was that?"

"Well, Neely Vanderbilt and I had some business to transact with General Crowder. He said, 'I understand you two were at Yale with Gayle DeRoman. Do you know him?'"

Both Billy and Neely replied they knew me well.

"'Does he speak French?'" asked General Crowder.

"'*Does* he speak French!'" exclaimed Billy. "'I should say so!'" Turning to Neely, he said, "'Do you remember *La Fille de Madame Angot?*'" Thereupon, Billy proceeded to sing for General Crowder a few bars of my song, with the appropriate gestures, and told the General that I was famous for the song. Neely nodded assent.

That is how I got appointed to General Pershing's Staff.

Back in 1912, when we were living in New York, some ladies asked me if I'd sing my Madame Angot song as one of the numbers of a Vaudeville show they were getting up for the benefit of the cause of Equal Rights for Women. I said I would.

On the night of the show I was well gotten up, with a blue skirt, an apron, and a white waist laced in with a velvet bodice; I had a blonde wig falling in two thick plaits. I looked a pretty tough French market woman. But as I didn't regard with reverence the cause of Equal Rights for Women, I'd composed for the occasion an extra verse in English, to follow the last verse of the French song.

The last verse of the French song ran thus:

Enfin toute sa vie elle voyagait—*mais*
C'est surtout en Turqué qu'elle eut un grand succes.
Parmi ses cinq cent femmes le Sultan certain soir,
Brulant de mille flamme la jeta le mouchoir.

Here's a translation:

And so all of her life she travelled—*but*

In Turkey especially she had a big success.
Among his 500 wives the Sultan, on a certain night,
Burning with 1000 flames of passion, threw her
his handkerchief.

Meaning, of course, that the Sultan elected her to his harem.

Here is the verse I added:

There then ensued a crisis the Sultan still regrets:
Madame and all his ladies became mad suffragettes.
They voted her Sultana, and, as Turkish men did flee,
She clapped twelve in her harem, crying,
"Equal rights for me!"

At the conclusion of my performance the Committee thanked me politely but with a frosty reserve.

I was pleased to hear that you graduated from St. Benet's and have decided to attend Orford Parish High School for several years in order to put your mind to work. I am not so happy to hear that Hen and the Heartwells want you to prepare to "come out" in Society. Don't become a Social Parasite.

Au plaisir,

FATHER

(Letter six)

Letter from Major Gayle DeRoman, dated June 12, 1917, from rue des Fossies St. Jacques, Paris, to Trinc DeRoman, Orford Parish, Connecticut:

Dear Trinc,

I intend to write to you as often as possible. Please save my letters so that I may refer to them in future when I am writing my memoirs.

Our arrival in Paris brought hope to a nation in the depths of despair. France! Nearly 700,000 buildings have been destroyed. Out of her population of about 9 millions of men between 19 and 50 years of age, a million and a quarter already have been killed, more than that number have been wounded beyond 30% of disability, and millions more have suffered lesser wounds.

As we rode in carriages from the Station, vast crowds greeted us with emotion too deep to be noisy, but in their faces and bearing its depth was apparent. Women with children in their arms would dart from the crowd to kiss our hands.

Soon after our arrival the French Government staged for General Pershing and his Staff an exhibition of the aeroplane defenses of the City. At the flying field we saw 300 planes take off at a signal to meet the supposed enemy.

The last feature of the program was to be a visit to a field three miles away where the newest combat planes were tried out and then sent to the Front, a large number every day. At the hour appointed for this feature I set out by automobile with two French officers, a captain and a major, to meet General Pershing and the other members of the Staff at this flying field.

Now, General Pershing had passed word that he could not take part in this part of the program. However, I was the only member of the Staff who was not told. The French officers at the flying field also were never informed. They awaited General Pershing's coming with a company of infantry and six buglers. Pershing was to be received with the highest military honors.

When we arrived at the field, the company of infantry presented arms, and the buglers sounded the notes of "Hail to the Commander in Chief." As I was not familiar with bugle calls, this one meant nothing to me. But the captain and the major seemed, for some reason, to be uncomfortable. Although the ceremony did seem rather elaborate for receiving me, a mere major, I reflected that the French were simply overjoyed to have us Americans on their side and that honors for any American officer were the order of the day.

As I descended from the automobile the officer in command stepped forward and saluted. He was accompanied by a young aviator dressed in red breeches and a light blue jacket. The officer in command presented this young aviator, informing me that he had downed six German *avions* and that he would have the honor of guiding me over the field. The youth's face shone with pride and joy as he took me in charge. Not another American officer had appeared.

It dawned on me that there was a mistake somewhere.

When, a moment later, the aviator answered a question I had asked with, *"Oui, mon général,"* my suspicions were confirmed. But I realized that to reveal my identity to the boy would not only be a blow to his pride but also would create an awkward situation all around. Even if I assumed that the officer in command eventually might learn the truth, he could be depended upon to hold his tongue lest he become the laughing stock of the entire French Army.

So I decided to bow to the circumstances which were making me Commanding General of the A. E. F.

When the tour of inspection was finished, I thanked my guide and, pointing to the medal of the Legion of Honor on his chest, said, "They tell me that your valor has well merited this honor." He blushed with appreciation.

When I was driving away with the captain and the major, I told them the story of the German general who died at the house of his aunt in a little village. The aunt died next day. The general's coffin was to be forwarded to Berlin for burial with military honors, whereas the aunt was to be buried in the village cemetery. Two days after the general's coffin had been shipped, the aunt's relatives took a last look into her coffin and found that, by mistake, the general, not the aunt, was in it. A telegram announcing this fact was immediately sent to Berlin.

The answer came back: "Aunt interred today with full military honors. Say nothing and bury the general in the village cemetery."

The captain and the major understood.

One day, if perchance your children's children come across this letter in the family archives, they will know that GreatGrandfather Gayle was for a few moments the Savior of France!

My first Courts Martial in Paris was of an officer who was so completely drunk that he was found incapable of creating a disturbance. So he was acquitted!

First Class Private James R. Miller, 16 U.S. Engineers, was found guilty of the charge that "he did throw his spoon on the floor and his plate of porridge into a serving pan of the same." He lost five days' pay for this naughtiness.

Here's a story told me by a friend, who has served three years in the French Army.

"Most descriptions of the Front are exaggerated. But there is one thing you cannot exaggerate—the mud. The high explosives of the shells pulverize the earth to a depth of from five to ten feet. The rain makes that a soft mess into which you sink to your knees, and wounded men drown in it.'

"There's a ravine at Verdun 800 meters long, and it's a mess of mud. A position beside it has been captured and recaptured, gained and lost a half a dozen times. It is an important position, and they say that there are 30,000 French and German corpses mixed with the mud of the ravine.'

"One of the entrenchments my Company on one occasion threw up was composed in part of corpses covered over with earth. They'd been buried by shell explosions, and the earth thus thrown up had been utilized as part of the entrenchment. The arm and hand of one deceased soldier projected from the parapet.'

"When the men filed by at the hour for relief, some of them

would shake hands with the projecting hand and say, 'Au revoir'."

Such is the brutality of war.

Au plaisir,

FATHER

(Letter seven)

Letter from Lieutenant Colonel Gayle DeRoman, dated February 3, 1918, from "The Front" to Trinc DeRoman, Orford Parish.

Dear Trinc,

Shortly after my promotion to Lt. Colonel, I requested and received permission to visit the battle zone. While there, I was asked to review the record of the Court Martial of an American Lieutenant who was on trial under a sickening charge, "Misbehavior in the face of the enemy"—in other words, cowardice. If the Lieutenant were found guilty, the penalty would be death by firing squad.

Since the trial had not yet taken place, I decided to attend. It was held in the messroom of the Division Staff, the only room in the village big enough for the purpose. The witnesses carried their rifles while testifying. This was according to regulations. The miserable accused, pale as a ghost, sat beside his counsel.

I had taken a particular interest in the case, though I was careful not to disclose this fact to the Division Commander because he wanted me to recommend approval, disapproval, or alteration of the verdict. The accused was no mere boy; he was twenty-eight years of age. Moreover, his record of service was a distinguished one. He had volunteered in El Paso, Texas, in 1916. Due to his having had a truly extraordinary education— he holds a Ph.D. Degree from Harvard in physics—he was commissioned and trained for Intelligence operations. It was not intended that he lead troops in battle. However, here in France, the officers of his Company were all killed. This First Lieutenant volunteered to take command. On three occasions he successfully led his men when it was necessary to attack entrenched enemy machine-gun emplacements. And on those occasions, it was said, he displayed such reckless courage that it seemed he was seeking to die in a hail of machine-gun fire. Finally, of some personal interest to me was the fact that the accused, one First Lieutenant Aeneas Caldwell, had been a Visiting Instructor at Vassar College. As you may know, Amelia graduated from this Yale and Harvard of women's colleges.

While there are some educated men among American officers, there are many more who, once the uniform is off, are quite ordinary men without refinement. This latter type was going to judge the character of a man superior to them, this Lieutenant Caldwell.

As I listened to the testimony, my imagination and nerves made my stomach cave in. I found myself experiencing vicariously some of the same terrors which Caldwell had experienced. I said to myself, "I am going into battle. Can I be certain that I might not act as he did?"

As if to place a punctuation mark to my thoughts, a couple of German bombing planes flew over the village and dropped scores of bombs, shaking the windows of the mess-hall and filling it with clouds of dust. I could see the officers, sitting rigidly erect, turn their eyes in the direction of the explosions. Wondering what would happen if a bomb scored a direct hit, I imagined the officers diving under the table, crying, "I vote for acquittal." Through it all, Caldwell stood unflinchingly, a look of almost angelic insouciance on his face.

According to testimony he had gone "over the top" with his first platoon. But then his feet got stuck in the mud. And then he lay on the ground while the battle went on and the shells burst around him.

When the prosecuting officer asked Caldwell to explain his behavior, he said that he'd been working "unconsciously" on a problem having to do with Einstein's theory of Relativity; that, just when he got stuck in the mud, the meaning to the problem had suddenly occurred to him; and that the experience so enchanted him, he completely forgot where he was. It was, he said, like seeing the face of God!

There was a sniggering of disbelief in the messhall. "Oh," said the prosecuting officer with a supercilious look, "the face of God? May I ask what He looks like?"

"It wasn't a 'he', sir," Caldwell replied in a dignified manner. "It was a light, like radium in pitch-blende."

"And did you converse with this, uh, radium?"

"I was spellbound, sir."

This line of response was obviously displeasing to the Court. Few of the officers, I surmised, knew anything about Relativity theory, and they probably thought Einstein was a German spy. I doubted that they knew that the Nobel Prize in physics was awarded in 1903 to Marie and Pierre Curie for isolating radium from pitch-blende. Who could explain why an officer leading his men into battle would be paralyzed by a "revelation" about space-time? Mysticism or poppycock?

But now came the most astonishing testimony of all. A medical officer of the Army Corps had examined the accused, and an appalling fact had come to light.

The accused, First Lieutenant Aeneas Caldwell, was for all intents and purposes a *castrate!*

At some time before he had volunteered in El Paso, he had suffered an injury in the genital area. The testicles, though not removed, were a mass of scar tissue. At the time of his enlistment, he had a document signed by a physician in Santa Fe, New Mexico, to the effect that the injury would not affect Caldwell's ability to lead a normal life, although he was incapacitated for sexual intercourse. He was permitted to enlist. The medical officer of the Army Corps, however, was of the opinion that a man without "manhood" was incapable of resisting the nervous terror which, it was alleged, had taken possession of him. Caldwell had literally been paralyzed with fear.

On this uncontradicted testimony the Court Martial was obliged to acquit First Lieutenant Caldwell.

The acquittal was a serious matter for the morale of a Division about to go into battle. Some of the men might be tempted not to resist the nervousness which brave men have to overcome in order to do their duty as soldiers. The General said to me, "Colonel DeRoman, I can't refuse to approve the verdict. But you must write me an approval which, when it is posted and read by the men of the Division, will make the faint-hearted hesitate to run the risk of having a similar record attached to their names."

I knew what the General wanted me to write—something to the effect that the Lieutenant lacked "force of character" and was "unfit to be an officer," and should be discharged dishonorably from the Army. The General felt personally repulsed by the Lieutenant's loss of "manhood."

Yet, to me, the Lieutenant was blameless. To damn the poor fellow for the rest of his life was hardly fitting punishment for someone with demonstrated patriotism, with courage tested under fire, and with the temperament of a genius. Moreover, the A. E. F. is not composed, for the most part, of men who have undergone the stern discipline that enables them to overcome a natural preference for avoiding danger. Crucifying the Lieutenant would not deter the faint-hearted. At the same time the General could not afford to make it easy for cowards to pretend that they were overcome by an irresistible impulse to avoid battle.

At the conclusion of the trial, after the verdict was read, Caldwell requested permission to speak to the Court. This was granted. He rose to his feet and stood to attention. A big man with dark greenish eyes, he gave an impression of singular *manliness*. Indeed, I thought that instead of blackening this man's record for all time, we might in other circumstances be awarding him the Distinguished Service Medal. He spoke in a deep, pleasant voice with measured tones.

"Gentlemen," he began, "it would be far better for the men to have me shot. I am not ashamed of what happened to me when we went over the top. I was seized by a power of apperception and possessed by an unconscious force. However, I do feel ashamed to be alive when others have died in the line of duty. Many of them have loved ones. The woman I love is denied to me forever. I request that your verdict be disapproved. Thank you."

He sat down amongst sibilant murmurs. I have never heard a finer speech.

I wrote for the General something like this:

"The finding of acquittal is approved. The evidence shows that the soldier was paralyzed with fear when confronted with the dangers of battle, so that he lay down on the ground until his men retreated to the rear.'

"Although the accused was incapable of conduct befitting an officer, he remains fit for service. It is ordered that First Lieutenant Aeneas Caldwell be reduced to the rank of First Class Private and assigned to another Division."

The General scowled at me but signed the order.

I was delighted to receive the snapshots of you in the "Isadora Duncan" costume, in front of that old firetrap, the Homestead.

Hastily,

FATHER

(Letter eight)

Letter from Colonel Gayle DeRoman, dated November 5, 1918, from Tours to Trinc DeRoman, Orford Parish. Enclosed with this letter are the originals of the letters from H. Dexter Heartwell and Mrs. Gayle DeRoman, dated April 28 and 27 respectively, to Aeneas Caldwell; and a copy of the letter of Aeneas Caldwell, dated May 15, 1916, to H. Dexter Heartwell:

Dear Trinc,

Today I am back in Tours with the Services of Supply, thankful to be alive and well, and to have a daily bath, and to dine at my favorite *estaminet*.

Something came up yesterday near Paris. Since it involves one of your Kodak snapshots, the story may interest you.

Do you remember that Court Martial business I reported to you earlier this year? Perhaps you don't, because your correspondence is brief and without commentary on my adventures. Well, yesterday I ran into the unfortunate Aeneas Caldwell again. One need not be surprised by such a coincidence: our American world in France is actually quite small. I had, in fact, expected Caldwell to turn up again in the course of my adventures. And, since I had saved his life, his story must have a place in my memoirs.

I had stopped at American Hospital No. 1 at Neuilly, the best in France, to visit Eliot Gates on Ward 65. He's the son of one of my Yale cronies; I wanted to report to his family about his wounds.

Eliot's a much shotup boy. His foot is partly off and must be amputated to make a proper connection for an orthopedic foot. But I ought to begin further back.

An ambulance driver, Eliot had orders to go out and bring in wounded soldiers. His Ford stalled. He began to jack up the rear wheel to tilt her forward and give her a start. He heard a cannon boom in Boche land and decided to crawl under the machine till after the burst. But he was only partly under the machine when there was a "Wram!" overhead—and when he woke up they'd taken off the pulpy flesh that used to be his toes and the front part of his foot. In addition, he had a fractured right upper arm, a fractured left lower arm, a shoulder full of shrapnel, and some scattered fragments distributed around his back. Evacuated to Neuilly, he has been nervously all out of gear.

When I visited Ward 65, one cheery boy whose leg is off close to the hip said to another cheery boy, who has two vertebrae of his spine shot away and pushes himself around in a wheel chair,—"Say, it's some class to have a colonel come down just to see you."

Next to Eliot was a blue-eyed Irish lad who's got holes in his stomach and bladder, made by machine-gun fire. He suffered a lot. He was writhing and groaning and clenching his hands so that the nails dug into his palms. I gave him a hand to grip on, then I wiped the perspiration from his brow and passed my hand over it gently. Eliot winked at me, grinned, and whispered, "He's a big baby." But I could not feel hard toward the poor boy.

I fed Eliot bits of chocolate and gave him cigarettes and talked of topics cheerful. As I talked, the others—poor, bored, suffering creatures—craned their necks to listen. They had no visitors, you see, and it helps to hear news of home. I got to raising my voice. To the ears of a dozen wounded boys I spoke of you, of your studies, your dances, your amateur theatricals, all your gay doings. Then I passed around the Kodak snapshots of you, to those who could use their hands, holding them up for inspection to those who couldn't. "She's a fine gal." This from Eliot. "My, but she's like an actress." This from Leg Off.

"Colonel DeRoman," Eliot grinned, "from now on we'll call you Mother DeRoman. What d'ya say, fellas?"

There were cheers of applause. It made me proud, the boys were so brave and cheery.

Then a voice rang out from a corner of the ward. "Sir! Colonel DeRoman! May I see the pictures?"

It was Caldwell.

Unknown to him, I was the one who had confirmed his acquittal of the sickening charge of cowardice. He knew my name only because Eliot had spoken it.

I left Eliot and approached the bed of this man whose head was wrapped in bandages. I didn't bother to read his chart. I made no small talk with a man of his intellectual stature. He held out his hand. I placed your picture in it.

He stared at the picture for quite a long time. His eyes glistened and his lip trembled. He said, "She is very beautiful, sir. She will make her husband a very happy man."

I said that you were not married. As I was about to retrieve the picture, he held my eyes in a steady gaze. Could he keep the picture? he asked.

I needed but a moment's reflection. Here is a brave soldier who can never marry and have children of his own. "Of course," I agreed. "Her name is Trinc."

He looked at me strangely. "Trinc DeRoman," he said.

It wasn't a question. I inquired about his wound.

"Near Abri du Crochet, Argonne Forest," he replied without further detail. I realized that he must have been in the thick of some of the fiercest fighting of the war. I half saluted him and turned to go.

"Colonel DeRoman, sir, may I ask you one more favor?"

It turned out that he had in his kit-bag a sealed envelope addressed to his cousin in New York City, a Miss Tabitha Van Dyke who lives on West Fourth Street, as you can see. He wanted me to enclose the envelope with the next letter I write to you, that you might forward the envelope, adding postage. I agreed to have you perform this favor. The envelope is hereby enclosed.

The war is almost over! Vive la victoire!

FATHER

(Letter nine)

Letter from Amelia Jay Ford (Mrs. Gayle) DeRoman, dated December 9, 1918, from Bar-le-Duc to Trinc DeRoman:

My dear Trinc,

Evidently when you telegraphed me in Philadelphia you were not aware that I had embarked for France, taking your little half-brother, Gayle, with me. Fortunately, my friend Maria Valdone, the former Contessa da Braga, understood the urgency implied by your telegram and had its message cabled to me here, care of the Vassar unit of the Y. M. C. A., where I have been since the Armistice of November 11th and your father is united with us as often as he can be relieved of duty.

Let me say what a great pleasure it is that a cordial relationship is established between us all, whatever the past wounds, given or received, may have been. Nothing could please me more. You have matured into a fine young woman of twenty who disavows the rancorous feelings of the Heartwell clan toward your father and his second wife.

Your father has always spoken highly of you. His generosity betokens that esteem. He knows what the Heartwells think of him, that he is an egotist. He knows, too, that he has neglected you in the past. To put the matter bluntly, he knows that his desire to have a son, recently manifested in his affection for our American fighting boys, may have caused you to feel you are second-best. He cannot help this; his family traditions and cultural predispositions could hardly have influenced him otherwise. Although he does not openly express his love, he loves his only daughter.

You requested that I visit a wounded soldier, a former Vassar professor named Dr. Aeneas Caldwell, in the American hospital in Neuilly. I was to impart to him your enigmatic message: THE FUR FOR PETER RABBIT'S WOUND AWAITS HIM BROKEN-HEARTED BY THE HAY-RICK.

Since fur does not have a heart, I realized that you relied upon my female intuition to understand that there are high, secret stakes in this matter, and that I should seek out Dr. Caldwell discreetly, without calling your father's attention to the matter. I went to Neuilly.

I regret to tell you that Dr. Caldwell is nowhere to be found. No one by the name of First Class Private Caldwell was recently on record as having been admitted to the hospital.

I shall continue my efforts to find him. Quite possibly there has been a mix-up in orders, as often happens. Dr. Caldwell may have already been "de-mobbed" (as the British say) and sent home. I'll write you as soon as I have any information.

Love,

AMELIA

Betrayed

THE SUDDENNESS OF HIS VANISHING takes her unawares. The more she ponders it, the more she feels akin to Hamlet. The world, out of joint, twists itself in her imagination into restless and elaborate shapes. She listens to the beating of the wings of her soul as it tries to sustain its flight in darkness. Alone in her room at the school, away from prying eyes, she sometimes shakes with fury. The vehemence of her feelings, lacking knowledge of why and how she has been betrayed, produces in her a sensation of a mad, headlong dash against the walls of entombment.

Someone, of course, must have betrayed her.

She had been summoned to Miss Bates's office and informed that she was strictly confined to her room. She was under surveillance. She must communicate with no one beyond the gates of the school. She could go to classes. She could eat at the Beanery. The stables were off-limits to her. Although there had been no explanation of the reason for these measures, Trinc realized that her affair with Aeneas had been discovered. Tubby Van Dyke had been expelled from school before Trinc could speak with her.

At first, Trinc believed Aeneas would find a way to effect her escape. If he asked, she would marry him. If he didn't ask, she would flee with him anyway. If he couldn't come at once, he would come eventually. With her money they could defy the world.

As soon as she graduated in May, if she hadn't heard from Aeneas by then, she would have Bruno Rancis drive her to Poughkeepsie. If she didn't find Aeneas there, she would learn of his whereabouts and let Bruno return to Orford Parish without her. She would follow Aeneas to the ends of the earth—even to New Mexico.

So it happened that Bruno Rancis loaded her steamer trunk and suitcases into the Rolls and took her to Poughkeepsie, as commanded.

She sees herself running to the cottage and rapping on the door, her heart beating wildly. When a woman comes to the door who says she has never heard of Professor Caldwell, Trinc loses her nerve, is flummoxed. Her heart frosts over out of season. It is as if the boundaries between life and death, as Aeneas had foretold, are no longer clearly defined.

She returned, bewildered, to Orford Parish.

One night in the middle of June she had retired to her third-story bedroom as soon as the evening torture with Grandpa Deck and his guests was finished. The maids had tidied up her room and turned back the covers of her bed. She undressed, slipped into a lace nightgown, crawled under clean-smelling sheets, and turned off the lamp. The casement windows had been opened to catch a breeze. As it was a warm night, she listened to the wind in the elms, watched moonlight printing trembling leaves on French wallpaper. She fell into fitful sleep. Then she dreamed as never before.

In her dream Aeneas leans against a tall tree that grows beside a sparkling river. He sees nothing before his eyes, not the long shadow of the tree across a place of stones, nor the men springing into black silhouettes against a magenta sky. These she sees, sees and tries to cry havoc, but a lance bleeds down its shaft and onto its bearer's hand until the hand is the color of the sky, and a shrivelled silver moon arises, holding in its cup the severed head of a horse, and Aeneas screams.

She woke, stifling *his* scream in *her* throat. She switched on the lamp. Muslin curtains swayed by the window. On the dresser was the picture of Father in his uniform at the Plattsburg Officer Training Camp. The alarm clock ticked. Shivering, she went to the bathroom and wrapped herself in a Japanese robe. Once so magical with its gold-plated faucets set in marble counter-tops, with its gilt-edged oval mirror, with its heady scent of perfumed soap, the room now was claustrophobic.

It was like everything in the house. There were dozens of rooms for family and servants. There were drafty corridors and broad, squeaky staircases. There was the oak-beamed attic, like the inside of a Spanish galleon, where once she had invented plays and operated a toy train to her heart's content. The house that had seemed so full of life had never, its magic notwithstanding, really been full. It reserved for itself some queer, empty spaces, as did Grandpa Deck himself.

What was she doing here? The mirror gave back answer: it reflected both the terror of her starkly staring eyes and the self-contempt of the sardonic smile at the corners of her mouth. She was living her life as a sham, not fashioning it from within. The life for which she was responsible had to begin by being responsible to itself. But these, she knew, were the reflections of someone who was barely holding on to reality. She needed all of her energy just to cope, just to struggle against the death of her heart.

She went, sat by the open bedroom window, and stared into darkness. She told herself to think calmly.

No Trust. That was the Heartwell motto. The family had it branded on their souls. Granny Ah, the Bostonian, remarked that Grandpa Deck "ground the faces of the poor," but Mother, flying into one of her Towering Rages, retorted that Grandpa Deck was a saint. Something crawled in Trinc's flesh when she thought about this patrician, the pillar of society, her benefactor.

He seemed appropriately kind and wonderful, this slender man with ice-blue eyes and silvery mustache and beard, but he didn't permit anyone to get close to him. He presided over an industry that reached its tentacles into the corners of the earth even though, it was said, the business of the mills was conducted in New York—ruinously—by Uncles Charles and Cliff, with Uncle Henry managing the mills themselves. What did Grandpa Deck do every day when he had himself chauffeured a quarter of a mile from his house to his office? What about Bruno Rancis? An ex-convict from the north of England, Bruno served no one but Grandpa Deck and lived alone in a loft over the garage adjacent to the house. During the years when he took Trinc to and from school, this squat, balding, pock-faced coachman with the impossible Yorkshire accent spoke only when spoken to, and then revealed little. If servants were mirror images of their masters—a platitude taught at St. Benet's as part of domestic economy—Bruno had certainly acquired the *No Trust* sign.

Looking out the window, Trinc spied the faint outline of the old Jouncing Board under a magnolia tree. The sight of it, for a moment, stirred fond memories. Pliant as a diving board at a swimming pool, the Jouncing Board was a sort of trestle between a pair of supports. You could sit in the middle and swing your legs up and cause vibrations that lifted your bottom up and spanked it down. Trinc and Aunts Edith and Dodo had often "jounced" together. Everyone squealed in delight. It was all innocent fun. Remembering those times, Trinc slipped under their spell. Then the scene repelled her.

She went and cranked the handle of her Victrola. She settled the needle in the groove of a new record. The room was filled with the screechyscratchy heartbreak of Orpheus and Eurydice.

"Stop that hideous noise!"

She gasped as a shock wave passed along her spine. Realizing that Mother had entered her room without knocking, she retrieved the needle and composed her nerves before turning to look at Mother, who was wearing the long silk "little dress."

It was remarkable how Mother's hearing had been completely restored since her divorce.

"This is my room," Trinc said with no effort to control her anger. "If you wish to see me, you can write a letter to me and slip it under the door." As soon as the words were out, she felt ashamed of her truculent tone.

Mother glared. "I'll not have my child telling me what to do."

"Oh? I'll not have a bitter old divorcée telling *me* what to do."

Mother flung out, "We'll see what Daddy has to say about that!" Mother slammed the door behind her.

Next afternoon Trinc found herself in the Homestead, Mother seated primly beside her, Grandpa Deck pacing the floor. Trinc thought he might knock the marble busts from their pedestals. He frightened her. She had never before been summoned to her grandfather's presence. The fact that some mysterious and God-like curse seemed about to be thundered through the Homestead made her sense that a Puritan jury had already brooded over her sins.

Grandpa Deck stopped pacing, balled his gnarled hands behind his back, and thundered indeed:

"You're not to see Aeneas Caldwell ever again. You're not to communicate with him in any way."

"We've had enough Southerners in the family," Mother chipped in, unfairly comparing the incomparable Aeneas to Father.

"We know all about him," Grandpa Deck's fulminating voice continued. He gestured to the ghosts of the Homestead. "You have a moral obligation to the family to do as we say. Else, there's hell to pay."

"You'll be cut out of our wills," Mother said.

"Lost," said Grandpa Deck.

Rudeness seemed the only way Trinc could express rage. She settled her glasses on her nose, stood up, glared at Mother and Grandpa Deck and went downstairs to the old keeping room. She rubbed its cool damp air onto her arms. How subtle of the family to choose the Homestead for the destruction of her happiness! The past, the past! As Aeneas had said, *there's no parting from one's own shadow.* Her attention was caught by the low-lying windowpanes. The original Heartwell in the eighteenth century must have had a difficult time clearing snowdrifts away from them in order to open up an unobstructed view of the wilderness, but the wilderness was in the blood all the time, savage and deep and dark. And the door to the room had once been much wider, so that hogsheads could be rolled directly from outside into the buttery—just as the door to the family soul must once have been wider before it conformed to a later, smaller age and the *No Trust* sign was erected.

Through the windows Trinc could see the magnolia tree in full spring bloom.

Bridal. It's bridal.

WHEN BRUNO RANCIS SPOKE, which wasn't often, he was quite a colorful character. Dropping his h's, he called his native town Uddersfield and began sentences with *Appen it's*, while calling human beings *buggers*. Given to being sententious, he would say, "Aye, where's there's mook, there's brahss," evidently meaning, the dirtier the job, the more the money. He had a way, too, of bringing up his criminal past:

"Appen I were down in th' mines and a pore bugger coom arter me with is pick. Appen it were dark and I ave the shoovel in me and. I never give a t'ought to urting the bugger, but I swing me shoovel to old im off. One cut of shoovel made im a capon."

A capon meant a castrated rooster, as Trinc learned from her dictionary.

Bruno looked a brute. His sleek gray uniform was fitted tightly against thick neck and shoulders. Black hairs sprouted on the backs of his hands. When oncoming headlamps molded his cheekbones into shadows, the tufted eyebrows and coal-black mustache looked as if glued on. Riding in the back seat of the

Rolls, she none the less felt at ease with him and often became talkative, though she expected no response.

He was driving her to Hartford for a debutante's ball. September leaves burst into silent flame. Seeing them as the car was crossing the bridge over the sparkling Connecticut River, she was reminded of the dream, how Aeneas was leaning against a tall tree beside a sparkling river near a place of stones, how men sprang, how a lance bled down its shaft, Aeneas screaming.

"Do you ever dream, Bruno?"

She heard him sigh heavily. "Appen it's mook I dream."

"I mean really and truly dream. A scary dream. I had a scary dream back in June. It was like this."

She told him the dream. He slowed the car.

"A place of stoones?" she heard him ask. "A bluddy and?"

Bruno drove on for a couple of miles before he abruptly pulled over to the side of the road near the Capitol Building and left the engine idling. He turned his head and studied her, wetting lips, touching the tip of mustache with flicking tongue. "Appen it's June, ye say, Miss?" he asked in a weirdly challenging tone.

"July or August," she lied quickly. "It was just a dream. It didn't mean anything."

His eyes narrowed for a moment before he turned around and engaged the gear. "Loovely day," he gestured to the sky.

FEBRUARY, 1918.

She receives Father's letter about the court-martial of Aeneas. His monstrous and mysterious wound is now her own.

SEPTEMBER, 1918.

Grandpa Deck had been taken to a hospital at an undisclosed location and had died of a mysterious illness in the spring. According to family custom, he was cremated and buried without services of any religious kind, just a gathering of the clan for distribution of booty. Granny Ah received the mansionhouse and the Homestead and like Mother and the uncles and aunts received shares of stock in the mills. Trinc received a pearl necklace that had belonged to a great-great-grandmother in Exeter, New Hampshire.

Now Grandpa Deck's portrait was to be placed in the most prominent position in the house.

After Augustus carried out the tea things, the women and Uncle Robin went into the Big Room to see if the electricians had finished their job. Where shelves of calf-bound books had risen to the ceiling behind the piano, there was a blank space with sunken light fixtures above and below. Mother and Edith and Dodo rustled about, straightening rugs and replacing vases moved while the workmen were busy. Rex, the old dog, sniffed the alien scent of boots on the polished floor and seemed to note the chairs which had been shoved from time-honored places. Trinc sat on the floor. When Uncle Robin sauntered past her, his in-the-closet homosexuality looking about as criminal as boiled custard, she knew he would like to exhibit his hands after tea. "Please play something, Uncle Robin." He sat at once at the piano. After running a few arpeggios, he played Grieg's "Hall of the Mountain King" while she watched his lean, tapering hands.

It was then that Granny Ah entered through the dining room archway. Seeming to rest on her full petticoats and black taffeta dress, she extended a tiny jeweled hand to Rex, who came over and pressed his head under it. Uncle Robin jumped up from the piano stool and led Granny Ah across the room to see the effects of the new lights in the portrait niche. "Do you like it, Mommy?"

Granny Ah frowned. "It changes the room. We shall see, when the picture comes."

"It won't make you sad, I hope," Mother said.

"Why, no, Hen," said Granny Ah. "If it is like him, it will be like having him with us again."

The portrait had been only half-finished when Grandpa Deck

died. Members of the family had had to go to New York to the artist's studio in order to pose for selected parts. Uncle Robin modeled for the hands, Uncle Henry for the hawk-like nose, Aunt Edith for the ice-blue eyes.

Trinc's memories of her grandfather had lately taken on a sentimental coloration. She remembered how he used to carry great logs to the fireplace, causing Rex to bark in appreciation; how, after the fatigue of a walk in the snow, he would bring Granny Ah a thimbleful of sherry on a silver tray, as if it had been a slight discourtesy to have it brought to her by one of the servants; and how, when he stood to carve a roast, he served children first. "Forgive me," he would say to the guests. "It is a family custom, because the littlest ones have the biggest appetites and the least patience." He would cut the children's meat in small pieces with the carving knife so they would not spatter grease on the damask cloth or take up their mothers' attention, asking for help with the heavy silver knives and forks. Trinc had been served according to the custom right through her nineteenth year.

The clearest memory of all was of Grandpa Deck on Christmas mornings. Everyone would gather on the stairs in the dark, the children whispering and shivering with excitement, the grownups not allowed to peek down into the Big Room where stockings were hung by the fireplace until the moment came when Grandpa Deck groped his way past them on the staircase, a box of matches rattling in his hand, and when there was a spurt of flame as he struck a match and lit a kerosene-soaked Cape Cod lighter, whirling the flaming torch over his head with a strangely diabolic glee before he cried, "Merry Christmas!" and everyone shouted, "Merry Christmas!" and rushed down the stairs.

"When you went to New York to pose for the hands," Granny Ah was saying to Uncle Robin, "was the head of the portrait finished?"

"No, not nearly," Uncle Robin replied, voice inflected by his usual drollery. "Henry was through sitting for the nose and Edith for the eyes. If it is not a good likeness of Daddy, it will be an interesting composite of the whole family."

"Interesting indeed." Granny Ah's eyes rested upon Robin and Mother, Edith and Dodo, each in turn. "If it is not like him as I remember him, it shall not be hung in this room. I shall destroy it at once with an axe."

Mother gasped. "Did you say an axe?"

"An axe."

Uncle Robin's eyebrows warned his sisters to hold their tongues. Aunt Edith burst out, "Re-ally, Mother! One does not simply destroy the work of a famous artist because it does not happen to express one's ideals." Aunt Dodo piped up in small voice, "The picture has not been paid for."

Granny Ah lifted round chin. "Write the check for me, dear, and I'll sign it."

Aunt Dodo pursed lips. "Two thousand dollars!"

Aunt Edith, the sister who, not having married well, thought a great deal about keeping up appearances, pursued the argument. "Now, Mother, oil paintings can be retouched again and again. Surely you can rely on my opinion, after all my years of art study in Paris? You always said, yourself, I had Daddy's eyes. There is no doubt in my mind that the artist reproduced them exactly. If you want them made dreamy, why of course they can be painted over."

"No doubt you want the nose made dreamy, too," Aunt Dodo offered with ill-concealed sarcasm.

Uncle Robin took Granny Ah's hand and gave it a lover's kiss. "I understand you now, Mommy. You want the artist to show Daddy's noble side. So do we all."

Aunt Dodo said, "We all know Father was a gallant gentleman." She turned and whispered to Aunt Edith, so that Granny Ah could not possibly hear, "But so was the Devil."

Rex's tail went thumpthump on the rug. They all looked up to watch the butler's stately march across the Big Room. He gave

Granny Ah one of his German bows and said, "The expressman is come with the picture, Mrs. Heartwell."

"Thank you, Augustus," Granny Ah raised her hand to her heart as if to quiet it.

"As soon as Henry and Charles and Cliff get home," Aunt Edith said brightly, "we can uncrate the picture."

Granny Ah shook her head. "Augustus is a skilled carpenter. He and I shall open the crate alone."

"Wait." Aunt Dodo took a checkbook out of her purse and stood at the piano as she wrote a check. Trinc guessed that she was trying to let the price of the portrait exert a restraining influence. Granny Ah took the pen from Aunt Dodo and signed the check. She then followed Augustus and Rex out of the room. Trinc and the others went to spy out of the window.

They could see the tool shed and the path leading up to it, but the crate had been set down beyond the porch, out of sight. They could see Rex but not Granny Ah and Augustus. Trinc wondered if the picture would reveal any secret about Grandpa Deck. "Aunt Dodo," she asked, "was Grandpa Deck cruel to the mill hands?"

"Well, no, dear. They hated him because he would not let them unionize."

"Uncle Henry lets them. Why shouldn't they if they want to unionize?"

"For their own good. Strikes are harder on the workers than they are on us. Poor Henry, I'm afraid, lacks Daddy's force of character. He is infected with modern ideas."

"Is he a dangerous radical?" No sooner had Trinc asked the question than she wished she had held her tongue. Uncle Robin heehawed. "When Henry comes home," he cried gleefully, "let's meet him at the door and say, 'Mr. Trotsky, I presume'! My brothers have already lost so much money on the mills, I dare say an uprising of the masses may be in order."

"Do hush," Mother said. Everyone looked at her. "On Christmas Eve we would all pile into sleighs with heaps and heaps of baskets of food and candy and toys. The harness had jingly silver bells, and there were two horses to every sleigh. Father would drive through the mill village, leaving baskets at the doors of all the people who were sick or out of work."

"I hear Rex barking," Aunt Edith interrupted.

"It's over! She's smashed it!" groaned Aunt Dodo.

"Nonsense!" Mother declared. "She had no axe with her. She's just pretending, the way she taught us to do."

"Well," said Uncle Robin, "here comes Augustus."

He was like an old penguin in his long-tailed black coat. He had emerged from the tool shed, holding an axe in one hand and a large white handkerchief in the other.

Aunt Dodo groaned again. "He's crying. Mother told him to do her dirty work."

"Don't be too sure," Uncle Robin muttered, rubbing his hands. "He cries when he's happy, too. He's been crying his way through every family wedding and reunion for as long as I can remember . . ."

"Those were not happy tears," Mother said, stiffening. She left the window and went to glance at the empty portrait niche. "The artist must have failed to show the kindness in Father's eyes." She half turned. Trinc saw her glaring at Aunt Edith, whose bitter blue eyes had served as the model.

MOTHER HAD FLINCHED AT THE PROSPECT of Trinc's descent into High School. Perhaps if Mother had not been so busy martyrizing herself, bending thin shoulders to tidy Trinc's bureau drawers in search of letters to or from Aeneas, the maternal foot might have stamped out Trinc's future as a scholar in algebra. As it was, algebra itself had Trinc fairly stumped, as did natural sciences—the studies invisibly marked For Men Only. She was good at literature and languages, history, music and art, and she didn't object to dissecting formaldehyde-embalmed frogs in biology lab. But when she was given an equation to solve, her mind wandered into poetry. You are standing at Point "A"

50 feet from Point "B" and 330 feet from Point "C"; a man has fallen into the river at "B" and been hauled from it a corpse at "C". How many feet has he traveled? Trinc wondered what the man's name was, what tragedy had brought him to despair, and whether bystanders had tried First Aid.

Still, Aeneas had inspired her at their meeting now more than two years ago. If she should ever meet him again, she was determined, it must not be as what Daddy had called "an uneducated woman." For this reason, St. Benet's having provided little serious education, she was going to Orford Parish High. She was older than most of her classmates and hated as a "rich Heartwell." Many of her classmates came from the mill village. She mingled with teen-aged boys and girls with surnames like Sadrozinski and McGonigal, Ginsberg and Kleinschmidt. A few classmates of her own age were National Guardsmen who had returned to Orford Parish having left a leg or an arm in places like Chateau Thierry. She found her classmates superior intellectually and personally to the wretched girls of St. Benet's.

As classes were ending one day in October, terrible news was announced: an influenza epidemic was spreading through town. School would be closed until further notice.

Earlier in the year, when Uncle Doc had been in charge of Red Cross headquarters on the Place de la Concorde, he had written to Trinc about the ravages of flu and pneumonia. They were killing off soldiers more quickly than German guns. "One lives a double life," he had written, "for always at the center of one's being is the thought of the slaughter sixty miles away, but the instinct toward life turns one back to a strange surface gaity in which life has never seemed so vital—and yet there before my eyes lie dying men."

She walked home from school. Even as she was thinking of Uncle Doc, suddenly there he was in the front driveway standing arms akimbo and calmly looking on while Augustus and a chauffeur were loading his new Packard with suitcases. Mother and Granny Ah were dithering about. "Uncle Doc!" Trinc ran and flung her arms around his neck.

Uncle Doc held her at arm's length. "What a sight for sore eyes!" He lowered voice. "I got news of the epidemic a few hours ago and thought I better fetch you and Hen and Ednah to New York while the going's good . . . The Red Cross was supposed to shut down your school over an hour ago. You Yanks are as slow to get fired as a cap-pistol in ice water . . . Run, pack an overnight bag, get back in a jiffy."

Trinc ran, stopped, came back. Where was Bruno Rancis when everyone needed him? When she asked this question, Granny Ah scowled, "Hard to find him now Deck's gone."

"He complained of a headache early this morning, Augustus told me," Mother explained. "No one's seen him since."

"Perhaps he has the flu and needs help," Trinc said. Uncle Doc explained that Heartwell Hall had been converted into an emergency hospital. "We'll stop and see if your man's there, on our way out of town," he said.

Trinc ran upstairs to her room. At last she was going to stay with Uncle Doc! She could talk with someone she trusted. What could medical science do about Aeneas's wound? Would Uncle Doc, especially now that Grandpa Deck was not around to enforce his rule, help her to communicate with Aeneas? The possibilities surged through her mind, and yet a rich girl's immobilized life was supposed to make it difficult for her hands to do servant's work, even to pack an overnight bag. She must try to be like Aeneas in valor, placing higher value on the lives of others than on her own life.

A few minutes later she was standing in the driveway. "I've decided to stay and help the Red Cross at Heartwell Hall." She had never before made such an impertinent declaration.

"Over my dead body! Get in the motor car this instant!" Mother's towering rage had erupted.

"The girl has spunk," Granny Ah said.

"Pishtash! She's just like her father. She wants to see how far she can go before there's hell to pay. Well, Billy?" Mother appealed to Uncle Doc. "The president of the American Medical Association seems to be the only person to whom the little fool will listen . . . Are you going to let a child with a weak chest die of pneumonia?"

His eyes gleamed as he challenged Mother directly. "Funny you mention the A. M. A., Hen, because I haven't been president for years. After I introduced my plan for national health service, my fellow physicians accused me of being a socialist and threw me out of office by the seat of my pants. . . Let me tell you something." He glanced swiftly at Trinc. "Your daughter has grown up. She can make her own decisions. As for taking risks, my dear Hen, you took a risk in bringing Trinc into the world . . ."

"That was no risk," Mother snapped. "That was a traffic violation."

"The point is, Hen, you can die from anything, even from drinking too much water. Trinc will make a fine nurse. Perhaps she'll consider nurses' training. It's a noble profession. I'm sure the Red Cross will see to her welfare. Ednah? All right with you if Trinc stays on here at the house?"

Everyone looked at Granny Ah as she straightened herself up inside a fur coat. "She can help Augustus keep an eye on the servants . . . I'd like to leave before I catch my death of cold."

Uncle Doc winked at Trinc. "Good! Coming with us as far as Heartwell Hall, Miss Cavell, Miss Nightingale, Miss DeRoman?"

"I don't think a person who is going to work should arrive at the door in a Packard," Trinc said.

Uncle Doc stage-whispered, "Bravo."

HEARTWELL HALL WAS USUALLY A LARGE Civil-War-period auditorium with stage at one end, organ loft at the other, tiers of seats in-between. Now the seats had been removed and bunk beds were everywhere. The blackness of walnut-paneled walls was broken only by pale squares of open windows. In the daytime, shafts of sunlight slanted across unshaven, haggard faces with glazed eyes. At night electric torches or lanterns would pick out a bed, turn upon a face flushed or deadly white—or, worst of all, a dull bluish color—upon delirious lips and blank eyes, gaze inward. Death was an actual presence in the room, a stirring in the troubled air of majesty and terror.

When Trinc first entered this hospital, foul odors repelled her until she heard the caterwaul of dying men, the gasping, the coughing, and dismissed her objections. She was met by a doctor who called her "Miss Derryman" and seemed to believe that anyone acquainted with the famous Dr. Knight already knew how to give hypodermic injections, take pulses, collect sputum cups, change sheets and wrap up corpses to look like mummies. He put her to work at once. She had done these things, soon moving as if in a trance as the first day became a landslide of nights and days that followed. Relief came at odd intervals. Sleeping at home was like touching shore when you had begun to wonder if you could swim any further.

There was a youngster of eighteen who called, "Rosy, Rosy, I need you." When Trinc went to him, he seized her hand and began to kiss it all over, crying, "Ma, take Sis away, she bothers me." He sat straight up in bed, whimpered, trailed off into feeble curses, asked for a glass of beer and died. There was a fine-looking boy who was not delirious and who seemed only humbly concerned not to be a bother. He said to her, "Don't feel badly," and died. There was a tough-looking Swede who said in dim light, "Hello, girl. I like you. I like you better than any girl I've seen. I'd like to go to town with a god-damned girl like you and have a hell of a time!" Trinc poured out some bitter medicine in a big iron spoon and gave it to him; he seized the spoon, tried to hit her with it. The doctor came and she helped him to tie the Swede's hands and feet to the ends of the bed, to fasten a sheet tight over his body, to tie the sheet under the bed. The doctor put a gag in the Swede's mouth. Trinc asked him not to do it. The doctor said, "Miss Derryman, a man who cannot move or curse becomes more tranquil." The muffled curses became fainter and fainter. The Swede died.

In the middle of her third night on duty Trinc, hearing a commotion, went to the entrance door to see if there were anything she could do to help move dying patients from Red Cross vans. Two policemen were trying to hold up the ragdoll figure of a man. A small man who smoked a large cigar was explaining to the doctor that this patient had been a prisoner at the county jail. He would have to be handcuffed to a bed at all times. The doctor raised the prisoner's head, examined his white, unshaven face with an electric torch. The prisoner's head was bald, face pock-marked. The bushy eyebrows and mustache, sickly white in the torch's glare, looked as if glued on.

It was Bruno Rancis.

SHE HAD STEPPED FORWARD, identified the coachman, and scolded the cigar-smoker for disrespect for the sick and the dying. She had said that handcuffs for a member of the Heartwell family were not to be tolerated. "Miss Derryman—!" The Red Cross doctor's exasperated voice she had ignored as she had ordered policemen to find an empty bed for Bruno. She had followed them with a lantern. When, after a while, she had taken Bruno's pulse, felt his burning, chalky brow, and listened to the rattle in his throat, she realized that his death was imminent. Then she had accompanied the policemen outdoors where she approached the small dapper man who wore a dark three-piece suit, white winged collar with black bow-tie, and a derby. He was rubbing his hands by a bonfire.

The chill air cleared her head. Some workers were emptying sanitary buckets into the brook. She almost ordered them to stop, to protest against pollution of an ancient stream which babbled past the Homestead, meandered through a forest primeval. In the flickering light the small man tipped his derby. "Buonsignori," came his gently inflected voice. "Detective Captain Buonsignori from Hartford . . . Miss DeRoman?"

"I hope you'll forgive me, Captain," she said. "I had no right to be giving commands. Please smoke. My nerves are piano wires."

He fluttered hands in practiced protest. "No no no . . . I was wrong. Handcuffs are, shall I say, superfluous. Nor should a gentleman of sensitivity be smoking in a charnel house . . . Now," he went on after blowing on his hands, "you will please forgive my asking questions, when you are obviously exhausted . . . but, you must know, you are the very person on whom I was expecting to call in the morning . . . You live in the home of Mr. H. Dexter Heartwell? Mr. Rancis also he lives there?"

She explained that her grandfather had passed away, that Bruno lived in a loft over the garage, and that she had been left temporarily in charge of the house and the servants.

"I should like to see the loft," Buonsignori nodded. "I need a search warrant?"

"That won't be necessary."

"Splendid."

"Has Bruno Rancis done something that involves me?"

Buonsignori looked at her sharply. "He has made a rather wild and improbable confession, Miss DeRoman."

"That," Trinc sighed on a note of dismissal. "He's always confessing to a crime for which he was jailed as a young miner in Yorkshire . . ."

"There's a criminal record?" Buonsignori cut in. "May I ask what he did?"

Trinc waited to get the indelicate words right. "He castrated a mine worker in a fight."

Buonsignori chewed on this information. "I *see*," he said with heavy emphasis. He tilted his derby back, pulled, studied, and pocketed a watch. "It's just past two. You're relieved of duty here, if you choose. My men and I would like to accompany you to the Dexter Heartwell house at once, rather than return in the morning . . . I would like to settle this confession business between the two of us, without scandal to your family . . . We were holding Mr. Rancis for drunk and disorderly and for assaulting an officer. Now that he's done for, it's a different ballgame."

"Wait." She turned and went inside. With the lantern she found the doctor and two nurses already wrapping Bruno in a sheet. She returned to the bonfire and told Captain Buonsignori she was ready to go.

They drove her home in the police van and waited outside while she knocked on the oaken door. Augustus opened it. She heard the crackle of logs in the fireplace in the Big Room.

"*Dear* Augustus! I am so sorry to tell you, but Bruno has fallen victim to the epidemic. The police have kindly offered to assist me in straightening out his affairs. Please, before you surrender to your tears, bring me the key to the coachman's loft, along with tea service for two. You may then retire for the night. I shall bolt the front door myself. There's a dear fellow. Thank you."

An hour passed.

She and Buonsignori were seated before the fireplace, drinking tea and eating scones while Rex waited at their feet for scraps. On a table beside her was Bruno's tin box for letters. Buonsignori had found it under Bruno's bed in the loft, exactly where he had expected to find it. Now that she had examined the letters, she realized that Grandpa Deck had given them to Bruno, expecting them to be destroyed. Bruno had kept them, evidently for the purpose of blackmail.

"Mr. Heartwell," Buonsignori was explaining, "promised Mr. Rancis a thousand dollars in payment for services rendered—a little arson here, a little assault and battery there, revenge for insults. However, Mr. Heartwell died without carrying out his part of the bargain. So Mr. Rancis, after brooding for some months and then feeling ill, went out and got stinking drunk and assaulted one of the officers here in Orford Parish. When he woke in a cell, he had a high fever and realized his time might be short. He confessed to a number of crimes, all of which he laid at the feet of the late Mr. Heartwell, and he gave the police the key to this box and information as to its whereabouts.'

"There was one crime in particular by which he felt haunted . . . Although our people had a devil of a time trying to understand the man's accent, eventually a statement was taken down. And since the particular crime was alleged to have occurred in New Mexico about two years ago, our Hartford office was called in to lead the investigation . . . Naturally, we wish to do everything possible to protect your family's reputation . . . What do you make of *this* letter?" Buonsignori leaned forward and gave Trinc a letter he had earlier removed from the box but not shown or read to her, as he had others.

It was from Aeneas—and Peter Rabbit—dated April 21, 1916 from Poughkeepsie, a SPECIAL DELIVERY addressed to her at St. Benet's. When she had read it, she learned at last that Aeneas had loved her and not abandoned her. And she knew by whom she had been betrayed: Grandpa Deck.

Buonsignori puffed up his cheeks and expelled air slowly in weary resignation. "It establishes motive . . . Proposal of marriage . . . He waited for you. He expected you to elope with him. All that . . . Oh, all right. You keep it . . . Do forgive. You don't see yet . . . The story is an indelicate one. But you strike me as a singularly strong person for your sex . . . Yes. I'll tell you."

He began the story without further ado, occasionally slipping stubby fingers through slicked gray hair. Images from his story had long been in her possession—the sunset, the tree, the sparkling river, the place of stones, the men who leapt and struck and the man who screamed—but now she knew them with a shock of horror that put her very soul in doubt. She also knew that the lance in her dream had been an ice-pick.

Bruno had been called to Grandpa Deck's office, given the

"Peter Rabbit" letter with instructions to destroy it, told to find Aeneas in New Mexico in the hamlet of Los Remedios, and commanded to await further instructions if Aeneas defied the family's wishes. One day these instructions arrived. After hiring local ruffians, Bruno and they tracked Aeneas down until they found him alone one sunset in a place called Turley's Mill. They bound Aeneas to a tree, removed his trousers. Bruno was supposed to "make a capon" with a knife but instead stabbed the testicles with an ice-pick. He lingered behind a boulder to make sure the man was not bleeding to death beside the stained, screaming river.

Trinc's glance wandered around the Big Room. Here she had opened Christmas presents from Grandpa Deck. Here she had played the piano and danced. Here the Will had been read that bequeathed her a necklace from 1812 . . . The empty portrait niche seemed to spring to life. Imaginary blue eyes stared from it as if to mock any real inheritance of honor and conscience and compassion.

"Wha-at?"

Buonsignori clinked teacup back in saucer. "Do you know if Aeneas Caldwell is still alive?"

"Alive?"

"If he died in New Mexico, there's an unsolved murder. I'll have to keep these letters and the Rancis confession."

"And if Mr. Caldwell is alive?"

"He may sue your family for malicious wounding and collect a great deal of money."

"Mr. Caldwell is dead," Trinc said evenly. "He was killed in action in France."

A sly smile crinkled the corners of Buonsignori's mouth. "I see," he said. "I'm sorry."

He picked up the tin box and stood close to the fire. One by one he threw the rest of its contents in, causing embers to burst into sizzling flames while Rex's tail thumpthumped on the rug as if a treacherous master were a palpable presence.

After a while, Buonsignori put on his derby and bowed to Trinc. "I'll inform the Orford Parish police that the dying man's confession was a hoax."

She saw him to the door. She watched him climb into the van from which clouds of exhaust floated on cold air like obscene cartoon bubbles. Presently she closed and bolted the door. She pressed her back against it and began to cry into her hands quietly, then violently, against family tradition and yet not loud enough to waken the servants in the house, or the dead and the damned.

7

A COLD-WATER FLAT

THE ARMISTICE HAD BEEN CELEBRATED in Orford Parish with parades of marching bands and tooting automobiles and with special shrilly blasts from the mill whistles. Heartwell Hall had been emptied of beds, fumigated, and restored to its function as a community center. Granny Ah and Mother had come back from New York feeling nicely fortified with purchases of Tiffany cut-glass and of silverware from Black, Starr & Frost. Trinc had resumed classes at the high school. Unknown as yet to the family was her decision to prepare herself for admission to nurses' training—for the "noble profession," as Uncle Doc had called it. The epidemic over, she had measured up to its test, found her vocation. That she could train for it in New York— and leave the family—contributed to a thrillingly private sense of future liberation.

If anyone had bothered to perceive in her face her inner feelings, they might have seen that the natural expression of exuberance in her eyes had been drained away. The man she loved could never give her children. The dictates of conscience nevertheless bound her to him forever. The burden of the family's guilt lay upon her if only because her surrender to desire had prompted Grandpa Deck to revenge.

Chancing to read Willa Cather's *My Ántonia*, she wondered

whether its rueful epigraph from Virgil were actually true, that "the best days are the first to flee." Ántonia had helped to transform a bleak wilderness into a garden and had raised a happy family. She was described as "a rich mine of life, like the founders of early races." Although Trinc deplored the sentimentality and nostalgia in Cather's novel, its heroic vision lifted her heart, only to dash it down. Would she ever be a rich mine of life? Her best "days" had been but a few hours with Aeneas. She struggled against the self-pity of this outlook, however, and was winning through to a philosophical stance—that she would do everything in her power to provide for Aeneas's happiness, irregardless of her own—when something happened that challenged her resolve: she received Father's letter of November 5th about encountering Aeneas in the military hospital at Neuilly and found enclosed with this letter Aeneas's envelope addressed to Miss Tabitha Van Dyke on West Fourth Street, New York.

She wept for joy. Aeneas was alive and not badly wounded in battle! Moreover, he had found a way to establish contact with her! She could not, of course, open Tubby's letter. Tempted though she was to shrug off the rules of restraint, respect for another person's privacy held her back and upheld the honor of love. Why, she could have Tubby's letter delivered in person! Intuition told her that Aeneas wished her to proceed in exactly this fashion. Acting at once, she sent a telegram to Tubby, advising her to expect a visit from her at noon the very next day.

It came, a Saturday. Daring as it had seemed to walk to Western Union in Orford Parish and send a telegram, how exhilarating it was to arrange for a taxicab to pick her up at nine o'clock in the morning in front of the Heartwell house! Sacred her mission, whatever Mother might do to obstruct it. When the taxi arrived, Trinc simply marched past Augustus, got in and drove off without having to explain herself to anyone.

She went to New York, to the street just off Washington Square, to the cold-water flat of Tubby Van Dyke. Eventually she would read four letters, one from Aeneas to Tubby, one each from Grandpa Deck and Mother to Aeneas, threatening him, and a slick carbon copy of his letter from New Mexico to them, defying them—and, as now she knew, bringing on Bruno. Since she already had Aeneas's intercepted love letter, the "Peter Rabbit" letter, now confirmed for her was his compassion: he had placed her happiness above other considerations. Then, too, he wanted Tubby to give Trinc the Heartwell-Caldwell letters, a gift that signified his forgiveness.

Expecting to find in Tubby the same plump schoolgirl whom she had known but slightly at St. Benet's, Trinc imagined she was going to meet a kind of full-bosomed odalisque in an opium den, wriggling eyebrows and prating about sex. Since Tubby had apparently told Miss Bates that Aeneas was an opportunist who just wanted to trap a rich girl into marriage, Trinc did not wish to cultivate a treacherous Tubby's acquaintance now. The curious thing was, Aeneas cared about his cousin and must have been writing to her for years. Perhaps, intelligent as he was, he really didn't understand the wickedness of women.

After instructing the cab driver to remain parked by the curb, Trinc stepped out into the raw wind-chill of West Fourth Street. With one hand she clutched tightly her old raccoon coat, with the other hand she tried to keep her cloche hat from blowing away. One glance around told her that the neighborhood was a slum. Brick tenements leaned into one another like crowded baby teeth. The fetid odor of sewerage seeped from manhole covers, and a greasy smell, like fried steak, seemed to come out of the very throat of the city. She mounted a flight of worn brownstone steps, pushed open a broken glass door patched with chicken wire, pressed a button beneath the name, "Van Dyke," on a mailbox marked "3rd fl". Somewhere above the ceiling of an unlit hallway there was a shuffling sound. It stopped, replaced from an interior tomb by the sound of a woman's lamentation, an eerie cry on tortured air.

"That you, Trinc?"

She located the person with the tired voice and climbed two

flights of stairs, uncertain of her tread. She saw Tubby in dim light, no fat floozy but a woman thin and pale who held in her arms a bundled babe. Forgotten for the moment was the vulgar Tubby she remembered. The two of them embraced. This Tubby was skin and bones. Beneath her shift Trinc felt shoulderblades that were stubs of wings. The child was beautiful.

"This is Karl," Tubby said. "We just had big din-dins. He's so cute when he sleeps . . . Look at his nose and his balled-up fists. He looks like a little Buddhist philosopher."

Trinc looked upon mother and child with envious eyes.

"C'mon," Tubby said, "before we freeze our asses off in this flytrap. I have a coalfire going in the grate, and I bought us a couple knockwurst sandwiches at the deli."

"Good work," Trinc said. Tubby, catching her own words of praise, looked startled but saved eyes for little Karl. "Yeah," she said.

"Let me give you my coat," Trinc said.

"Oh," said Tubby, "I'm sorry we don't have the girl today who's supposed to check it."

"I didn't mean that. I want you to have it."

"That coat? I wouldn't be seen dead in that coat."

"Please, Tubby. I don't need it any more."

"Well, maybe Karl can use it, seeing as how you want to get rid of it."

All this time the walled-off sobbing of a woman kept on filling the air.

Tubby tossed her head in its direction. "They oughta do something about that dope. She drinks rubbing alcohol and wails for her demon lover."

The flat consisted of one room, its single window giving a view of a brick wall, its coal-burning grate affording little warmth. Strung drying on a piece of string before the fire were diapers, ammoniac odor thickening the atmosphere, vapor fogging up the window. There was no furniture save for things on the floor: a coverless mattress with one blanket and a pillow; a couple of paper bags for storing clothing; a coal bucket and a kerosene lamp; a small stack of books; a filmy hand mirror; an orange crate for a table and on this table an assortment of bottles and kitchen utensils and Trinc's telegram and, just unwrapped from newspaper, two knockwurst sandwiches with pickles.

Eventually, Trinc would learn Tubby's story, though it came in bits and pieces as the two of them sat on the floor that afternoon.

When Tubby's parents on Long Island found her too unruly to cope with, they sent her with a governess to live in Manhattan in a furnished apartment on lower Fifth Avenue. When she wasn't at St. Benet's, that apartment was home, the idea being, she was to receive psychiatric care in the city. She was placed under the care of a middle-aged German doctor, Dr. Karl, an intellectual who talked of revolution and free sex. Gradually during therapy he convinced Tubby that she suffered from a hysterical desire to commit incest with her father and to bear him a child. Although Dr. Karl was married, he escorted Tubby to fashionable, late-night drinking parties in Greenwich Village dives. He introduced her to gin-and-bitters as part of "therapy" sessions. After he raped her, she became his mistress.

Aeneas appeared in the summer of 1915, practically penniless after completing graduate studies at Harvard. For a few weeks Tubby put him up at her apartment, and soon Dr. Karl was taking him to Mabel Dodge's avant-garde salon for artists and intellectuals, to the parties and the dives. Aeneas thought of Dr. Karl as a kindly professional who wanted his patient—a typically hysterical woman with a normal fixation on her doctor—to learn to be at ease with men. Of her real predicament, Tubby revealed nothing to Aeneas. Who would possibly believe her story? The old goat was not only a married man presumed to be past the age for sexual violence but also was her oath-bound physician.

She had indeed been pregnant at St. Benet's. She had indeed had a miscarriage on that afternoon. If she had not become panicky, she would not have permitted Trinc to go riding forth in search of help from Aeneas. Midway through the next day, as she lay in bed recuperating, Tubby was summoned before Miss Bates. She went down to the headmistress' office and was promised that nothing would happen to her if she agreed to portray Aeneas as an opportunist who was using her to pander to his plans.

"I couldn't do it," Tubby said. "Aeneas's *father* was an opportunist, as all the Van Dykes know, but Aeneas an opportunist? *Never!* But Bates said, 'Like father, like son'."

Tubby was expelled from school. When she arrived at her apartment in New York, she found her father waiting for her, the governess having been discharged. Miss Bates had telephoned Mr. Van Dyke and revealed the fact of the pregnancy and miscarriage. Mr. Van Dyke demanded to know the name of Tubby's lover. She refused to give it. He beat her, he threatened her, then he disinherited her and had her physically thrown out of the apartment with only such clothing as she could gather in paper bags. She wandered the streets for three days, sleeping and eating at a hostel operated by the Salvation Army, and then she went to Dr. Karl and begged for help.

It came, briefly. He installed her in a small flat in the Bowery. He visited her on weekends, sometimes taking her on the ferry to Staten Island, but no longer to parties. Every Sunday he gave her a five-dollar bill. When she again became pregnant, he deserted her, albeit he despatched an errand boy weekly to bring her money. With the help of a mid-wife, she gave birth to little Karl and shortly thereafter moved to the cold-water flat on West Fourth Street. Where now the five-dollar bills from Dr. Karl? They ceased when she moved. She feared that as soon as Dr. Karl discovered she had been delivered of little Karl and was now more than ever dependent, the creep would come knocking at her door.

"Tubby," Trinc asked, "what are you doing to support yourself?"

Tubby lowered eyes. "Me and little Karl go over to Washington Square to the subway entrance. I let people see how beautiful he is. I hold out my hand. You know."

What if, Trinc thought, Tubby received help? Couldn't she start a new life uptown, buy clothes, hire a maid, get a job and, like Cather's Ántonia, meet a good man to marry and take care of her and the child? Here she was, Trinc, with money she hardly knew what to do with, and here was Tubby friendless and floundering, resilient perhaps and proud, not lacking in dignity but floundering. "Tubby," Trinc asked carefully, "what would you do if you had $5,000?"

"Me? You've got to be joking."

"But supposing you had money enough to help you for a few years, like a loan you could pay back without interest once you're on your feet, what would you do?"

Tubby laughed on a false note before she bowed head over Karl and rocked him in her arms. "Oh, me and Karl could get by on a couple hundred. I mean, we could blow this flytrap and go somewhere nice like California. Start again." She lifted head, smiled. "Five thou is more money than there is, but if I had $5,000, we'd go to England and take care of Cousin Aeneas. He's fixing to go to Cambridge to study the new physics, come hell or high water, but he's flat broke and needs taking care of. Yeah, I'd do that . . . Would you like to see the letter he wrote me?" She rose from the floor, fetched Aeneas's opened envelope from the mattress, and squatted beside Trinc. "He said you're to have the other letters, the ones that show how your family played Abelard and Héloise with your relationship, but this one's for me. You don't have to read the personal stuff . . . Start where he got himself in trouble, and how he changed his name and got wounded . . . There," Tubby pointed.

Trinc began reading to herself.

". . . After the acquittal, I returned to my company and found that the men whom I had formerly led into battle now considered a victim of attempted castration as an abomination. Men who had bayoneted enemy soldiers as dispassionately as children swatting flies crowded me into a corner and began to close in, their eyes lit with hate. Part of me wanted to resist, another part to let them have their will, whatever it was. I found myself crouching like a wrestler who gets ready for his opponent's attack. Before the men attacked, however, we were called to attention. It was the Captain who had just been assigned to my company.'

"I followed the Captain to his bunker. Since it had been ordered that I was to be reduced to the ranks and sent to another combat Division, I believed that the Captain would be executing that order. To my amazement, though, he, or some higherup officer, had decided that the best way to get rid of a 'eunuch' like me was to toss me overboard, like Jonah. On the spot I was given a medical discharge!'

"At one moment a man is about to be executed by firing squad, the next moment he is set honorably free.'

"A citizen again, I could have gone to Cambridge immediately, to study the new physics there under the supervision of great men—Rutherford, Bohr, Jeans and others. I decided, however, to permit myself no retreat from the war, not that I had a taste for it or believed it served any purpose. I'd become so indifferent to my own death that I assumed a disposition toward it. When I arrived in Paris, I volunteered under a false name to drive an ambulance for the French.'

"There's a story here. My Grandma Floride in Columbia, South Carolina, once took me aside and said, 'Aeneas, your great-great-grandmother was the sister of the mother of John C. Calhoun. Don't you ever forget it!' Well, I thought the connection was as disagreeable as it was obscure. Like it or not, I mustn't forget that my old Upcountry ancestors are connected to a madman whose defense of slavery led to the Civil War. I served the French under the alias of John C. Calhoun. I am presently in the American hospital at Neuilly.'

"Quite early one morning, during a frightful barrage of mortar fire, I was busy evacuating casualties. The woods were cracking in fury all around me. I was about a hundred yards from my ambulance, making a crouching run for a stone wall where a

French officer was huddled over a body and waving for me. I heard overhead the *Wram!* of a shell, and the next thing I knew I was bowled over by a stunning blow to the head.'

"I lay on the ground while shrapnel fragments burned themselves out in my head. The French officer came and peered down at me. 'Quelque chose?' I could tell by the tone of his voice that he had better things to do than worry about me.'

"After a while, I stood up, walked to the ambulance, got in. I remember reaching my hand up to test gingerly what was left of my skull. When all I found were a few shallow holes about the size of buffalo nickles, I began to feel deliriously happy."

When Trinc finished reading, she squeezed Tubby's hand. "Tubby, I'm ashamed to admit I've misjudged you. I love and trust you as a sister. Promise me you won't refuse to listen to what I have in mind."

Even as she proposed a loan of $5,000, Trinc had the sinking feeling that she was going too far. She trusted Tubby. That was not the problem. The problem lay in herself, that she had no right to meddle in other people's affairs. Deep down, she suspected that she wasn't going to do anybody any good. Still, her feelings for others were more important to her than fear of failure. She was acting on her feelings, intrepidly taking down any No Trust sign.

"A loan, huh?" Tubby said. "Like the coat, huh?"

"The coat is a gift."

"Jeez, Trinc. I don't know what to say."

"Don't say anything. We'll take my cab to a depositor's bank that opens on Saturday. We'll set up an account in your name. You can start drawing on it today. There is one condition. Do you hear me?"

Tubby nodded.

"Aeneas must never, ever know where your money came from. Tell him it came from Dr. Karl but not from me. Ever."

"Why are you doing this?"

Trinc could have revealed, then and there, the dictates of

her conscience. It seemed her heart had reason enough. "I love Aeneas," she said.

It was as true as any words she had ever spoken to anyone save Aeneas himself. He mirrored the moving spirit of her life, whether or not they were ever to share a life together.

Later that afternoon when the banking business had been settled and Tubby and Karl had been returned to the cold-water flat to begin a new life, Trinc ordered her driver to stop by a Western Union office. She didn't believe Aeneas would still use the Calhoun alias after being admitted to the American hospital. She telegraphed Amelia in Philadelphia in hopes that she would cable Father, that he might give Aeneas Caldwell the long-delayed response: she would wait for Peter Rabbit by the hayrick.

THE PROBEYS

GRANNY AH'S NEW 1920 CADILLAC glided over the grid of shadows cast by the El. The young chauffeur, a Negro named Jim, seemed to regard other cars with a mild disdain.

"The subscription dances begin in September," Mother was saying.

"Then I'll come home for them," Trinc said, "*after* I graduate from nurses' training." She stretched a silk-clad calf. Mother leaned over and straightened Trinc's skirt. "Sit up, child!"

Jim eased the Cadillac down a dismal side street, turned a corner, and brought the car to a stop under an ornamental brick arch with a sign, "New York General Hospital." Barred windows, meretricious turrets, and brick blackened by soot accentuated the impression of sheer ugliness. Trinc had somehow formed the impression that Uncle Doc worked in an elegant building like the Waldorf-Astoria.

"If you change your mind before October," Mother continued at the hospital entrance, "you can still get home in time for the Junior League Ball."

Now that Trinc was no longer participating in what she regarded as the shallow, impertinent life of Junior Leaguers, Mother wanted to treat her as an outcast of the leisure class.

A faint odor of ether and Lysol met her at the entrance to the hospital. There was something mysterious and exciting about the odor, like that of the Cunard ocean liner she had visited the year before when Tubby and Karl were sailing for England.

"We're looking for the Training School Office," Mother said to a lynx-eyed woman who sat inside the wire cage to which a series of porters had conducted them. The woman nodded to another porter, who led them through a maze of white-tiled corridors to a door marked "Superintendent of Nurses." Trinc's knock was answered by a gaunt woman in a white uniform, its collar so high it gave her a giraffe-like appearance. "Miss Dean is busy at present," said Giraffe. "You may wait in her private sitting room." She showed Trinc and Mother into a room darkened by velvet curtains and containing a tea table and sofa.

"This would be quite homey," Mother snorted, "if it were not for that queer stink."

"I like the stink," Trinc said. "It's romantic."

Mother hooted. "If you think hospitals are romantic, you won't last two weeks. With your weak chest you'll be spitting blood in less time than that . . . Poor Robin, dying at the sanitorium in Colorado Springs with nothing to look at except Rocky Mountains." So much, Trinc admitted, was true: some Heartwells sometimes died of TB. Mother, though, seemed less concerned about Uncle Robin's imminent death than about its occurrence in what she considered culturally impoverished surroundings.

A nurse dressed in blue and white, with tired lines about her mouth, slipped into the room, set the table with tea and sandwiches, and noiselessly departed. "Will your uniform be like *that*?" Mother drew herself up stiffly as if she were about to be surrounded by immigrants fresh from Ellis Island.

"Oh, no," Trinc said evenly. "Probationers wear dirt-gray, without bibs or caps. Uncle Doc told me they used to wear pretty pink dresses, but the ward maids copied them, and nobody could tell the difference between probeys and maids. The probeys had to choose a style that the maids wouldn't want."

"I must say," Mother remarked after a depressing silence, "they are not very attentive here. Remember, I told you to do your training in Hartford where the family name is respected."

Trinc stood up. She had caught sight in the doorway of a woman with beady eyes and a mouth set into a professional smile, obviously Miss Dean. She rustled forward, took Trinc's hand and gushed, "Is this the little girl who wishes to join our new class?"

"As I told you in my letter, Miss Dean, Susan has set her heart on becoming a nurse. I'm sure you won't find her strong enough to do any of the hard work."

Mother's pronouncement caused Miss Dean's smile to tighten. "Has Susan a chronic complaint?"

"Oh, no, it's not that. Girls of her fragile type should not take up such an exhausting hobby."

"Mrs. DeRoman, I trust she will find more in our profession than a pastime?"

Mother, looking absolutely crestfallen, said, "My poor little girl has never darned a stocking or scrubbed a floor or washed a dish. There won't be anybody to take care of her here."

"We keep a strict watch over all our girls." Miss Dean patted Mother's arm. Mother drew back quickly as if to avoid being infected with some deadly disease. Miss Dean turned to Trinc. "Are your school credits complete?"

Trinc explained that she'd only recently graduated from high school.

"No college credits?"

Trinc looked down at her high heels, felt toes squirm in hot silk. "Are there no other students here without college credits?" With Uncle Doc in support, she didn't think Miss Dean would object to a lack of preparation. She was relieved to hear Miss Dean's reply. "Quite a few, Susan. I'm sure you'll get on well with the other students."

"She's so democratic," Mother cut in. Miss Dean's beady eyes narrowed. "Susan will doubtless have much to teach her classmates," Miss Dean said, "due to her superior advantages. What does *that* mean, Susan?" She pointed at a fire-opal ring Trinc was wearing, a graduation present to herself.

"I won't wear it on duty, if that's what you mean, Miss Dean."

"I should hope not. There is no use in your entering training school if you wait to marry a fiancé. That's the way the girls do. As soon as they are trained to be of use to society, they want to have babies. We're not going to waste our time in making you into a housekeeper!"

"Susan is not engaged to be married," Mother put in.

"Well," said Miss Dean, "I always quote the wise doctor who said, 'Every nurse who is not engaged when she enters training comes either to forget a man or to look for one'."

"I really must go," Mother said.

"No tea?"

"We are not accustomed to drinking embalming fluid . . . Susan? A telegram will reach me when you change your mind." Mother swept out the door without closing it. Trinc shut her eyes, hoping that when she opened them again, she would be free. Miss Dean was saying, "I will detail a nurse to show you to the Nurses' Home."

Trinc opened her eyes. "Thank you, Miss Dean. I can't thank you enough."

A few minutes later she picked up her suitcases where Jim had deposited them at the hospital entrance and followed the tired nurse to the Home. A group of girls was sitting on suitcases and giggling as she appeared. She wished she hadn't worn high heels, silk stockings, and the pale organdy dress, the pearl necklace and fire-opal ring.

When the tired nurse told everyone to rise and stand at attention, the girls scrambled to their feet. The nurse read out a list of names and room numbers, grouping the girls alphabetically three to a room, and told them to follow her to the probationers' quarters two blocks away. A short while later Trinc stood with two other girls inside an old tenement building in what might once have been its parlor. It was a high-ceilinged room with stained wallpaper and furnished with cots, desks, and one bureau with mirror. From the sash window they could see Lexington Avenue.

She and the other girls burst into peals of laughter.

The alphabetical probeys were soon good friends. Mallie Devine was a large, crimson-faced girl from a New Hampshire farm and a woman's college. Dora Downey of Boston concealed a ready wit under the aspect of a Christmas card angel: her cheeks needed no cosmetics, for they were rose petals, and her mouth was a holly berry.

That night, when Dora slipped off her clothes and took the pins from her hair, gold ringlets fell across a full white body to the waist. Trinc thought she had never seen anyone so beautiful, yet so simple and unaware of her beauty. When the three D's went to bed, they tried in vain to sleep in hot stale air as mosquitoes whined in from the open window. Finally Dora got out of bed, went to her knees, and buried face in hands.

"Do you think anything is the matter?" Trinc whispered to Mallie.

"She's praying," Mallie whispered back. "She's never been away from home before."

Nor had Trinc ever seen anyone praying before. She wondered if things happened because you prayed them into reality or if human destiny were beyond supplication. No idle question, it made her think of Aeneas's wound. When, almost daily, she wished for its cure, she must have been praying without knowing it.

Dora, having risen from her knees, came and sat on Trinc's bed. "Will you hold me till I fall asleep? At home, I always sleep with my sister." Without waiting for answer Dora lay down next to Trinc, flopping an arm across her breast. A small Heartwellian flame of aversion burned at Trinc's temples, but the thought of how Mother loathed to be touched cooled protest. The situation was, she decided, really quite amusing. Dora, angel, was a dead weight of about one hundred pounds of meat and bone. The doll who belonged in silent films was snoring in snorts and gasps and relieving herself of flatulence.

Trinc eased herself from bed. Finding purse, she removed silver cigarette case and matches, went and sat by the window, and lit up an Old Gold. Mallie came and sat on the floor beside her. "Are you mad?" she whispered. "Any nurse caught smoking gets sent right home."

"I quit." Trinc flipped the cigarette out of the window. "Strict rules."

"Strict rules and scrubbing," Mallie said.

"What do we scrub? Patients?"

"Floors. Floors and beds and things."

"Whatever for?"

"So the hospital won't have to hire scrub women."

"The noble profession."

"That's what they call it," Mallie said.

They looked at one another and giggled.

AT FIVE-THIRTY THE NEXT MORNING there was a pounding on the door as someone called out, "Uniforms! Breakfast in the nurses' dining hall at six-thirty sharp!"

Trinc had spent a sleepless night on Dora's bed. She sprang to the door, slid it open, and found a box of clothes.

Half an hour later the girls were dressed in identical uniforms. Long, gray dresses. High, stiff collars pinned in three places around the neck. Aprons fastened on with studs. The girls took turns at the mirror, giggling and gasping at what they saw. They climbed on a bed to get the reflection of their feet in the clumsy black boots and cotton stockings.

Dora made a clown's face. "It keeps us humble."

"Drab," Mallie said.

"Noble," Trinc said. The pocket of her apron was deep enough to conceal her ring and pearl necklace.

The girls walked two blocks to the hospital and down a maze of corridors to the dining hall where they and the other probeys received derisive stares from various Juniors, Seniors, and Graduate Nurses. A breakfast of lukewarm coffee, porridge, soggy bacon and cold toast smeared with rancid butter awaited them. Neither Trinc nor Dora had any appetite. At seven o'clock the probeys were escorted to an assembly room where the nurse with the tired droop to her mouth, a Miss Snavely, formed them into military ranks and showed them how to keep their hands clasped behind their backs.

Miss Dean appeared. Gone was yesterday's professional smile. In its place was the tight-lipped grimace of a tortoise at the Bronx Zoo.

"My first warning to you," she began without preamble, "is not to get into the habit of calling one another by first names. During your years here, those of you with the stamina to train for our noble profession will address one another as Miss So-and-So. If you use first names with one another in the dining hall or the classroom, you will find yourself doing it on duty in the wards—and that is not to be tolerated. We are to maintain objectivity at all times. It is the foundation of scientific morality. As for the upper-classwomen and doctors, you will not speak to them at all . . . *Who* is that, fingering her apron? Put your hands behind your back, Miss Downey! . . . Now, you are to follow me for your first demonstration of bed-making."

Dora blushed as tears started to roll down her cheeks. "Don't let the old hypocrite bother you," Trinc whispered to her.

"She's down on me."

"She's down on me, too. She admitted me to training only because my uncle used his influence. Then my mother pretended to be Queen Victoria and insulted her . . . We'll just be good little machines on duty and little devils off duty." Trinc squeezed Dora's hand. Dora sniffed up her tears.

The probeys followed Miss Dean to a hospital room that was so small that the bed alone used up half of the available space. Probeys were packed against the walls for Miss Dean's demonstration of bed-making. The sheets must be tight as a drum. The bed-spread was to be placed just so . . . The pillow was to be smoothed . . .

Trinc began to wish she had eaten breakfast. Her head swam with dizziness. Uniformed bodies swayed before her eyes. She tried to straighten her shoulders, wishing someone had opened the window. Miss Dean's nasal whine penetrated her consciousness at irregular intervals . . . Her tortoise face went out of focus . . .

"Miss DeRoman?"

Trinc lay sprawled on the floor, looking up at Miss Dean. Pearls from a broken necklace were bouncing and rolling across the floor in a Lilliputian hailstorm. The eyes of dozens of probeys seemed to contemplate Trinc from a height to which she was aspiring in vain.

FOR WEEKS THE PROBEYS SPENT SEVERAL HOURS a day and all of Sunday mornings folding gauze compresses as they sat at long wooden tables in a small, poorly ventilated room barely large enough to move around in. A sharp gauze-cutting machine had to be avoided if one were not going to be sliced like a sausage.

Miss Dean had impressed upon the probeys the importance of turning in correctly the rough edges of surgical dressings. Probeys were to count compresses in piles of twelve, evenly stacked, and put elastic bands around them. "While you are using this room," Miss Dean warned, "you may converse in low tones, provided you do not take your eyes off of your work. When a member of the Operating Room Staff comes up here to mend rubber gloves, respect and courtesy require your absolute silence. The doctors are gods not to be trifled with."

The probeys soon discovered that the Operating Room Staff liked to relax in the Bandage Room for hours at a time. Whenever the probeys settled down at the tables with mountains of cut gauze before them and nothing to break the monotony of hand motions except idle talk, it seemed that the door would open and another blood-spattered "god" would come in from surgery. A silence suitable for such Olympians was then metaphorically disturbed by many a girl's beating heart. Miss Snavely also came snooping. When she entered the room the probeys had to stand to attention until she seated herself at the glove table with her back turned to them.

One morning as Miss Snavely was mending gloves, Dora whispered to Trinc, "Be good little machines on duty and little devils off duty." The joke was wearing thin. After weeks of training—bed-making with Raggedy Ann dolls for patients, cleaning bed pans, scrubbing floors, folding compresses, listening to lectures—the "D" probeys were too tired to have fun. Usually they spent off-duty hours trying to catch up on sleep, only rarely taking a subway to Times Square to see a movie or to Carnegie Hall to hear the Philharmonic. On several occasions Trinc had gone to parties thrown for her by Mother, who had rented an apartment on Park Avenue so that she could leave Orford Parish on certain weekends precisely for that purpose. Although Trinc thus came to meet F. Scott Fitzgerald and other new writers, loved their wit and bold diatribes against convention—she thought Edna St. Vincent Millay's erotic poems some of the best since Shakespeare's—she hadn't the time or the heart to consider some of the "romps in a taxicab" that, unknown to Mother, were being proposed by Ivy League writers not for a nurse probationer but for a "gal" with Heartwell riches attached.

Amelia had corresponded with Trinc regularly since receiving the ill-fated cablegram that arrived too late for its message to be delivered to Aeneas. Although Trinc told her that there had been a mistake, that the Caldwell in the hospital at Neuily was not the man for whom the "Peter Rabbit" message was intended, Trinc wondered what would have happened had she asked Amelia to look for an ambulance driver called John C. Calhoun.

It was water under the bridge now. Aeneas was in Cambridge, with Tubby there to take care of him. More importantly, where Trinc was concerned, he would never again propose marriage to her: *precisely* because he loved her, he was too much of a gentleman to ask her to share in an unconsummated union. Or so Trinc reasoned. But now that Father and Amelia had settled permanently near Paris, the temptation to visit them there— and to go to Cambridge—loomed large. She would have to quit training, though. And Father would, like Mother, have liked nothing better than for her to quit. Amelia's letters gave a picture of Father that Trinc knew only too well. He had "entertained" Marshal Foch to dinner and was promised, in return for this subterfuge, the Ordre National de la Légion d'Honneur. Through the Reparations Commission, he had come to know that "charming" man, the Duke d'Aosta, Emmanuel Philiberto de Savoia.

Mother of god.

FINALLY ONE DAY TRINC WAS ASSIGNED to a hospital ward where, she hoped, she could care for live patients. However, she had not counted on Miss Mock, a bat-faced sadist, before whose desk she came to stand at attention.

"Make that bed over there!"

Ward patients were craning their necks to watch an Alice-in-Wonderland performance.

"Look at it!"

"I know which bed you mean," Trinc said.

"Say 'Yes, Miss Mock' and don't fidget with your apron!"

"Yes, Miss Mock." Trinc went and took particular pains with the bed, stretching sheets so tightly she could have bounced her opal ring on them. Before she had completed the task, Miss Mock descended on her. "That bed spread is two inches longer on the left side than it is on the right. If this is your standard of work, I have no further use for you on the ward!" Trinc ripped blankets and sheets off the bed. A nearby patient with a gravel-throated voice grinned at her: "Jeez, probey, learnin' ta noyse?"

"See this mattress?" Miss Mock pointed at the stripped bed. "Take this mattress up to the roof."

"Yes, Miss Mock." Trinc gave the mattress a fierce tug, pulled it upright, and started dragging it through the ward.

"Don't drag it on the floor, Miss DeRoman!"

"Yes, Miss Mock."

Patients guffawed.

Trinc carried the mattress down a long corridor. When she was safely out of Miss Mock's sight, she dragged it. At the elevator she rang the bell, and when the operator came, she asked him how to take a mattress to the roof.

"Ain't a-going to be takin' it alone, are ye now, miss? Well, it's the Medical Roof what's allus askin' extras, the place top o' hospital for the TB . . . I'll take you to First Floor. Then you go length o' the two buildings and up five flights."

After stumbling off the elevator at the first floor, she was halfway through the first building when she was stopped by a head nurse. "What are you doing on the Private Floor with that thing? You can't go dragging mattresses through here. Suppose a stretcher or a wheelchair wanted to get past. You're blocking my hall! Take it through the basement."

Trinc struggled back to the elevator. This time she rode it to the basement, but when the elevator cage rattled shut, she was left in the dark. After a while she could see well enough to work her way down the length of a narrow brick passageway that had the Homestead's odor of dry rot. This passageway led to a storeroom. She returned the way she had come, tried another passageway, and saw at its end a light under a door. She opened it and gasped in surprise.

There under a dangling lightbulb Dora and a Russian she recognized as Dr. Nicovich stood locked in an embrace.

Dora's cherry lips parted. Dr. Nicovich's lips curled. He struck Trinc as being a pasty-faced Lord Byron with a pencil mustache and a patch of pitch-black hair that fell over his eyes like a housepainter's brush.

"Sor-ree." Trinc closed the door, found yet another passageway, dragged the mattress down it, and finally arrived in a paved courtyard where odors from the Diet Kitchen directed her to a passageway that led to an elevator cage for the second building. She rang the bell and waited, conscious of cool air on her sweat-soaked uniform. Some minutes later, having reached the Medical Roof, she stood at attention before the nurse in charge.

"What in Sam Hill have you brought that thing up here for?"

"Miss Mock sent it to you."

"You take it right back to Miss Mock. I have no use for it."

Down the elevator . . . through the basement of the Medical Building . . . into the courtyard . . . through the basement of the Surgical Building . . . up the elevator . . . down the corridor and back to Miss Mock's ward: Trinc had lost her hair pins and collar button.

"Really, Miss DeRoman," Miss Mock snorted, "I shall have to report you to Miss Dean for wasting time. Go and get an orderly to carry the mattress for you, as you should have done in the first place. Direct him to the Surgical Roof—one flight up."

ONE NIGHT DORA DOWNEY WAS MISSING from her bed. Mallie Devine explained what had happened.

She, Dora, and other probeys had been working in the Bandage Room. Miss Snavely was there, keeping watch through the eyes in the back of her head. In walked Dr. Nicovich, a White Russian émigré said to have been 134th in succession to the Czar.

Making directly for Dora, Dr. Nicovich put his arm around her shoulders and pretended to listen to her heart with his stethoscope. He whispered something in her ear and flashed perfect teeth. "No, Nicky," Dora said, blushing.

Miss Snavely turned her head, grinding her teeth. "Excuse

me, Dr. Nicovich, I should like to have a word with Miss Downey."

Dr. Nicovich wet his mustache with tip of tongue. "We are making examination," he said. "We lizzen to beautiful breathing. She has pain in heart." He placed a blood-stained hand over his own heart in an affected manner and smiled at the probeys. He clicked his heels and bowed to Miss Snavely. "I continue examination layder." He left the room.

There was a sharp scream.

It seemed that Dora, alarmed by the look on Miss Snavely's face, had attempted to run around the long table where she had been sitting. She stumbled against the gauze-cutting machine. Blood spurted from a deep gash on her arm. She was taken to the Emergency Ward.

"Last I heard," Mallie said, "the doctors are fighting for her life. She's lost a lot of blood and has a temperature of 104 degrees."

Mallie had no sooner finished her explanation than the front doorbell of the Probationers' quarters was rung. While Trinc put on wrapper and slippers, Mallie went to answer the door. She returned to the room accompanied by Uncle Doc, who was wearing a starched cotton coat over his three-piece suit.

"Is Dora worse?" Trinc asked, divining the reason for his visit.

"No worse but no better. She severed a vein near the carpus. She needs a blood transfusion right away."

Both Mallie and Trinc offered to give blood, but Uncle Doc shook his head. "No, no. I just wanted you to know that everything has been taken care of. There's no time to test out what group your blood is in." He paused to cough politely in a cupped hand. "I must say, my opinion of certain folks has gone up. Guess who offered blood for the transfusion?"

Trinc thought and exclaimed, "Not Miss Dean!"

"No. But Miss Snavely. Also Miss Mock."

"Can vampires give blood?"

Trinc's sarcasm was ignored. "Also Miss Dorking, the graduate nurse. Snavely, Mock, and Dorking."

"Sounds like Father's old law firm," Trinc remarked. "Anyone else?"

"Dr. Nicovich," Uncle Doc beamed. "It seems that the hospital is teeming with human beings, after all. . . Guess which one of our heroes and heroines has been chosen to give blood? Miss Downey has group two blood, and all of the donors on the list are group one or four. Except one." He lifted a finger for emphasis. "Dr. Nicovich. He's group two."

"Oh," Trinc groaned. "She's too pretty for him."

Uncle Doc shrugged shoulders. "He's a petticoat chaser, a drunk, and a degenerate aristocrat. But he's a damned good doctor, and his older brother, whom I met in Paris during the Great War, is a world-famous specialist in glandular and neurological diseases. Nicky has royal blood, you know." Uncle Doc winked at Trinc, reached inside his coat, tossed her a box of Whitman's Samplers. "Come and see me sometime, princess," he said as he turned to go.

TRINC HAD SELDOM VISITED THE KNIGHTS since she began training. He had been influential in having her admitted for it, and she felt obliged to him as ever, but she wanted to prove to herself that she could make it in life on her own. There was something else: it annoyed her that the role of nurses was to serve at the beck and call of the doctors, all of them males. Then, too, she had begun to think that Uncle Doc might be too good to be true. He certainly had the power to make things go his way, and he was solicitous of everyone's welfare. Perhaps, though, he had a flaw, not the inability to appreciate someone else's feelings, for he was courteous and urbane, but a habit of taking things for granted as long as he controlled them. Even his gifts now seemed to be ritual designed to remind a female of her subordinate place. It troubled Trinc that a doctor so famous for treating alcoholism as a disease would so "objectively"—a local term of praise—ignore the problems of Dr. Nicky Nicovich.

More than once now she had found Dora and Dr. Nicovich

together, though not embracing as they had been the first time. Once, when Dora was still in a private room recovering from blood loss, Trinc happened to see her and Nicky there, both of them kneeling at the foot of the bed. Praying together? The tableau irritated her: golden-haired Beauty, wearing little but a knee-length cotton chemise, and decadent Beast out of Anna Karenina.

By the time Trinc was through with Diet Kitchen and Massage Room duties and had graduated from the Baby Formula Room, she was assigned to Miss Mock's ward for full-time duty.

"We need a probey up here," Miss Mock said. "The lavatory has not been scrubbed thoroughly for weeks. Mary, the maid, will teach you about the trays. Have you given medicines?"

"No, Miss Mock."

"Baths?"

"No, Miss Mock."

"Enemas?"

"No, Miss Mock."

"What did they send you to me for?"

Miss Mock's face was covered with freckles that gave her the look of a bat. Trinc wondered if she, herself, were beginning to appear to others as less than human. "To learn, Miss Mock," she replied truthfully.

"The first thing to learn is not to be insolent! Go and practice on Miss Smithers in the semi-private room."

She knew about Miss Smithers by reputation. A retired nurse who was now a non-paying patient, she was said to be very demanding. Trinc went down the hall and knocked on the door of a semi-private room before entering it. She was not prepared for the specimen she found there, a great tub of a woman with the jowls, pink and flaccid, of a permanently inflated blowfish.

"I've been ringing my bell for twenty-three minutes. Why didn't you answer it?"

Trinc explained that she had just received assignment from Miss Mock.

"Sent me another probey, has she? Can't spare a real nurse for me? Anything will do for old Smithers. I might as well be dead."

"Is there anything urgent, Miss Smithers?"

"Of course it's urgent! Put fresh water in my flower vases."

With three vases balanced in her arms Trinc went down the hall and was just entering the pantry when a dwarf with wizened face started bellowing. "Get your feet off my floor! Can't you see I'm scrubbing the floor, you bitch! Miss Mock! Miss Mock! Get this probey off my clean floor!"

Miss Mock came flying. "Be quiet, Mary. As for you, Miss DeRoman, why can't you get along with Mary? Aren't you accustomed to servants at home?"

When Trinc apologized, Miss Mock softened tone. "Mary *is* insane . . . You must have provoked her. Why, Mary was a ward maid when Miss Dean was a probationer like yourself. Mary is a tradition. If Miss Dean learns that you have provoked Mary, your goose is cooked . . . Now go back to Miss Smithers."

A minute later Trinc found Miss Smithers ringing her bedside bell violently, like an obese Salvation Army matron at Christmas. "Where are the vases?"

"I had to leave them. I'm not allowed to get water from the pantry until the floor is dry."

"It took you long enough. Didn't you hear my bell?"

"What do you want, Miss Smithers?"

"I want a hot bath. The powder is on the bureau. I don't care for your hospital powder or soap. See to it that I have two clean sheets and four clean pillow cases every day. Today I have my table towels changed, and a fresh gown . . . My pulse has gone up to 122 from having to ring my bell so much. I shall be so upset I can't eat . . . Don't forget to take my temperature. Always heat the bed-pan before giving it to me. My medicine is due in six minutes. I get an aspirin tablet every two hours, a glass of sherry before meals, and bicarbonate of soda after meals. I'll tell you how I like my tray fixed. If my food is not properly prepared, I shall have a very aggressive B. M. . . ."

MALLIE DEVINE WAS A CERTAINTY to get to wear the blue uniform and cap of the Junior class. If she sometimes forgot to turn on a patient's radiator now that it was winter, she could compute calories and mix medicines with perfect accuracy. Dora Downey, however, had earned the displeasure of various nurses. Not only did they not forgive her the angelic complexion, but also they wanted Dr. Nicovich's attention diverted from Dora to themselves.

Trinc figured that she'd been reported too often to Miss Dean to have much chance for a cap. Her popularity with patients, even with Miss Smithers, would probably not be weighed in the balance. Still, she had been transferred from Miss Mock's ward to Miss Dorking's. There might be a last-minute reprieve.

The probeys, she among them, stood at attention before Miss Dorking's desk. Their hands were clasped firmly behind their backs while Miss Dorking, a pretty young woman with a hard look to her, looked over a memo in front of her daily calendar. "Miss Downey can learn Medicines today. Miss DeRoman can take her place on Diets. We have a transfusion at ten. Miss Grady? You and Miss Tabor go to Massage Clinic at nine, Miss Bond to Basal Metabolism. There will be Doctors' Grand Rounds on Sadie Steinberg, so save a clean gown for her . . . Miss Downey, help Miss DeRoman with the trays. That will be all."

In the ward pantry Dora helped Trinc to set the trays and to dish out cold breakfast food. "That's Sadie's tray," Dora indicated hurriedly. "She isn't allowed salt. Mrs. Schwartz takes an apple and two slices of toast. There's an extra dish of oatmeal. Let Mrs. Gruber have it. She's always hungry."

Presently Trinc pushed a five-tiered tray carriage and was distributing trays to patients that she didn't know. When the last patient had finished complaining about the food, it was already time to collect the first trays served and the water pitchers that needed washing. She took these to old Molly, the ward maid. She asked where she could wash the pitchers.

"You may wash them in hell, for you'll not use my sink."

"I'll wait until you are through, of course, Molly. But please show me how to turn on the sterilizer, so I can be working on something while I wait."

Molly folded red arms. "If you're too goddamn dumb to manage that old boiler, you're too goddamn dumb to waste me breath on."

"That's right, Molly, I am dumb. But I've got to share this pantry with you for a long time. Let's be friends."

"Friend with a probey bitch? Don't pester me. And don't soil no extra dish or spoon. And promise to stay out of me way."

"I promise, Molly. And you promise not to swear at me. You may call me a dummy but never a bitch. I'm not a bitch, am I, Molly?"

"Oh," Molly said as her face relaxed into a partly toothless grin, "get along with you, Miss . . . Come now. I'll show you about the old dish-boiler. Satan's own machine, it is. She'll hiss and spit scalding water at you if you touch the wrong handle . . . Don't mind me bad language. It's me sore feet tawkin' through me worn-out slippers."

Annie, Trinc thought. Old Annie again. The thought gave her an idea. "Molly? I'll give you a fine pair of shoes and silk stockings to wear. O. K.?"

Molly's frown changed into a sunny smile. "Lord bless you, Miss," she was saying just as Dora rushed into the pantry with a frantic look on her face. "O Trinc DeRoman, you're in for it now! They say Dr. Knight is furious because he came two hours early to give that test on Sadie Steinberg and ever so many doctors are waiting for the report on that test. Remember? It was to be discussed at Grand Rounds . . . Miss Dorking says you're to go to her at once!"

Trinc could hardly remember Sadie Steinberg's name, there had been so many names to get straight. She recalled that somebody was supposed to save a clean gown for her in order to make a good impression on the doctors. "What test are you talking about, Miss Downey?"

"The metabolism test."

"What has it got to do with me?"

"They say you spoiled the test."

"She ain't spoiled no test," Molly declared hotly.

"Shut up, Molly," Dora said. "Since when did you start being nice to probeys?"

"Since I took a tick off the dog to catch rain, mavournin." Molly pushed her face at Dora. "She's givin' me shoes and silks. It's more than ye give me, darlin'."

Trinc rolled down sleeves and went with Dora to Miss Dorking's desk. Dr. Nicovich was there, looking bored, and Miss Dorking, beside him, was smiling sweetly and saying, "Let me take care of this, Nicky . . . So!" She turned the hard look on Trinc. "Here's the Diet Nurse. I suppose you gave Sadie Steinberg a large breakfast on purpose to get me in trouble with Dr. Knight and the other doctors?"

"I gave her the usual breakfast," Trinc said.

"The usual breakfast." Miss Dorking's repetition was laced with sarcasm.

"Perhaps she don't know there is test."

Everyone looked at Dr. Nicovich who was looking at Dora. Miss Dorking went on, "I read out the morning's program to all assembled. I told Miss DeRoman there would be a basal metabolism test on Sadie Steinberg. Are you deaf, Miss DeRoman?"

"I heard you say, Miss Dorking, there would be Doctors' Grand Rounds on Sadie Steinberg. You didn't say Sadie Steinberg was to go without breakfast."

"That," Miss Dorking declared through clenched teeth, "is a lie! You can tell it to Miss Dean and to the doctors whose time you have wasted. They are waiting for you . . . And what do you think you are doing here, Miss Downey? You're supposed to be learning medicines today. . . This is an important matter, don't you think, Nicky?"

"Important madder?" A thin smile twitched his mustache as he looked at Dora. "Suddenly I remember to go to Dr. Knight. With both ladies. I teach medicines to Miss Downey in elevator."

"That shut her up," Dora said a few minutes later in the elevator.

"Shud her up good." Dr. Nicovich looked pleased with himself. "She don't like Nicky, I think, now."

Although Trinc had to smile to herself, she thought Dora had also made an enemy of Miss Dorking. "Dora," she said in a worried tone, "you're not to mix yourself up in this. My Uncle Doc—"

"—Uncle Doc?" Dr. Nicovich queried.

"Dr. Knight," Trinc corrected herself, "has a right to be furious about the spoiled test. I'm sure he'll take my side if Miss Dorking is trying to shift the blame."

"I ask question?" Dr. Nicovich broke in. "Dr. Knight is uncle?"

Trinc's secret was out. She bit her lip, nodded in the affirmative.

"Very good. He is great man."

"I hear, Dr. Nicovich, that your brother is a great man."

"Oh, yes. He is not a bastard like me. He's worse: a shaman."

"I hear he treats glandular and neurological problems. Is that correct?"

"Is correct," Dr. Nicovich replied. "His research so mystical he will one day going to jail. Also too expensive. How much French franc to dollar? Anyway, about ten thousand dollar for operation."

"Ten thousand dollars!" Dora whistled. "You're poor, Nicky. You could make money, too."

The elevator bounced to a stop.

A few minutes later the three of them were seated in Miss Dean's office. When Uncle Doc came in, Dr. Nicovich sprang up and shook his hand, took him aside for a few words in private. Then he turned to Trinc. "Dr. Knight, he permit me ask question . . . Miss DeRoman, why we here?"

"I spoiled a basal metabolism test."

"Is correct. You know what is basal metabolism?"

Trinc shook her head at words she had heard without understanding.

"Miss DeRoman has been in the Diet Kitchen," Miss Dean said. "She is in charge of diets now on Miss Dorking's ward. She ought to know about metabolism."

Dr. Nicovich exchanged a glance with Uncle Doc. "Metabolism not duty of Diet Kitchen. How much time you on ward of Miss Dorking, Miss DeRoman?"

"Since seven o'clock this morning."

"You know patient, Sadie Steinberg?"

"I have not had time on the new ward to know the patients by name, Dr. Nicovich."

"Is correct," he said, then turned to Dora. "Miss Downey. You are present when Miss Dorking read morning program . . . Do Miss Dorking say Sadie Steinberg not have breakfast?"

Dora wet her lips before replying. "No, doctor."

"Please to step outside office," Dr. Nicovich said, a wave of hand followed by his holding open the door. "Dr. Knight have something to say to Miss Dean."

Out in the corridor Trinc looked at Dora with new eyes. She had some sand, after all. And Dr. Nicovich had the confidence of Uncle Doc for good reason.

Miss Dean emerged from her office smiling so pleasantly that she seemed transformed to a creature in the primate category. As they answered her beckoning finger and returned to the presence of the doctors, she positively glowed. "Congratulations, Miss DeRoman and Miss Downey, you and Miss Devine also, all may call at the sewing room in off-duty time tomorrow to be fitted for your blue uniforms."

9

Do You Like T. S. Eliot?

MALLIE WAS ON DUTY. Trinc, alone in their room in the Nurses' Home, studied her reflection in the mirror while the Victrola played a tune from George White's *Scandals*. The eye-liner made her look mysterious with just a touch of vamp. The permed hair glowed as it fell across her long neck to exposed shoulders. Uncoerced by a camisole, her breasts poked nipples into the flimsy organdy dress. The jewelry—new dew-drop pearls for earrings, the repaired pearl necklace, the fire-opal ring—would have to do.

She leaned forward, stretched and puckered her lips, and applied color lightly. She crinkled her eyes, frowned, raised eyebrows, examined teeth, added dabs of Toujours Moi to the cleavage of bosom. Standing up and placing a silk-stockinged leg on the footstool, she pulled her dress above the knee, tightened a garter strap. Straightening up, she inspected the firm, uptilted abdomen, the slim waist.

Jumping a groove and scratching the record, the phonograph needle made her realize how nervous she was. She went and lifted the needle and turned off the phonograph. After grabbing her new fur-trimmed overcoat, she locked the door and headed downstairs. High heels tapped on marble stairs.

Troy Turner was meeting her at the subway entrance to escort her to his bootlegger's . . .

She, Dora, and Mallie had been appointed for duty under the direction of Dr. Troy Turner, their professor in surgical nursing. Sitting in the back row of the lecture hall, prior to her appointment, Trinc had exchanged scribbled notes with Dora. "Do you suppose he's a good dancer?" Dora replied, "His legs are too long." Trinc wrote, "How old?" Dora replied, "All of thirty," with lots of exclamation points. They decided that they liked the doctor, even though his lectures were boring. He had dark, soulful eyes and wore prim Arrow collars.

The bell by the ambulance gate clanged. Orderlies carried in a patient.

Dr. Turner opened the door of a small operating room. "In here, please. Easy there, men! Put him on the table." He gave instructions for washing the patient and shaving his head. When the orderlies were finished with their task, he rubbed his hands in lime and soda and signaled to Trinc that he was ready for a towel from the sterilizing drum. Trinc took it out, handed it to him with forceps. He seemed to look at her with sudden interest.

"You're Miss DeRoman, aren't you? You're in my surgical nursing course."

"Three hours a week."

"I've often seen two girls in the back row, who take so many notes . . . Let's see how much you know about surgery, Miss DeRoman. Do you want to manage this case?"

She glanced at Mallie, surprised to have been preferred over the most competent girl in Junior class. Mallie looked pleased for her. "All right," Trinc said.

"He needs about twenty stitches in his scalp. You sew him up. I'll play nurse. Miss Devine will serve the towel and gloves after you've scrubbed up." His dark eyes studied her.

"Needlepoint or cross-stitch, doctor?"

"More like sewing rawhide on a baseball, Miss DeRoman."

An anaesthetist arrived with gas and oxygen tanks. While Dr. Turner observed Trinc's technique at the scrub-up basin, Mallie served her the towel and gloves. The three of them stood over the unconscious patient.

"Hold the forceps like this," Dr. Turner demonstrated. "Now, put your needle in like this . . ." Trinc set to work. His voice murmured through his mask. "Good . . . I'll tie the knot . . . You're quick with your hands, Miss DeRoman. Do you play the piano?"

"Halfway between Chopsticks and Chopin."

"Put your needle in this side. Don't let the knot slip . . . Did you hear Kreisler at the Carnegie?"

"Wasn't it beautiful!"

"Thread the needle again . . . Now, stick it in . . . Do you dance?"

"I'm the second Isadora."

"That leaves me out. I'm the second Abe Lincoln."

When the twentieth stitch was taken, Trinc followed Dr. Turner out to the hall of the Emergency Ward, her cheeks flushed with triumph.

"Thank you for letting me take that case. The nurses so seldom get a chance." She meant to say that doctors *never* gave nurses a chance to practice medicine but stopped herself short of the truth. "Doctors so seldom have the time to teach us."

"That's all right, Miss DeRoman. You did a good sew-up." He paused. "Would you mind if I asked you . . . ?"

"Asked me what?"

"Asked you to go out with me tonight?"

"We're not allowed to go out with doctors."

"We could dance at a hotel."

Trinc was intensely, almost breathlessly aware of him. She thought and said, "Why don't we ask Miss Downey and Dr. Nicovich to join us?"

"Splendid!" he said. "Nicky's a pal of mine. And I know he gets in the pants of the little movie star who sits beside you in class. . . A deal! I'll meet you at the Lexington subway entrance at seven o'clock. Two blocks down and one to the left." He reached for Trinc's hand but drew himself back. Miss Snavely had entered the ward. "As I was saying," Dr. Turner said in changed voice, "I'll need that chart before seven."

Everything was easily arranged with Dora. At six o'clock the two girls raced off duty, hoping to be the first to use the bathtub upon which Juniors depended for washing. As Trinc undressed in her room, Dora came in shaking her head and pouting. "Ada's in the tub. Marie's promised her turn to me. You may use my bath water after me."

"We'll be late," Trinc said.

"Oh," Dora half laughed, "Nicky doesn't mind my being late. When I stay out with him after midnight, he helps me climb up the fire escape . . . I just wish he wasn't so poor."

Trinc believed all the young doctors were paid skimpy wages. "One would suppose that a distant successor to the Czar would have a few items to pawn?"

"He's so poor he borrows from Dr. Turner just for a couple shots of gin. Your Dr. Turner, though, is another story."

"*My* Dr. Turner?"

"I don't mean that money would interest you," Dora said. "I mean that Turner's no churchmouse."

"You amaze me," Trinc said as a call from down the hallway announced that the bathtub was free.

Half an hour later the girls were dressed in sleeveless black satin dresses and cloche hats. They stopped by the Training School Office to collect late passes. Miss Dean stared at Trinc and ordered her to go into the inner office.

Trinc whispered to Dora, "Go on to the St. George and explain the delay to Dr. Turner at the subway entrance." She went and stood at attention before Miss Dean.

"Please remove your hat. An embarrassing matter has been brought to my attention by Miss Snavely."

As she removed her hat, Trinc wondered if Miss Snavely had overheard Dr. Turner's conversation with her.

"Is it true, Miss DeRoman, you have dyed your hair?"

"And if I should dye my hair, Miss Dean?"

"Girls with dyed hair cannot take our Florence Nightingale pledge and wear the Nightingale pin. Please put your head near the light."

After taking Trinc's head in her hands and pulling it beneath a dangling electric lightbulb, Miss Dean could be felt examining it with her fingers as if she were searching for lice. "Well," she finally said in vexation, "I can't imagine how the rumor got started. Your hair is a natural, albeit unusual mixture of red and black . . . Goodnight, Miss DeRoman."

When she arrived at the subway station after seven, Dr. Turner was nowhere in sight. With a sick feeling she realized that he and Dora and Dr. Nicovich had taken her at her word and gone on to the St. George. She flagged down a taxi and settled in.

Why was she so excited about Dr. Troy Turner? He was not charming. His smile was private, not sociable. He yawned when he read his lecture notes. He liked to embarrass the girls with irrelevant questions. "Miss Downey, describe the psychology of the normal man." The answer to this riddle, known only to himself, would be revealed by him: there is no normal man. "Miss Healey, you are going to tell me, are you not, that depressed patients are not suicidal?" There was no answer from Miss Healey because Miss Healey had dropped off to sleep.

She alighted from the taxi by the hotel's awning, pushed through revolving doors, and found Dr. Turner in the lobby, leaning against a pillar, smoking a cigarette. He dropped the cigarette into a potted palm and ran to clasp her hands in his. "Dor said you were detained. How on earth did you manage to escape that old witch?"

"Miss Dean thought my hair is dyed! She pulled it for inspection. Isn't that ridiculous? Where are the others?"

"Nicky and Dor went in to start dinner. They're saving places for us. They say your name is Trinc. May I call you Trinc? Call me Turner." He offered his arm. "Let's go, Trinc! There's a redhot jazz band, I'm told."

Arm in arm they approached the faint rumble of a band

until they entered a large dining room. There they were met by the screechy blare of trombones, the urgent oopy doopy of saxophones, the bop of drums, by candlelights on tables and a swirling of dreamy dancers. After checking her coat, Trinc put her hand lightly on Turner's shoulder and let his arm gather her to him. They swayed and whirled, his breath thrilling to her hair, his body moving as part of the rhythm. She closed her eyes and let him guide her according to the up-tempo beat until a drum was rolled and bright lights flooded the room and couples returned to their tables.

Turner squeezed her hand. "Oh, Trinc, we mustn't dance like that!"

"We didn't know." She caught her breath. "It just happened."

"I didn't know anyone could dance like you!" They found the table and sat down. "Hullo, Dor! Hullo, Nicky! O my baby baby baby—yeah! Have you ordered for us?"

"We're budgeting," Dora smirked at Dr. Nicovich. "Oysters for everybody."

"Do you want oysters, darling?" Turner asked Trinc in a dreadfully earnest voice.

Darling?

"Thank you."

"What did Miss Dean want with you?" Dora asked. Turner piped up, "Oh, yes, darling, tell them how Miss Dean tried to pull off your wig!"

Wig?

"She almost pulled my head off! She." Trinc wondered why she was laughing so hard. The story wasn't funny. "She said . . . my hair . . . is dyed!"

Everybody laughed.

Oysters were served, dozens of them. Trinc put Tabasco sauce on hers, mindful of her Louisiana heritage. When the waiter brought glasses of ginger ale, Dr. Nicovich—she considered it unprofessional to think of him as Nicky—produced a hip flask and mixed vodka into them. After a while Turner said, "I say,

Nicky, I think Dostoevsky and Tolstoy are swell."

"Don't get high-brow," Dora said.

Lights were dimmed. The band struck up a frantic number. At a nod from Turner, Trinc stood up, and then she was in his arms again. It seemed that their feet did intricate things, whatever the music prompted, and there was no need to talk when he smiled down at her. When the music stopped she felt that they had spanned a year of intimacy together. As they returned to the table Turner spoke softly in her ear, "Let's go around to my place."

Place?

"Oh," Trinc groaned. "Does dancing have to stop?"

"It's not far, darling," Turner said with a glance at Dr. Nicovich. "We'll get you girls back before curfew."

"Unless we ask Miss Dean to act as chaperon," Dora said, breaking the ice.

Trinc went to collect her coat. When Turner was helping her on with it she gave the coat-check girl a dollar, thinking, *he's poor as a churchmouse.*

The four of them walked for about six blocks before they came to Turner's apartment building near the El. After they climbed two flights of dimly lighted stairs, Turner unlocked his apartment and they entered a dark room that smelled of stale tobacco. Turner switched on lamps, passed out cigarettes that "Dor" and Dr. Nicovich accepted, lit a fire in the grate and went to a kitchenette to crack ice and pour cocktails. The mood of the evening was slipping away as Trinc sank into a leather chair near the fire and appraised the apartment, to see what she could learn about Turner.

He didn't strike her as even comfortably off. That, for her, was one of his attractions. There were books everywhere, on shelves, on the floor, on a table covered with a gold batik. This survey earned him good marks even though she considered authors such as Michael Arlen and Edgar Rice Burroughs trash. On a wall there was a photograph of Turner in a football player's uniform, the pointy leather helmet giving him some resemblance to a Babylonian in D. W. Griffith's *Intolerance*. Among other possessions, a Royal typewriter, a Victrola, a stack of records. Good.

When Turner came in with a tray of cocktails and placed it on a table, he was smiling his private smile. Not until then did Trinc realize that they were alone. Dora and Dr. Nicovich had disappeared into a bedroom.

All of a sudden Turner lunged to a kneeling position at Trinc's feet and buried his head in her lap. "I do love you, seriously I do," he sighed deeply against her belly. "I fell in love with you this morning between stitches."

Love?

"Where did Dora go?" She tried to toss off the question diffidently.

"Oh, let's not worry about them." His head lay heavily between her thighs. She noticed that where his hair was thinning there was a rim of dandruff, like a dried salt-lick at the zoo. Gently pushing Turner away, she stood up, brushed off her black dress, and went to look at the record collection.

"'Song of India,'" she said nervously. "Would you like me to dance?"

"Good-o," he said without enthusiasm. She placed the record on the Victrola, went to the table, and removed the batik from under the tray. "I'll change in the bathroom," she said over her shoulder.

The peer-glass in the bathroom informed her of what she already knew: her heart belonged to a time long, long ago, when she had danced for Aeneas without music. Could she ever recover that feeling? She removed everything but her camisole and panties and wound the gold batik around her hips, like a Javanese sarong, taking her time. When she heard Dora and Dr. Nicovich talking to Turner, she reappeared in the living room. They were sprawled on the floor, drinking the cocktails. Turner had loosened his Arrow collar. Dora's lipstick was smeared around the mouth. Dr. Nicovich's paintbrush hair looked bedraggled.

"This," Trinc announced with a flow of hands, "is a garden with a lotus tree." She went and wound the Victrola, starting "The Song of India," and let the pantomime in her head translate itself into the gestures and movements of a maiden's prayer for love. When the last phrase of the music died away, she stood poised and solemn. Everyone applauded. Turner came to her and carried her hand to his lips. "I know you love me now," he whispered.

"Bravo!" Dr. Nicovich leered. "Have nother drink. Don't mind I do."

She ran to get dressed. Before the peer-glass in the bathroom, she tossed warm hair from her face and studied it to see if the feeling-tones of love had risen to the surface. She recognized a look of nervous fatigue which bore little resemblance to natural vivacity.

"I swear I didn't do that to make love to him," she protested to herself . . .

NOW HERE SHE WAS, letting Turner take her to Guiseppe's in Little Italy. He called it "my bootlegger's" with a curious air of proprietorship.

He was smoking a cigarette, waiting for her at the Lexington entrance to the subway downtown. "Darling!" He pecked her on the cheek. "I'm afraid I can't afford a taxi."

Trinc gave him a twenty-dollar bill that she had already removed from her purse and kept folded in her hand. It would more than pay for everything. "Good-o," he said, taking the bill and hailing a passing taxi. It took them to a market square where women wearing black shawls squatted on doorstoops.

Everything was going to be very romantic.

They mounted a flight of ornamental iron steps that led to a green door on which Turner knocked nine times in a rhythm of threes. An unshaven man opened it and let them through. They passed through a corridor and an empty room decorated with artificial vines, from there through a door in the rear of the building. When Turner opened it, Trinc saw a steep spiral staircase that led down to a brick-walled courtyard with an Old World appearance. She could see candle-flickery checkered tablecloths, tables occupied by well-dressed couples. Although she had seldom seen anything so corny, she had to admit that Prohibition would cast even the sleaziest joint into a favorable light. She squeezed Turner's hand as they descended the stairs.

After they were seated at a corner table, Turner ordered two plates of spaghetti, then exchanged a secretive look with the waiter. He brought them two teacups filled with an oily, clear liquid.

"To us," Turner toasted. "Down the hatch, old girl!" He swallowed half a cupful. His eyes were watering when he put the cup down. "Jesus! Just what the doctor ordered."

Old girl?

Taking a tentative sip of the gin, Trinc gasped from the burning sensation, "Your bootlegger has a sense of humor!"

She took another, bigger sip. This time the sensation passed through her throat and warmed her belly. She took a big swallow. After the pain-fog cleared, she was being offered one of two cigarettes that Turner had lit. She had quit smoking, but she took the cigarette and inhaled deeply. Candles flickered in bottles under a small sky. The feeling of intimacy seemed to be returning.

The waiter brought two steaming plates of spaghetti. Later, after the plates were cleared away, Trinc wondered why Turner had spoken so little. Perhaps he was sparing her the small talk about the hospital. Perhaps he was just shy. He drew his chair close to hers. He took a book from his pocket.

"Listen to this, darling." He began to read in a reverent tone: "'O the waves, the skydevouring waves, glistening with light, dancing with life, the waves of eddying joy, rushing forever . . .

The stars rock upon them, thoughts of every tint are cast up out of the deep and scattered on the beach of life . . . Birth and death rise and fall with their rhythm, and the sea-gull of my heart spreads its wings crying in delight'."

He drank his third gin. "It's perfect, Trinc, don't you agree?"

Beach of life? The sea-gull of my heart spreads its wings?

"I think," Trinc said, "it's for the birds."

"Oh," Turner shifted, "I'm no judge of poetry. I'm just starved for beauty . . . I don't say there's no beauty in a hospital. I remember an old woman's dying, how beautiful I thought her courage, and I remember holding a new-born baby." He paused to look up. His eyes reflected candlelight. He brought them down to rest on Trinc. "Your face is beautiful. Like my mother's face as she sat beside my bed whenever I was sick. There's beauty in our noble professions. That's the real reason we stick to them. But we need to escape reality."

"How?" Trinc asked, curious as to how reality could be separated from itself.

"With poetry and jazz and alcohol and love," he replied. "We have all four."

He leaned in. She let him kiss her, briefly, on the lips. He moved his hand under her dress. She felt its progress as if she were hypnotized—slowly past the knee, past the garter snap, then to the moist inner flesh of the thigh. "Do you like T. S. Eliot?" she managed on an intake of breath.

"Don't look now," he said, withdrawing hand, "but it's that old fart, Dr. Knight. He's at the top of the spiral staircase. Mrs. Van Dine is with him."

Old fart? Mrs. Van Dine?

She covered her face and peeked through fingers. Huddled couples. Guttering candles. A waiter wiping his hands. The staircase. At its top a woman in a black fur coat, swept-up hair unnaturally blonde, like spaghetti. There, too, a tall man in a Chesterfield, top hat a-tilt above Uncle Doc's leonine features. Trinc turned her head away quickly.

Turner spoke in low voice. "The waiter's bringing them a bottle in a paper bag . . . They're leaving. He didn't see us."

Half an hour later, as she and Turner were headed uptown in a taxi, she reviewed what he had told her.

"They say, after Dr. Van Dine divorced her years ago, Dr. Knight has been keeping Mrs. Van Dine in a love-nest on Murray Hill. It's all very discreet. But everyone in the hospital knows she is his mistress, because, once in a while, when there's an emergency and Dr. Knight has to be called in, the staff is instructed to dial the operator and give her a certain secret telephone number."

Trinc had feigned sophisticated disinterest. "Oh? You mean he has a wife and a home?"

"Sure. He's married to some rich society dame. Know what they say?" Turner had paused to finish his fourth gin. "They say the old fart's wife is so Victorian, she's never slept with him, ever. For over forty years. Imagine . . . Man has to have a piece of ass. Makes you feel sort of sorry for the old guy."

"And his wife? Don't you feel sorry for her, too?"

"Oh," Turner had shrugged, "she's probably frigid, so she's in on the deal. Besides, they've got lots of money."

Now in the taxi Trinc turned her head and spoke into the scent of Turner's threadbare smoking jacket. "Do you mind my having more money than you?"

"Me mind?" He chuckled softly. "I had an uncle who made a fortune in bananas and lost it on the stock market. So he went to Seattle and made another fortune in salmon. Lost it, too. So he went to Cripple Creek and made another fortune in gold. Lost it, too. Last I heard, he's trying to strike oil in Wyoming . . . Easy come, easy go. That's me."

"Do you think it's ethical for a doctor to charge ten thousand dollars for an operation?"

"Why do you ask?"

"Oh, Dr. Nicovich has a brother who charges that much for an operation. Maybe in Paris the ethics differ from ours."

"I dunno," Turner said. "It depends on value. If the doctor's that great, that's one thing. If the operation is so important that the patient wants it more than anything, that's one more thing. It's all relative . . . Of course, the doctor shouldn't be paid unless the operation is a success."

"That's a point," Trinc said.

It was also, she thought, a point in Turner's favor. He wasn't quite as sentimental and thick in the head as she was coming to believe. On the other hand he seemed to resemble T.S. Eliot's portrait of hollow men.

JUST AFTER COMPLETING JUNIOR YEAR, Trinc arranged with Uncle Doc's secretary for an appointment in his office during off-duty hours. When the time came, she was ushered into his office a few minutes early and told to wait.

She had been right to think that he worked in the Waldorf-Astoria. A thickly carpeted, pine-paneled room with a polished mahogany desk, the office had on display many oil paintings and photographs, most of them revealing his love for the West. Here was a picture of him on horseback with Teddy Roosevelt in Yellowstone Park. Here was another one with Teddy in Oklahoma, the two of them standing over a mound of slain wolves and coyotes. In both pictures Uncle Doc was, of all things, a handsome middle-aged man with blond Van Dyke beard and handlebar mustache, a jaunty cowboy right at home in the environment of majestic mountains and vast plains. He had had an adventurous life all right. But had he been happy?

That same dear man, beginning to slump slightly with age, entered the office and closed the door behind him. She did not run to him and put her arms around his neck, but he pressed her hand in his with his usual warm greeting before he sat behind the desk, folded hands and waited. Trinc had made it very clear to the secretary that this was to be a business meeting, not a family matter.

"What can I do for you, Trinc?"

"Do you remember," she began, "telling me that you knew Dr. Nicovich's older brother in Paris?"

"Serge. That's right."

"I have a friend in England whose cousin was mutilated during the war. In the scrotum. It seems that he may be castrated. I was wondering, you see—because this man wants to get married—whether it's possible for two people to be married happily without, uh—"

"—carnal intercourse?" Uncle Doc's eyebrows shot up. He unfolded hands, spread palms. "If they love each other with all their hearts and souls, anything is possible. They can satisfy one another physically without penetration. They can adopt children. They might even find in restraint the path to a higher spirituality . . . To those who love each other, sex is gratifying, fulfilling. I would add—" Uncle Doc seemed to look Trinc directly in the eye—"I would add that sex, without love, is nothing. You're going to get the blues."

"I think I know what you mean," Trinc said. "My friend's cousin, though, has the blues for another reason. It's my opinion of the case that he will never marry the woman he loves unless he is healed. Which brings me to the point: do you think this Dr. Serge Nicovich would be willing to treat my friend's cousin as a patient? My friend is rich. She's willing to pay anything . . ."

Uncle Doc folded his hands again. "Of course. Especially as you seem to be aware, as I am, from our own Nicky, that his brother is as greedy as he is brilliant . . . I can't say that Serge is the right specialist, but he'll know what's to be done, if anything—that is, if there's any possibility of successful treatment . . . You do understand, there are no guarantees."

Trinc thought of Turner's advice and said, "If there's an operation, and it isn't successful, does my friend pay the fee anyway?"

"I'm afraid so, Trinc . . . I'll ask Dr. Nicovich for his brother's current address, and I'll write Serge myself on your friend's behalf. I'll let you know what happens."

"Uncle Doc?" She knew that the Heartwell tradition of frankness had its ambiguities, but now that she knew, too, about Uncle Doc's sadness of soul, she felt that she had to let him know that she shared it, and understood. "I saw you a few weeks ago in the company of Mrs. Van Dine. I thought my idol had fallen. I was wrong. I'm sure she means nothing to you. . ."

"Sally Van Dine is, well, a legacy," Uncle Doc sighed after a pause. "I wish we were all better men."

"You're a great man, Uncle Doc! You're a wonderful man! You're my true father, and I love you!"

It was sad to see him hanging his head. Then it was wonderful to see him raise it. "Among my failings, princess, is the lack of a present to give you today."

"You've given me all I could ever hope for," Trinc said. But Uncle Doc had fallen from a great height. She could not pretend otherwise to herself. "Do you love this Sally Van Dine?" she asked, voice barely audible.

Uncle Doc frowned, cleared his throat. "All right, Trinc," he said, "you'll have to know the truth. Sally is my half-sister, my father's bastard with his mistress on Murray Hill . . . I am her sole source of comfort and support since her divorce."

10

Scientifically Moral

TRINC HAD COME TO NEW YORK to serve people, but there seemed to be a blank spot between her profession and the world. She was taught to treat symptoms rather than their causes. The medical profession, as she was coming to know it from the inside, seldom allowed considerations of conscience to prevail over those of power. It was all done in the name of "scientific morality," a sort of disciplined blindness to the evidence of weal and woe. She was working in an environment of diminished care—of diminished consciousness.

Uncle Doc's revelation about his illegitimate half-sister, however, had taught her a lesson about herself that was hard to swallow. She had distrusted and misjudged the dearest man she had ever known, the very man whose proudly concealed code of honor and conscience had always provided for her soul a feeling of hope and sanctuary. How could she ever again completely trust her own judgment unless, first, she were aware of all the facts and, second, drew conclusions from them in a spirit of faith? Uncle Doc's sadness, which she had mistaken as a sign of guilt, had, she now knew, at least two sources, compassion for the suffering of others and restraint of, possibly renunciation of, his natural desires. It was probably true, as Turner had said, that Uncle Doc and Auntie Em had had a marriage without sex, but who was anyone to judge, let alone she, that it was not a true marriage of love and respect? Thus reflecting, Trinc realized also that she didn't want a man—Turner, for instance—whom she couldn't love—and that a happy marriage with Aeneas was possible—and that she had been blaming Mother for complicity in a crime against Aeneas of which she might be blameless. Trinc decided that when opportunity arose she would confront Mother with the facts.

One morning she was "specialing" a patient who had frequent epileptic fits. Holding a gauze-wrapped tongue depressor in her hand, she stood by his bed waiting for the next seizure, ready to thrust the depressor between his teeth to keep him from doing violent injury to himself. Because his fits disturbed other patients on Miss Dorking's ward, Trinc had screened off his bed.

"What about the party tonight?" she overheard Dora say on the other side of the screen.

"Dr. Van Dine's taking us to a road-house," came another voice. It was Miss Dorking's. Trinc would have recognized that scratchy phonograph needle anywhere.

"Nicky can't go. He's on call."

"Try Turner."

"He's too high-brow."

"You better rope him in before that DeRoman bitch lands him. Not that she needs his money."

"He wouldn't fall for me."

"With your looks, honey? Men only want one thing. We'll get him drunk."

They left the ward still talking.

Two weeks later Trinc and Turner went for a Sunday stroll in Central Park near the crossing where as a little girl she had seen the horse shot. When she told him the story, he stopped and stared at her with his mouth oddly twisted. "I wish they'd shoot me," he said.

"Turner, what's wrong?"

"I can't tell you what a fool I've been." He shoved his hands in pockets and looked at the ground. "I'm so rotten . . . You know I love you . . . Here, read this."

He pulled a crumpled paper from a pocket and glanced away as Trinc read. It said that the State gave permission for Troy Turner to marry Dora Downey.

"You're *married* to her?"

"Last week."

"Will she make a good mother for your children?"

"Don't torture me, Trinc! I don't know anything about her. I'm a fool. That's enough. Why be a cad as well?"

"Did you go to a road-house party with Dr. Van Dine two weeks ago? Did you date Dora?"

"Yes."

"Did you drink?"

"I did nothing but drink."

Trinc looked again at the date on the marriage license. "You got the license the morning after?"

Turner nodded.

"The first three acts of this farce are clear," Trinc continued in a voice she didn't like. "You got drunk. You slept with Dora. You went to get the license . . . Now, the last act. Why, cold sober, did you marry her a week later? Is she pregnant?"

"God damn her, no!"

"But she said she was."

He sighed hopelessly. "Yes. She said she was."

"And your objective, scientific opinion, based on the fact that you were so drunk you couldn't see, and fortified by your conviction that billions of sperms automatically fertilize an egg, and that you know the results immediately, turns out to be rot."

Trinc spun around and flagged down a taxi on Fifth Avenue, taking care not to seem hurried, or to look back.

Next morning she went to Radiology where Dora was working. It was one area of the hospital which Trinc feared, so little was known about x-rays. It was true, as Aeneas had said, there were new worlds of energy and mind, invisible but always there, like stars in daylight. She found Dora taking x-ray pictures of a patient strapped on a table. Her little fist pressed a button, then the patient put on shorts and left the room. His penis had looked like a strange, melancholy sort of vegetable. $10,000 for *that*?

"May I speak with you for a moment, Mrs. Turner?"

Dora was caught by surprise. "You know."

"He has no money," Trinc said. "How is he going to support you?"

Dora looked outraged. "The creep told me to earn my own living."

"You tricked him. You told him you're pregnant, then you denied it . . . But you are pregnant, aren't you? By Dr. Nicovich . . . Turner will probably believe it's his baby, if you deny the affair which he's observed with his own eyes. He'll make you a good husband."

"Why did Miss Dorking tell me he was rich?" Dora pouted.

"Because just about everybody in this noble profession is an idiot! . . . Now, go down to Miss Dean, resign your position here, and make Turner support you. Tell him that I expect him to protect you to the best of his ability."

That night Trinc received a note from Turner.

"'Darling'," she read. "'Dor has told me everything. I don't see why she said first she was pregnant, then that she wasn't, and now again that she is. I suppose it's some hysterical behavior that men should understand but don't. I've taken her back. We're going to announce the marriage formally tomorrow. I'm going to make a decent home for my wife and child. Goodbye, darling. Bless you for helping us get through this crisis, with your wisdom and compassion, even though none of this would have happened if you weren't such a prick-teasing, snooty, frigid bitch!"

If there was one oasis of sanity in the Nurses' Home, it was Mallie Devine. The crimson-cheeked farm girl and college girl from New Hampshire was bright, well-adjusted, and kind, the only true Nightingale in the lot. Although others found her about as interesting as wallpaper, Trinc was drawn to her idealism. After graduation, Mallie was going to work in a clinic in China.

Mallie was washing stockings in the bathtub.

"Mallie," Trinc said, "I'm through with men. Will you teach me to live your way?"

Mallie chuckled as she fed the stockings through a wringer. "I don't live in any special way."

"No, Mallie, you're special. Why are you going to China?"

Mallie shrugged. "Oh, it's not what you think. I'll not be a martyr among the starving masses—though there'll be plenty of those. I just want to learn more about the oriental idea of death."

"Tell me."

"Well," Mallie said as she hung the stockings on a string to dry, "it's like we think of our bodies as occupying a particular space, so that when we die we must cross a boundary into personal extinction. But in the Far East, I'm told, there is no such boundary. Instead of our rushing toward annihilation, we are already mingled with the earth and the air and the stars. . ."

It was what Aeneas had said, except that he was speaking in scientific terms about energy and matter, not in mystical terms. Perhaps science and mysticism were mostly two ways of describing the same thing. When Mallie finished speaking, Trinc proposed that they go to a movie.

"But the Anatomy exam!" Mallie exclaimed.

"I know the bones and the cranial nerves," Trinc said, "and I also know that Gilda Grey is supposed to be terrific in *South Sea Love*."

Mallie's grin dimpled cheeks. "That's anatomy. Let's go."

Trinc spent three months in O. R.—the Operating Room. The first day there, Miss Snavely took her aside for instructions. She opened closets and cupboards, showing Trinc the many instruments on many shelves, the sterilizers, the doorways "entered from the left, during an operation, but never from the right," dressing rooms and anesthetic rooms. She spoke of laparotomy, cystectomy, nephrectomy. "You must remember all I say. If you don't, you may be responsible for the loss of a life."

There was a madhouse atmosphere in O. R. When the doors of an anesthetic room opened and the operating table was pulled into the theater, the unconscious patient lay covered by sheets except for the iodine-painted flesh that the surgeon's hands would cut and sew. No one but the surgeon and the instrument nurse saw that patch of flesh up close. No one but the anesthetist saw the patient's eyes or felt the pulse.

Compresses and flasks of salt solution were done up in bundles. The surgeon would murmur to the instrument nurse; the instrument nurse would signal with gloved hands to the "clean nurse"; and the "clean nurse" would signal to Trinc, who would fetch the right bundle and send it up the chain of command to the "operating field."

One operation followed another. The surgeons swore or pleaded for speed and cooperation. Some of them performed antics for medical students in the gallery. Now and then a Great Man flew into a tantrum, ripped off his gloves, and swept instruments onto the floor. Nurses were knocked out of the way or rapped on the knuckles with instruments or cursed for having the "wrong size cat gut." Once, a surgeon sobbed like a child. All through the morning and often late into the afternoon the surgeons and nurses stayed close to the operating field, whereas Trinc scurried about, valet to surgeons, errand-girl to the anesthetist, messenger to the "clean nurse," telephone girl, scrub lady and, at times, stretcher bearer.

When the last basin was scoured, the last instrument returned to its place, the last needle polished, the O. R. team retired to a small office, lay down in their clothes on the floor, and waited for the telephone to announce the arrival of an emergency case. Then they would spring up, lace their shoes, run and set up the Room. Hours would pass. Sometimes a dim dawn light could be seen sifting through cigarette smoke under a glass dome, showing the lined white faces of nurses bent over, polishing steel knives, their bare arms and stained fingers working steadily, their lips parted, their eyes red-rimmed with fatigue.

It was during this period that Trinc arranged to have $10,000 transferred from Lazard Frères, her bankers, to Amelia's bank in Paris, Amelia having agreed to have Dr. Serge Nicovich paid this sum in secret through the agency of yet another person. Amelia, it turned out, had already made the acquaintance of Dr. Nicovich in Leysin, Switzerland, where she had gone to a TB sanitorium near where he directed an Institute. Dr. Nicovich, she assured Trinc, was the right specialist for Aeneas, and she would herself persuade Aeneas, once she had his address, to have his Wound treated. Strange, how Amelia and Father always ended up meeting the "right" people. This was an opportunity not to be missed.

Once the transaction was completed, Trinc tried to forget about it. Somewhere in Europe an operation would be performed, or had already been performed. Like the work of the 0. R. team, it was unreal, magical, a kind of witchcraft without spells and owls.

Suddenly it was 1923. She would be twenty-five years of age in November. She might even be graduated as a Registered Nurse.

SHE WAS TRANSFERRED TO THE MATERNITY WARD where Mallie had already served for a month. Even as she arrived Trinc heard a woman crying, "Help me! Help me!"

She found Mallie brushing her teeth in a cubicle of the wash room. "Do you hear Mother Goldberg?" Mallie asked without looking up.

"I hear nothing else. She can't have been in labor all night?"

"But she was. All yesterday afternoon, too. Dr. Van Dine is almost never here when he's needed. And waiting for Baby

Goldberg is not the half of it." Mallie lowered her voice. "The husband has syphilis, the grandmother has TB, and this is Number Eight for Mother Goldberg."

Trinc had seen patients dying the horrid death of syphilis. It was against State law to teach birth control. When she remarked that she believed the doctors were teaching it anyway, Mallie snorted. "Not Dr. Van Dine. Last month in Pre-Natal Clinic . . ."

Mallie had noticed a frail-looking woman on a bench outside Dr. Van Dine's office just as Dr. Van Dine came with a clipboard. Write down your name and age for the record, Mother, he said. You write it down for me, said the mother. Seven little ones and all in their coffins. I'm Mrs. Goldberg. About thirty-five. So here's Mother Goldberg again, said Dr. Van Dine. Have you gone and done it again? Mother Goldberg blurted out, Please, Doctor, tell me how I can keep from getting another child! Dr. Van Dine threw back his head and laughed. Take a big drink of water and go to bed—late, he said . . . "Is he moral, immoral, or amoral?" Mallie finished.

"He ought to be fired," Trinc said.

"Haven't you noticed, Trinc, that gods almost never get fired?"

After working for a week in the First Stage Room that adjoined the Delivery Room, Trinc learned to distinguish by the sharpness of a woman's cry whether she was nearing the end of labor. One night, the nurses and Dr. Van Dine went for a midnight supper on nearby Lexington Avenue. Trinc was left in charge.

"Jesus . . . Jesus."

Trinc went to a bed to investigate the special cries and found them coming from a small dark head on a pillow. She picked up the patient's chart. Darlene Smith. Admitted 10:00 p.m. Race: Colored. Age: 12.

She smoothed the child's brow. "You must tell me when the next pain comes, Mother Smith," she said in a carefully controlled voice. She placed a hand on the hard little abdomen and counted contractions every five minutes. After half an hour she asked, "Does it hurt you, Mother? "

"No, Teacher."

Suddenly Mother Smith started up, white eyes protuberant, threw off bedcovers, and began rapidly grunting her baby out. Trinc ran for the emergency bell. As she did so, Mother Smith screamed. An infant's black hair was poking into the world. On her way back to the bed Trinc grabbed a towel. Presently, doing as she had been instructed by Dr. Van Dine, she pushed the baby back against the next contraction. She megaphoned her mouth and called for the elevator man. "Mike-hell! Mike-hell!"

Michael, like his name, swiftly like an angel came. He was to get Dr. Van Dine urgently. Meanwhile, Mother Smith's sobbing screams filled the ward. The infant could no longer be held back.

Trinc received the tiny, coffee-colored child in the towel, waters warm on her hands, just as Dr. Van Dine came running, followed by Michael and the nurses. "Stop that!" the doctor exploded, stethoscope swinging under gray beard. "You know you're forbidden to deliver babies!"

SHE WAS NOT ON DUTY the day that Dora was admitted to a private room on the Maternity Ward. It was Mallie who told her about it that evening in the Nurses' Home as she was flopping on her bed. "I better tell you something. Dora has gone into labor."

"Is Dr. Turner with her?"

"No. But Dr. Nicovich is."

"Mother of god."

Trinc dressed in uniform, hurried over to the hospital, and took Michael's elevator to the ward. She went directly to the private room. Opening the door, she was met by a haze of cigarette smoke and a stench of liquor. On the floor were overturned bottles. On the bedside table were several empty bottles of what looked like vodka. Dora, who was wearing a pink negligee, sat up in the bed with her mouth open in a slatternly leer. Seated on the foot of her bed was Dr. Nicovich, naked except for a pair of cotton skivvies. He squinted against the curling smoke of a cigarette dangled from between his lips. He clutched a flask in one hand.

When Trinc swam into his focus, he let the cigarette drool from his lips to the floor and raised a finger to pale lips. "Shhh. Leedle party."

Dora's belly still bulged. Her face was dough-colored and bloated.

Trinc gathered Dr. Nicovich's clothes from a chair, bundled them in her arms, marched to the door and threw them in the corridor. She came and stood, arms akimbo, over Dr. Nicovich. She wanted to slap him with all her might. "Get out, Nicky," she hissed. He took a swipe at the hair that fell over eyes, wiped mouth with the back of hand. "I am doctor here."

"Oh? I didn't know that the hospital employed abortionists."

He flung an arm over Dora. "Bye bye, baby," he said in sing-song. Stood. Swayed precariously. Pushed back shoulders. Studied the floor as if it were tilted. Offered the flask to Trinc. "No? Trinc don't drink. Funny. Don't mind if I do." Said. Took a swallow. "Muzz give blood to Dor." Said.

And stumbled out the door.

Trinc stood over Dora. "You've been trying to kill your baby, Mother Turner. Are you still having pains?"

Tears welled in Dora's eyes. "I get so scared," she said.

Trinc bent over and hugged her, drew back from the odor of Dora's breath. "You miss your sister," she said. "I know. I'll have the doctor called."

"Dr. Van Dine?"

"Dr. Van Dine."

"He said Nicky could be here."

Trinc went to the charting desk where a nurse she didn't know did the paging. "Doc-tor-Van-Deen, Doc-tor-Van-Deen" was squawked through loudspeakers. When the telephone rang, Trinc picked up the receiver and held it against her ear.

"Van Dine. What is it?"

"Second Floor Private, Dr. Van Dine. Miss DeRoman speaking . . . A patient of yours has been drinking heavily. She shows no signs of having labor pains. Someone needs to listen to the fetal heartbeats right away."

"Is it Mrs. Turner?"

"Yes."

"Is Dr. Nicovich there?"

"No."

"I'll be right up."

She returned to Dora's room, threw open the window, and hid the bottles in a closet. When Dr. Van Dine burst in, he ordered her to wait for him by the charting desk.

There, she tried to collect her thoughts. Nicky's baby, Nicky's blood. No more Dr. Nicovich for Trinc. Probably his brother no better than. Turner? Off fuzzing up his mind with the poetry of Tagore. Maybe Dr. Van Dine thought Nicky would be needed. For what? For blood transfusion? Not very likely. For abortion? Drinking for hours. Did Mallie know? This Van Dine. Former wife Uncle Doc's sister. Took Miss Dorking, Dora, and Turner to a roadhouse and watched Turner do nothing but drink.

This scientist, this Dr. Van Dine, was a short, balding man with a gray beard. His intimidation tactics included wedging a monocle in his right eye and looking at you as if you were an insect.

Now he came toward her, scowling. "The baby's dead," he said. "I'll have a nurse get Mrs. Turner ready for an emergency O. R., and we'll tell the Office to put her on the critical list and to notify Dr. Turner." He had been pacing in front of the desk. He stopped, took his monocle out of a pocket, lifted it to eye, and scrutinized Trinc. "What were you doing in that room, Miss DeRoman? You're not on duty."

"I'm a friend of the Turners, Dr. Van Dine."

"I know all about that. I suppose you'll say you have no wish to avenge yourself upon Dr. Turner because he jilted you? Who let Mrs. Turner get that booze, Miss DeRoman?"

"A visitor brought it."

"I asked *who!*"

"She worked in x-rays. Perhaps the baby died from effects of radiation."

"I didn't ask for your medical opinion, Miss DeRoman. Who brought the booze? Did you—?"

"—I can't in all conscience, doctor—"

"—Conscience be damned! There is no such thing as conscience! There is only your duty to science!" He let the monocle drop on its string, left it dangling. "Answer me."

"Dr. Nicovich," Trinc said.

"Nicovich, Nicovich." Dr. Van Dine brought his face up close to Trinc's. "He wasn't in the room."

"I threw him out."

"Oh? A likely story. You, a student nurse, throwing a doctor out of a room? You wouldn't be jealous, would you, Miss DeRoman? He's bedded half the girls in this hospital. You wouldn't ruin a man for life just on a vague suspicion . . . Listen to me." Dr. Van Dine's face looked hot. "You don't mention that name to anyone. Do you understand? You are not to speak to anyone about this hysterical charge of yours!"

"It's not a charge," Trinc said. "It's a fact."

He moved away from her but swung around, smiling pleasantly. "You let me decide about the facts . . . If anything happens to Mrs. Turner . . . due to complications following still-birth . . . I won't mention to anyone, unless pressed, that an off-duty nurse-trainee . . . was aborting a child in a certain room on my ward . . . the niece of my old, good friend, William Nathaniel Knight . . . I suggest that you take a long walk to clear your head. Good evening, Miss DeRoman."

11

Sun Dance

Letter from Amelia Jay Ford (Mrs. Gayle) DeRoman, dated June 15, 1922, from Brunoy, France, to Dr. Aeneas Caldwell, Harvey Road, Cambridge, England:

MY DEAR PROFESSOR CALDWELL:

Let me introduce myself. I am Amelia, wife of Colonel Gayle DeRoman whom you met at the hospital in Neuilly at the end of the Great War. On that occasion he gave you, at your request, a photograph of his daughter by a previous marriage, Trinc. I am the mother of Trinc's little half-brother, Gayle DeRoman, Jr., and I am a graduate of Vassar, where you taught. Because my native city is Philadelphia, I occupy neutral ground between North and South, and because I come from an old and respected family, I have never been impressed by the pretensions to aristocracy of any American family which has risen through trade and manufacturing. I refer to the Heartwells of Connecticut.

In the course of correspondence with Trinc, I have learned much about you that Colonel himself does not know, and I have obtained your address from her, who has it from your cousin, Miss Tabitha Van Dyke. Your relationship with Trinc is your own affair. Your health, however, is my affair. That is, I am making it my affair. *J'ai votre affaire*, as the French say.

You are the victim of malicious wounding and have a right to feel resentment and self-pity. I do not, however, infer from this right that you wish to punish Trinc, who is innocent; rather, I infer, you have withdrawn yourself from relationship with her because you are possibly unable to give her children. Come now, dear Dr. Caldwell, is a woman's love to be so gallantly dismissed? Have you sought her opinion about your Wound? Do you really believe that all you have to offer Trinc is your natural member without its erective capacity? Shame on you, dear Dr. Caldwell. You are surely too refined to believe that the power of love is limited to sex. What are you doing to have yourself cured? Are you neglecting your own health and happiness because you have convinced yourself that you are permanently injured? Or is it that you are too poor to seek the help of the best physicians?

Although Colonel DeRoman is totally in the dark about your relationship with Trinc and about the cause of your Wound, he joins with me in the desire to see you healed. Here, parenthetically, may I rely upon your discretion to reveal to him nothing about the iniquity of the Heartwells. His soul is too light, too gay, to suffer reminders of Yankee "domination." We must all shield this great-hearted Quixote from knowledge of this wicked world, lest he tilt at windmills. That said, he does know about the nature of your Wound, and he does admire your character. He was, you see, unbeknownst to you, present at your court-martial. As a judge advocate on General Pershing's staff he was given responsibility for reviewing your "case" and for making the final recommendation, death by firing squad, dishonorable discharge, or reassignment with reduction in rank. In recommending the latter, he saved your life. To be frank, you owe him something in return: a willingness to seek a cure.

Can you be cured? Colonel DeRoman was never satisfied with reports from a New Mexican doctor and from an Army medical officer. We believe your problem may be a mental one. He on the battlefront, I with the Vassar unit of the YMCA/Red Cross are all too familiar with incidents involving soldiers with "shell shock," with effects of fright so sudden as to make one's very soul seem lost. If your Wound is akin to shell shock, as we believe it is, your underlying "illness" represents a loss of spiritual vitality. Your Wound, we believe, may be curable by means of symbolic healing.

Last year when I was ill with TB I was obliged to spend seven months at Dr. Jacquerod's Sanitorium in Leysin, Switzerland. Gayle, Jr., stayed nearby with his governess in Vevey. Colonel DeRoman had to remain in Paris as a representative on the Reparations Commission. Still, every weekend he came to visit me, that I would not suffer alone. Terrified that I would die of this disease, as once his mother did, every weekend for twenty-eight weekends he took the Simplon-Orient express for fifteen hours (one way) to Leysin. Together we shared the magnificent view of the snow-clad Alps, in the distance the jagged peaks of the Dents du Midi gleaming in sparkling air.

My dear Dr. Caldwell, I am not going to allow you to suffer alone. What is more, it is a small world over here, and I am in a position to help you. While I was at the sanitorium, I happened to strike up acquaintance with a doctor who is a specialist in the treatment of glandular and neurological diseases. His name is Dr. Serge Nicovich, a Russian émigré. Part of each year he maintains a clinic in Paris, the rest of the year he spends near Leysin as Director of the *Institut de Conscience Universelle*, which he has founded for the purpose of symbolic healing.

Serge traveled for twenty years all over Russia and Asia as far as Tibet in search of methods of healing based upon psychic energy. He studied in the lamaseries of Tibetan mystics, in the huts of Siberian shamans, and in the libraries of Balk and Bokhara, traditionally the region where the culture of China and the East has mingled with Arab and Western cultures. After returning from his travels, he was convinced that scientific medicine is in itself not enough and that symbolic medicine is often called for. Whereas the practitioners of scientific medicine work with facts, the practitioners of symbolic medicine are less concerned with specific symptoms and bodily organs than they are with a process of renewal in which the patient comes to identify himself with the prodigious energy of Creation. The patient treated only in a scientific way often feels left out of the treatment, his suffering an intrusive, alien force; he lives in a spiritual desert. Symbolically treated, the patient feels that his suffering is given significance as he breaks through to powers latent in his psyche, powers that bring him back into harmony with natural forces. He perceives that the whole universe is alive—"endowed with conscience," as Serge says—and that our only importance as human beings lies in our relation to this living universe. This perception frees the patient to confront the underlying causes of his suffering.

What Serge calls "conscience" is not what we call "morality" in our usual sense of the word. Morality is relative to time and place, but conscience is eternal and universal, an organized power present in every person though buried in the unconscious. "Conscience," Serge says, "makes us sensitive to the workings of the universe where there is nothing arbitrary and all is meaningful." Thus conscience, once the patient receives its energy, forms the basis for his rejuvenation therapy.

The method of healing at the Institut de Conscience Universelle is dance. Let us not think here of dance as a form of idle amusement. Dance, as defined by Serge, is a spontaneous linking of feeling and movement, a breathing. By means of breathing, then, in a state between consciousness and trance, the spiritual body renews communion with living nature. Specifically, the dance performed by a patient at the Institute is designed to be a physical ordeal. The patient dances for several days and nights without refreshment of any kind save for brief intervals for sleep; he may neither eat nor drink. With the assistance of Siberian drum-beaters and chanters, he is constantly reminded to stay awake and to sacrifice his body. At the conclusion of the dance, he is voluntarily subjected to torture, his body suspended from a beam. He acquires power that comes from compassion, all resistance to bodily and spiritual change having been overcome. The patient, according to Serge, "becomes extremely virile."

Trinc informs me that you are already intellectually predisposed to think of the universe as a living one. That is good. You are an ideal candidate for treatment by Dr. Nicovich. Moreover, though his fees are large, there are philanthropists in Europe who support his research and thus make it possible for him to treat selected patients free of charge. You have been selected. I have written to the doctor, currently in Paris, concerning your condition, and he has waived the fee. He requires of you that you be willing to train for a period of six months, such training to include fasting and body-strengthening to prepare yourself for what he calls "a new world." You will need to meet with him no later than the First of July for preliminary examination and thereafter place yourself under his guidance. You must tidy up your affairs in England and come to live in France for six months.

Colonel DeRoman and I hereby invite you to be our guest in our new home at Brunoy, twelve miles from Paris.

Perfectly suited for guests, our place at Brunoy consists of an acre surrounded by a high stone wall. The resulting privacy permits any kind of dress (or undress) and any kind of noise the inmates choose to indulge in. Inside the walls are great, ancient trees, and in the far corner of the grounds, hidden by trees and bushes, is a bully tennis court, near it a swimming pool. Rays of sunlight slash cool green waters. Sizzling tennis players swim to cool off before the pre-prandial cocktail. We often wine and dine out of doors. After dinner, if you have not eaten too much of Germaine's *cuisine*—you won't be fasting all of the time—you may go down the Chemin de Soulins, under a tall avenue of poplar trees, to the XVII-century stone bridge over the little river called the Yerres. At the *bordeau* beside the bridge you may embark in our red canoe and drift down the lovely stream to an open glade enclosed in a semi-circle of oak trees where surely you'll abandon skepticism about the ancient gods—for nymphs and satyrs disport themselves in the twilight.

The conversation at dinner is varied. When the stomach is comfortably filled, mild sallies produce hearty laughter, and there is nourishment for the soul at twilight: the French horns of the village band, unaccompanied by other instruments, are sounding from afar the old hunting airs—"Le Bon Roi Dagobert," and the like. There is no telephone or radio.

Our visitors are usually from Yale and usually arrive inebriated from the Ritz bar and usually stay that way. To assist them in finding us, Colonel DeRoman has painted a two-story, blue symbol on the side of the house, thus:

Yet is it ever our custom to share our *pantagruelism* with any guest who is, like us, for a certain gaiety of spirit and Rabelaisian indifference to all the accidents of life.

Your friend,

Amelia DeRoman

1947

Excerpts from "Sketches for a Memoir" (1947), by Aeneas Caldwell:

My grandfather, Horseshoe Robertson Caldwell, Major, C.S.A., came from Pickens County, South Carolina, in the Upcountry where everyone is born with manners and pride and in the image of God—or at least of a father. His very distant relative, Vice-President John C. Calhoun, precipitated

the Civil War because he was too proud to pay the price of Union. These Upcountry folks would rather die than lose their personal honor and live in disgrace. Grandpa Horseshoe died at the battle of Gettysburg. His young widow, my Grandma Floride, was left poor and pregnant with an unborn son to raise in her family home on Laurel Street in Columbia. My father, Calhoun Caldwell, was born and raised in that house without a father's presence.

I was born in 1890, the only child of Calhoun and Elizabeth (née Van Dyke). My parents had met at the Art Students League in New York where she was studying to be a painter and he was looking for someone to support him. Because Elizabeth came from a wealthy family on Long Island, my father eloped with her. They cut her off without a penny. Indeed, my father had an uncommon knack for miscalculation. As a result of this one, he brought my pregnant mother from New York to move in with Grandma Floride, who supported them.

The house on Laurel Street was a large, two-story white clapboard structure with three brick chimneys and a shaded porch with eight wooden columns. On the night of February 17, 1865, General Sherman's troops had set fire to the roof, but Grandma Floride had clambered on to the roof and extinguished the fire with pails of water handed up to her by the cook. Often as a boy I was to lie in bed in that house imagining, as just outside my window, the thunderous trampling of Yankee horses, the flung torches, and the tiny, demonic figure of Grandma Floride pouring pails of water and bellowing defiance. The scene impressed itself upon me as a kind of moral triumph, though I'm not sure why.

She was a remarkable woman. Educated in Classics, she it was who insisted—in exchange for board and lodging?—that I be named after the Virgilian hero who survived the sack of Troy. Apparently I personified her hope for a new world to rise from the ashes. After the war, cramped by poverty, Floride supported herself and infant son by writing popular novels about the Old South, like Longcane, a chilling tale about how John C. Calhoun's grandmother got herself scalped at Longcane in 1760. From her endeavors Grandma Floride accumulated some money, and to her generosity I owe my education, including seven years at Harvard and a post-doctoral year at Cambridge (she died in 1916, leaving me $1,000 which I put to that purpose). Unfortunately, she never bothered with Father's education. He did poorly in school. I guess, having no man in the house, she spoiled him.

Those who know me best, know that I've no great objection to sentiment. As I pen this sketch in 1947, during voluntary exile in England, I confess that not long ago I had a great weep for Grandma Floride. I was reading David Copperfield and of his youth and his mother, and I thought of Floride and let myself go. There's something terrible, I thought, about being a mother. Here was Grandma Floride with every intention of making a happy childhood for her son, and yet Calhoun turned out to be a stranger. And then I had a great weep for my mother—known to the family as "Ma-Betty." She endured a loveless marriage. How terrible and how beautiful, I thought, is this business of living.

Major Horseshoe's steel sabre was hung over the mantelpiece in the living room. I often entertained myself simply by staring at this sabre. One day I noticed on its cutting edge a dark spot and asked Grandma Floride about it. "What's yonder spot, Ganny?" I pointed.

Her eyes blazed. Drawing herself up stiffly in that black, lace-trimmed dress of hers that sagged from thin shoulders as if from a coat-hanger, she replied in a passionate hiss: "Yankee blood!" I got the idea all right, but hatred and vindictiveness have, for some reason, seldom boiled in my veins.

Unfortunately for my mother, Calhoun was a tall, dark, and handsome fellow with deep-set green eyes that smouldered under heavy brows. Much as I dislike having to stress the point, he was a brick made without straw. When I was about five years old, I ran to our backyard privy in urgent need of its "two-holer." Flinging open an unlatched door, I found my father already installed, his buttocks squashed over a potty-hole next to the half-keg of lime, his face clearly visible against the background of whitewashed walls. He was rubbing the stubble on his weak chin. His face was unmasked, not yet surprised or annoyed. Never before or since have I had such a feeling of peering straight into someone's lost soul. His whole countenance revealed despair, complete lugubrious despair. I suppose he knew the discrepancy between potentiality and achievement, felt worthless, and feared rejection because, expecting to be found out and rejected, he explosively discharged blows upon the person who most loved him, Ma-Betty. He suffered from lack of a father—or of a God.

Grandma Floride must have decided that the only way to kick our family out of her house was to put Father to work. In 1895 she had him set up as owner of a pottery, "Throstle's Nest," in the Pine Barrens of Moore County, North Carolina. Off we went in a mule-drawn wagon to live in a gloomy forest isolated from the modern world. Our home was a log cabin and a pottery shed in a clearing connected to civilization by a single muddy road. We slept on corded beds; ate fatback with sorghum syrup, as well as candied yams, spoon bread and rabbit stew; spun our own cotton, wool, and flax; and made our own footwear, using wooden shoe lasts. Once in a while, though, Mother would bake a cake, mixing eggs, sugar, flour, milk, salt, vanilla, baking powder, chocolate and butter. The secret of her success was to remove the cake from the wood-stove's oven the minute a broom straw came out clean. I have often tried without success to copy her recipe. Only once did I succeed in baking the perfect chocolate cake, the night I met Trinc in Poughkeepsie.

The local potter was a man named Sheffeld whom everybody called Old Joe Shuffle. After Old Joe Shuffle had kicked a kick wheel and kicked out a jug, it was said, he got his kicks by drinking forty-rod and listening to God. The thing was, God talked to him. My father envied his workman and said to the family, "I wish God would talk to me, god-damnit."

When Old Joe Shuffle had kicked out enough pots, we'd take a wagon full of them to market in Carthage, N.C. Those are trips I'll always remember fondly, as the most charming I have ever known. The wagon would be piled high with vessels of pottery for sale—crocks, churns, telegraph insulators, pickle jars and whiskey jugs, all glazed in "tobacco-spit" brown. While Father inched the mule over rutted road, I would sit with Mother on top of the vessels and observe the picturesque landscape. In June, as we broke from the forest we would see small fields of wheat being harvested. The men cut wheat with old-fashioned cradle-scythes while the women, having parked their babies on quilts under shade tress, bound the sheaves. Boys in faded blue overalls ran back and forth to the fields to refresh the thirsty harvesters with large water jugs and gourd dippers. Having no talent myself, I once pleaded with Mother to draw the scene and later capture its rapturous beauty on canvas. She declined, saying the Barbizon School had already done such things to perfection. She was, I guess, too careworn to paint.

With a watermelon to devour on the way home from Carthage, I felt rich in delight.

Our neighbors took life as they took the rain—without an umbrella. If tragedy happened to them, they accepted it with stolid plainness, without introspection. For example, one of our neighbors shot himself to death on a Friday. Early on Saturday morning Ella, his daughter, came over to our cabin to deliver our milk. Mother said, "Ella, I declare, I am so sorry about your father. When is the funeral?" Ella replied, "We gawn er git 'im in the ground to-day cause we gawn er go jerks to-morrow, be pleasured." In other words, she wanted her father buried on Saturday so that she could go to church on Sunday and "jerk" her head backward and forward rapidly, causing her arms to move in the manner of a ragdoll playing the violin. Well, they did git 'im in the ground, and at the church his wife sat on the steps and howled at the top of her lungs to show what a good wife she was.

Unlike our neighbors, Father seemed to want a God who was personal and perfect. On one occasion, when we were in the shed together with Old Joe Shuffle, and Father was reading his Bible to himself, licking his thumb to turn pages, Old Joe Shuffle stopped his kick-wheel and turned his head to me. "'Neas," he said with a frown, "you're a right sensible sort of boy. Did you ever study about them Ten Commandments?"

"Right smart," I said. I was "ball boy" picking clay clean and shaping it into balls ready for turning on the wheel.

Old Joe Shuffle went on. "Did you ever study about how long it taken God to write them Commandments? Well, it taken forty days —think of it—forty days. What puzzles me is that a man like God done did the world in seven days, so why it taken more time to do them Commandments than it done to make this world?"

A loud oath from Father caused us to look in his direction. He was glaring at Old Joe Shuffle as if thunderstruck. "I gotta go talk to Him," Father declared. "Get me some of your forty-rod, Joe."

Father took his Bible and a jug of whiskey and disappeared into the woods. When he came back three days later, he looked as if he'd been wrestling with an angel. Mother had a black eye the following morning.

Once in a while fiddlers showed up at our clearing and played, with old-time energy, songs like "I'm Agoin' Down the Road Afeelin' Bad" and "Keep My Skillet Good and Greasy." Times like these, I was happy in the Pine Barrens and had no urge to prepare myself for further education. I read books because they were magical, not because I was looking for self-improvement. Every morning before dawn, before it was time for me to stack pots in the ground-hog kiln, I would read for a couple of hours from Mother's books that lined the walls of the cabin. By the age of twelve, I pretty much had a handle on such absorbing works as Simpson's Euclid, Dryden's Virgil, Cicero's Orations and Milton's Poetical Works. But when I was thirteen Grandma Floride came to visit. Finding me to my astonishment unfit for civilized life, she took me away and had me boarded out at the nearby Euphronia Academy. The curriculum there consisted of English, French, Latin, Greek, geography, music, natural and moral philosophy. While singing to myself "Keep My Skillet Good and Greasy," I wrestled with the angel called the Subjunctive Mood in Latin—and lost.

Home for Christmas of '05, already having set my heart on eventually going to Harvard, the Headmaster's alma mater, my hopes were dashed: Father had sold the pottery business and was moving the family to New Mexico. "A ten-gallon jug is bringing in only 40¢ on account of them Prohibition rascals," he explained. "I'm going in for Indian trading, like that Richard Wetherill."

Even in the backwoods of the Pine Barrens we knew from magazines about Richard Wetherill. He had discovered the ruins of an ancient American civilization, that of the Anasazi or "Old Ones," in places like Mesa Verde in Colorado and Chaco Canyon in the Territory of New Mexico. At that time Wetherill was not considered the pioneer archeologist that he is today. In fact, some people in Washington thought Wetherill was looting Indian lands of antiquities. Apparently what Father called Indian trading was really the looting business, although he confided his schemes to no one. He promised to settle Mother and me in a fine house in the Taos Valley while he went "trading" in the desert country to the west of it.

I might add at this point that on June 8, 1906, Congress passed the Antiquities Act to protect Indian lands from looters. Father had miscalculated again.

Off we went. We arrived in Denver in March of '06 and from there rode the Denver & Rio Grande Western Railroad—

known locally as the "Dangerous & Rapidly Growing Worse"—to Tres Piedras, from which whistle stop we took the stage coach eastward some forty miles across the Rio Grande into Taos Valley. There being an ever-present danger of being held up by bandits, Father rode with the driver, pretending he knew how to use his newly-purchased Winchester.

The "fine house" promised us turned out to be a crumbling old adobe morada, i.e., a small chapel formerly used by the Penitentes sect for ceremonies of self-flagellation. The light from slit windows was poor, the floor earthen. Only when Ma-Betty had a fire going in the kiva fireplace did we see that the vigas and latillas of the ceiling were saturated with bloodstains. Moreover, the morada was situated a long way from what a New Yorker like Ma-Betty was accustomed to consider "civilization": we were the only Anglos in the Villa de Nuestra Señora de los Remedios, a hamlet six miles from Taos on a rim overlooking the Rio Hondo and the ruins of Turley's Mill where Anglos had been killed and scalped in 1847 during an uprising by Indians and Mexicans. Father abandoned us there, taking his hat, Winchester, and Bible and leaving us $100.

We lived close to starvation.

Yet we lived in paradise and felt an immense sense of belonging. To the west lay the deep black gorge of the Rio Grande, to the north and east the dramatic Indian-bow curve of the Sangre de Cristo Mountains, the pyramidal Taos Pueblo, at least 800 years old, nestled below the towering snows of Wheeler Peak. From the top of our shoebox home, a sort of eyrie, we could watch brilliant light turning distant, pitched, tin rooftops into crystals that flashed beneath cobalt-blue skies. We could follow the sweep of the desert southward for some seventy miles in the direction of Santa Fe, a day's treacherous journey away. Our eagle eyes feasted on the Hondo Valley below us, the green of its irrigated orchards like little patches in tawny hills thickened by giant, ochre-gray cottonwoods, low-growing piñon, and putty-colored aspens.

Ma-Betty began to paint again. She planted a garden, too, growing tomatoes, beets, turnips and beans, oregano, cilantro, mustard, chives and yerba buena. Against the mud-and-straw walls of the morada she planted tiger lilies, red and white hollyhocks, and rose hip bushes, adding civilization's touch to that which grew profusely wild around us: Indian paintbrush, Apache plume, blue flax. Storm or shine, she baked our bread outdoors in a horno. She collected amole for shampoo, broomgrass for brooms, ocha for colds, chamisa for fevers, lanten for wounds, clover for toothache. She carded and spun our wool, beating up the wool so that it could be used for the mattresses. She went with the village women to the acequia to wash our clothing and linens. And, once a week, she took our two horses—one with a milky eye—hitched them to a wooden-wheeled wagon, and went to Taos to collect staples and mail and gossip. Our neighbors, mostly ranchers and sheepherders, were gentle and courteous and friendly. Far from yearning for a return to the East, Ma-Betty felt that she had found heaven on earth.

I felt the same. I cut our firewood near the ruins of Turley's Mill, often lingering there beside the Rio Hondo to contemplate 1000-year-old petroglyphs. I fed the chickens, knowing I could trade one egg in Taos for a candybar. In the village I bartered for mutton, pork, milk and cheese, "refrigerating" these by lowering them thirty feet by rope down our well. I fed and groomed our horses. I filled our bronze lamps, each holding a gallon of coal oil, that were suspended from the good red ceiling of the morada. Of course, I had to go to school. Five days a week I rode Tiresias, the half-blind horse, to the Taos plaza where some Presbyterian teachers had put together the semblance of a school. They had agreed with very good grace and little confidence to get me prepared for entrance to Harvard.

Father came home to us the winter of '06-'07. He presented

Ma-Betty with a few hundred dollars, "for the year," he boasted. He had grown a thick gray beard. His eyes darted about restlessly. One detail stands out from this visit: a red bandanna. He wore it continuously. On wintry evenings as he sat before the fireplace he tucked the bandanna beneath his disguised weak chin, but at night, as he lay down to sleep, he tied the bandanna around his eyes. I asked him why he did this.

"Old Nick can't find me," he replied with a strange smile.

The winter of '07-'08 he didn't come home to us. Instead, he sent us a letter scrawled in pencil. I have that letter still to this day. Business would have been good, he wrote, except that "savages" had "robbed" him of an Anasazi pot for which "I could of got a fortune from this feller down in Albuquerque." The letter took a misanthropic turn: "I ain't fond of no civilizations, old or new, I don't care for humanity they just rob and cheat you, no respeck." Then an ominous turn:

> I am alright only have arthyritus cos I am holed up in a clif by a bute I go hongry alot. I kilt and et the mare. Come spring I speck trade for blankits and turkoise to pick up right smart Have decided that God is a monster.

Finally an ugly turn:

> I aint coming home no more. I dont want to see you all ever agin. Eliz., marry a good man. I am sorry.

Came June of '08 and Ma-Betty, one day, returning from Taos and standing on the buckboard waving a piece of paper at me, shouted, "Praise God and Little Aeneas!" I didn't know what God and I—not so little at six-foot-three and 165 pounds—were being praised for until she added, "You're going to Harvard! Hallelujah!"

My heart skipped a beat for joy until I realized that Ma-

Betty would soon be living alone. It was necessary for Father to come home. Early in July, I set out in search of him. I went by rail to Durango, Colorado, by wagon to Farmington, New Mexico, there hired a horse and bought supplies of grain, food, and water for the three-day journey to Chaco.

It was the loneliest and most beautiful land I had ever seen. What "trail" there was consisted of wheel ruts meandering off into sand and buffalo grass. Stretched out as far as I could see was a waste-land of spiky, olive-green greasewood and sagebrush. A dazzling sun printed running blue cloud shadows over high, flat-topped mesas, deep canyons, and fantastically eroded sandstone cliffs. My skin assumed a red color: I'd forgotten to wear a hat. Once some Navajo shepherds on horseback, rifles carried across their saddles, paused on a hill and impassively watched me as I invaded their land. That was all the human companionship that was tossed my way. Otherwise I could just as easily have been a castaway in the midst of an ocean.

As I lay in my bedroll at night, while cooking odors still flavored the dry air, I watched millions of stars flashing pale fire in a broad band from horizon to horizon and felt as never before how much I was a part of things.

Quantum theory shows that we cannot decompose the world into independently existing smallest units. The whole universe appears as a dynamic web of inseparable energy units. Out in that waste-land, of course, I knew nothing about physics, astronomy, and depth psychology, at least as we understand these subjects today. Pondering the stars and the mystery of myself, though, I intuitively understood that the universe was one, I one with it. It had to be that mind and matter sprang from a common background source, as Eastern philosophy had speculated for thousands of years. If so, God was not "up there" waiting for me to establish relationship with Him but "within" all things already, here and now. This was a world new to me, if not to sages.

On the third day I rode through a wide low gap between mesas into Chaco Canyon where the late afternoon sun deepened the hues of red rock formations. Shadows spread from 200-foot-high canyon walls until they consumed the brave green of cottonwoods lining Chaco Wash. In the distance I could make out the crescent shape of Pueblo Bonito—in the eleventh century, as I knew from the Wetherill articles, the largest and most progressive center of civilization in North America—and the buildings and windmills of the Wetherill trading post. Perhaps Father would be there, I hoped.

. . . I found a young hand in the bunkhouse who remembered my father. Back in March a grizzled-looking man who called himself Horseshoe had appeared in a snowstorm, riding a gaunt mare, a man with the crazy look of an Old Testament prophet. He wore a low-crowned hat, a red bandanna, and galluses and carried a Winchester. This man who called himself Horseshoe paid the hand a silver dollar to have a letter sent by the supply-wagon to Farmington. I asked the hand if there was nearby a butte—Father's "clif by a bute." The hand pointed south and said I would find a great butte about ten miles down the Wash. I bedded down in the bunkhouse that night, it being cold even in summer, having first smeared my sunburned face with axle grease.

Before dawn I rose and headed south. At daybreak the top of a purplish-red butte in the distance loomed out of mists like the funnel of an ocean-liner shrouded by fog. By noon I was dismounting at the base of this wreck, opposite a canyon wall about 200-feet high. Shielding my eyes from the scorching sun, I scanned the cliffs for any sign of human habitation.

All was still, stifling hot and still. After a while the stillness was broken by murmurs from the Wash, by the brittle chirp of insects. I had an eerie, claustrophobic feeling—canyons do that to me, as do cities. At my feet a crew of ants busied itself building their pueblo bonito. Above me, swallows darted in and out of the protective ridges of out-jutting rincón, against the backdrop of a fathomless blue sky. All was still and yet teeming with life, the silent stone and wind-scoured cliffs telling a tale of mythless eons.

Something fluttered to my feet. I picked up a few threads of red cloth, curious autumnal leaf. And looked up. There about sixty feet up the face of the canyon wall a swallow appeared with something in its beak, flew up with it, up to a rincón, then, without it, down again, down the face of the wall, and disappeared as if into a hidden chamber. Thus I discovered a recess in the rockface, poking from it the tip of what seemed to be masonry, then down from this recessed spot a chimney with toeholds that must have been cut there by the Old Ones.

Cupping my mouth with bright red hands, I shouted, "Father!" The canyon echoed thuh thuh. I remembered what the hand had said; I knew Father had assumed his missing father's name. "Horseshoe!" I shouted. The canyon echoed oo oo . . .

A few minutes later, after a giddy ascent, I stood sixty feet above the Wash outside an arched cave entrance about ten-feet-high and twenty-feet-wide, the cave half blocked by the mud-bricks of a dwelling that had weathered the vicissitudes of a thousand years of nature and civilization. Pecked into walls of stone were strange whorls and rabbit-eared figures playing flutes; in the dust were rusted tin cans, potsherds, charred firewood scraps. I stopped and entered the cave, peered inside the dwelling even as its fetid odor rushed to gag me.

There he was.

He had been dead for several months. Blue jelly-flesh sagged off bones. The red bandanna had slipped from forehead to jaw, exposing Oedipus eyes. Part of the bandanna was torn, shredded —in order for a swallow to build a nest.

Father had blindfolded himself before putting the bullet through his head. The Old Nick in himself had found him at last and dropped the Winchester on the blood-dark longjohns.

A search of the cave turned up evidence that he could have

continued to live: unopened tins of corned beef and beans; a box containing 100 rounds of ammunition; under a buffalo robe, a pile of Navajo rugs worth hundreds of dollars; a flour sack stuffed with silver dollars. But the Holy Bible on the floor of the cave spelled out his belief he had reached his last oubliette. Opposite the book's dedication page "to the Most High and Mighty Prince, James, by the Grace of God," etc.—my father had scrawled in pencil,

Cant seek no more He gone. Dont tell Eliz. & the boy.
C. Caldwell

It was my father's final miscalculation.

I buried him as best I could by wrapping the corpse in the buffalo robe and piling upon it the stones of a lost civilization. His impedimenta I tossed to the canyon floor. The rugs and silver dollars would provide Mother with enough money for years to come, the Winchester with protection, and the Bible with words to grieve on. The hat I put on. I would still be wearing that low-crowned hat eight years later when I first met Trinc and another seven years after that, when we became engaged.

MY MEMOIR IS IN MANY WAYS A STORY OF WOMEN, good, brave, intelligent, resourceful, loyal, loving women. A pivotal moment in this story was 1916. That was the year I was teaching at a college for women, Vassar, because, it seemed to me, the next stage in the development of modern world civilization was going to be the liberation of women. I wanted to be in the vanguard of the movement, urging its necessity. That year I attended the salon of Mabel Dodge, a precursor of the new world. That year I went to Columbia to attend the funeral of Grandma Floride and had ample time to reflect upon her indomitable spirit. That year I met Trinc.

Prior to meeting Trinc, however, I had committed myself to returning to Los Remedios to visit another remarkable woman, Ma-Betty. Always she had implored me to remain at Harvard, never to take vacations when I could and should pursue my studies. I had arrived poorly prepared. I was not to leave until the sterile curriculum of the university's waste-land blossomed into fresh thought, new directions. I stuck to my guns. And Ma-Betty flourished. First, she trained herself as a photographer with the new Eastman Kodak. Second, by selling photographs of Pueblo Indians to *Leslie's Illustrated Weekly*, she had earned a small but steady source of income. Third, she met Phillips Blumberg, who had studied *plein-air* painting at the Académie Julien in Paris and recognized in Taos the perfect locale for eventual establishment of a new American style. They were engaged to be married late in May, and I had happily received the honor of giving away the bride.

Cruelly deceived into believing that Trinc rejected me, I drove my Ford cross-country to Los Remedios, arriving in mid-May only to find awaiting me a packet of letters from Trinc's grandfather and mother. They had a poor impression of my character. And insinuated threats. I was jubilant: Trinc was true! But what to do? Should I return at once to the East, armed with Father's Winchester and a renewed proposal of marriage? On the other hand, what was to deter Trinc's family from doing to her what the Van Dykes had done to Ma-Betty, leaving her disinherited and abandoned? Trinc, I felt, had the sand to defy her family, good, but by what right could I act to cause her turmoil and misery? By right of love, I decided. If she still loved me, she would be content with what I could provide. My mind was made up. As soon as Ma-Betty's wedding had been celebrated, I had my own bride to carry away.

The wedding was held in the village of Arroyo Hondo in a little breadloaf-shaped adobe church surrounded by willows and apple trees. When its bells peeled gloriously and the ceremony was over, I felt such an enormous sense of well-being that I neglected my philosophy of *carpe diem*. Instead of putting on a coat of armor, saddling old Tiresias, charging quixotically into the country of the Heartwells to rescue an imprisoned maiden, I put on that symbol of Authority—my father's hat—and accomplished nothing in the country of the Heart. For while I had inherited my share of Southern rebelliousness, I had also inherited an unromantic compulsion toward responsible and prudent action. In short, I couldn't think of marriage without first thinking of poverty—that is, how to avoid it. Consequently, I spent the first two weeks of June in applying to universities for a job.

One afternoon I informed the housekeeper at the *morada* where I was staying that I was going for a drive to Turley's Mill. I had always loved to meditate there, collecting firewood and watching the Rio Hondo, its waters flowing past stones of the old whiskey mill.

It came to pass that at Turley's Mill, at sunset, I was assaulted by a gang of masked men who seemed to spring out of nowhere. I was tied to a tree, stripped naked below the waist, and stabbed several times with an ice-pick, then untied and left to bleed into the river. Before fainting, I heard the masked man with the ice-pick muttering in a strange but unmistakably English accent, "A rum do, a rum do," as if he were ashamed. Had he not spoken, I might have assumed that savages were responsible for this assault, as they had been for the scalping of Turley after Americans conquered this part of Mexico. But his speech—and the threats from Trinc's family—threw suspicion in the direction of the Heartwells.

I fainted away. When I woke in twilight, I could see at eye level a party of buzzard-hawks pecking at the blood-soaked ground, contemplating me in the sleek blue-black patina of ravening ways. I rose to my feet with remarkable agility, found my trousers, put them on. I was astonished to find nothing missing from my pockets and wallet. Eventually I staggered to where I had parked my car and drove to Arroyo Hondo, to the home of a *curandero* of my acquaintance. He was with a young Hispanic woman who, as far as I could tell, wanted to have her bowels removed so that they could be cleaned. After a pause the *curandero* shook his head and said, "You will need too much assistance in putting them back again." At this point I fainted again. When I came to, the *curandero* was already treating my wound with *aceite de lampara*—kerosene. It was the same treatment that is used in rural New Mexico for cauterizing animals after castration.

THE EUREKA-MOMENT OF DISCOVERY, the culmination of other moments in the act of creation, is, it seems to me, one of the varieties of religious experience. It need not be, but it certainly can be, an experience of ecstasy so profound as to cause time to stand still and to relegate to the shadows whatever it is that has been occupying the mind up to that moment. Such a Eureka-moment seized me in the most unlikely of times and places—on a battlefield in 1918 in France, during my platoon's more or less suicidal dash "over the top" and into withering machine-gun fire, bombshells bursting all around. I found my mind in a new world, pondering Einstein's curved space-time as an explanation of gravity, which stretches and distorts space and time. As poor luck would have it, just as I led my men over the top, I fell down in the mud and felt as though enchanted, physically unable to move while my spiritual body was bathed in incredible light as if in the glow of the fiery birth of the universe. Rather than thinking of galaxies as moving apart through space, one could think of the space between galaxies as expanding. Thus the universe didn't have to expand into some external void. Perhaps at the unbelievable energy of the first brief moment of the universe's existence, a tiny residue of unbalanced matter survived. This thought raised the question as to whether the cosmos itself had erupted spontaneously into existence without God. Or was God the Light?

Just as I snapped out of my spell, I saw that my men, my dear comrades, were being lifted and carried past me by stretcher-bearers ...

THE ARRIVAL OF COUSIN TUBBY and her little Karl enabled me to continue research at the Cavendish Laboratory under the general supervision of the great physicists at the University of Cambridge. For the first time in many years I had a home and family and didn't feel as alienated from humanity as I had been. Still, not unlike my father, I couldn't bring myself to feel much empathy with it.

We moved to a three-bedroom flat on the ground floor of a white-brick-and-slate Victorian house only a few minutes away, on my bicycle, from the laboratory and the Backs of the Cam. The upper story of the house was let to a Trinity don named Playfair, a man about my own age who was a Tutor in Medieval and Renaissance English Literature. We all of us became fast friends. Playfair's fresh pink cheeks and merry blue eyes belied the depth of his experience—he had served in the Admiralty during the war—and the extraordinary care he took to avoid hurting people's feelings exemplified the best of English life: decency.

Those were revolutionary times at Cambridge. Ernest Rutherford's experiments on the disintegration of atomic nuclei by bombardment with alpha particles had opened up a new epoch in natural philosophy in that for the first time the artificial transformation of one element into another had been accomplished. Also frequently at Cambridge was Niels Bohr, whose name ranks alongside such names as Galileo, Newton, and Einstein. Bohr made it possible to understand and to calculate almost every phenomenon in the world of atoms. By means of passionate discussion, he groped his way forward to an understanding of how things must be in the universe. As we students sipped our coffee after dinner, some of us literally at his feet, on the floor, so as not to miss a word, there, I felt, was

Socrates come to life again, tossing us challenges in his gentle way, lifting each argument out to a higher plane, and intoxicating us with the heady spirit of radical new ideas. Bohr's interest in reconciling mind and matter and in viewing the entire universe as an indivisible whole represented a complete break with the "classical" physics which had dominated thought for centuries. The traditional ways of modeling nature in largely mechanical terms were doomed to failure when it came to the atom.

Exhilarating as my life in Cambridge was, it was not a contented one. If my destiny, like that of Virgil's Aeneas, was the discovery of new worlds, I still lacked the wholeness of love. Perhaps by inheritance of Upcountry pride and honor, I could not accept the disgrace that impotence might bring.

Then in 1922 my complacency was shaken. First, Tubby and Playfair came to realize their love for one another and became engaged. Although Tubby considered herself a pariah, little by little Playfair had shown her that her being an unwed mother had its advantage: he loved little Karl, too. But as long as I was around, Tubby was not going to set a wedding date, so determined was she to provide me with support. Second, late in June, I received an extraordinary letter from Amelia DeRoman urging me to come immediately to her home near Paris. I was to begin preparations for what she called "symbolic healing" under the guidance of a physician and a shaman whom she had met in Switzerland and wholeheartedly recommended. I decided to go.

The night before my departure, we had a party. Playfair and I rented tuxedos; I wore my hat. Tubby appeared in a low-cut, full-length evening gown that was better suited for Windsor Castle than our mouldy flat. At dinner it struck me that this once-destitute, mistreated, and undervalued girl had been transformed by luck, freedom, and love into a sort of Jamesian heroine, an independent American lady fully capable of coping with European manners.

Playfair stood and proposed a toast. "Lady and gentlemen," he began, beaming upon Tubby, me, and Karl (who had been given half a glass of the wine), "in keeping with this solemn occasion, I wish to remind you that, not so long ago, all the sewage from colleges along the Backs was emptied into the river. When Queen Victoria was shown over Trinity College bridge by the Master, Dr. Whewell, she looked down and said, 'What are all those pieces of paper floating down the river?' To which, with great presence of mind, he replied, 'Those, ma'am, are notices that bathing is forbidden '. . . The departure for France of a dear cowboy of our acquaintance is relevant to the subject of decay. All those smelly little atoms to which he has devoted stern endeavors will rot from neglect. Furthermore, unless he gingers us up to martial prowess, the decay of morals will set in here . . . I swear, however, to eschew wicked intentions until January, provided he return for the proper nuptials. Have we, sir, your promise?"

I stood, lifted my glass to Playfair, and said, "You have my promise, sir, and my admiration. One must not be overly zealous in jumping into bed, as I have learned to my dismay . . . I miss you and Cambridge already. I miss the strolls along the Backs by the river; discussions at the Kapitza Club in which one has approached the deepest riddles of nature; the companionship of friends whose generosity I can never repay. I shall return because I can never leave."

"Jolly good," said Playfair, still lifting his glass. "I give us Aeneas." We drained our glasses. He remained standing and lifted a book from the table. "For the *benedictio*, I shall read from the poetry of John Donne, in the edition provided by our good neighbor, Grierson.'

"As you will recall, Donne took a trip to the continent in 1612, leaving behind, with much foreboding, his wife Ann. In this, his 'Valediction: Forbidding Mourning', he expresses the very paradox to which you allude, namely, that the separation of bodies cannot diminish the wholeness with which souls are united . . . I shall give you two stanzas only. I would be chuffed if you would do me the honor of removing your hat to Love, to show proper reverence."

I took off my hat to Love.

These were the verses Playfair read that evening. I have them still by heart:

> *But we by a love so much refined*
> > *That our selves know not what it is,*
> *Inter-assurèd of the mind,*
> > *Care less, eyes, lips, and hands to miss.*

> *Our two souls therefore, which are one,*
> > *Though I must go, endure not yet*
> *A breach, but an expansion,*
> > *Like gold to airy thinness beat.*

As I lay in bed that night, repeating the verses to myself, I reflected that the paradox of wholeness-in-separation liberated my affectionate hopes with respect to Trinc DeRoman and expressed the essence of my belief with respect to the nature of the physical universe.

Wholeness in separation. Could it be that Donne's two souls "which are one" were analogous to quanta? Since the quantum is indivisible, we never know exactly where it comes from; positioned nowhere, it could be everywhere, like the soul. Did distance matter? Could it be, in a way of thinking alien to the push-pull concepts of gravity and magnetism, that everything in the universe is instantaneously connected? If so, the world cannot be divided into separate objects, with events in one region of space uncorrelated with events in another, remote region of space. Could it be that the quantum does not depend upon strength to create an effect but upon aliveness, a kind of underlying activity of the universe in which all events are mutually contained? If so, each part contains all. Similarly in the faith of love is one soul correlative with another soul and is the other in fact—separated though Trinc and I had been in time and space, suffering as we had the anguish of distance, and yet through wholeness beaten like gold to airy thinness.

SERGE NICOVICH HAD A PUSHBROOM MUSTACHE and an ace-of-clubs nose; the expression of his face was beautiful and sweet. Following his physical examination of me in Paris, in which he discovered that my wound might be curable, I submitted myself to his Olympian regime. For six months at Brunoy I ran bare-footed ten miles daily in order to strengthen mind and body; repeatedly got myself sunburned in order to toughen the skin of my chest; and fasted for extended periods in order to become less conscious of hunger and thirst. As instructed, I rose before dawn each day and prayed for the sun to bring new worlds to mankind, and increase of life.

This regimen for a thirty-three-year-old academician sterilized from obeying the Authority of universities and armies—instead of the inner voice of Experience—would not have been possible without the encouragement of the DeRomans. Amelia applied balm to more than torn feet and aching limbs, and Colonel, as he liked to be called, bucked me up with charming stories and gay French songs. When I returned to their home after a run in the countryside, bleeding, exhausted, and so thirsty I could spit cotton, Colonel would pretend that my paltry exhibition had been a legendary one, comparable to scoring a touchdown in the Yale-Harvard game. On the day I completed training, Colonel with tears in his eyes insisted on temporarily placing his Order of the Legion of Honor around my neck. I had been made to feel that I was an accepted member of the family—even though in all this time Amelia and I had spoken not a word about Trinc.

I arrived in Leysin on the 27th of December and was greeted at the station by Serge Nicovich. We went at once to his Institute, a secluded, high-walled estate nestled in a snow-mantled forest in the mountains. I was ordered to rest for several days before the dance.

The dance would be held in an open area behind the Institute. Erected in the center of this area was a pole about twenty feet high; from its top a thirty-foot rope with thongs snaked to the snow-covered ground. About ten feet from the base of the pole a circle of a path had been trampled down, and here, I was told, I would be dancing for three days and nights, 11:00 a.m. to 3:30 p.m., 8:00 p.m. to 7:00 a.m. from December 29th to January 1st. I was to dance by lifting knees and raising arms, hour after hour, as I circled the pole slowly and acknowledged the four directions of the earth, four being the number for wholeness. In spite of freezing temperatures, I was to wear only a loincloth. I was not permitted to wear my hat.

Having heard from Amelia DeRoman that my dance would be accompanied by Siberian drummers and chanters, I was curious, the first day, to see them, and out they came as I stood shivering: eight men clad in bearskins and astrakhans, tough-looking lads who in another life might have been impassively piling up pyramids of skulls for Genghis Khan. After setting up a wooden platform with a huge thunderdrum in the middle, four of the Siberians squatted around the drum and began to beat it with leather-bound sticks. Booming, frenzied, deafening—200 beats to the minute, I later learned—the thunderdrum made the Alps shrink from consciousness. Then the other Siberians began to chant in a high-pitched tremolo a monotonous round of meaningless words.

I began to dance to the frenzied beat of the thunderdrum and the meaningless words of the chanters. Soon I was sweating and so a-thirst that every mud puddle I had ever seen seemed to manifest itself before my eyes. I was occasionally approached by Serge who asked cheerfully, "Remember your last drink?"

The second day I was no longer thirsty. On the third day I felt dismembered, as Serge had told me would happen. Evidently the energy of my ego was no longer dealing with external events and had nowhere to go except to increase my other energies.

Still I danced to the frenzied beat of the thunderdrum and the meaningless words of the chanters.

In the final phase of the dance, before sunrise on New Year's Day, servants carried me by torchlight to the pole and had me lie in the snow. Serge came and peered at me, touched my face. I looked up and loved this man's sweet, beautiful face that understood my suffering. He put a wet towel between my teeth. "Bite on it," he said gently. He rubbed my chest above the pectoralis major and breasts, raised loose skin with thumb and forefinger, and pushed a scalpel through the skin, twice. The pain was excruciating. Then he thrust wooden skewers through the incisions, one skewer inserted over each breast, and he attached these to the thongs on the rope that dangled from the pole. When the servants lifted me up, my blood poured out on the snow.

"Pray now," Serge commanded me. "Pray that the sun will bring new worlds to mankind, and increase of life. Give your heart to the children of the future."

I clung to the pole and prayed.

"Go now," Serge commanded me. "Lean back and pull on the rope."

I leaned back and pulled. The skin pulled away from my chest. Such was the ecstasy of pain, I no longer danced to the thunderdrum and chanters. I heard nothing. I was in another time and place. Then, feeling as if I'd been hit by a thunderbolt, I had a vision.

It was a headless horse, pale with a twenty-foot wingspan. He grabbed my body with his wings and flew with me into an abyss where rings appeared with color and feeling in them, each ring a memory, ring after ring of memories, my whole life in an instant, my whole unconscious in an instant, ring after ring, all of history. I felt no pain, no fear, only resolve: the world and I must be healed! My whole being felt suffused with compassion. Spinning before me on a wheel with luminous spokes were myriads of faces, sweet and beautiful. I saw the sweet, beautiful faces of my mother and my grandmother, saw the sweet, beautiful face of Trinc who was suffering the day of my return, saw the sweet, beautiful faces of the lost, my father's face there still faithful to a god that failed, saw not the face but head of a masked stranger with an ice-pick still bleeding. And then the wheel vanished and the headless horse released me and the horse suddenly had a head seamlessly fused to the body and the horse had a milky eye and he disappeared into my loins in a sunburst of energy.

I heard my skin breaking. I felt the skewers as they were jerked from my chest. I saw the rope uncoiling from me. I fell as if I'd been slammed from a great height into the good red snow.

12

Homecomings

THAT SHE HAD DOUBTED UNCLE DOC'S INTEGRITY humbled Trinc so much that she began to review other relationships in which she may have been jumping to hasty conclusions. In particular, there was the question of her relationship with Mother. When she tried to look at this relationship as a complex one, as if it were the pattern in a magical oriental rug, she had to discard her image of Mother as a monolithic ogre.

Mother upheld a fixed standard of conduct. Instead of resenting it, Trinc felt she should try to be thankful for having a parent who let you know where you stood. A daughter's upsurges of rebellion were hardly in themselves above reproach. She should accept Mother the way she was. This was not to say she should submit; while Mother's happiness was important, it was not an alternative to her own.

Nevertheless, while Trinc felt that much could be said in Mother's favor, Mother's behavior toward Aeneas rankled like a boil. Mother had threatened Aeneas and all but destroyed his and Trinc's happiness. But had Mother been Grandpa Deck's knowing accomplice in malicious wounding? The enlightened procedure would be to let Mother know the charge and defend herself as best she could.

Trinc's private correspondence she kept locked in a suitcase in her room at the Nurses' Home. Late one night after long hours in O. R., she took out the Bruno Rancis collection of letters and went over them. Sure enough, Mother had written to Aeneas in 1916 that she and Grandpa Deck had "methods" to use against him, methods that would be used. Aeneas had defiantly, even arrogantly replied from New Mexico that the family's "authority" was secondary to consideration of Trinc's happiness. As she re-read his letter, it vexed her that she had neglected to have translated his quotation, *Felix qui potuit rerum cognoscere causas*. In showing off his erudition Aeneas had been deliberately exposing Grandpa Deck and Mother as anti-intellectuals. Was there anything more to the Latin than that?

Next morning she showed the quotation to Mallie. "Here," she said, affecting indifference, "I suppose, since you went to college, you can read Latin. Can you?"

Mallie rolled her eyes. "Can I read Latin? I read *The Aeneid* of Virgil in the original. The Latin I didn't mind. It's the story of an idiot who forsakes love in order to found an empire. Poor choice, don't you think?"

"Can you translate this for me?"

"Well, what do you know," Mallie whistled after a pause. "It's Virgil, I think. 'Happy is he who knows the causes of things'. Are you investigating the moral order of the universe?"

"Sole purpose of translation," Trinc said.

It was true enough, that phrase. Happy was the person who knew the causes of things. Aeneas had seen through the Heartwells' pretenses. He had made a carbon copy of his letter, saved it during the war, and mailed it to Tubby, that Trinc might decipher its message. It seemed to Trinc that she was indeed obliged to discover the truth.

A few days later she wrote to Mother that she was coming home on the train for Christmas and that the two of them needed to talk frankly about the family's conduct in regard to Dr. Aeneas Caldwell and herself. She went shopping and bought thoughtful presents, a Cape Cod lighter which Granny Ah could add to the collection of lighters in the Homestead, oil paints, brushes, and stretched canvas as an inducement for Mother to rediscover her talents, various trinkets for aunts and uncles, and, for Augustus, a monogrammed silk handkerchief large enough to accommodate copious tears.

On the afternoon of Christmas Eve she arrived in Hartford at the New York, New Haven & Hartford Railroad station and was met by Jim, still Granny Ah's chauffeur. It was a cold, cloudy day with recent accumulations of snow throughout the Connecticut River Valley.

Jim, as he drove, gave her the news from home. Mr. Robin Heartwell had died of TB at the sanitorium in Colorado Springs. Rex had died and been buried with a headstone next to the grave of Mr. H. Dexter Heartwell. Augustus still flapped about in his penguin suit. Sad to say, Mrs. Heartwell was full of the miseries. She had lost a lot of weight, was using a wheelchair, and was attended full-time by a nurse from Hartford, a Miss Potter. No, no one was giving big dinner parties anymore. In fact, more than half of the servants had been discharged for want of work to keep them busy. The mills, it was said, were losing business, and controlling interest in them was being sold to strangers. No, Christmas was going to be a quiet affair restricted to members of the immediate family. All in all, however, things in Orford Parish were about the same, just fine—except that Dutch Elm disease was spreading. There was talk—just talk, mind you— that when Mrs. Heartwell died, Mrs. DeRoman was going to donate the Homestead to the Orford Parish Historical Society as a museum open to the public. 50¢ adults, children free.

"You didn't mention Mother before. How is she?"

"Oh," Jim said, "just fine. Only, she sort of running things now Mrs. Heartwell got the miseries."

"Bossy, is she?"

"Bossy?" Jim grinned. "Nome. She's a sweet lady if you know how to get along with her. She been good to me. Raised me to a hundert a month. But you might could say she's kinda bossy."

"How do I look?" Trinc had wanted to wear her Senior's uniform but was afraid that Mother would look upon it as an affront to the leisure class. She had decided to wear the sleeveless black satin dress, with cloche hat, silk stockings and high heels, with fur-trimmed coat for wintry weather.

"Just fine, Miss DeRoman. Fine-lookin' high-class young lady."

"Now, Jim, don't go condescending to me. We're about the same age. Besides, I'm sick and tired of being called 'Miss DeRoman' at the hospital. As if I were some kind of old maid. Call me Trinc."

"Yessum," Jim said. "Miss Trinc."

Trinc had to laugh. "Oh, Jim, you're hopeless! Now I feel like a little girl."

She liked Jim, he was so naturally open and considerate. Why did most people have to be so secretive all the time? Some people, some of the best people, kept secrets as a matter of probity and discretion. Uncle Doc was like that. She had learned her lesson, there. Some other people, Turner for instance, wanted to keep themselves at a safe emotional distance, free to walk out of any relationship. Still others, like Father, were hidden from themselves. Still others hid their faces because they were ashamed. Could Mother's face be one of them?

They had crossed the river a few miles back. It reminded her of her vision of a river, her single, frightening experience of telepathy or clairvoyance—whatever it was called—and of her talk with Bruno Rancis many months later. More than six years had passed since she had met Aeneas. She was unlikely ever to see him again. And yet she could still see him clearly in her mind's eye, tall and intense and warm, the green eyes that radiated a sensitivity absorbed in the depths of space-time. What a mystery, Time! It seemed only yesterday that she had begun nurses' training. Now she was close to graduation. Her feeling for Aeneas hadn't moved at all. It was beyond Time. It endured. It made experiences which separated themselves into now and then, here and everywhere, bow down before the unity of here and now.

Jim, she noticed, had swung off the main thoroughfare onto a little-used country road. She knew it avoided the main streets of Orford Parish and led directly to the Kingdom of the Heartwells through the old forest of towering pines, spreading oaks, and pointed firs. For years the road, though in reality only two miles long, had promised a special sort of enchantment. One left behind the modern world and entered a forest that must have been ancient before the first settlers arrived in New England. Mists rose through beams of sunlight to a cathedral roof of limbs and foliage. The small-birdsong silence made one's scalp tingle with excitement. Often in the past Trinc had enjoyed imagining the forest as inhabited by fairies with whom she could dance—she, like her nickname, a sprightly soul meant for gaity and companionship, for poetry and song and the old, high adventures.

On the occasion of this homecoming, though, the snowy woods beckoned her not. To them, she realized, she was bringing the city where there was suffering, always suffering, and where she was needed, always needed. The forest, too, looked subdued as if it had discovered its own mortality. Then the car was out of the forest, and Jim was driving through a maze of deserted streets on either side of which rose not the battlements of some enchanted palace but walls of red-brick buildings covered with soot and no longer as high as she had remembered them, their paned-glass windows seeming to mirror vacuously dancing devils of blowing snow. Silenced for the holidays, the mills seemed to be x-rays of doom, perhaps doomed since before they came into existence, before the first foundations had dried in the ooze of mortar, before the building of the Homestead, before the first Heartwell converted his pilgrimage into a sojourn in a strange land. The founders of this lost civilization must sometimes have wondered, Trinc thought, whether it all came down to a dream and delirium. Grandpa Deck must have seen the doom approaching, heard it speak as if in the voice of the old gods who made him feel contemptible. He repudiated them as shameless impostors and tried to prove them wrong by being always right, his soul astir with rage and impotence, himself, at last, a little god.

They passed the entrance to the Homestead, a shabby little clapboard cottage exposed to the elements, some long-familiar elms, she saw, cut to stumps; circled once-vast lawns now resembling a golf course abandoned to snow; and entered the driveway to the mansionhouse just as horizontally driven snow obliterated it momentarily. Then there it was, not as grandiose as she had remembered it, no longer impertinent and somehow frail.

"Wait," she said. Perhaps the sentiment of Christmas was pulling her heart back to the warmth of homefire. She was feeling at that moment that no mother in whatever earthen hut or mythic barn could reject the decisive splendor of her womb. Resentments seemed to be blowing away like veils of snow. The assumed degradation of dependence on a mother's iron rule was revealed as a fear of love; the fear was gone. She loved Mother. She ought to call her "Hen" to her face in a grownup's way. She was home.

Jim came and opened the door for her. She stepped from the Cadillac.

It all happened as in a dream of misty elms when sunlight bursts from concealment. Augustus had opened the great oak door. There stood Mother wearing her "little dress" like some queen in a myth, slender hands uplifted and clenched as if in answer to a prayer. Trinc ran and hugged Mother as seldom before.

Mother did not draw back.

THE UNCLES AND AUNTS CAME TO WELCOME TRINC and to kiss Granny Ah on the shrunken cheeks beneath the drug-glazed eyes, most, though not all, of their fires out. Miss Potter, the fat nurse, told Trinc that Granny Ah had arthritis and colitis, could still move her tiny body about without using her wheelchair, and was taking codeine. Trinc could see for herself that Granny Ah was seriously ill and becoming addicted to something stronger than codeine, probably morphine. She didn't want to discuss these observations with the family.

Granny Ah was surprisingly kittenish. After a dinner of turkey with champagne, she rose from her wheelchair and declared, "Now that Deck's gone, we won't have to wait till morning to open presents. We shall open them now!" Everyone looked at Mother to see if she would raise a protest on behalf of the Ghost of Christmas Past, but Mother, saying nothing, pulled up skirts and led the stampede into the Big Room where gifts for family and servants were arranged on the floor next to the Steinway piano.

Now it was ten o'clock on Christmas Eve. Opened boxes were strewn about the tables of the Big Room. The uncles and aunts had departed, and old, white-haired, rheumy-eyed Augustus, after poking the fire into a blaze, had retired for the night, leaving Trinc, Granny Ah, and Mother seated by the fireplace in highback French chairs in needlepoint. At Trinc's request Miss Potter had been excused from the room.

Before she began her speech she studied the faces of the women. Round, delicate faces with complexion like orchids that blushed. Mother with graying hair pinned into a bun. Granny Ah's white hair covered with a net. Both women with tight, cupid's-bow mouths. Both with good, kind eyes behind the spectacles.

She began.

"When I was a little girl, Miss Bridgit took me to Central Park. As we crossed Fifth Avenue where ice made the footing precarious, I saw some horses which were pulling a heavy cart fall down and break their legs. The driver killed the horses with a shotgun. I felt great sorrow for the horses and for a long time had nightmares about them. Eventually I understood that pain, that which we give and that which we receive, is inescapable. Life is suffering and love. And so I want you to know, whatever painful truth emerges from our talk, I love you.'

"This talk concerns you, Mother, and Grandpa Deck in regard to me and to a man you've never met, Dr. Aeneas Caldwell. Since you insist that Granny Ah represent Grandpa Deck's side, I must respect your wishes. I warn you, I am going to tell the truth with complete candor. I rely upon the Heartwell family's tradition of frank, open talk.'

"As evidence of what I am about to reveal, I have some letters which have come into my possession. If need be, I could ask Captain Buonsignori of the Hartford police to verify the facts. . . An attempt was made to have a certain man castrated."

"Oh," Granny Ah interrupted with a grimace, "the poor man!"

"This same man," Trinc continued, "served his country in some of the fiercest fighting of the war. Father, who met him in France, believed this soldier, on account of his wound, was deliberately trying to get himself killed in action . . . That man is Dr. Aeneas Caldwell."

"Was this Dr. Caldwell wounded in battle?" Mother asked.

"Why do you ask, Hen?"

"I was under the impression he wished to avoid military service," Mother said.

A familiar flame of resentment caressed Trinc's cheeks. After taking a deep breath, she doused the contamination. "Father thought Dr. Caldwell deserved the Distinguished Service Cross. And, yes, he was wounded in the line of duty. The wound of which I speak was inflicted on him in New Mexico, not long after you and Grandpa Deck forbade me to communicate with him . . . I have a question for you, Hen . . . In your letter to Dr. Caldwell, you threatened him. You said you had 'methods' to use against him, and that you would use them. What did you mean by 'methods'?"

Mother stiffened. "I don't know what you're talking about . . . Of course you needed protection. The police would protect you from this man, if I couldn't."

"So your method of protecting me from the man I loved would have been to call the police?"

"I did call them," Mother said, "the constabulary in Poughkeepsie. We were ready, Daddy and I, to swear out a warrant for the fellow's arrest, but he wrote from New Mexico, some godforsaken place. We supposed we'd run the opportunist off. We had Miss Bates's word."

Again Trinc took a deep breath. "Miss Bates lied about Dr. Caldwell's luring me into his trap. She was only telling you what you wanted to hear . . . Did Grandpa Deck ever suggest to you that he had methods of his own for restraining Dr. Caldwell?"

"Of course."

"Oh?"

"He wrote Dr. Caldwell's employers at Vassar to learn more about his character."

"That's true," Trinc said. "And he learned that Dr. Caldwell was a brilliant professor of exemplary character. Grandpa Deck ignored this evidence and ordered Bruno Rancis to go to New Mexico and find Dr. Caldwell. . ."

Mother looked anxious. "What on earth for?"

"For the purpose of castrating Dr. Caldwell."

"Daddy?" Mother's eyes were widening.

"Grandpa Deck. And Bruno almost succeeded in doing his dirty work."

Mother and daughter studied one another. Mother looked bewildered, fingered rings nervously, finally shook head. "I don't know what to say. I'm very sorry, Trinc." Hearing a low moaning sound, they turned to see Granny Ah who was squeezing shut her eyes and holding a skeletal hand on breast. Who moaned, "Ayii, Ayii," almost inaudibly.

TRINC SPENT A SLEEPLESS NIGHT, deeply glad to have Mother cleared of suspicion but worried about Granny Ah. Who knew the measure of reality which people could stand? She had rushed to Granny Ah, hugged her and said that she was sure that there had been a mistake somewhere — that, in spite of what had been said, Bruno Rancis had acted on his own. "Bless you," Granny Ah had said. When Miss Potter came with the wheelchair and took Granny Ah upstairs to bed, Granny Ah had clawed at the air violently like someone falling from a skyscraper.

Not long after going to bed, Trinc had heard a commotion in the house, followed by the sound of an automobile outside in the driveway. Afterwards, all was quiet again. She went to the window-seat in a mood of reverie that was heightened by the effect of moonlight on snow. In the distance she could see smoke uncoiling from a Homestead chimney. Probably the caretaker was there, though what he would be doing on the night before Christmas she couldn't imagine. Moon-blanched snow on lawns had a portentous glow. Under the nearby snow-laden magnolia tree stood the Jouncing Board. It needed a new generation of children on whom to work its magic. Mother had been the last Heartwell to bear a child, and Trinc's own chances of motherhood seemed marginal at best. After a while her room grew cold. Fortunately, Mother had knitted her a thick sweater for Christmas. She pulled it over her nightgown and went back to bed. Warmed, she still couldn't sleep for more than brief intervals. She wished the house were full of servants and visiting relatives and children. She wished that six o'clock would come so that everyone could sit on the stairs in the dark, waiting for Grandpa Deck to strike a match to a Cape Cod lighter and thunder, "Merry Christmas!"

Some hours later, a small figure in a rustling silk gown came into the room and stood looking down at Trinc in moonlight.

"Hen?"

"Did I wake you up? I'm sorry."

"No. Stay. I haven't slept a wink."

"Nor I. Granny Ah is dying. I suppose you've seen for yourself. The doctors say it's nothing to worry about. It's something mysterious. I have a strange feeling that Granny Ah knows what it is, herself. . . Did you know that she decided to go to the Homestead with Miss Potter?"

Trinc sat up in bed. "Why would she do that?"

"Oh, she gets sudden impulses, as old people do. She said she wanted to take the lighter you gave her at once to the Homestead, to build a fire there where she and Daddy were married. Miss Potter had to wake up Jim. He drove them down there and left them . . . Trinc, I am an odd, sickly, disagreeable woman, my life suffused by a loneliness for which I cannot account. I've made my soul my citadel. I've shut myself up in it and turned a deaf ear to the world. This was very wrong of me. I have been wrong to dwell upon my own moral purpose and to give you so little of my love. But I do love you, and I'm proud of you."

"I love you, too, Mother, I mean, if you don't mind, Hen," Trinc said in a kind of awe.

"I've been reading Marcus Aurelius all night," Mother said in quiet voice. "Marcus says, no soul is willing to be robbed of the truth. You were right to speak frankly with entire candor. I know you have spoken the truth. You have never been an under-handed person . . . But, don't you see, we must beware of indignation against Grandpa Deck. We must learn to be imperturbable, even though we know he stumbled. Is it not, Marcus asks, the property of man to love even those who stumble? Shall I love my kinsman less?'

"Marcus says, we must habituate ourselves only to thoughts about which, if someone were suddenly to ask, 'What is in your mind now?', we would at once reply that all is simplicity and kindness in our heads, nothing there that we would blush to put into words.'

"I do not consider myself free of wrong-doing, though I never dreamed that physical harm would come to the man you loved . . . As your mother I was born to protect you. My actions have served this purpose. Even in protecting you I may often have done you wrong.'

"But we must remove our indignation. We must not surrender to it. We must not meet evil in another by evil in ourselves, with resentment and hate. Marcus says, the noblest kind of retribution is not to become like your enemy.'

"Only kindness is invincible."

"Are we kind people?" Trinc asked.

"Yes," Mother replied, "we are kind, all save one, and he is dead."

They talked quietly for several hours. Mother had spent a happy childhood with her six brothers and sisters. However, when she went away to art school in Boston and fell in love with one of her fellow students, Grandpa Deck had her removed from school and sent home. She had seldom painted anything since. Trinc, for her part, revealed that Aeneas's wound might yet be healed. While she believed he had forgiven the family, she doubted he cared for her enough to see her again. She might, after graduation, seek work in a hospital in China.

By and by, crimson dawn pressed against leaden skies. Faroff churchbells tinkle-clanged. As Trinc was glancing out the window, she saw a spurt of orange flame in the distance. Up it shot, then fell away to blackness. A gray cloud of smoke was billowing toward the dawn. Jumping out of bed, she ran to the window in hopes that the fire was other than what she already, on a thrust of panic, knew it was, and then another burst of flame came and rose higher than the first, a mad Bunsen burner's flame that made the woods shrink back.

Mother, who was standing beside her in the "little dress," exchanged with her an inference beyond words.

Granny Ah.

Trinc would find the two of them safe and unharmed, Granny Ah and Miss Potter huddled under the magnolia tree away from the Homestead, its roaring blaze and ruin. For, leaving Mother to call the fire brigade and to send Jim in the car, she had put on her coat and a pair of old riding boots and run as fast as she could across the lawn, lacerating hands when she stumbled on snow, gulping frigid air thickened by acrid smoke. She knew as she arrived in the driveway that it was already too late to save the house, its walls making a see-saw motion before collapsing. All she could see through an opened front door were burning beams and twisted pipes and fragments of plaster—and weirdly upright pairs of marble Ionic columns, one with a "Winged Victory" figure in bronze, and a headless dressmaker's dummy, enamel breasts and belly exposed. She thought she could hear the clanging of a fire engine from far away before she heard a shriek, glanced toward the frozen brook, and saw Miss Potter's waving.

She would hear Miss Potter's story before Jim's Cadillac and the fire engine arrived, how she had been sleeping on an Empire sofa when she heard Granny Ah crying, "Merry Christmas! Merry Christmas!," not from the bedroom but from the keeping room, and went there; how she found the keeping room ablaze from kerosene spilled from Cape Cod lighters; and how she saw Granny Ah whirling a lighter, torched, above her head, throwing it under the stairs. "I had to carry her upstairs, put her in the wheelchair, and cover her with the blankets. By that time," Miss Potter finished with a whimper, "I was so scared I don't know how we got out alive."

"Miss Potter," Trinc would say, "don't tell anyone what you just told me. Just say the kerosene was spilled accidentally near the fire in the fireplace."

Trinc looked at the fires reflected in Granny Ah's eyes and knew that the ghost of Grandpa Deck had been smouldering in them all along.

JANUARY, 1923.

She hears good news from Uncle Doc. The operation in Switzerland on a man named Aeneas Caldwell has been a success. Dr. Serge Nicovich is convinced that the patient's psychology has been a primary cause of trauma. There was neurological lesion, gross ulceration of the scrotum, negative indication of glandular coarsening in the testes. . .

WHILE DORA WAS UNDERGOING EMERGENCY SURGERY to remove the dead child from her womb, Trinc went for a long walk near the East River.

Dr. Van Dine's lies and threats of a few minutes earlier had directly challenged the dictates of her conscience. At first her impulse was to report Dr. Van Dine and Dr. Nicky Nicovich to Uncle Doc. On further reflection she decided to leave Uncle Doc in the dark. If she forced him to choose sides, he would probably throw his support behind males, no matter how venal they were. Besides, it was time to stop leaning on him. So, alternatively, she could stand on principle, go to Miss Dean, and resign her position. But quitting solved nothing. She would have to admit to herself she was just a spoiled rich girl unable to persevere through thick and thin. The only practical course of action was to complete nurses' training and to keep her mouth shut. At least as a Registered Nurse she would gain the power to be of service to people.

Seated on a bench, she watched lighted boats crisscrossing the river, leaving knife-cuts painlessly healed. A tugboat honked its laryngitic giant's horn. An aeroplane droned above the glittering city. She saw the plane against a broad glowing band of stars, watched it dip its wings, glide down and land on the river, a tiny seaplane churning up a chiaroscuro of silvery ripples on black water.

One didn't have to escape from reality to find beauty. There was beauty in everything. By the same token, however, there was also terror in everything, the terror of the unknown life, the terror of the insubstantial pageant of Time. One grew used to terror and assigned it to childhood, as she had once done with Jack the Ripper, or learned to pretend that it was visited upon strangers down on their luck. The seaplane she had just been watching might have crashed, its occupants an instant statistic. In truth, she was herself alone in an isolated, dimly-lit city park in the early hours of morning, an even more likely victim of violence than they.

These thoughts sent a sudden chill of apprehension down her spine. Somehow she had grown so accustomed to late-night relief from work that she expected the city to grant her immunity from danger. Now, senses pricked alert, she rose from the bench, and looked about—and looked about—until it seemed that every tree, every bush, every parked car, every concrete abutment concealed the proverbial beast in the jungle.

"Wha—?"

Thinking she had heard a threatening sound, she wheeled around, startled suspiration accompanied by excited heart. She scanned a line of trees by the river, the pitch blackness there a hundred feet away, unpenetrated by the light of the single lamppost.

Nothing there.

And yet there was *something* there.

Something crashing through brush.

Something *white*.

A man came running, springing out of darkness, sprinting under the lamppost, and for a moment she was sure he was wearing the uniform of a doctor in O.R., gown, cap, and mask. As he was a tall man thick-set in the shoulders she thought she recognized him.

Turner.

Then he was gone, disappearing behind parked cars in a direction away from her.

Turner? Absurd. She had been thinking about knife-cuts. She had been recalling Turner's proposition that one must escape reality to find beauty. Turner would be at home, waiting for news about Dora. As for someone running around in the middle of the night in New York, there might be a thousand explanations. As for his wearing surgeon's garb, that didn't mean he was a surgeon or that he wasn't an actor who had been playing the part of a surgeon, or that he wasn't one of the countless nut-cases who could crawl at any moment out of a billion rat-holes. But *masked*? And not just running, but running as if for his life?

She shook herself to dispel further doubt. Starting back toward the Nurses' Home about five blocks away, she might have been remembering Uncle Doc's prescription for Jack-the-Ripper avoidance: she ran as fast as she could. She had gone about two blocks when she slowed down to allow a pair of mounted policemen to clatter past her. They went in the direction from which she had just come. Had there been an accident? Or something worse? Was there anything logically to connect the running man with the appearance of mounted policemen?

Turner?

On Lexington Avenue two o'clock was struck in a church tower. The sound lifted her gaze again to the night sky. She couldn't remember when she had ever seen so many stars shining so brilliantly over New York, not even when she had danced on a rooftop and opened herself to life as a nymph-bringer of Light.

From far-off in the city came the sound of a siren. Police? Fire? Ambulance?

She entered the vestibule of the Home. Just as she was mounting the stairs she glanced at her mailbox. A yellow envelope was inside it.

A few minutes later she was shedding tears both unhappy and happy. The telegram in her mailbox had read: *Grandmother Ednah dying. Imperative you come home tomorrow morning with Jim. Who is Dr. Peter Rabbit? He is in Orford Parish and asks my consent your marriage to him. Your loving Hen.*

Clever, clever Aeneas! There was serious purpose in spite of the facetious incognito. Using a name coded for Trinc herself he had penetrated the No Trust defenses of Mother's citadel! He was home! He was home! Trinc rushed back outdoors to thank the stars for his blessings. She could hardly see stars, so warmly blinding her tears. She knew they were there, though, the stars to which in her innermost being she was related. Why should she doubt that stars influenced relationships? There was more to life than the rationalities of science. Aeneas had taught her that. Experience confirmed it. Happy indeed was he or she who knew the causes of things.

Presently, having dried her tears, Trinc crossed the street and went to the O.R. to learn what had happened to Dora. The operation was over, the patient recovering. Dr. Turner wasn't answering his telephone but would undoubtedly be on his way over soon. She went to Miss Dean's office and left a message that she was called home for a few days due to an illness in the family. One day she would prove to all the Miss Deans that a nurse could be a wife and a mother without neglecting her profession. She would soon be wearing both a Nightingale pin and an engagement ring.

Next morning she went home with Jim.

"Have you met Dr. Peter Rabbit?"

"Nome," he replied cautiously. "Mrs. DeRoman says we-all mustn't scare him away, on account he might could get cold feet."

"That," Trinc said, "is enough out of you . . . He just showed up at the house, did he?"

"He sent a calling card. Old school. Sure funny name. I had to pick up drugs for Mrs. Heartwell. I didn't see the man. They say, though, Mrs. DeRoman took a shine to him. Seems like she is most peculiarly curious to know what you been doing to get this man to come a-courting."

"Why," Trinc teased back, "I haven't done anything. Peter Rabbit liked the cabbage patch."

Once she was home Trinc was immediately joined in her room by Mother, who proceeded to inform her that Dr. Peter Rabbit was everything a girl could wish for in a man—a young Uncle Doc.

Trinc feigned annoyance. "Yes, Hen. Dr. Rabbit's a Doctor of Philosophy. If you plan to pester him for medical assistance, you'll get a lecture on time and space . . . Didn't he tell you how we met?"

"I don't like to pry," Mother said. "He said he hoped I would consent to let him propose to you . . . How did you meet?"

"We corresponded," Trinc said.

"Oh," said Mother, "you inherited your literary talent from our painters a century ago. But," she went on, look puzzled, "I was under the impression you were breaking your heart over that Dr. Caldwell. Now it seems you have two beaux to every string. Whom do you love, Dr. Caldwell or Dr. Rabbit?"

"Oh," said Trinc, "I love them both. Whom do you think I should prefer?"

Mother pondered the question in solemn seriousness. "Marcus Aurelius," she said, "advises us to remember that all mortal life is small and transitory. In the circumstances you would be well-advised to accept Dr. Rabbit as your future husband . . . Of course you'll have to support him for a while. Although he has taken employment at a suitable university, he tells me, he regrets that he will not immediately be in position to support you in the style to which you are accustomed. In the circumstances you may overlook a man's obligation to provide support. Granny Ah will be leaving you something in her will. Are you persuaded?"

"Oh," said Trinc, "I'm quite fully persuaded."

A few minutes later she went to see Granny Ah in the master bedroom and arrived just as a doctor was injecting her with a hypodermic needle. Miss Potter stood by.

Lying in a nightgown in a tall post bed was a skeleton with nothing left over the bones but a little flabby skin and swollen blood vessels. She clawed the air, apparently beseeching the doctor for another injection. The doctor ordered Miss Potter to change the nightgown, then left.

Granny Ah's hands seemed to be without direction from a conscious mind. When Miss Potter had slipped off one sleeve of the gown, Granny Ah grabbed it, sobbing, and had to have her fingers disengaged before Miss Potter could roll the little body over in bed. When Miss Potter drew off the other sleeve, Granny Ah clutched it with both hands and twined it around her bones. When the nightgown was off at last, she hugged it as if it were a child, her sharp bones protruding, limp breasts hanging, jaw and teeth opened to a grin like a skull's.

Trinc recognized the symptoms of a disease which was ravaging the country. The very name of the disease was blue-pencilled by editors and was taboo in movies and over the radio. Now she understood why Granny Ah had avenged herself on Grandpa Deck by burning down the Homestead.

She stood by the bed as Miss Potter was getting a clean gown whisked on the woman who was writhing in pain, the hands still busily clawing the air, still begging for morphine. She watched as Miss Potter pinned the body down with a sheet. Trinc left the room. Obviously, Grandpa Deck had also died of syphilis. She wondered if his features at dying were like those of the wife he had infected. During the time his portrait had been painted, there must have been so little of the New England aristocrat left that his children could not possibly have recovered a likeness.

DR. RABBIT WAS EXPECTED TO ARRIVE FROM HARTFORD at any minute for a late lunch. Trinc told Mother she would be waiting for him on the Jouncing Board, under the blossoming magnolia.

It was there, soon afterward, she and Aeneas met, and the meeting was as meaningful as a dream in the mysterious dimension of the timeless. He wore his old hat and some English tweeds. She hardly noticed if he had changed, he seemed so wonderfully like to the man she had loved and now loved anew. She hardly noticed what they were saying to one another as they jounced on the Jouncing Board. It was possible that there was too much to say and that they said only what needed saying. She heard, almost certainly, that Aeneas had been summoned to see a famous doctor in Paris and had had an operation paid for in advance by an Italian philanthropist named Contessa da

Braga. Almost certainly she heard news of Tubby's recent, happy marriage to a Cambridge don, a decent fellow named Playfair. Aeneas's own proposal of marriage did seem to be wonderfully satisfying, even though she was distracted by the magnolia blossom he was handing her just as he spoke the words she had waited to hear for so long. Her engagement ring was quite the most beautiful one ever purchased from a pawn shop in London. She was glad he hadn't been extravagant, just as she was glad that he remembered to remove his hat when Augustus came and announced that luncheon was served. Her jubilant Aeneas hurled his hat into the air.

Aeneas was seated, at Mother's insistence, at the head of the table. After Augustus poured three glasses full of claret, Trinc lifted her glass and met Aeneas's gaze. It was true, the cliché about his "penetrating" eyes, and she was planning to lose herself in them once Mother got her comeuppance.

"I am very happy," she began. "Thank you, Hen, for the gracious welcome of my future husband into the family . . . He is my prince, my hero, a scholar and a gentleman too indolent, as the saying goes, to harbor malice. I propose this toast to him— not to Dr. Peter Rabbit, but to Aeneas Caldwell."

Mother neither flinched nor blinked her eyes. She drank the toast as if the iceberg which a water-fairy named Trinc had slipped beneath her hull had melted away. Mother lifted her glass. "To Aeneas Caldwell, my son," she said simply.

Suddenly there was a sound like the trumpet of an elephant followed by the *queek* of a guinea pig. They all looked up at Augustus who had ceremoniously blown his nose into his new silk handkerchief. They were just in time to watch him folding it as if he had found in its happy tears a pearl.

PART II

The Physicist

13

Leviathan

1.

1947

Extract from "Sketches for a Memoir" (1947) by Aeneas Caldwell

IN AMERICA THE AMAZING NEWS ABOUT FISSION was disclosed at a meeting in Washington of the American Physical Society on January 26, 1939. Niels Bohr, chomping on a cigar, and Enrico Fermi, grinning through his gap tooth, announced that the uranium nucleus fractures into two parts when it absorbs a neutron. In the resulting split a force of 200,000,000 electron volts is generated. Although 200-million electron volts is not a large amount of energy, it is an extremely large amount of energy for one atom—about 100-million times as much energy as that released when an atom of hydrogen burns in oxygen. Furthermore, the fragments which Bohr initially called "splitters" must emit neutrons. If enough neutrons were emitted, a chain reaction might be sustained.

Science is a battle to set men free, a battle directly related to a discovery of this magnitude. The Real in nature, hidden and unknown except to introspective philosophy since ancient times, had been revealed, or, to put it more dramatically, Leviathan had been pulled to the surface, gasping on its hook! If Leviathan's store of energy comes from the nuclei of atoms, we reasoned, how could we find a way to set it free that mankind in turn might reap the benefits? And so when I say we were working frantically to build an atomic bomb, driven by fear of Nazi Germany, I must add that many of us were also driven by the excitement of discovering Leviathan. Only gradually did some of us come to realize that scientific research without control by scientists might determine the fate of civilization in unimaginable and tragic ways.

After the Washington conference we rushed back to our universities to verify the discovery. The situation was urgent and also called for self-imposed secrecy. As a consequence a scientist's increasing isolation from those closest and dearest to him placed his family relationships under an almost unbearable stress. He, himself, moreover, was subjected to stress. His two duties, that to science and that to his country, would gradually come into conflict. A third duty—a planetary imperative—was and still is only just beginning to emerge into consciousness. Clearly, if we had been fully aware of all the consequences of our acts, we might have seen it as humanly necessary to throw Leviathan back into its universal sea. But that is wishful thinking.

One nucleus of a uranium atom is to its atom as a small marble is to the earth. A neutron is ten thousand times smaller than that nucleus. To measure the behavior, then, of such infinitesimal objects was a matter of indirection and conjecture at best, and to build a coherent theory of their behavior was necessarily a process of testing and thinking. Initially, too, we were working in a situation in which only the smallest amounts of the most relevant substances— e.g., uranium—were even available. Thus the theoretical possibility of making an atomic bomb encountered from the outset enormous practical obstacles. How much material could be assembled in one bomb? What stuff could be used to surround that material? The stuff would have to hold the explosive together for a while so that it wouldn't blow itself apart, stopping the chain reaction. What explosive power could you achieve from all of this? These were questions of immediate concern to the scientists.

My own thinking early took an apocalyptic turn: How were we going to control Leviathan's released power? Might not the enormously high temperature of an atomic bomb explode hydrogen? Might the explosion of an atomic bomb set off an explosion of the oceans? Would an atomic bomb trigger the explosion of the nitrogen in the atmosphere? Would we be risking the transformation of the Earth into a star?

At Trinc's insistence I took the family for a week's vacation at a beach during the first week of September, 1939. For seven months I'd been working feverishly at the university, often from 7:00 a.m. to midnight. We all needed a break. The plan was to get as far away from Poe's Hill as possible. I rented a cottage at an isolated resort, Cherry Grove, about ten miles from Myrtle Beach, South Carolina. The cottage would have no indoor plumbing, no electricity, no telephone. In order to relieve Trinc of housekeeping chores, I hired a cook, Mary Christmas. We would be celebrating my son Billy's tenth birthday. Because Ma-Betty was going to be in New York for an August exhibition of her paintings, we invited her to join us from there.

Try as I might to empty my mind of its preoccupations while I was at the beach, I remained intensely focused on them. Thus it came about that during a dangerous hurricane, as I was engrossed in observing waves driven by winds well in excess of one hundred miles per hour, I arrived at my theory of a controlled nuclear reaction. When the first atomic bomb was detonated at Trinity Site in New Mexico less than six years later, the theory proved to be the correct one . . .

2.

1941

Letter from Mrs. Elizabeth Blumberg, Taos, New Mexico, dated December 23, 1941, to Aeneas Caldwell, Poe's Hill, North Carolina

Dear Son:

The sun is bright, the weather mild. Today I am sitting in the patio garden looking past frost-withered hollyhocks and tiger lilies by the adobe wall. Across a yellow sea of sagebrush toward the naked gorge of the Rio Grande as defined by the setting sun, I can clearly make out the serpentine range of the Jémez Mountains and the truncated volcano shape of Georgia O'Keeffe's famous mountain, Pedernal. I wear a turtleneck sweater over my paint-spattered coveralls and am happy to stay outdoors for a little while under a New Mexican sky that is, as ever, bluer than Van Gogh blue in the air that is, as ever, high-altitude thin and vibrant. Indoors, dear Phillips has cocktails ready and piñon a-blaze in the *kiva* fireplace, while Felicidad, who glides on moccasins as lightly as Ariel in order to show respect for what she walks on, is preparing us a supper of *chile relleno*, peppers as hot as a *ristra* is red. Everything seems immeasurably lovely.

But the world is dark.

I cannot say I am entirely surprised to hear that your marriage to Trinc might be breaking up. In your letter you say she has taken Diana and Billy to New York with her; your only companion is the cocker spaniel, Roguey. Everything, you say, is your fault. You've compelled her to live for fifteen years in the South where she feels "about as welcome as Darwin's monkey." Your income "from a notoriously underpaid profession" does not provide enough to put the kids through private schools, or "to support

Trinc in the manner to which she was accustomed." Above all, you blame your work as responsible for her "unhappiness."

Grasshopper molasses!

Whistling maids and crowing hens never come to no good ends, as they used to say in the Pine Barrens. Now, Ma-Betty is not someone to come between a man and his wife. I'm not a sower of discord, swinging my severed head like a lantern. I'm not going to tell you Trinc has witch cradles in her hair. I'm not going to play the part of a mother-in-law who puts all the blame on her. I reckon there's something in what you say. But you can't be the only one at fault. That's point one. Point two is, stop keeping score. She'll probably come back to you once she has had a bellyful of New York. Look a-here. I've been a Trinc-watcher for a long time. Here's what I think.

Remember our vacation at Cherry Grove two years ago? I kept a diary. I'll remind you of what happened before, during, and after the hurricane, and I'll tell you about the shark incident about which you probably know nothing. Here we go then, you, Trinc, Diana, Billy, me and Roguey, setting out from Poe's Hill in your Ford . . .

Those were heart-wrenching sights we saw as we drove toward the coast. Whitewashed cabins from which melancholy black faces peered. Derelict tobacco farms, silent cotton mills. Impoverished little towns with no hope for the future except Roosevelt—or Jesus. Along about the time we stopped for lunch in Fayetteville the Depression had me too upset to eat. The rest of you ate right heartily. I make no nevermind about that: ever since your Daddy left us to starve in Los Remedios, you've been hell-bent to make up for the insufficiency by stuffing yourself. You and the children helped yourselves to fried chicken, hushpuppies, cole slaw, bisquits and peach cobbler and washed everything down with buckets of iced tea. It bothered me having to listen to Trinc argue with the waiter about over-charging. Sure, $2.37 is a lot of money. Somehow it didn't seem right for a wife to be contradicting her husband in public. When we arrived at the cluster of CCC-built shacks called Cherry Grove, the eye-puckering glare of the lime-white sun and the close-by dirge of surf-boom stole upon my soul and ravished it with swift, pristine, and rapturous delight. As for our cheap accommodations, I found them charming. Sure, the cottage was only a paint-chipped wooden box on two-by-four stilts stuck into a sand dune near the ocean. Sure, there were those two bedrooms with the mildewed mattresses on rusted iron bedsteads and with the Monkey Ward dressers and mirrors. Sure, the kitchen had only an ice-box and a wood-burning stove, and the front room was furnished only with broken chairs and tables, a couple of kerosene lanterns, and a sofa that washed up after the Fall of the House of Usher. And, yes, we had to use a privy out in the swamp grass. But there was a Pawley's Island hammock on the deck. Luxury enough for Gauguin.

So when Trinc took one look at our charming accommodations and said, "We're proving our liberal convictions by living like sharecroppers," I just kept my trap shut. Ma-Betty's no interfering mother-in-law.

All went well the first three days. It did my heart good to see you paying attention to the children. There you were with a twelve-year-old girl and a ten-year-old boy, holding their hands as you ventured into deep water and tossing them over waves and shouting, "Whiskey-Wow-Wow!," the way your Daddy used to do, and catching them as the waves crashed over their whoops and screams. When Trinc saw Diana and you, she remarked, "Diana has an Oedipus Complex." Stupid me, I thought it was just love.

On the fourth day a red sun had water in its eye. That was the day we visited the Brookgreen Gardens and the Waccamaw River country. I had such a happy time taking notes for future paintings! At the old rice plantation I breathed fragrances of myrtle and magnolia and discovered the green bronze of Mercury, his sandals wings, motionless while a butterfly fluttered down to rest on them. *A butterfly sleeps on Mercury's wing.* Up river, I noted these: *Cypress trees reflect dragon-shapes in mirror-*

swamps; blue herons stand on one leg and contemplate the lazy lidded gaze of an alligator; live oaks droop behind plumes of Spanish moss, mottle with spots of sun the deep well of overhung roads; by ruins of a plantation house, doors and windows a-gape and jalousies askew, Time rests and His scythe rusts in the river, His hourglass is no longer turning. We returned to Cherry Grove to find that low tide had become high tide and a quiet rain was beginning to fall. I scribbled again. *Saltgrass has the brilliant, almost electric hue that presages storm. Spotted white globs glitter on the beach, stranded by tide beneath screeching gulls. The children run in mock terror from the jellyfish, but consider, O Lord, the thrift of the jellyfish: they are sting-y.* I felt so happy that day, I made the rain stop.

Now it's the fifth day, Billy's birthday.

Thunder in the morning, all the day storming. As you will recall, the Florida hurricane was not supposed to hit the beaches north of Charleston. You put on your new swimming trunks and your father's old battered cowboy hat, went out on deck, and sprawled in the hammock. You stayed there all afternoon even while big waves came ramping up the beach and swishing underneath the cottage. You stayed outside even while rain pelted the tin roof and window panes with a sound like drumfire. Trinc was getting anxious, and Mary Christmas, the Gullah cook, was less festive than her name. You—you lay in the hammock under some kind of spell.

At three o'clock Dr. Springer, that dentist with Parkinson's Disease, brought his two little girls over from next door for Billy's party. Trinc dressed the children in masks and paper hats and entertained them with New England games like Black Spider, Miss Ginia Jones, and All the Great Men. She needed someone to assist her.

"Want me I should fetch Aeneas?" I offered.

"No," Trinc replied. "When he gets into one of his space-time trances, he leads the band while the ship sinks."

I allowed she might be right. How does anyone conjure up

logarithms and powers-to-the-tenth during a hurricane? Beats me. Anyway, I figured, lightning won't kill us unless we kill a lightning bug. Sure was plenty of lightning, though. By four o'clock the rain was leaking through the roof and leaving puddles in the bedrooms. Finally Trinc went outside, and I heard her yelling at you in exasperation, "Are we having a nervous breakdown like King Lear?" Only, I guess you didn't hear her. She came back inside looking kind of ticked off because she'd gotten her party dress, the one she made herself from a bolt of Cheney Brothers silk, soaking wet. Another hour passed. Outside, the high-pitched whine of the wind and the lightning's irradiation of twenty-foot waves colliding did seem to suggest that the hurricane had not passed out to sea between Savannah and Charleston but was heading directly toward us. But we women know the men know best, don't we? Like, for instance, that Dr. Springer told me, "Cherry Grove never has bad storms." I wondered what it must be like to open your mouth to a high-speed drill held in the trembling hand of a dentist with Parkinson's. I mean, after he has punctured your windpipe and opened up an artery or two and drilled an oil well in your sinuses, would you still trust him? A Springer girl asked me in a worried voice about the storm, and I just said, "The faster the wind blows, the sooner we'll have a change in the weather."

Mary Christmas baked a cake and topped it with 5¢ Hershey's chocolate bars. We ate. Billy opened presents. I gave him *King Arthur and His Knights*, the only edition I could find in New York. Unfortunately, because it had pre-Raphaelite illustrations of flimsily-clad nymphs and effeminate champions, it was not a suitable book for a boy old enough to masturbate. Luckily, Billy's eyes widened with innocent pleasure as he threw his arms around Ma-Betty's thick neck and gave me a big wet kiss.

Well, about six o'clock I happened to glance out of the window and past your darkly blurred shape and saw a huge, churning avalanche of waves rising high above spindrift and slouching toward the cottage. Those waves broke thunderously beneath us.

The cottage shook violently. A mass of spray splattered against the window as if hurled there by a flick of a sea-monster's flukes.

"Lord-a-mercy!" This utterance from Mary Christmas.

"A-roooo!" This wolf-dirge for the end of the world from Roguey.

"Shithouse mouse!" This exclamation from Trinc. Where, I wondered, did *she* learn to swear? I couldn't recall her having worked as a scrubwoman in the men's rest room of the bus station in New York. Of course, I couldn't recall her having worked, period. Is it work to raise children, two beautiful, happy children?

She clapped her hands sharply. "All right, children," she commanded. "Diana, tell Daddy to take Mary Christmas home to Myrtle Beach. Now! Springers? Party's over. Billy? Tell Roguey to shut up and start behaving like a dog!" Trinc went to the kitchen. Mary Christmas was moaning there in the flat, quacking tones of the Gullah, "Miz Cal'wells, we's hatter been gawn! Miz Cal'wells, we's hatter been gawn soon!"

Then you put in your appearance, ducking your head under the low deck door. "Ah," I said, remembering a line from *Aeneid* that Grandma Floride and I used to read out loud to one another, "'Mercury splits the winds to the sand bars of Libya and alights tiptoe'!" And there you were with your wild mane of graying hair, your waist as slim as a twenty-year-old Olympian's. I saw Buster Crabbe swimming in the aquatics show at the New York World's Fair and I decided to buy you swimtrunks just like his and the salesgirl at Macy's couldn't believe that a fifty-year-old man wears a size thirty-four. And there you were holding in your hand your father's old snapbrim Stetson and I thought what a handsome man Calhoun was in his prime before he got whiskey and religion. Anyway, there you were. You lifted one Springer girl into your arms and went to the kitchen where Mary Christmas was wringing her hands as if the *Titanic* were sinking again. You had a tease-smile at the corners of your mouth and said, "It takes 200-million electron volts to convert mass into energy."

That was really on the ball, son, to give us a physics lesson just before we drowned. Mary Christmas rolled her eyes. "I ain't studyin' no 'lectrons, Mr. Cal'wells. I studyin' God!"

"Split an atom with a neutron, Mary," you said, "and God does the rest."

"We all's God's chi'ren, I speck," Mary said with a thoughtful expression on her face. There's nothing like a lunatic professor for calming folks down, I guess?

"Everybody out!" Trinc said.

"Wait," you said. "I'm taking the Springer girls home first. Then I'll take Mary home."

"Are you telling us to wait for you here?" Trinc asked in apparent disbelief. Her dripping wet white silk dress was smeared with chocolate. She bit her lower lip and said, "You decide. I don't care anymore."

You lifted the other Springer girl into your arms. "You and Ma-Betty pack the suitcases. When I return, we'll leave right smart," you said. I could tell you were angry with Trinc for almost arguing with the Head of the Family, but I kind of agreed with her, I just kept my trap shut because I didn't want to be a meddling mother-in-law. After you opened the kitchen door for Mary Christmas and followed her outside into a shrill blast, Trinc and I watched your shapes bending into a rain blowing horizontally and helter-skelter. You disappeared behind violently swaying palmettos; then you reappeared, having dumped the girls with their Pollyanna tooth-quack father. You opened the passenger-side door of the Ford for Mary to get in, and I was right proud of you for being such a gentleman, and you splashed around to the driver-side door and started the engine and turned on the headlamps and spun the car out of the path of the privy, which was just then blowing away, leaving a hole the shape of Ohio. The storm swallowed the car. The tail lights made red dots on a palimpsest of parchment-yellow sandclouds. I thought of a joke. "Gone with the wind," I said.

Trinc gave me a hot look. "I hate it, I hate it!" she muttered. "It reminds me of my father's abandoning his family by taking off in a rainstorm." She went to the children's bedroom to pack things.

Me, I went into the other bedroom. Rain was pouring through the roof and showering on my face. Now, look. I wasn't snooping around. I was throwing stuff into suitcases, minding my own business. How could I know that when I opened a dresser drawer full of panties and stockings and bras and corsets and Kotex pads I was going to find a leather belt and holster and a six-shooter? I was about to toss these heavy items into a suitcase when I said to myself, I said, Whoa there, Ma-Betty, what if that revolver is loaded? I spun the chamber. The gun was loaded all right. I said to myself, I said, What in Sam Hill is Aeneas doing with a loaded gun? Why is he hiding it in a bunch of ladies' underwear? It didn't seem right somehow. I emptied the bullets into my hand and stuck them in my pocket. I put the gun, etc., into the suitcase. After I finished packing everything I took a look at myself in the mirror. I didn't want my face to look worried or suspicious. I didn't want it to look shocked either — but it was. Just because I'm a bit over twenty-one, it's not fair to have gray hair, a widow's peak, crow's feet around my eyes, and a nose that looks as if it has been permanently pressed against a candystore window. I went into the front room, lit the lanterns, got the kids to cuddle up with me on the sofa and started reading to them about Merlin and Excalibur. After a while Trinc came in and slumped in a chair. "'What the hell, Archy, toujours gai, that is my motto'," she sighed dramatically, "'there's more than one dance in the old dame yet'."

"Grasshopper molasses," I looked up and said, recognizing that line from *Archy and Mehitabel*. "We've got two tense kids and a dog who believes the world is coming to an end, and you've got alley cats and cockroaches on your mind."

When the kitchen door flew open, you came in looking like the Ancient Mariner. "We're getting out damn quick!" you bellowed. You put out the lanterns and grabbed suitcases, Trinc grabbed the children, and I grabbed Roguey. Out we scrambled into the storm and piled into the car, me with the kids and dog in the back seat, you and Trinc up front. Roguey puked in my lap.

"Forgotten anything?" Trinc asked.

"My *King Arthur!*" Billy wailed.

"I'll get it," Trinc said, opening her door to get out. Although she managed to stand up in the wind, she was not able to move. For the first time I noticed that she had strapped that gunbelt around her waist and that the gun was in the holster. I said to myself, Smart girl. Just then the roof of the cottage was torn loose. It fluttered up and spun off, like an enormous butterfly, and crashed into palmettos about a million miles away. Trinc got back in the car. You accelerated it like Barney Oldfield roaring out of the pits at Indianapolis. I looked back. Rising from the sea was a tidal surge like a range of blizzard-blurred mountains. It rose and it rose and crashed on the cottage and the next thing I knew the cottage was just a bunch of flotsam and jetsam poking from the ocean like toothpicks.

We made for Conway, you'll recall, figuring to go inland *from* Myrtle Beach, but halfway to Myrtle Beach a man with a flashlight waved us to a stop. It turned out he was fleeing from Myrtle Beach and we couldn't go there now because huge trees were blocking the road. Just then, part of a tree somersaulted over our car. We had a choice left between two roads, one road inland and lined with trees, the other road along the coast for eighty miles to Wilmington, but because your gauge was broken and you thought you didn't have enough gas to go eighty miles, you took the inland road. I thought to myself, Ma-Betty, maybe you don't look like Venus, mother of Aeneas, and you didn't go to Harvard, but sometimes this boy of mine doesn't have sense enough to buy a tank of gas when the going's good. Anyway, giant trees were snapping and crashing on either side of the road. We hadn't gone five miles before you skidded to a stop. The road was blocked by a monster tree. I saw in a flash of lightning that Trinc's hands were curling up like lobster claws. In the same flash I could see, beyond the *swish-swop swish-swop* of windshield wipers, a man waving a flashlight at us and running toward the beams of our headlamps. He was a big barefooted white man in bib overalls. As he passed directly in front of our lightbeams I thought I saw feral eyes popping from sockets and jagged teeth protruding from his mouth, like a shark's. What was all that about King Lear? Why, here he was, Lear on the heath, stark, raving mad!

You—you're such a trusting soul, son, sometimes you don't know a shit hill of beans—you rolled down your window. "Evening," you said to the man, "do we have to go back?" The man—if he wasn't King Lear he sure as shootin' resembled Paul Muni in *I Was a Fugitive from a Georgia Chain Gang*—spoke in a strange, deep-throated voice. "Beasts outside know High Wee back!" That's what I thought he said. "What did he say?" I asked you. You said to me, "Beastly outside, no highway back . . . It's Scotch-Irish dialect."

When I thought about it, I reckoned you might be right. While you were shaking the man's hand and thanking him and giving him a dollar, and while I was studying the birthday cake in my lap, puked up there by your neurotic dog, no one saw Trinc slip out of the car until suddenly she appeared in the light beams in her white silk dress, screaming at the top of her lungs and pointing the gun at this man: "Son of a bitch! Get out of here or I'll shoot!"

That man's shark's mouth made the letter "O." Slowly he backed away from Trinc and from the car. Then he ran and leapt into the swamps like a startled deer and you got out of the car and lunged at Trinc and knocked the gun from her hand and she fell down, rain pelting her, and I got out of the car and ran, too, and you were panting hard and Trinc was shielding her eyes and the wind was howling.

"He might have killed us!" she said.

"He was trying to help us!" you said.

"You hit me!" she said.

"I hit the gun!" you said.

"Why do you care about him instead of us?" she shouted.

"He's a sharecropper!" you shouted. "What got into you? Snap out of it!" You pulled Trinc to her feet, picked up the gun, examined it. "Thank God it wasn't loaded!"

And she said: "Who's been messing with my pistol?"

"Me," I said. I fetched the bullets from my pocket and handed them over. I felt sheepish for some reason even though I had accidentally averted what might have been a tragedy. "Sorry," I said.

Trinc looked at me and you as if the whole world had turned against her. She just grinned like a chimpanzee in a peanut factory. And climbed back into the car and sat saying nothing. We climbed back in, too.

"Bitch bitch bitch," Billy was saying quietly to Roguey. "Bitch bitch bitch."

Trinc whipped around and hissed, "Don't ever use that word again!"

And you said: "He doesn't know what he's saying. He's only repeating what you said."

And she said: "You're going to get it, Billy." She hopped from the car, came and jerked open the back door, pulled Billy out, dragged him with hands like claws, bent him over her knee even while the rain is coming down on them like a waterfall, and spanked him until he cried. Billy crawled into the back seat, into my arms, but Trinc jerked open your door and said, "Move over. I'll drive."

It didn't seem right somehow. I thought you would straighten her out, especially with your kids watching. But, no. "0. K.," you said.

Grasshopper molasses, I was saying to myself. This is real grasshopper molasses.

I'm not saying Trinc was a bad driver. She shifted gears and clutched down as quickly and smoothly as a bank robber in the getaway car. I'm not saying she didn't have a sixth sense about where to go. Because, remember how she got us on the road to

Wilmington and not fifteen minutes later swerved off the paved road and onto a rutted sand road, where I expected any minute to meet Blackbeard searching for women and rum, and how she found at the end of the road that fishermen's village called Little River and that tourist home sheltered from the wind? Beats me how she did it. Remember how we all tramped into the tourist home and an old woman told us the dog would have to spend the night outside, and Trinc slapped an extra ten-dollar bill on the night desk and just said to the old woman, "Bull"?

And then for the first time all day Trinc began to laugh her warmly humorous laughter. Somehow in all the commotion we hadn't noticed before that you were wearing nothing but the swimtrunks and the old hat.

There were other folks there in the lobby, refugees like us, and when they joined in the laughter, you had the good grace to bow to them. You always were a bit of a clown, whether acting at Harvard in the Hasty Pudding or trying to keep your students' attention in the classroom.

We stayed at Little River for two days. The clouds were soft and feathery, tinted with rainbows in the afternoon. On the second day you hired a trawler to take us deep-sea fishing. At the last minute you decided to take Diana to Charleston to buy her new clothes for school, so after the two of you and Roguey departed, Billy and Trinc and I boarded the trawler. It rumbled down an estuary past uprooted trees and some drowned cows that had gotten tangled in branches of cypress trees. As it plowed over breakers and headed toward the Gulf Stream, Trinc and I had a chance to talk things over. "Ma-Betty," she said, "I'm a very insecure person, but I've never before been out of control the way I was the other night. It was a crack-up, and I'm sorry."

I told her that in the circumstances just about anybody might have mistaken the sharecropper for a crazy man threatening our lives, and that she had acted in defense of the family. As for her reason for spanking Billy, his using her own cussword, she had been altogether in the wrong, but a few good whacks now and then might instill in a child the concept of redemption: we have to work through pain and violence in order to find peace with ourselves.

The more we talked, the more I realized this wife of yours is a brick. Especially when you are not around to assist her she's not just a wife and lover, she's a father, chauffeur, policeman, plumber, electrician, garbage collector, grocery shopper, cook, laundress, house cleaner, home nurse, banker, P. T. A. committee woman and general repository of the wisdom of the world collected since Adam and Eve ate apple pie. Sure, she'd like some fun now and then. She spoke of introducing the children to cafés in Paris, of seeing the palaces of Venice, the Uffizi Gallery in Firenze, the glory that was Greece and the grandeur that was Rome, all the things that you and she saw on your honeymoon, but, as I've said, the world is dark now. She can't go. I can understand her wanting to take the children to New York for a spell.

Although she says she is "insecure," I think she has learned to be a pretty tough gal.

We had anchored out in the Gulf Stream. I had helped Billy to bait his fishing line. He would shout gleefully, "I've got one!" In an hour he caught a dozen mackerel. Then, one time, as he shouted "I've got one!" the line was jerked out of his hands. He recovered it, tugged. Whatever he had hooked, though, tugged back. It looked to me as if Billy might be pulled overboard. I grabbed the line, too. The thing almost pulled me overboard— and I'm 1-7-0 pounds of Venus, tough as cougar meat and twice as nasty. Seeing us in trouble, some crewmen came and took the line. They had their hands full. Someone shouted, "Shark! Shark!"

Billy and I peered into a glassy ocean. By and by we detected just under the surface a most awesome sight: the sleek white body of a shark was thrashing and flailing about in primordial fury and anguish at having been discovered.

When the men had the shark hauled on deck, it was only about five-foot long, maybe less than a hundred pounds. Still it refused to die. The men tried to beat it with shovels. In retaliation it lunged at their feet with wicked teeth. The men tried to beat it with Coke bottles. Still it wouldn't die.

"Stand clear!"

We were all startled by this command from Trinc, even more startled to see her aiming her gun at the shark's snout. She fired point-blank a crack of lightning.

Sure, at the time it didn't seem right for a woman to be doing a man's job. Now I realize someone had to put the brave fish out of its misery in a swift, clean manner. Trinc was as disgusted as I was to watch a bunch of men slowly torturing Leviathan with Coke bottles.

Billy went and looked down at his catch and turned his head away.

"It ain't the same," he said.

Trinc put her pistol back in a tote-bag and came and gave Billy a big hug and said, "Billy, it was too late to throw it back. I can have it mounted for you, if you'd like. We'll put it back the way it was. Would you like Mommy to do that?"

Billy shook his head. He was fighting back tears. "It ain't the same," he said.

Look a-here, son. Nothing ever does remain the same. What's done is done. Don't look back. My other advice to you is this: Remember that love has more kinds than Carter has liver pills. The only kind that lasts, though, the only kind that teaches us to take the forward step, is compassion.

Cocktails! Phillips is calling.

Your loving

Ma-Betty

14

The Lady in the Chapel

AENEAS BELIEVED IN THE PURSUIT and conquest of happiness
and was appalled by human suffering. When happily married
friends got divorced, or a married professor ran off with a co-ed,
or a brilliant Rhodes Scholar sailed through the air from the top
floor of the Bright Leaf Hotel in Poe's Hill, he wished with all his
heart that he could have prevented the disasters. He and Trinc,
after all, had managed to stay married for seventeen years.
They had love to spare. Although they had come from different
backgrounds, almost from different cultures, they shared not
only the same values but also, or very nearly, the same feelings.
They were so close to one another in spirit that they had grown
accustomed to thinking one another's unspoken thoughts as if
spiritual communications were an a priori fact.

Now their marriage showed symptoms of fissioning.

Trinc had never forgiven him for "hitting" her during the
hurricane. She had, he recalled, over-reacted to the sudden
appearance of a sharecropper and threatened to kill him; Aeneas
had struck not her but the revolver from her hand. If she wanted
to make him feel guilty, she had nevertheless only to say, "You
hit me," and he would suffer remorse. It was better to take the
blame than to argue, even though he had to subtract a measure
of misery from the sum-total of happiness.

Matters worsened. First, about a year ago, she introduced the Perfume Ritual. If she placed her Toujours Moi next to his bottle of Listerine in the bathroom, it signified that sex-tension had reached critical mass, and it was make-love time. Second, for the past six weeks he'd been banished from Trinc's bed and sent to sleep alone in the attic. Were fifty-two-year-old husbands supposed to be hidden from sight, like fugitives or illegal immigrants?

But he had long been practically hidden from sight anyway. From 1939 through 1940 and 1941 he had been working on the problem of fast neutrons, how they might create and sustain a chain reaction in fissionable materials. Working at the university from early every morning until late at night, he must have seemed a stranger to the family, indeed. He couldn't seem to escape the prison of his duties even though they were making him sick. Quite often a sensation like that of hot skillet grease was spattered beneath the surface of his scalp.

Ironically, it had been his attempt to find extracurricula relief that had led to his banishment.

The University Playmakers were producing Lillian Hellman's *Watch on the Rhine*. Aeneas had taken the family one weekend by train to New York to see the play—yes, he had sacrificed himself!—and now that an amateur production was opening in Poe's Hill he decided it would be relaxing to try out for a small part. He hadn't expected to be cast as Kurt Müller, the leading role. One evening, home early for dinner, he was sharing his excitement with Trinc.

"It will do me a lot of good to get out of the lab for a few weeks in the evenings. I'm perfect for the part of Kurt Müller. He's a middle-aged German leader of the anti-Nazi movement, come to Virginia to collect money for his cause."

"His menopause?"

He cringed. "He plans to return to Germany and to use the money to barter for the lives of captured comrades."

"Is he a communist?"

"I thought you *liked* the play."

"I liked the play in New York. I didn't know you were an actor."

"Hasty Pudding once upon a time at Harvard." He felt like apologizing for his amateur status. "A Romanian aristocrat, a Nazi sympathizer, threatens to expose Kurt to Nazi diplomats in Washington, meaning certain death for Kurt and his, er, friends. Unless Kurt pays blackmail. Which he won't do. So he has to kill the Romanian."

"How thrilling, darling! You get to kill somebody."

"Backstage. With a cap pistol."

She placed a hand over heart. "I thought you had a moral obligation to devote all your time to work."

It was true. At least he had used the argument about "moral obligation" in order to disguise the Top Secret nature of his work. He shrugged shoulders. "I can fit rehearsals and performances around my work."

"And when will you be coming home?"

He thought. "Midnight," he said. "Well, about two."

"And you get up at five."

"That's right. Three hours of sleep. Just for a few weeks. Not to worry. I'm in my prime."

"Are there women in the play?" Trinc was smiling a frosty smile. She already knew the answer. "Me," Aeneas parried, "constant as Planck. I'm faithful as a cuckleburr in sheep's wool. The play's the thing. O. K. with you?"

"You won't be angry?"

"I won't be angry."

"I was thinking," she said in softly inflected voice, "so that the family won't be disturbed, would you mind sleeping on a mattress in the attic?"

"Mind?" He smiled without heart. "I'll come downstairs on perfume nights."

"No perfume."

Now that he slept in the attic, Aeneas had been wondering of late whether he were becoming as weak and contemptible as his father had been.

Nothing in family tradition could account for Calhoun Caldwell. Other Caldwells, men, women, and wives, had been tough, uncompromising Carolinians proud of their Scotch-Irish heritage and protective of their sense of intimate honor. Calhoun's mother, Aeneas's Grandma Floride, was a tiny woman with such a touch of austerity in her face that she could have sat for the central figure in a Confederacy group in bronze on the grounds of the state capital in Columbia. Widowed early in the Civil War and confronted by starvation, she had developed a talent for writing romances, had prospered, and had given her only child every opportunity to grow up a cultured and courteous gentleman. But Calhoun was proud of being "ig'rint hillbilly trash," unfortunately endowed with good looks. He persuaded Elizabeth Van Dyke, a New York artist, to marry him. Her family disowned her. He took some of Floride's money and with Ma-Betty, his bitter wife, and precocious son Aeneas removed the family to the Pine Barrens of North Carolina, a region so isolated from the modern world that folkways persisted unchanged from those of medieval Europe. Aeneas could remember people who slept with forks on the chest, prongs up to spike witches as they crawled toward the neck, other people who saw the Devil once in a while—an itty bitty black rascal in a wide field of snow. After settling in "Throstle's Nest," Calhoun revived the local pottery trade, but prohibition ruined the whiskey business for which he made jugs. He took to drink. He battered his wife. He discovered religion. He sold "Throstle's Nest", moved the family to the Hispanic hamlet of Los Remedios in the remote Taos Valley of New Mexico, abandoned them, disappeared into the wilderness and found neither God nor fortune and one day in a cave in Chaco Canyon put a bullet through his head. It was the boy, Aeneas, who discovered the corpse and buried it in that cave. The boy, who was on his way to Harvard thanks to money provided by Floride, would never be able to erase from memory that grinning skull with a shredded red bandanna tied across the eye sockets. The boy, though terrified lest he be destined to repeat Calhoun's pattern of disintegration, carried his father's ghost around as if on his back, a curse that impelled him to feel inordinately responsible for perfecting an impious world.

Of late, without intimacy to set as a bulwark against the onrush of nightmares, he'd been sleeping with a red bandanna tied across his eyes. He didn't want his nightmares to escape through their portal and infect the people he most loved.

It was the morning of Sunday, November 23, 1941.

Awaking in the attic in darkness, he had a moment's panic before he remembered to remove the bandanna. A neighbor's cock crowed. It was five o'clock, he knew that. He lingered in bed in order to put to flight the nightmare images still chiseled into his brain like petroglyphs scratched on a cave wall by an aboriginal humorist: Calhoun's skull, a headless American corporal, a German machine-gunner, a bloated French boy and a dog. Gradually the images faded away. He could look forward to the exercise of daily routine. Tiptoe downstairs to the bathroom. Shave, dress. Eat a breakfast of coffee, orange juice, Post Toasties, grits, hash-brown potatoes, scrambled eggs, toast, and bacon. Out of the house by six-fifteen, walk to campus, be at work by seven at the latest. Suddenly he remembered what day it was: *Sunday, November 23.* "Oh," he groaned aloud, "noooo."

Three weeks ago, after he had given his final performance in *Watch on the Rhine,* he had been cornered in the Green Room by Peregrine Pinker, an Englishman and Dean of the School of Divinity, who wanted him to deliver the annual "Faculty Sermon" in the University Chapel at eleven o'clock on the 23rd. Aeneas was removing Pan-Cake with cold cream and Kleenex when there appeared over his shoulder and in the mirror Perry Pinker's plump and apple-cheeked face, beady eyes boring through wire-rim spectacles, the almost perfected look of complete sincerity oozing from a heart corrupted by politics. Aeneas felt he must greet Perry effusively, with imbecilic grin. After the small talk Perry mentioned the sermon.

"You're not serious," Aeneas demurred with the requisite modesty. "Talk moral rot in the Chapel? There will be a thousand good people present who probably regard scientists as practitioners of witchcraft. You'll get me burned at the stake."

Perry roared with the requisite guffaw. "After the sermon you may reconsider your apostasy."

"Like Galileo?" As Aeneas still had traces of make-up at the hairline, he wondered whether Trinc would scorn him for having a hot bath and shampoo when he got home at 1:30 a.m. In the meantime, in order to get rid of Perry Pinker, he would have to agree to give the sermon. "I should warn you about the principle of unpredictability in physics," he said, standing up and looking the Dean straight in the eye. "It means the universe may be self-creating. We'll have to abolish your supernatural spook."

"Oh, dear," Perry said, drawing back as if shocked. "Another Pagan suckled in a creed outworn . . . Didn't one of your chaps —Einstein, I believe the name is—declare that God doesn't play dice?"

"Touché, Perry. Why me?"

"Your Kurt Müller, my boy, your Kurt Müller. He's a chap who must bring evil into the world in order to save lives. It occurred to me as I was watching your simply marvelous performance, you naturally innocent colonials must eventually fight and help the King's men win the war. You will corrupt your consciousness in the process. You will bring evil into the world in order to save lives. . . Give us Paul, *Epistle to the Romans*, 3, verses 7 and 8, and don't flinch from the Pauline Principle. Give us Martin Luther. Here I stand. That sort of thing. November 23 in the Chapel. Eleven o'clock. Don't forget, dear boy."

Aeneas had not forgotten, but since giving the Faculty Sermon was the last thing he wanted to do, he had put off preparation until now, five in the morning of the absurd day.

The neighbor's cock crowed again. Was the son of Calhoun fit for the role of moral leader? Calhoun had probably covered his eyes with a bandanna in order to prevent the soul from escaping into the contagions of humanity. That was an old superstition, that one could deceive death itself. Aeneas had on the contrary always desired to let souls communicate through the eyes. This was the mystery of love. Banished to the attic he was shut inside himself, the prospect of happiness growing dim. Why so swiftly guttered the obscene candle of romance? Next to his bed were cobwebbed steamer trunks with labels from the honeymoon abroad:

FIRENZE

PARIS

NOT WANTED

ON VOYAGE

ROMA

LIVERPOOL

He rubbed his eyes. Still etched behind them were those familiar images, his corporal decapitated by whispering machine-gun bullets and the German machine-gunner who, seeing Aeneas leap over sandbags, screamed as Aeneas killed him with a Browning .45-caliber semiautomatic pistol.

The images were Not Wanted on Voyage.

He left the house at six-thirty. The dark three-piece suit he was wearing was the one Trinc hated. It reminded her, she said, of *The New Yorker* advertisement for Calvert's booze, of the Saville Row stuffed shirt with a preference for it. As he was walking through a wooded stretch of the university's campus, he observed, as was his custom, ordinary things. Predawn golden light lined the dull, even masses of clouds. Small birds made weather-gossip in the branches of waxen magnolias. A hawk canted in the sky above pinnacles of the Chapel. It was curious how religious were the feelings of a scientist, how one stood before a mystery out of which all things were created. In that stance the mind was free, free of myth and dogma, free to reach beyond appearances into reality itself and to inscribe for the benefit of mankind a sacred view of life. Perhaps the threat of becoming as weak and contemptible as his father had made him resolute in defense of intellectual freedom.

At South Hall he climbed a flight of worn wooden stairs to the Physics Department, unlocked his office door, went and sat in a swivel-chair and lit his old, carbonized Sherlock Holmes pipe. After a while he submerged himself in thought.

His soul had a wild life of its own. How did the soul stand in relation to conscience? Hackneyed as the question was, it none the less pulled him from his chair and sent him to his shelves of books. What was it? Ah, here. This was the book. He had placed a marker for D. H. Lawrence's remarks on Cooper's Deerslayer. Yes. Here. *The essential American soul is hard, isolate, stoic, and a killer.* The idea, like its author, was repellent but not easily dismissed. Aeneas had been reflecting upon it recently in relation to *Watch on the Rhine*. He returned to his chair and cold pipe.

Doubtless as a boy in the Pine Barrens of North Carolina and in the Sangre de Cristo Mountains of New Mexico, when he squeezed the trigger on a deer, he had experienced a thrill of gratification. Doubtless as an officer in France he had been glad to kill the German machine-gunner who had killed his corporal. But he had respected his victims. Perhaps the so-called essential American soul—hard, isolate, stoic, and a killer—was evolving toward a new world of conscience. Freedom unbridled by moral effort gave no regard for the generations of children yet to be born.

He sat up alertly. Here was the connection with *Watch on the Rhine*. Some of Kurt Müller's lines surfaced from memory. He repeated them silently to himself, in sum, there were everywhere men who will fight to make the world good for children he loves. That was it! Kurt Müller had not intended or desired to kill. Kurt

Müller had not done evil that good might come of it. Hating the sickness of the violent, Kurt Müller had murdered a man in order to save lives . . . No wonder that Peregrine Pinker, Dean of Divinity, had divined in the play the subject for a sermon: preserving one's humanity in war.

A stress-pain burned where fragments of shrapnel had once been embedded in Aeneas's scalp. He ignored the pain, leaned across his desk, and plucked from bookends his father's Bible.

A few minutes later he began to write.

"Today's Scripture lesson is from Paul's *Epistle to the Romans*, 3, verses 7 and 8. 'For if the truth of God hath more abounded through my lie unto his glory: why yet am I also judged a sinner? And not rather (as we be slanderously reported, and as some affirm that we say), Let us do evil, that good may come? whose damnation is just.'

"Many people acknowledge that in course of doing good it is sometimes necessary to bring evil into the world. As our nation is drawn inexorably into war, this Pauline principle, that one must not do evil that good may come, is certain to be severely tested.'

"Let us suppose that an American army has pushed its way across France in pursuit of a retreating German army. Let us suppose that an American commander has halted his troops outside a small French village occupied by a German artillery unit. And let us suppose that the German artillery unit has our American troops pinned down. The commander estimates that in a frontal assault fifty American soldiers will probably die. But if the village is bombed from the air, there will be no American casualties. He estimates, however, that five innocent French civilians will probably be killed in the bombing. He asks himself: Is it morally permissible to kill innocent civilians in order to save lives?'

"For the killing to be morally permissible, certain conditions must be met. The commander must not intend or desire the deaths of those who die. The killings must be a necessary condition for the saving of lives. The commander in this example, though he foresees the killing of innocent civilians, does not intend or desire that they be killed. Some lives will probably be lost that a greater number of lives may be spared.'

"But now let us suppose that German scientists have developed a secret weapon, a superbomb. This superbomb is so powerful that it can destroy an entire city in one explosion. Let us suppose that the Nazi leaders have selected their first American target for destruction by the superbomb. The target, in fact, is our own city. And now let us suppose that we are all gathered here in this Chapel, the pinnacles of which signify our human aspiration to escape spiritually from fetters of the earth. Without warning the bomb is dropped. These glorious stones are instantly reduced to smouldering rubbish. Our city and all of its inhabitants are instantly vaporized. The Nazi leaders demand on the basis of demonstrated terror that the United States surrender.'

"Are the conditions of the Pauline principle met? They most certainly are not. The Nazi leaders intend and desire the murder of innocent people. Part of the proof is this: the power of the superbomb could have been demonstrated in an open area and in conditions whereby no one would have been killed.'

"The greatest evil is the loss of consciousness of evil. In war, horrors accumulate. It becomes increasingly expedient to use evil as the means to a good effect. Although moral numbness may prevail, to save our humanity we must make a moral effort. Let us remember these words from the *Codex Bezae*: 'Man, if thou knowest what thou doest, thou art blessed. But if thou knowest not, thou art accursed and a transgressor of the law'."

Aeneas finished the sermon at ten-thirty, dissatisfied. Should he have written something edifying? Perhaps he could have told the story of the French boy and the dog.

At the end of the First World War he had supplied himself with bread and cheese and taken a slow train to Le Havre. When the train made a stop next to the bombed-out ruins of a village, he alighted onto a platform and began to eat. As he was eating, a mangy, emaciated dog crawled from under a barbed-wire fence and stared at him with soulful eyes. He threw the dog a piece of cheese. The dog wolfed it down, begged for more. When he tossed the remainder of the cheese, the dog did not eat it but carried it in his mouth to the other side of the fence. A minute later the dog returned. "Sure beats all, fella," Aeneas said. "Reckon you'll want the bread, too." He tossed the loaf of bread to the dog. The dog ran with it and disappeared on the other side of the fence and did not return. Curiosity aroused, Aeneas went to the fence and looked over it. In a bomb crater full of twisted blocks of concrete were the dog and a little French boy with famine-bloated belly and with, it seemed, blinded eyes. He and the dog were sharing bread and cheese together, ravenously.

No, it wouldn't do, that story. Since the dog, not the boy, seemed caring, people might consider the story cynical.

He rose, went to a coat rack, donned his Harvard-crimson academic robes and mortarboard, locked office and soon emerged from South Hall into bright sunlight as carillon bells in the Chapel tower began to peal. In front of the Chapel a crowd made way for him as if he were the anachronism he looked. Even though he resembled a bishop setting out for the Crusades, he was resolved to carry out the role of Authority assigned to him, worthy of it or not.

During the First World War there had been an incident when the light of a vision filled his soul with awe. He was leading his men out of trenches and toward enemy lines. As moths swiftly rushing toward flame, so he and his men rushed into the *wram wram blam* of exploding shells, into the *ugga ugga* bursts of machine-gun fire. Suddenly he fell in mud, his senses in abeyance. Moments before, he had been absent-mindedly pondering Einstein's mass-energy equation, $E = mc^2$, thinking *If energy can be created from matter, matter can be created from energy.* Rapture seized his mind, vision came. The universe must have evolved from a spontaneous, inconceivably hot burst of light. From this light were thrown all stars and galaxies, all life. Like a small, fluttering bird put into a nest where it might be quiet, his soul had on that occasion rested in an infinite tenderness. Everything was light, light, light!

He was waiting in a choir-stall for his time to speak, thinking, *The Chapel is a testament to light. The colonettes soar until they arrive at a pointed, ribbed vault of ceiling. They deny the weight of stone. The stained-glass windows, gem-like and smouldering, flood with ruby-blue colors the gray stone walls of the nave and cast upon the air a palpably splendid glow. The Rose Window patterned after the one in Chartres proposes through the power of art the irradiation of earthly love by divine.*

It was time. The organist had concluded playing a toccata and fugue by Bach. Aeneas went and mounted steps to an oak-canopied pulpit. A sea of faces splashed up to him. As dark clouds suddenly break above an alpine peak and shafts of a sublime radiance transform snow into sheer dazzlement, so light from the Rose Window beamed down and flooded a section of the nave in the middle distance. Although he was reading his sermon, his voice appeared as if from a periphery of consciousness. Where light fell, as in a dream of a Byzantine madonna in the basilica of Santa Maria Maggiore, there appeared the head of a lady with golden aureole. Warm and sweet and sad was her face. She lifted her gaze to meet his. She lowered her gaze only to lift it again. She penetrated his soul. His soul cried out in amazement.

"Splendid, perfectly splendid!"

He barely heard Perry Pinker's gush as they left the Chapel by a side portal after the service was over. Mumbling thanks to Perry, he shielded eyes from the glare of sun and surveyed the crowds going home. If only he could get a real-life glimpse of the Lady, he could break her spell. Of what use to him was this soul-stuff? It was less real than certain subatomic particles that existed for one-millionth of a second. Yet she was like some previously unimaginable physical law suddenly emerging at the point of criticality.

"Daddy, Daddy!"

Diana and Billy were calling and waving, running to greet him on the flagstone terrace by the Chapel's front portal. He hugged them, kissing their eager faces. "What on earth are you two doing here? Where's Mommy?"

Billy made a face. "She said we could come to hear you as long as we don't get seduced by religion."

Aeneas tousled Billy's hair. "I hope I haven't contributed to your delinquency."

"It was scary," Billy said.

"Yeah," Diana said. "Is there really a superbomb?"

Aeneas replied carefully. "A writer named H. G. Wells made that up."

"Daddy?"

"Yes, Diana?"

"Play football with me."

"You're on my side," Billy said.

"Hold on," Aeneas laughed. "We'll play on the same team."

They went home. For the first time in many Sundays he devoted himself to the children.

Late that night as he lay on the mattress in the attic he prepared for the next day's lecture on thermodynamics for his freshman Intro to Physics class. With flashlight in one hand, fountain pen in the other, he sketched in the main points he would make about the Second Law, the theory that the universe was losing energy over the eons and would eventually come to nothing. But the image of the Lady in the Chapel kept intruding upon his thoughts until he began to doubt if the Second Law, the cornerstone of physics, were entirely true. If there were a continuous Genesis, as the ancient Chinese believed, nature, instead of inexorably running down, would reverse itself and create a balance. And if a timeless creative spirit pervaded the universe, he might as well personify it, as the ancients often did, as female. He would play at worshipping at Her shrine if only because nihilism—the Nothing Nothing Nothing of the modern age—made chaos the whole ballgame.

He decided to write the Lady a letter.

Putting his lesson plan aside and finding a clean sheet of paper, "*Dear Lady in the Chapel,*" he wrote.

Or dear goddess—mi muy querida y misteriosa señora de alegrías, dolores y mercedes.

Now I come to happiness.

Your image warms and uplifts me. I've waited for it a long time, and now that your beauty fades not from mind I prize it the more highly. Love has done it; and I do love you. We shall lose nothing, but gain everything if only Beauty has its way with us. Of course I regret you didn't pick out a more reasonable man—or just a whit less sentimentalist. I'm scared to death of you, to tell you the truth.

I cannot concentrate tonight on the Second Law of Thermodynamics. You refute it. Also I think of how you adore me, and of your yielding to me the unspeakable passion of your love.

Oh, Lady, damn it to Hell! It's so confusing, and it's not a bit funny. I wouldn't mind it so much if I knew definitely what my role is. I have to confess that you irritate me a great deal. But love takes the sting away. Love is more than my pride. I'll gladly swallow my pride if you give me assurance you won't turn a cold shoulder if ever we meet.

One observation needs to be made: a gentleman never inflicts pain. This serious reflection bobs up and down in my head. I wish I were reserving what I have to say against the day of our meeting. Even then, like as not, you will be terribly amused. I hope so, because love encompasseth all things, and in love there is no superiority.

Until now I must have hated womankind in general, its lust for children, its tyranny, its foolishness, and so on. I was not at all happy and was rather distrustful of the whole business of sex. It was an honest distrust. But now there's no pretending that I'm unhappy, or that I'm cold and don't need you: I'd crawl on my knees to you and ask forgiveness.

I regret nothing tonight, not even my love for you, by God's Hat, No! Believe me, my darling, damnable, lovely Lady, I love you very tenderly.

He hid the letter under the mattress.

15

Love Tests

HIS MIND WAS ABSENT FOR THE NEXT FEW DAYS. Trinc's forty-third birthday was coming up on Thursday the twenty-seventh. There was going to be a party with relatives arriving to celebrate the occasion, Uncle Doc, Colonel DeRoman, and DeRoman's son, Gayle, Jr. He couldn't risk forgetting that, lest the you-hit-me hallucination become unforgivable through neglect. He had purchased in New York a hard-to-find bottle of Toujours Moi. Perhaps she would take the hint.

He also couldn't risk displeasing her relatives. He did make a concentrated effort to review their circumstances. After Auntie Em died of cancer five years ago, Uncle Doc had retired from medical practice. He was driving south to spend the winter in West Palm Beach, with a stopover in Washington along the way. Colonel DeRoman, too, was a widower; Amelia had died of TB at least ten years ago, leaving Gayle, Jr., to be raised by his doting father. Colonel and son were driving north from Cuernavaca to attend debutante balls in Philadelphia and New York. At least there would be no Heartwells with whom Aeneas would have to contend. When he and Trinc were married in Orford Parish, most of the Heartwell clan had treated him with a formal reserve. Only Hen had welcomed him into the family in spite of his being a pauper, a Southerner, and an intellectual. Hen had died of cancer three years ago.

The morning of the birthday arrived. He rose as usual and tiptoed down from the attic to the bathroom. As he was groping his way along the dark, narrow corridor he stubbed his bare foot painfully against a large object that had no business being there. He went and bathed and shaved and dressed, noting in dim light that the object was a steamer trunk. Trinc must have hauled it down from the attic, *his* attic! He had not forbidden her to go there; she at any time could change his sheets and collect his dirty laundry. But what if she had discovered his letter to the Lady in the Chapel? A furious feeling came, molten as an earthquake. How could he have been so careless? He remounted the stairs to the attic, lifted his mattress. Thank God the letter was still there! He folded it and thrust it in his pocket.

Half an hour later, precisely at six, he was polishing off a breakfast of coffee, juice, cereal, bisquits, grits, scrambled eggs, waffles and sausages and contemplating a peaceful morning in the office where he could write another letter to the Lady—when an apparition entered the kitchen, a sleepwalker in a beauty salon, facial cream glistening, hair done up in curlers: Trinc. He observed her dumbshow as she opened the refrigerator door, peered inside. She removed a big pink turkey, plunked it on a counter and began to scoop entrails out with her bare hands.

"Hi!" He decided to try for the Peace-in-Our-Time tone of Neville Chamberlain after his meeting with Hitler.

"Morning." She didn't look at him.

"Happy birthday. Guests come at noon?"

"You knew that."

"So I did. Dr. Knight?"

"Uncle Doc," she said. "Everyone calls him Uncle Doc but you."

"Colonel DeRoman and son?"

"Colonel. He wants everyone to call him Colonel." Trinc half turned to look at him. "He saved you from the firing squad."

"You make it sound like a mistake," Aeneas said.

"I'm Trinc," she said with a tight smile. "Also known as Mrs. Caldwell. You may remember me."

"I remember you well, Mrs. Caldwell," he said. He decided upon praise. "Loyal. You stuck by me during our years of separation . . . Plucky. You defied your family to become a nurse. Long-suffering. You threw in your lot with a pauper. You live with him in the boondocks. You're cooking in a mortgaged flytrap only two stories high—three, counting the attic . . . I remember things we have in common: conscience and honor and old-fashioned rectitude. Fanfares for Trinc."

If a man were to flatter a woman on the grounds that she stood for conscience and honor and old-fashioned rectitude, he doubted whether she would be altogether pleased, but he wasn't mocking her. He was spelling out a long-standing high regard.

She rinsed bloody hands in the sink. "Do you suppose I don't care for my honor?"

"That's not what I said. I said the opposite."

"I used to, when I was a girl, keep everything inside my insecurity. I'm strong now, Aeneas Caldwell, I'm strong. I'm not going to spare you the consequences if my demands on life are unfulfilled."

"You approve your anger in advance?" he chided. "What have I done? Why don't we make up? Come heart to heart with me. I'm a candid person in the old sense of the word."

"Innocent?" Trinc spun around and glared. "Do you think I'm stupid? Do you think I don't know what you're doing when you stay away from home, pretending to be an actor?" She struck a pose. "'Until now, I must have hated womankind in general, its lust for children, its tyranny, its foolishness, and so on' . . . I love that 'and so on'. It sounds to me as if you want to go to bed with the Virgin Mary."

Aeneas chuckled soundlessly at the ridicule he could have aimed at himself. So she had read his letter. So he was a jerk. "Trinc, that's a poem addressed to the Goddess Mother of the Universe by a supplicant, a troubadour!"

"It sounded horny to me," Trinc said, glared. "First, you're an actor. Now you're a troubadour." Her voice relaxed. "True, you once wrote me a poem. In your very first letter to me. It was sweet."

Aeneas sensed a weakening. "Look," he said, "this Lady in the Chapel, as she's called in the poetic epistle, is not a rival. She's Everywoman. She's you. If you won't let me make love to you, at least let me express my yearning for an unattainable woman."

"Aeneas?"

"Yeah."

"Aeneas?"

"Go on."

"There's no profiting from another's unhappiness."

"I want you to be happy."

"Well," Trinc said, "I asked Father and Uncle Doc to come for my birthday party because I need to know who loves me."

"You have me," Aeneas said, a sensation of betrayal passing through his heart. Was she going to consult with her relatives about breaking up the marriage? "They have enough troubles of their own," he essayed. "They're lonely old men."

Trinc glanced away. "Our 'troubles', as you put it, are none of their business. I want them to show their love, their respect for me. They'll bring gifts."

"Gifts? Of love? Let me get this straight. Uncle Doc has loved you all your life. You don't need further proof. Colonel loves only himself. If you put him under pressure, he may try to humiliate you . . . Let's be friends. Let's serve one another. Let's grow."

"You do whatever you want," she snapped.

"Guilty. My work is important."

"All you do is work. When you're not working, you act in a stupid play."

"0. K., it was stupid."

"You didn't invite me to the play."

Aeneas bristled. "I gave you tickets. You didn't use them. You said you didn't want to see the play a second time. You said you couldn't stand watching me make a fool of myself. Maybe I made a fool of myself. Why does that lock you in to a desire to exclude me from your respect?"

"What about Sunday's sermon? I read about it in the papers."

"I honestly didn't think you'd be interested." Aeneas took a deep breath. "I apologize . . . For years you've praised your stoical mother and other Heartwells for not being, I believe the phrase is, seduced by religion, whereupon Grandpa Deck made himself into a god and tried to have my balls cut off."

"Thanks," Trinc tilted her nose. "Thanks for reminding me how much we owe you."

"I didn't say that," Aeneas said hotly. "I've never tried to make you feel guilty."

"You've always resented the Heartwells. Did you marry me to get revenge on them?"

He almost broke a silence by saying, tritely, he had married for love. The validity of that protest seemed overshadowed by evidence of his present neglect. He had carried off the patrician to a cramped kitchen cluttered with dirty dishes and bloody entrails. New to him was the idea he had married for revenge. "If I had wanted revenge," he said, "would it not have been simpler to sue your family for damages related to malicious wounding than to carry off the princess to life as a scullion? I'm sorry I can't support you as well as I'd like."

"I could use my own money if I wished," Trinc said, seemingly mollified. "I could hire servants. I could have my children educated in private schools. Have I ever complained about living within your means?"

Aeneas took this opening. "I never married you for money. I want no part of your money. I am happy to provide whatever support I can, and for reasons. One, my father was a scoundrel and I refuse to sink to his level. Two, I take my responsibilities seriously. Three, your family, what's left of it, would love to believe I was a fortune-hunter from the word go. We're talking rot." He rose from the breakfast table. "Look, Trinc, I do listen to you. And I don't do whatever I want. Perhaps you have a notion I'm selfish, a greedy egotist like your father. Obviously, I don't see myself that way. If I neglect home life because work life is demanding, should I suddenly neglect my duty and devote myself entirely to home life? I'm a great believer in happiness. But the way to your happiness does not include self-abnegation on my part."

"Then go work," Trinc said. She turned her back to him. "I don't care."

Aeneas straightened his necktie. "I'll be back by noon to help with the party . . . And don't worry about my work. All I do at the university is write love letters."

"Not to me," Trinc said.

HE HAD SPOKEN IN EARNEST, though obliged to keep secret the nature of his work. Half an hour after the hassle with Trinc in the kitchen he was in his office with, on his desk, a brown manila envelope inside of which were letters to the Lady that he had had the great good fortune to compose away from home. The first letter of the series, the one Trinc had discovered, he now took from his pocket and slipped into the envelope.

It was dangerous, what he was doing, a kind of infidelity, even though he had spoken sincerely when he tried to explain to Trinc that *she* was the Lady. In surrendering to the undertow of passion, especially *this* passion so alien to Puritan and excessively masculine culture, he was hypocritically abrogating the rules of Authority. But he was faithful to individual experience of life. It had to be entered upon in a kind of dread, with possibilities of fulfillment or of deep unhappiness, and he wasn't going to forfeit his chance to drain the cup. What to him was quantum physics except an esoteric way to know oneself as a participant in all things? The Lady seemed to signify something similar. She encompassed. She united. She harmonized. She redeemed. She was not an object out in space and time, not a

Being to be glimpsed in a state of self-transcendence but the light of an indwelling power projected from his own wild soul.

He took fountain pen from breast pocket of his tweed jacket, paper from a drawer. Then as a climber buffeted by wind-driven snow, who suddenly lunges for the shining summit of his dreams, he began to write:

Dear friend,

Love, as the Sonnet says, can bear Time out to the edge of doom. So must it be that your presence preserves me, else would I be divided against myself and pitted against the world. You unite me with life. You make me a part of all things. You lead me to rejoice in the stream which has no death. I give you my love without effort. Once I enjoyed the spectacle of the universe through the lens of the rational mind. Now I perceive with my soul and have come to happiness. Will you allow my affection for you to liberate your affection in return? Our reciprocal happiness exists beyond space and time. We are one.

Putting down pen and slipping the latest letter into the envelope, he leaned over desk and buried head in arms. Over his heart there floated a cloud of wistfulness, as of a mourning without end for losses that had once seemed plenitudes. Never had he doubted his love for Trinc. From the first moments of their meeting he had known she was the moving spirit of his life, and she had often told him of her same feeling in the same words: he was the moving spirit of her life. Now, it seemed, she was an unstable element, lacking binding force.

After a while he raised his head. On the desk were two letters, both opened yesterday. He picked up one of them, read it again. A young physicist in the Bell Labs in New York had been asked to invent a small, half-inch-square screen with a half-million holes in it so that the uranium-235 isotope could be separated from uranium-238. The physicist wanted advice.

Was nickel the right metal to use with uranium hexafluoride, or were other metals and alloys also impervious to the erosion caused by the gas? Aeneas considered the question. Splitting an isotope off from an element, however unstable, was no easy task. Collecting that isotope in beneficial amounts was a long and painstaking process. Well, he would recommend nickel as the solution to the barrier riddle. Did the physicist understand the hidden significance of the engineering task assigned to him? Did he know that unless U-235 could be separated from U-238 in pure, large quantities, no atomic bomb could be built in time to save the world from Germany's conquest? In his reply he would avoid all mention of an atomic bomb.

The other letter, a long one, was from Cousin Tubby, mostly with news about her son, Karl, adopted by Playfair. Karl had so distinguished himself in physics at Cambridge that he had been retained as a Fellow at St. John's College and elsewhere as a research assistant to Chadwick, discoverer of the neutron. Consequently Karl was being spared military service. As Aeneas re-read the letter he felt especially warmed to Karl, whom he'd previously known only as a little boy. The Playfairs had gone one summer to spend the Long Vac at Hexham on the Tyne, near the ruins of Hadrian's Wall, and the windswept, rolling hills and dales had ignited in Karl a passion for history and music. He conjured up pictures of savage hordes sweeping over the Roman wall and down upon the startled cities of Arthurian lands to the south. He went hiking in Scotland and he struck up acquaintance with an old piper and singer of ballads, whose language he set down for Tubby: 'After finding I had the genuine lilt o' the air, we had a gude snaiker o' whiskey, and he drank weel and nae sooner was he prodigiously animated than he made the awfuest and uncoest howling sound ever I heard'. Back in Cambridge, Karl found someone to teach him the bagpipes. Now, as Tubby described him, "he marches up and down and his abdomen pumps like a bellows and he gingers up every party."

It seemed nothing short of miraculous that a girl once thought to be mentally disturbed, and who had an illegitimate child, had married a Cambridge don, and that the child had already grown up a scholar, a dreamer, another troubadour!

By God's Hat, he would go and ginger up Trinc's party!

Walking home just before noon, he changed the mind from which he had recently been absent. He disliked gifts with strings attached. It might be better to give Trinc nothing at all than to give her the perfume. On the other hand, the perfume did not necessarily have strings attached. She had a choice. Until now she had chosen to live with him in a manner far, far less than that to which she had been accustomed. Their home, as he approached it, presented a case in point. A two-story brick house with only four rooms—two bedrooms, one bath, kitchen and combined living and dining room—was certainly no fairybook castle. If he were Trinc, confined to this chicken coop for seventeen years, without servants to help with housekeeping and raising children, he would have complained. She had never complained—not at any rate about it.

A shiny black Lincoln Continental drew up to the curb and parked in front of his Ford. A gray-uniformed chauffeur, a small man about thirty, stepped out briskly and opened the curbside rear door. From it emerged, struggling with a silver-tipped cane to pull himself to his feet, was a tall thin man with white mustache and white Van Dyke beard. Wearing a Chesterfield, a silk scarf, and a homburg, he looked like an emissary from the Court of St. James.

"Dr. Knight!" Although Aeneas thought of him as "Uncle Doc," he did not wish to presume upon acquaintance.

"Hell-O, Aeneas!" Uncle Doc beamed. "Where's Trinc? Where is my namesake, Billy?"

Because Washington to Poe's Hill was a six-hour drive, Aeneas thought the old man would be tired. "I'm sorry about the long drive down."

"Naaaw," Uncle Doc said, leaning on his cane. "Left yesterday. We were staying, Jun here and I, with Stimson in Washington."

"Henry Stimson? Secretary of War?"

"That's the fella. Old friend of mine. A most wonderful man even if he is a buzzard-pissin' Republican!" Uncle Doc threw back his head and laughed. "Yup, arrived last night. Pulled into a little tourist home. White-washed cabins in the pines. Had'em a big lit-up sign, said MORALLY CLEAN. I said to Jun, let's go pick up a couple of fast women and a bottle of corn liquor and get registered for the night. Anyway, our room was clean enough for a monastery. I slept with the enormous consolation of knowing I was morally clean for the first time in my life . . . Say." Uncle Doc beckoned to the chauffeur. "Jun, come on over here. Meet Professor Caldwell."

Jun had an open face lit from within by amusement. He gripped Aeneas's hand tightly, with a slight bow. Aeneas liked him.

"Let me tell you about Jun." Uncle Doc rubbed his chin, flashed blue eyes. "When Em passed away, I needed a chauffeur, valet, chief cook and bottle washer. Who should turn up but this California fella who had been barred from entrance into medical school on account of his being Japanese American. Well, I looked the fella over. By golly, there was something wrong with him! No yellow skin. No slant eyes. No spectacles. No buck teeth. Didn't say Ah So or Flied Lice. Wasn't a monkey. So I said to him, I said, if you can stand my company for a couple of years, I'll see to it you get into Cornell Medical College. I'll foot the bill. It was a deal. Right, Jun?"

"I'm the Yellow Peril," Jun remarked. The look of amusement, Aeneas saw, was edged by a frown.

Aeneas invited Jun to come in for dinner. "Obliged," Uncle Doc intervened, "but Jun wants to wax and polish the car . . . See here. Where's that rascal, Gayle DeRoman? Haven't laid eyes on him since your wedding. He had packed up and left France after Amelia's death. This was even before I was in Spain with the International Red Cross . . . Let me tell you, we had to perform some pretty ticklish operations over there. Hacked limbs off soldiers without administering anesthetic. Had no choice: no supplies. For instance, in the Alcázar of Toledo . . . Whoa! I'm wandering. We were speaking of Gayle. From what I've heard on the grape vine, he's spoiled his son rotten."

Aeneas told him what he knew about Gayle, Jr., how he had been kicked out of a succession of private schools for smoking, drinking, and fornication, and how Yale had refused him admission in spite of Colonel DeRoman's attempt to bribe authorities. "He ended up," Aeneas concluded, "at a college in Alabama where Colonel stipulated, Gayle's roommate must be the quarterback of the football team . . . The past few years, father and son travel from Newport to Pasadena to Cuernavaca, with stopovers in Philadelphia and New York, evidently for the purpose of introducing Gayle, Jr., to society girls susceptible to charm, money, and good looks. Colonel supplies the charm and the money, Gayle, Jr., the good looks. The poor guy!"

"Imagine," Uncle Doc shook his head. "A father who insists that his son room with the quarterback, as if to confer romantic respectability upon a weakling! This 'Colonel' business! Gayle's exhibitionism has never failed to get my goat. Say, d'ye think Trinc will be spoiled if I give her a somewhat extravagant present?"

"Frankly, Uncle Doc," Aeneas began and stopped. "May I call you Uncle Doc?"

"Delighted."

"Frankly, Uncle Doc, I don't understand why she suddenly demands these shows of love."

"Menopause," Uncle Doc said in a stage whisper, leaning in with a sly wink . . . "It's a mink coat from Sak's Fifth Avenue. You can't afford to buy it yourself. I hope it won't offend you if I give this deal to my favorite gal?"

"I'm thrilled for her," Aeneas said. "She doesn't have a mink coat because she hates to spend money on herself. A gift from you . . . What's that?"

Off in the city an air raid siren began its spiraling blast into stridency. Uncle Doc took off his homburg and scanned the sky.

White hair thinning out. Cheeks hollow beneath prominent bones. Neck muscles like catgut. It seemed to Aeneas that the sound that stained the sky was ringing the death-knell for Uncle Doc—for the vanishing days and ways of princeliness.

"Trumpets of folly make smaller skies," Uncle Doc said, resettling the homburg and putting an arm on Aeneas's shoulder. "I want to meet my namesake, William Knight Caldwell, before the cow jumps over the moon."

"THAT WAS FATHER," TRINC SAID TO AENEAS in the kitchen as she cradled the receiver of the telephone. She was still dressed in a bathrobe and had curlers in hair. "He and Gayle, Jr., spent the night at the Bright Leaf Hotel. They threw an impromptu party at the bar, with Colonel buying drinks for college boys and their dates. He sang what he calls his 'gay' French and Yale songs. He told his usual stories, how he impersonated General Pershing, how Marshal Foch gave him the Croix de Guerre. Gayle, Jr., got drunk. He is only now up and about after downing three hair-of-the-dog gin martinis. Shall we lock up the liquor?"

An hour had passed since Uncle Doc's arrival. Because Aeneas was busy in the kitchen, trying to prepare the dinner that Trinc had neglected, he had had to leave the old man alone with the children in the living room. At least, now, the turkey was in the oven. The yams, cranberries, bread and pumpkin pie—ingredients he had bought at the Piggly Wiggly yesterday–had yet to be cooked. "We should lock up our daughter," he replied lightly. "Just because Diana is Gayle's fourteen-year-old niece, we shouldn't ignore a masher with the looks of Lord Byron. So I'm told."

He managed to make Trinc smile, even to relax her voice as she spoke. "The reports come from Father and may be slightly exaggerated . . . Do you remember my telling you, Father took Gayle to Hollywood and got him an audition for the movies? When the day of the audition arrived, Gayle was nowhere to be found. He turned up a week later at a hospital in Honolulu. While Father had been busy ingratiating himself with Cecil B. DeMille, Gayle was invited by a starlet to a party with Charlie Chaplin at the castle of William Randolph Hearst. But instead of going to San Simeon, Gayle drove to Burbank, bought an airplane on Colonel's credit, and flew with the starlet to Hawaii. He was too drunk to make a proper landing. He crashed. The starlet was killed. Father had to pay a fortune to her family to keep the scandal out of the papers. No more auditions for lovely brother."

Aeneas had heard the story before and was as usual annoyed by the DeRoman penchant for dropping the names of famous people. Although he had never envied the rich and the powerful, their success served to magnify an impression of his own inadequacies. Trinc was opening the oven, inspecting the turkey, and seemed so flummoxed that his heart went out to her. "Look," he began.

"I know what you're going to say," Trinc interrupted. "You're going to say I'm uneducated."

"I wasn't going to say such a silly thing."

"You thought it."

"Look, Trinc," he said gently, "it's your birthday. Now go and put on your glad rags. I'll take care of dinner. Anything else I can do? You're just having an off-day."

"Yes." Trinc shot him a distracted glance. "You're right. I'm having an off-day. Thanks. You're sweet." She leaned in and pecked him on the cheek. "Give Uncle Doc a glass of sherry. He must be bored to death with the children. Put Roguey in the back yard before he shits on the carpet." She thumped out through the swing door.

Aeneas set to work at once. He poured the sherry, took the glass to Uncle Doc who was seated on the sofa with Billy and Diana snuggled in his arms. Back in the kitchen he put yams and bread in oven, cranberries on stove. Discovering that the turkey had no stuffing, he made it with bread, onions, celery and lemons. He made gravy and coffee. Finally he scooped Roguey up and dumped him outdoors. "Old man," he said, "mark how the verb 'to shit' has been added to American family values." The one thing he wouldn't do, he decided, was set the dining room table. Trinc knew the whereabouts of the linen tablecloth and napkins, the engraved silverware that had belonged to Hen, the seldom-used Crown Derby chinaware that had come as a wedding present from Amelia DeRoman. If Trinc set the table, she would have a sense of accomplishment—of being cherished.

He poured himself a bourbon highball, went into the living room, and sat down. Uncle Doc was speaking to the children in a slow voice that wrapped words in wonder.

"Didn't I tell you about the time I took President Teddy Roosevelt's son for an elk hunt? Well, it was like this . . . Night overtook us before we could return to camp. We had to lie down where we were, on hard ground with stones. Of course, I was a pretty big fella in those days. Didn't mind sleeping rough. But that night I couldn't buy shut-eye for all the tea in China. I lay awake under a sky so dark it was like the blackest black bean soup you ever saw, with millions of tiny stars like snowflakes sprinkled on top. The wilderness was so quiet the crickets must have taken aspirin. Now, usually the wind tells stories in the leaves of trees—you know, don't you, that the wind tells stories?—but on this night the wind-stories were only whispered in a bright moon's ear. Then . . . everything still and quiet . . . Ever take a Saltine cracker and snap it in two? I remember a silence once. Up in the Yellowstone it was. Teddy and I heard a wee itty bitty sound like your Saltine cracker snapped. Know what it was? It was a great big old grizzly bear's stepping on a twig. *Shhhick*. Again: *shhhick*. If we hadn't have been listening to the silence we would never have heard that *shhhick*, never have readied our rifles in time. Because here he came just a-chargin', that great big old grizzly goin' ninety miles an hour!"

"What happened to the boy?" Diana murmured.

"Yeah," said Billy, "what happened to Presdent Teddy

Roozyfelt's boy?"

Uncle Doc looked around as if he'd lost something. He saw Aeneas and winked. "Didn't I tell you about the boy? . . . I lay awake half that night, but the boy slept so soundly that, next morning, I rather enviously said to him, I said, 'I see the stones didn't interfere with your sleep'. And the boy said, 'Well, Dr. Knight, you see, it isn't long since I used to take fourteen china dolls to bed with me every night'!"

While Uncle Doc was making a clown's face, opening mouth wide and bulging out eyes, the doorbell rang. He drew a watch from vest pocket, consulted it, frowned. "That'll be the playboys of the Western world. I better go tell Jun to bring in the booty."

BALD, THICK-NECKED COLONEL DeROMAN, medals dangling outside rumpled white Palm Beach jacket, sat on a divan, highball in one pudgy, liver-spotted hand, cigar in the other, ashes falling on an old "Y" sweater under the jacket. Next to him, dressed in a preppy suit and regimental necktie, sat Gayle, Jr., who was holding highball glass in two hands at chest level and bowing his head over it from time to time as if he were contemplating Holy Communion. On the sofa sat Uncle Doc, a large carton beside him. The children, wary as kittens, stood in a corner of the room and whispered behind their hands like a delegation of observers from Mars. It all, to Aeneas, made a tableau except that the central figure in it was still missing: Trinc. It was after two o'clock.

Dashing back and forth between living room and kitchen in order to refill drinks and to monitor progress on dinner, he had caught only snatches of the conversation. When Uncle Doc said something about the Red Cross in the Spanish Civil War, Colonel said something about Communists. When Uncle Doc said that the dream of his life since the early 1900s had been the inception of a National Health Service, Colonel said something about Socialized Medicine. Uncle Doc had countered, "Access to the means of attainment and preservation of health is a basic human right. Of every hundred men who are twenty-five-years-old in 1952, eleven years from now, sixty-five will live to the age of retirement. Of these, one would have to have above-average means, as we do, and nine would be able to scrape by—but the fifty-five others would become public charges. By 1970 there will be 20-million people sixty-five-years-old and older, and most will be unable to feed, clothe, and house themselves adequately, let alone pay a doctor. By the year 2000 the number of elderly and retired people will be staggering. Who is going to pay for the care of aged relatives? Not the buzzard-pissin' capitalists, that's certain!" During this speech, Colonel had shaken his head in vehement denial as if the former president of the American Medical Association were talking treason.

Aeneas left the room, returned a few minutes later. Standing, Colonel was waving his cigar like a metronome in Uncle Doc's face. "No doubt with your friends in Washington you'll get my taxes raised, but what you conceal behind your statistics is the un-American greed for free lunch. The public charges to whom you refer are like that chink outside, waiting for manna to drop from heaven!" Colonel placed fingers on his temples and stretched the skin around the eyes so that he resembled a caricature of Asian peoples.

Uncle Doc's eyes blazed. "You son of a bitch, what d'ye think you're doing?"

The children giggled. Gayle, Jr., stuck out teeth and said, "Ah so, Ah so." The children giggled.

Aeneas stepped in, clapped Colonel on the back. "Say, Colonel! Tell us about your adventures in Mexico. How's the good life in Cuernavaca?"

"Ah, Cuernavaca." Colonel rolled his eyes. "Dwelling place of Cortés and the Empress Maximilian! . . . We stayed at the Hotel de la Selva. Splendid view of Popocatapetl. Tell the story, son."

"You tell it, Dad," said Gayle, Jr., "and may I have another?" He handed his glass to Aeneas, who smiled without heart and said, "Don't tell the story until I get back." Aeneas dashed to the kitchen, filled the glass with ice, bourbon, and water, dashed back, handed Gayle, Jr., the highball. "Thanks," said Gayle, Jr., with a lovely smile and drank. "That's sure swell whiskey."

"It's an amusing story," Colonel said. "Gayle was taking a girl home late at night. They were stopped by the mounted police of the night patrol and robbed at gun point. When the next night Gayle was taking the same girl home, he thought he was being followed by the same patrol. He resolved to grasp the thistle firmly. He turned back toward the hotel. The patrol followed. As he neared the hotel, he stopped and waited for the patrol to come up. He invited them to come in and have a drink. They accepted and dismounted and took possession of the lobby. Gayle banged on my door and called out very loudly, 'Colonel, I want to introduce you to some swell guys'. I got up and went to the lobby. There, Gayle presented me ceremoniously to half-a-dozen mustachio'd boys wearing baggy uniforms and bandoleers. 'El coronel, mi padre', Gayle said. That did the trick! The police returned the stolen money, with profuse apologies for their 'mistake', namely, they had, they said, mistaken Gayle for a 'tourista'!"

Colonel finished the story and looked about the room to measure its effect. Gayle, Jr., chimed in, "They were swell guys. They provided me with a horse and a carbine. They took me out with them on many night patrols."

"Did you help them rob the tourists?" Uncle Doc's question was inflected by sarcasm. He struggled to his feet with a big grin and bellowed, "Hell-O! Hoo-ray! The princess is here!"

There stood Trinc at the bottom of the staircase. Wearing a long, light blue, silk evening gown with sleeves, a pearl necklace, and a diamond tiara in swept-back coils of shining hair, she looked as if she had just posed for a portrait by John Singer Sargent. Here was the lovely Lady whom Aeneas had married, but there was a catch: this was Henrietta DeRoman's "little dress," enlarged for the occasion. Trinc was her mother's ghost in the act of making guilty the man who had divorced her.

"Well." Uncle Doc cleared his throat and rubbed hands. "I have my little surprise for you, dear Trinc. Not a hand-me-down. It's brand new . . . Here, my love, open it, please."

Trinc took the box he had given her. "It's heavy," she smiled. "*Dear* Uncle Doc. Sak's Fifth Avenue! . . . Oh! I can't believe it! Is it?" She peeped under the lid, drew back with a gasp. "A mink coat! Thank you, thank you!" With that, she placed the box on the coffee table and went and threw arms around Uncle Doc's neck. "Put it on," he said. "I'm pleased as punch you like it. Of course I had to guess at your size . . ."

Diana ran forward as Trinc lifted the coat from the box. "Can I touch it, Mommy?"

"Stop."

The room grew quiet.

Colonel, who stood in the center of the room, swaying on his feet and perspiring, and chewing an unlit cigar, again commanded everyone: "Stop. You haven't asked me what my gift is."

"Yes?" Trinc was almost trembling.

Removing an envelope from his jacket and waving it at Uncle Doc, Colonel took the cigar from his mouth and struck a pose. "I hold in my hand a legal document," he declared as if addressing a jury. "A piece of paper. A blank piece of paper. But when it is written, signed, and properly witnessed, it will be a legal document, as follows . . . Under terms and conditions thereof, I, Susan Caldwell, née DeRoman, do solemnly swear to have the name of my son, William Knight Caldwell, changed to Gayle DeRoman Caldwell. Under these presents, I, Gayle Thomas DeRoman, Colonel, United States Army, retired, do solemnly swear that upon receipt of a Court Order effecting aforesaid change of names, I shall give Susan Caldwell the sum of $25,000 (twenty-five-thousand dollars). . . Furthermore, if my son and heir, Gayle DeRoman, Jr., should predecease me, Susan Caldwell, and William Knight Caldwell, aforesaid change of given names being effected, I bequeathe to Susan Caldwell, in my Last Will and Testament, my entire estate. To be signed, dated, etcetera . . . My current worth is five million dollars."

Colonel put the cigar in his mouth, found a match, lit it and puffed. Uncle Doc was first to explode. "What kind of a buzzard-pissin' gift is *that*?"

"*El coronel, mi padre!*" Gayle, Jr., saluted the ceiling with highball.

Aeneas looked Colonel in the eye. "Billy's name is his own affair, sir. We don't accept bribes, sir. And I'll thank you not to humiliate my wife."

"Well spoken," Colonel smiled, "but the choice is not yours. It is Trinc's. She makes the choice . . . Billy can call himself Billy. No skin off my nose. But his name shall be mine . . . Trinc? You know it's not my money you want, it's my recognition. When have you, a woman, ever been consulted about what you really want?"

What with all the commotion, Aeneas had hardly glanced at Trinc until now. She was chewing her lower lip and smiling at the same time. "That's right," she said. "When has anyone ever asked me what I really want? It's a principle—choice—and you understand me very well, Father . . ." Her eyes danced. "I understand you even better. You're bluffing. You despise us all, a woman most of all. Very well. I shall call your bluff. I accept."

"You *what*?" Aeneas felt a pain in his scalp.

"I accept."

"This is ridiculous!"

"Don't interfere, Aeneas."

"You don't need his money."

"Oh? The money is part of what we owe you."

"Fetch my coat and hat!" Uncle Doc was shaking his cane at Colonel and heading for the door.

"Don't go, sir," Aeneas tried to protest. "Dinner will be ready soon. Let's all sit down like civilized people."

"Civilized?" Uncle Doc squared his shoulders. "I'm off to Florida where even the alligators are more civilized than you lot.

At least an alligator doesn't bother to invite you to dinner before he eats you alive!" Opening the door, he hobbled out, slamming the door behind him. After getting the old man's Chesterfield and homburg from a closet, Aeneas, too, hurried out.

Jun was holding open the back door of the Lincoln. Seeing Aeneas, he quickly came and took the coat and hat while Uncle Doc turned about and let flaring eyes meet Aeneas's look of dismay. "Don't apologize, Aeneas. It ain't your fault . . . All Trinc ever wanted was to get the attention of that egotist. She wants to strike the father dead." He stooped, sat down. Jun shut the door, ran forward, started the engine. Uncle Doc rolled down his window, gestured to the sky. "Maybe that siren was telling us something. Maybe no one cares anymore who gets hurt."

16

Throstle's Nest

After watching the Lincoln speed out of sight, Aeneas went inside and found everyone where he had left them. Trinc sat stiffly on the divan, mink coat in lap. Colonel stood in the pose of an orator, one hand on the medal of the Legion of Honor on his lapel, the other hand and smoking cigar lifted as if to accept a nation's gratitude for electing him to the S.O.B. Hall of Fame. Gayle, Jr., clutched highball glass with two hands, flushed and blowzy face ablaze.

"You haven't set the table, dear," Trinc said.

In spite of a throbbing headache for the next several hours he acted the part of host. He set the table, served the dinner, replenished cocktails, cleared table, washed and dried dishes, fed Roguey, made turkey sandwiches, wrapped them in wax paper inside the children's lunch boxes and put these in the refrigerator. He reappeared in the living room in time to see Colonel and Gayle, Jr., staggering arm in arm out the front door boozily singing, "Boola boola . . . sarsapa-roola . . . E . . . li . . . Yale!"

"Oh," he said. "Here's your present. Happy birthday, darling."

He took the bottle of Toujours Moi from his tweed jacket and presented it to Trinc with a bow. She *did* seem to glance at him in a certain way. But said, "I've got The Curse. I'm going to bed. Will you please take the steamer trunk back to the attic with you as soon as I've put Mother's gown back in mothballs?" Gathering the folds of the gown, she went upstairs while he put himself to work again, opening windows, vacuuming carpets, dusting furniture and folding the mink coat up in its box. Then he went outdoors.

At last he felt himself again, felt like a seismograph the subterranean movements of his soul. It was about to explode with its invincible affection for freedom. His wish to hallow his whole life with love still restrained the impulse to run away. After a while he went indoors and upstairs to say good-night to the children. Already dressed in pajamas, they were sitting up in their double-decker bunk, listening to their Philco radio from which was coming a familiar voice speaking in sepulchral tones. "Who knows what evil lurks in the hearts of men? The Shaaaadow knooows."

"Call me Shadow," he said. "Goodnight. I love you."

"Dad?"

"Yes, Billy?"

"I just love Uncle Doc."

"So do I, son."

"I feel real sorry for Grandpa Gayle, though."

"Why is that?"

"I dunno. Dad?"

"Uh?"

"Are they really going to change my name?"

"A long, long time ago," Aeneas parried, "when I was living in England, I knew a girl named Pig. Miss Pig. She was very pretty. But she was horribly unhappy because everybody teased her about her name. She made up her mind to marry the first man who proposed to her, so as to change her name to his, and one day along came a chap by the name of Wilfred Arthol. He proposed. She married him and changed her name to Mrs. Arthol. Alas! Now everybody teased her even more unmercifully than before. Why? You see, instead of calling her Mrs. Arthol, they lisped her name and said, 'Mitheth Arthol'. . . It's best not to worry about your name. Just worry about the sort of person you are."

Billy giggled. "Daaad, you said a bad word."

"Don't snigger during a sermon," Aeneas said.

"Why do you sleep in the attic, Dad?"

"Let me ask you a question, Billy. What do cows do on Saturday night?"

"I give up."

"They go to the mooo-vies . . . Don't worry about Grandpa Gayle and Uncle Gayle. Some grownups never grow up."

"Diana is going to marry Uncle Gayle."

"Brat! I am *not!*" Diana's face peered from the upper deck. Her long, combed black hair startled Aeneas. She was almost a young woman. "Brat!" she hissed. "Daddy, tell Billy to stop lying."

"O. K., O. K.," he said. "Sleep tight." He kissed the children, went and dragged the steamer trunk in the hallway up to his attic. Was Uncle Doc right? Was Trinc trying to dominate the fathers? She was playing games, destructive games. Or was she still struggling to assert herself? If that was all there was to it, she had a friend in support—himself. Although it was early for him to try to sleep, he undressed and covered himself with blankets and let his mind go wandering to pick up traces of the old life.

As a young post-doc in New York, celibate as a seminarian, he had attended Mabel Dodge's salons and listened to avant-garde Freudians chat about free love and the defiance of taboo. It had all sounded pretty childish, to make conscience into a kind of tumor that needed to be removed. For when he met a beautiful and witty seventeen-year-old schoolgirl named Trinc and made love with her, he had felt committed as well as liberated. Love made him feel a right and proper part of everything real and good. Now that love was not being made, however, should he be ashamed for remaining faithful to his first and only partner and his wife? His acceptance of exclusion from Trinc's bed certainly made him look a fool, were others to know about it. But it didn't matter what others might think of him as long as he conducted his life according to a code impervious to shame. It was not a Puritan code he lived by, not a code of fear and exclusion . . .

As he peered into the dark a picture came to mind, a picture from England in the early 'twenties. He saw himself in a Cambridge pub near Parker's Piece, saw himself drinking a pint of bitter ale, saw himself seated in a booth with Cousin Tubby Van Dyke and her fiancé, the dapper Trinity don, Playfair. And the voices, he could hear them again, especially the voice of Playfair who was always teaching . . . "It should never be forgotten that St. Augustine, for nine of the most formative years of his life, was a Manichaean and saw life as an eternal battle between the forces of darkness and light. For the Manichaeans, this world was not created by God but by the Prince of Evil. Physical matter was incurably corrupt, though each man had a particle of divine light imprisoned in him. Thus, since procreation merely imprisoned more and more particles of the divine light, it was best to depart this vale of tears as soon as possible and to regard sex as an abomination. In holding explicitly that Adam's sin was carnal, St. Augustine brings to full stature the fear and exclusion of our own origin which have dominated us ever since. That's why, whenever the subject of sex is approached even subconsciously, we exclude certain words, we forbid certain actions, we set ourselves apart from people of other cultures, other races . . ."

And Tubby: "I always thought St. Augustine was a smelly little man, hanging out his laundry for everyone to admire. But how do we get at the light?"

And Playfair, lifting his pint of ale: "Light permeates all. Blake said, 'And we are put on earth a little space that we may learn to bear the beams of love'. Let us not forget that humanity evolves from the same root, and it is not a completely base one, this root of the human animal. I propose a toast. Let us drink to the development out of puritanism toward a higher consciousness of ourselves in relation to all the other selves. Cheers!"

Next day Aeneas had gone to a book shop in Petty Cury, purchased a copy of *Songs of Innocence and Experience*, and immersed himself in reading it as he sat in the Copper Kettle coffee shop on King's Parade. From "The Little Black Boy" he took and memorized a stanza:

> *And we are put on earth a little space*
> *That we may learn to bear the beams of love,*
> *And these black bodies and this sunburnt face*
> *Is but a cloud, and like a shady grove.*

Now in the attic he was thinking, *The body is a cloud. It shades the soul from direct exposure to God. But we must none the less move from innocence to experience and seek true divinity on earth, in human beings, and gradually through compassion we may hope to learn to bear the beams of love. These beams, both exposure to the radiance of the light of truth and the weight of suffering as in the bearing-up of a rood-tree, make us supportive of one another and recall a purposive source, be it God or creative evolution.*

As the picture from the pub faded, Aeneas recalled how Trinc had twice alluded to a debt she owed him because of Grandpa Deck's persecution. Had she married him from an inveterate sense of honor linked with shame, a payback for his wound? He didn't believe that. He couldn't. She had, it was true, loaned Tubby money to be spent on advancing his career at Cambridge. Tubby had revealed the secret. Trinc had, it was true, paid for his cure in Switzerland. Amelia had revealed the secret. But secrets they were, and, if Trinc paid off a debt, she had not only paid it in full but also surrendered hopes of ever seeing him again. She had sacrificed herself for his happiness. So, now, what could he infer? There was a debt, but it was a debt that he owed her, not she, him, a debt whereby he must hold her even while her resentment of his secret and epoch-defining work seemed to be sweeping her from his grasp.

NEXT DAY IN THE OFFICE he continued to pick up traces of the old life.

From the window he could see beyond the granite buildings of the university all the way to the outskirts of a forest where he often walked in spring, delighting in dogwood's white flame, in sudden violets, in listening for whippoorwills. Now that it was winter in the forest, patches of red clay amongst the rolling hills of pine resembled sores on the flanks of some bristlehaired animal. This earth-mood kindled in him a visceral yearning for which the English language had no precise word. *Mi tierra*, the Mexicans called it. My earth, my mother. How he yearned for his *tierra*! How he yearned for Throstle's Nest.

Throstle's Nest! The very name evoked remembered laughter. Ma-Betty had once remarked, "The only thrush I ever saw in those boonies was an oral infection." Apparently the name had been given to the pottery in the Pine Barrens by a homesick English potter in the eighteenth century. Generations of potters, including Calhoun Caldwell, had retained the name just as they retained expressions such as "I'd be pleasured" and "might could." Throstle's Nest! The name conjured up the log cabin where he had spent most of his childhood, the pottery where he had prepared clay and kicked a kick wheel, and the groundhog kiln where he had baked jugs with a glaze called "tobacco-spit brown."

After consulting a calendar, he selected the weekend of December 6 for an expedition to Throstle's Nest. Walking home that night he felt a rush of exhilaration. Everything seemed to beckon him to emerge from self-confinement, the drooping pods of a persimmon tree trembling in the wind, the far-off rumbling of a freight train. Home, he went straight upstairs, knocked on Trinc's bedroom door, entered and began to speak at once.

"You're right. All I do is work. I'm going to camp out in the Pine Barrens for a few days."

A vague shape on the bed responded in a voice that showed she had not been sleeping. "One day you'll come home and find us all gone."

"What do you mean?"

"I mean what I say."

"You'll leave me if I go camping for a few days?" He could hardly believe she was threatening him. Over the years he had sometimes traveled to conferences or visited institutions where the New Physics had taken hold—to Princeton and Columbia, to Chicago and Wisconsin, once to California to inspect Lawrence's cyclotron —but now a camping trip to a place no further from home than a couple of counties constituted desertion. "You know," he said, anger rising, "during the Civil War my Grandma Floride used to cut up sweet potatoes into little squares, dry them, toast them and grind them—to make coffee. She sweetened the stuff with sorghum molasses. My people find a way to live. We don't budge beyond a certain point. If we are threatened, we stand where we are and fight."

The words were no sooner out than he realized his mistake: he had not consulted with her, had not invited her to come along, had not given her a choice. But she had stirred his anger and pride. Even if she went camping with him, he assumed that she with her provincial outlook, whereby anything south of Philadelphia or west of Albany was supposed to be culturally inferior, would disdain the Pine Barrens, a vast gloomy forest of majestic pines, an area where in the old days one could travel from dawn to dusk on a carpet of pine needles, where creeks were named Wet or Greasy or Devil's Gut. He had seen in his youth a bunch of native, salmon-colored orchids of such entrancing beauty that nothing in a Fifth Avenue florist's window could possibly have rivaled them. Trinc would dismiss such evidence of genuine culture, wouldn't she?

He turned to leave.

"Close the door."

Close it yourself.

He closed the door—quietly.

A few days later he set out in the Ford on pilgrimage to Throstle's Nest. He stopped for breakfast at the Carolina Inn in the sleepy college town of Chapel Hill and picked up a pint of Old Crow at an A. B. C. store. Below Chapel Hill a flat country spread out, an ocean of hoar frost atop pines, here and there tiny tin-roofed barns like crystal sailboats. He took a narrow blue road to Pittsboro, then to Carthage, and from there a red clay road wound past clearings for corn, wheat, and tobacco, fence railings laden with vines that would be honeysuckle in summer, a rutted road winding through sheltering woods, glistening thickets in mist and a freshness in the air like beeswax and cedar. Then it was not even a road anymore but a trail of sand full of potholes and rocks like a dry creek bed, and there was such a silence all around him that the rest of the world was but a rumor, a sea in a conch shell. When he emerged from the forest, before him lay the sundappled dingle of his youth, two hundred yards downslope the cabin, shed, and kiln: Throstle's Nest.

He switched off the engine.

Little had changed from what he remembered. Two pickup trucks in front of the cabin had replaced Calhoun's wagons. The bright orange flower pots on the cabin's long porch might well be the very ones Ma-Betty once filled with purple petunias because she wanted a "Japanese" feeling that would blend refined taste into semibarbarous surroundings and, as she said, "bring an individual into harmony with them." Evidently, too, pots were still being made: a wisp of smoke from the chimney of the groundhog kiln indicated a firing. As a boy, he, his parents, and the hired help, when the kiln was fired, had roasted hot dogs on pronged sticks held over the chimney, warmed rolls on the kiln itself, and had a picnic with slaw and cold drinks and wild cherries, these from a pail of freshly picked ones. "Save the cherries for last," Ma-Betty had always said.

Today he would not introduce himself to the new owners. He would save for last the visit, like the cherries, because a returning native would be embraced as someone just naturally better at heart than the rest of mankind! Today he would swim. There was a creek a mile or so back in the woods; in it, a muddy swimming hole, deep and cold. Over the hole Calhoun had attached a rubber tire by rope to a weeping willow, and Aeneas, swinging out on the tire, would release and splash into the water while Calhoun shouted, "Whiskey-Wow-Wow!" That was a good time with Calhoun.

Aeneas reversed the car and parked it in a thicket out of sight from the trail. After collecting his gear, he walked into the woods, feet guided as if by instinct. Twenty minutes later he heard the creek murmuring its reposeful arpeggio. Soon he found the swimming hole. Brown water sparkled as beams of sunlight penetrated thick overhanging branches. Dangled from the willow as if by some imperative resistant to time was the tire. He dropped gear and studied the surface of the water for the ripples of water moccasins. Calhoun had taught him to do that. Everything looked safe. Though the weather was cold, he flung off clothes, walked gingerly on soggy pine needles, climbed on the tire, pushed off from the bank, swung out, out, out—and it seemed he could hear Calhoun shouting, "Whiskey-Wow-Wow!"

Late the next afternoon he drove to Throstle's Nest, pausing to inspect a metal mailbox inscribed in black letters,

Skye

R. R. 74

Rollins, N. C.

Back in the old days mail had been delivered once a week by a mounted courier who stopped at every dwelling-place to exchange gossip and to sample the whiskey. Back in those days, too, a visitor to Throstle's Nest would find himself surrounded by a roiling, yelping mass of hounds named for opera singers like Ruffo and Caruso. He parked the car next to the pickups. No dogs greeted him. On the long porch there was an old woman in a rockingchair. He waved to her. She ignored him. She had a stringless violin tucked under her chin; a bowless right hand rested in her lap. Her neck was encased in delicate lace. She wore a two-piece dress, wrong side outwards, and cotton stockings and low-heeled shoes.

"Afternoon, ma'am."

The old woman lowered the violin and gawked at him with sucked-in mouth and crinkly eyes. "Where is my baby?" she implored. Spotting an undressed rubber doll on the floor next to the rockingchair, he pointed. "That your baby there, ma'am?" Her eyes followed his finger. "Oh," she cooed to the doll. "There you are, Bygie. Thank the gentleman, Bygie."

"My pleasure, ma'am." Aeneas picked up the doll and gave it to the old woman. "Is the man of the house around?"

"He's knee-deep in the radio," the old woman replied. She stuck out a gnarled, skinny, blue-veined hand. "I'm Flora Skye." She had a soft accent and smiled with toothless gums.

He introduced himself and shook her hand lightly. "I used to live here, Miss Flora."

"Well," said Flora matter-of-factly, "you know your way. Just go on in. Archie's in the settin' room. Blevyn's in her room, just a-cryin' her eyes out. There's a pot of hot beans on the hearth. We're fixin' to have rabbit stew this evenin'. Are you previously engaged? What did you say your name was?"

He told her again.

"Caldwell? Are you a game warden?"

"No, ma'am."

Flora's eyes studied him. "If you're a Caldwell, what kind of a Caldwell are you?"

"Seneca River country. Originally. And you, Miss Flora?"

"Columbia."

He nodded. "My grandma was from Columbia. Floride Caldwell. Widow of Horseshoe Robertson Caldwell. Laurel Street."

"Laurel Street Presbyterian?"

"Nome. Marion Street Presbyterian."

"I declare," Flora smiled. "I knew the pastor there when he was a little boy." She raised her voice. "Archibald! Archibald! There's a Ca'lina boy out s'here!" Suddenly she looked at the doll with an expression of utter desolation. "My baby!"

"What is it, Mama?" asked a little old man in coveralls as he pushed open the screen door.

"My baby! He isn't breathing!"

The little old man gave Aeneas a sideways glance. "There, there, Mama," he said soothingly. "Why don't you play your violin for a little bit more?"

"I don't know how to play it no more, Archie."

"Yes, you do, Mama. Just raise it up. The music will come to you by and by . . . Archibald Skye." He held his hand out. Aeneas grasped it, introduced himself. Archie guided him toward the screen door. "My wife used to be a concert violinist. Now she's forgot ever'thing, even what a violin is used for . . . Say, mister. I've been listening to H. V. Kaltenborn. This morning the Japanese bombed Pearl Harbor. Ships burning there. Hickam Field bombed. Lots of casualties. Clark Field, too, in the Philippines. Sounds like another one of them Orson Welles hoaxes. It ain't . . . How be you on, Mr. Caldwell?"

THE NEWS DID INDEED SEEM TOO FANTASTIC to be true. At no time had Aeneas believed the first blow of war against the United States would be struck by Japan. It was, in spite of a decade of ruthless expansion in the Far East, a fairy island on the other side of time. Japanese emissaries were in Washington having talks with President Roosevelt . . . He had followed Archie Skye into the low-ceilinged living room with the wide-board wooden floors. Together they had been sitting in front of a crackling radio. The high-pitched voice of H. V. Kaltenborn began to drone in his ears. He rose and wandered about the room. It was remarkable how little had been changed. Walls of roughhewn logs and plaster, open hearth with pine logs blazing in it, old brasses and lit candles in tall holders on the mantlepiece, split-bottom chairs, one wall devoted to shelves of books and on the top shelf some small, blue-green pots: all save the pots could have come to the Skyes from the old days. The pots were nothing like the crude jugs that Calhoun and his helpers had made. The shapes and glazes had been made by a true artist.

Photographs on the bookshelf drew his close attention. The photo labeled "Bygie, The Citadel, 1895" showed a clean-shaven, bright-eyed young man in military uniform. Another photo showed a silvery-haired middle-aged man, also in uniform, mustache clipped and horned-rim glasses prominent above a proud countenance. Penned on this photo in a flowing hand was an inscription: "Brig. Gen. Hampton Bygie Skye, U. S. A., Bronze Star, Silver Star, Distinguished Service Cross, Philippines campaign, A. E. F. France, Born 1875 Columbia, Died of the Swine Flu, Presidio of San Francisco, 1920, *In Grand Mansions Above.*"

"Sir," Aeneas said, "I reckon I better get going. Pleasured to meet you."

"So soon, Mr. Caldwell? We ain't got the good out of you yet."

"Another time, Mr. Skye."

"Come back tomorrow. We don't have visitors since Flora took sick. It's hard on Blevyn, having to look after a couple of old pigtracks like us . . . See here, mister. The President is addressin' the nation 'long about noon tomorrow. You come on over. Rabbit stew today, squirrel stew tomorra."

Aeneas thanked him. "I told your wife that I used to live here. I hate to put you and Flora . . . and Blevyn . . . to trouble."

"Blevyn's the dearest lady," Archie beamed. "My only grandchild. She's takin' the news real hard, sort of angry and ashamed at the same time on account she's a third-generation Japanese American. She'll feel better tomorra. See you right smart."

As Aeneas turned to leave, a movement at the kitchen door

caught his eye. A lovely young woman of about thirty, wearing denim shirt and handwoven skirt, had emerged from shadows into candlelight in a golden aureole, raven-dark hair loose about shoulders, pale face lifted toward him in blue-eyed gaze. "Professor Caldwell," she said in soft voice, "we're honored by your visit . . . I saw you in *Watch on the Rhine*. Twice," she laughed lightly, blushing.

"My second performances are rarer than my first," he blurted out.

"I heard you in the Chapel, too," she said. "I'm Blevyn."

He felt too shy to shake hands. He lowered his gaze, went to the screen door, and walked out into breathless sunset. He glanced at Flora in the rockingchair, violin tucked under chin, doll at her feet. The beating of his heart told him that he, too, just might be enchanted.

Blevyn was the Lady in the Chapel.

17

Last Pastoral

ONCE AGAIN, though this time in the field of mortals, she had appeared and dissolved the world around him. He felt like a boy again, a boy under a spell, and wanted nothing more than to be with her forever, not in a state of self-satisfied elation but in one of simple adoration. And yet, he admonished himself, nothing must ever come of this infatuation. He was already descending the ladder of life while she was still young. Perhaps with luck the spell would be broken tomorrow according to unwritten rules of the heart.

Upon returning to camp, he built a bonfire, fried up dinner, drank half the bottle of Old Crow and settled into his sleeping bag. With a flashlight he would write Blevyn a little note . . . never to be sent.

Letter from Aeneas Caldwell dated December 7, 1941, to Blevyn Skye

Dear Blevyn,

When I was fourteen and living in your very cabin, I loved a girl like you. I composed a poem about her. It has no merit as poetry, but I'm safe from criticism because you'll never read

The Ballad of Little Lumbee

In Carolina where I was born
By Big Sad River one sunny morn,
The hounddogs barked the moon away,
Whippoorwills sang at break of day,
And my Mammy called me Little Lumbee
Beneath the sighing willow tree,
And the earth was good, the sky so blue,
My heart was light as the world was new.

The woodsmoke curled around the pines,
Pappy got drowned in the fishing lines,
Winter came, the hounddogs died,
No birds sang by the riverside,
But my Mammy called me Little Lumbee
And sang me a song of the willow tree,
We ploughed and reaped till I grew strong
By Big Sad River where I belong.

Then along one day when the corn was high
A lonesome boy chanced to pass me by,
Saying, "Little Lumbee, won't you follow me
Down Big Sad River to the Glory Sea,"
And my Mammy waved from the riverbend,
Disappearing at a rainbow's end,
Her very last words were, "Little Lumbee,
Look in your stocking if he truly loves thee."

The years have slipped beneath the moon,
Days flow down to glory soon,
And every spring with first whippoorwill
I hear the hounddogs barking still,
And I go to bed backwards, look in my shoe,

No sweetheart's hair—no love is true—
And my heart is wasting with a song I know
Of Big Sad River of long ago.

Local folklore has it that after the first whippoorwill you hear in the spring, you should go to bed backwards, take off your left shoe, and inside your stocking you will find the hair of your sweetheart. The Little Lumbee of the ballad longs to return to a childhood when the sadness of life did not come from experience but from the heart of things. As for her name, she is a Lumbee Indian from the Lumbee River over there in Robeson County. Some people believe that the Lumbee mixed with survivors of Sir Walter Raleigh's "lost colonists" from Roanoke Island. The original of my Little Lumbee was proud to claim "first" ancestry among Americans.

Her name was Lillian Brandon Oxendine—Brandy for short. When her family's farm failed during a drought, her father scraped together a living by distilling liquor. They came into the Pine Barrens in the summer of 1904. He was making a brew known as "stumphole."

I had been for some years boarded out at an academy for boys. Our heads, stuffed with Latin, English, Natural Philosophy and the like, were ripe for girls. We knew little about them except what we surmised from books or from observation of farm animals. The only girl at the academy was the sixteen-year-old daughter of the Headmaster. Full-bosomed as a Brobdingnagian, she inspired considerable awe when she appeared at Sunday church services.

One day in the summer of 1904, while I was home on vacation, I had been roaming barefooted in the forest when I came to a clearing and discovered in the middle of it a towering magnolia tree. Its blossoms filled the muggy air with a heady fragrance like musk. Its thick, sagging limbs were as inviting to this boy's heart as the beanstalk was to Jack. I started climbing up. When I was about thirty feet above ground, I heard a voice just above my head.

"Would you like me to hold your hand?" the voice said. "It don't mean a shit hill of beans to me."

This was a Miranda-voice for my Caliban-ears! *The clouds methought would open, and show riches ready to drop upon me.*

I looked up. On a branch above mine some bare feet and skinny brown legs were poking out of a homespun white calico dress. The dress belonged to a divine creature whose long black hair tumbled wantonly over coppery-colored neck and arms. This creature was a Girl. She had quietly alert, snapping black eyes set in a soft round face. From a corner of her mouth dangled a wrapped, smoking leaf. *Had I wak'd, I would have cried to dream again.*

"It don't make a shit hill of beans to me neither," I said pretty gallantly. I extended my hand. Grasping it firmly in her own hand, she hoisted me up to sit beside her on her branch. Before she let my hand go she squeezed it. "I like to hold hands," she said.

"Reckon," I said. She asked my name. I told it to her. "Well, Neas," she said in a most friendly manner, "Brandy. Want some rabbit tobacco? I got lots." With a free hand she passed her cigarette over to me. I took a big puff.

Now, I had never smoked any kind of cigarette before. Smokers at school were expelled. I had only studied the art of smoking from a distance, amongst the farmers. It seemed to me all you had to do was close your eyes, get a good suck, and snatch the cigarette from your lips with a debonair flick of wrist. I did all that. The next thing I knew, I was falling out of the tree. Only, Brandy saved me. Maybe she saw my eyes roll back into my head. She had the presence of mind to throw a hammer lock around my neck, and she was a pretty strong girl for her size. My head cleared. I looked at the ground far below and said, "I usually smoke Bull Durham." I returned her the cigarette, glad I hadn't dropped it. She took an easy drag on it and blew a smokering in my face. "If your eye itches," she said, "you will see the one you love best."

"Honest?"

"I shit you not," she said. "If your nose itches, you will kiss an old person before the end of day."

This was the funniest thing I had ever heard. I laughed so hard I thought I might fall again. I said, "When animals and vegetables are dying, you can cure them by cutting off the head of your best chicken." I said this because I wanted to make Brandy laugh.

"Shoot," she said with a disgusted look, "that's the wastin' sickness." She dropped the cigarette through limbs to the ground. When she glanced at me again, her eyes were snapping. "After the first whippoorwill you hear in the spring," she said, "you got to go to bed backwards, take off your left shoe, and inside the stocking you'll find the hair of your sweetheart."

I pretended I wasn't impressed. "Shoot," I said, "if you spit in your hand and say, 'Spit, Spat, tell me where my true love's at', and you hit the spit in your hand with your middle finger, the spit will fly in the direction of her home."

"Honest?"

"I shit you not," I said. By this time I figured she loved me a whole lot.

"What does your daddy do, Neas?"

"Potter."

"My daddy's a bootlegger," Brandy said. She was proud of her daddy. I could tell by the way she was scrunching up her mouth. "Right now he's making hisself some stumphole."

"Ain't that against the law?"

"It don't mean a shit hill of beans to me," she said.

"Me neither," I said.

She sprang to her feet, leaned into the tree, and began taking things from a hole there, one by one. "Rabbit tobacco. Corn husk. Arrowhead. See? And this s'here is my box of sulphur matches." She put everything back in the hole and sat down. "Know what, Neas?"

"What?"

"If you want to write me a poem or just give me a diamond ring, put 'em in this s'here hole. K?"

"K," I said. "I got a Latin book at home."

She was impressed, I could tell. "Say something in Latin," she said.

"*Omnia Gallia est divisa.*"

"I'm an Indian," she said. For emphasis she nodded her head up and down a couple of times. "Lumbee from Robeson County. Sir Walter Raleigh and Elizabeth Throgmorton, the lady-in-waiting to Queen Elizabeth, they had 'em a love-child. She got lost with the lost colony. She married into a right friendly bunch of Indians. I am d'rectly descended."

I could tell that Brandy had a lot of nobility going for her. It made me feel humble in view of the fact we were going to get married. We sat in the tree for a little while longer and held hands and then we went home. I guess she was living in the woods.

I didn't see her again until church on Sunday.

It was a good three-mile wagon ride to church, the only time of the week when my father was full-sober and high-spirited and singing in his baritone voice. I always enjoyed that ride immensely. We clip-clopped down the trail, and he sang songs with stately words, and vague and beautiful thoughts would form in my mind of Greenland's icy mountains and of every creature, every tribe, on this terrestrial ball.

The church itself was just a gaunt whitewashed structure teetering on brick footers above eroding red clay. On Sundays it came alive. The people seemed, like their clothing, to be made out of some plain, sensible material that would never wear out or change. Pews filled up. An untuned piano would be played with a strong, unwavering beat. Fans fluttered like a regatta of gigantic moths. Everything smelled deeply and thickly of ladies.

That Sunday, after we seated ourselves in our pew, Brandy and Mr. Oxendine sashayed down the aisle and took seats in the pew in front of ours. Mr. Oxendine was a tall, black-haired man with bushy eyebrows and a red, weathered neck above the starched white collar. Brandy wore shiny store-bought shoes and white gloves and a handmade blue silk dress with a narrow white neckline. When she turned her head and smiled at me, I made a little clenched fist to show I was still holding her hand.

Just as service was about to commence along comes this Mr. Jasper, the deacon. He rushed panting up the aisle and stopped where the Oxendines were seated. With a handkerchief he dabbed at beads of sweat on his bald head. His gold-rimmed spectacles slid down his nose. "Folks," he declared with a nervous but sly smile, "you'all'll have to worship back yonder with the Colored. No offense, you pre-chate. It's human nature." When he had finished his speech, Mr. Jasper looked all over the congregation. He wanted us to know he was standing on India's coral strand with instructions from the spacious firmament on high.

There was gasping and murmuration. Fans ceased to flutter. Like everyone else I turned around and had a look-see at the last row of pews, the one reserved for "Colored." It was funny, but I had never thought there was something special about the folks there, just some kindly old people, people who groomed horses and did cooking in the county. Then like everyone else I turned back and watched to see what the Oxendines would do.

He, Mr. Oxendine, stood up slowly, a little quivering smile on his face. Brandy also stood up slowly. She yanked a glove from her right hand, and before Mr. Jasper realized what she was going to do, she hauled off and slapped his face so hard you could hear the THWACK, like a whip being cracked at a mule. Well, his spectacles had been sent skittering across floorboards, and while he was on his knees, groping around to find them, the Oxendines walked slowly down the aisle, past the last row of pews, and out the door. The door was pulled shut, gently.

"You can't boss an Indian," my father said. "There might could be burning crosses."

There was burning all right but not crosses. That day and for three days afterwards I ran to the magnolia tree. Brandy was never there. On the night of the second day, though, the church was burned to the ground.

Of course everybody believed that Mr. Oxendine had done it. But, it turned out, he had been all that night out in the woods serving stumphole to some of our leading citizens, my father among them. Me, I suspected that Mr. Jasper had burned the church down in order to cast suspicion on Mr. Oxendine.

On the third day, the day after the burning, I climbed up in the magnolia tree and took out the treasures Brandy had buried in the hole. Everything but one thing was accounted for: the rabbit tobacco which I now know was a kind of low-grade marijuana that grows wild in the Barrens, the corn husks, an arrowhead. But the box of sulphur matches was missing.

She knew I could be trusted with her secret. There in the treasure hole I found a scrap of paper with a pencilled message for me. "Neas," it read, "remember, I am holding your hand."

I never saw her again. Folks said Mr. Oxendine returned to Robeson County. For the rest of my youth, indeed for the rest of my life, the spirit of Little Lumbee lingers on,

Far on the forest skirts, where none pursue.

That's from a real poem with which I'm sure you're familiar. Mr. Matthew Arnold wrote it.

"**Yesterday, December 7, 1941**—a date which shall live in infamy—the United States of America was suddenly and deliberately attacked by naval and air forces of the empire of Japan . . ."

Flora had served the squirrel stew early so that everyone could listen to the President's broadcast. Aeneas had taken it upon himself to steer clear of the topic of war. He repeated the joke about Throstle's Nest, that the only thrush hereabouts was an oral infection. He remarked upon his finding everything much as he remembered it. To bring Blevyn out, he mentioned the blue-green vases on the bookshelf and learned from Archie that she was making pots as a hobby, using designs based on Ming vases she had seen in the Metropolitan Museum in New York. Aeneas had pushed back his plate with a sigh of contentment. "I'd sure like to kick a kick wheel again," he said. "I can't make a Ming vase, but I can turn out a tolerable mudball." Only then had Blevyn lifted downcast eyes, eyes almost as blue as the sky, and said, "I'll show Professor Caldwell around the pottery shed after the broadcast, if that's all right."

"Are you married, Mr. Caldwell?" Flora piped up. Her purchase on lucidity was something to watch for.

"Now, now, Mama," Archie cautioned as if embarrassed.

"Yes, ma'am." Aeneas tossed hands in air in a time-worn gesture of male horror and defeat. Blevyn, he noted, almost laughed. "Now now, Mama," Archie repeated, "let the man be in peace." Flora leaned over and patted Aeneas on the arm as if to affirm that her geese were always swans.

After looking at his wristwatch Archie had rushed from the dinner table and turned on the radio in the living room. As Flora cleared away dishes, Aeneas's gaze caught Blevyn's. His soul cried out to him. Quickly, he had followed Archie into the other room.

"... The attack yesterday on the Hawaiian Islands has caused severe damage to American naval and military forces. I regret to tell you that very many American lives have been lost ..."

The President's deeply enraged, slightly tremulous voice, its arch and aristocratic intonations in place, struck home to Aeneas's heart. He must go at once to Selective Service in Poe's Hill and volunteer for the Army. Perhaps his old honorable discharge on medical grounds would not be counted against him; with luck, the records were lost. It was disconcerting, though, to listen to the President sounding like a patriarch in a myth. Roosevelt was only eight years older than he.

". . . No matter how long it may take us to overcome this premeditated invasion, the American people, in their righteous might, will win through to absolute victory."

"Yes, sir!" Archie erupted, leaned back in chair, and hooked thumbs in straps of coveralls.

"I ask that the Congress declare that since the unprovoked and dastardly attack by Japan on Sunday, December 7, 1941, a state of war has existed between the United States and the Japanese Empire."

"Archie, turn that radio off."

"It's the Commander-in-Chief, Mama."

Tears glistening on sunken cheeks, Flora walked unsteadily forward. "It ain't going to do you a God's bit of good, Archibald, to listen to that talk. You sent Bygie to the Citadel and made a soldier of him. Where is he now? We got to get down on our knees and bow our heads and pray."

Blevyn went and put her arm around Flora. "Time for your nap now, Grandma. We'll pray together in the bedroom. We'll pray for our American boys . . . Give me your hand." As Blevyn was guiding Flora, the old woman whimpered, "I'll fall," and gave Aeneas a helpless look over her shoulder. "I'll fall!"

"No, you won't fall, Grandma. Hold my hand. Remember, you're holding my hand."

Brandy's words now Blevyn's. Aeneas wondered if the coincidence might be meaningful.

THE POTTERY SHED LOOKED MUCH AS HE REMEMBERED IT: dirt floor, kick wheel installed by the pale light of the single window, board shelves for drying ware, old cast-iron stove. On the shelves, though, there were pots of a new and original kind. Vases, pitchers, bean pots, bowls and crocks, most of them orange-glazed, glistened in the light. A few "Chinese" pots, their fluted edges touched with blue-green glaze, stood out from the rest. All the pots were so simple in effect, so unaffected, so modest in technique, so beautifully shaped for service that he sensed genius in them, like a soul in music.

He asked Blevyn questions in a matter-of-fact manner. Little by little the story of the Skyes began to emerge. Archie had been an insurance agent in Columbia. When he retired, he looked for a place in the country where he and Flora could live quietly and cheaply. Late in the Depression, when the farmer who owned Throstle's Nest declared bankruptcy, Archie learned about the property through a bank in Fayetteville and bought it. Still intact were the remains of a pottery business, and even the antique furniture belonging to previous owners had been left behind. Then Flora became senile. Archie consulted with Minnie Skye, his Japanese American daughter-in-law in Los Angeles, and two years ago she had sent Blevyn to help look after Flora. Although Blevyn had B. A. and M. A. degrees in English from the University of California and had planned to become a schoolteacher, no one would hire a Japanese American. With time on her hands at Throstle's Nest she put the shed and kiln in working order, taught herself pot-making by means of trial and error, and spent one vacation in New York studying vases at the Metropolitan.

"You're an artist," Aeneas said.

"It's just a hobby."

"We're keeping a firm hold on anonymity." Aeneas used a professorial tone he reserved for students lacking in self-confidence. "Perhaps those paranoid idiots in California got you to feeling you don't fit in. Well, that's nonsense . . . I have an idea." He went on to tell her about Ma-Betty's career as an artist, how she and her second husband, Phillips Blumberg, had access to New York galleries and dealers. "Your work might be sold anonymously, Blevyn. May I have your permission to write to my mother about your work?"

"You're very kind, Professor Caldwell," Blevyn said in a voice so shy he wondered whether she would have the guts to grow as an artist. Suddenly her eyes danced and she shook back her hair and laughed, "I want to see *you* work! I'll bet you haven't forgotten anything!"

"You'll lose your money," he said. "I was just a boy."

"You're still a boy!"

"Thanks for that." He moved to the wheel and sat down, tested the lever with foot, massaged hands. "You do realize, Blevyn, that I spend most of my time studying the monotonous green lines on oscilloscopes, calculating on slide rules, and punching keys on adding machines, not to mention talking to students and colleagues about energies, alpha particles, and beta decay?"

"This will be child's play," she said in a teasing tone, "after your cyclotron."

"Ah, Berkeley," he said. She had gone to university there. Of course she would know about Lawrence's cyclotron. "Did you like it at Berkeley?"

"Very much."

"Sometimes I think, Blevyn, I buried myself in the South. Not that I would have been invited to Berkeley."

"You're quite a famous man," she said, apparently without mocking.

He clutched his stomach. "O my *gawd*! The star of *Watch on the Rhine*! Ta-Tah!"

"Don't deprecate yourself, Aeneas."

Aeneas? Professor no more?

"You were wonderful in the play," Blevyn went on. "And you were selected to give the Faculty Sermon. The newspapers spread the word, even down here in Moore County . . . I got in my truck and drove to Poe's Hill to hear you. You were excellent. Everyone was talking about it."

"I saw you in the Chapel," he confessed before considering what he was saying. After a pause, he was clowning again. "Now, maiden, my kingdom for a bit of clay."

"Not a horse?"

"I had a horse once in New Mexico, a half-blind horse named Tiresias."

"And what did he foretell for you?".

"You're good," Aeneas said. When was the last time he had met a student who picked up on literary allusions? "The clay, please."

She went to the old pit in the floor, brought back a chunk of creamy clay mottled with a yellowish-brown iron oxide, and slapped it on the wheel head.

Half an hour later he had erected something tall and coiling with resemblance to the Leaning Tower of Pisa. He threw up slimy hands in surrender. "Think Pisa," he sighed. "Think Galileo. Think Galileo denounced for heresy . . . and I'll ham up a quotation for you! . . . 'Whereas you, Galileo, son of the late Vincenzo Galilei, of Florence, aged seventy years, were denounced in 1615, to this Holy Office, for holding as true a false doctrine taught by many, namely, that the sun is immovable in the center of the world, and that the earth moves' . . . Quaint, don't you think?"

"Quaint."

"'See here, Galileo! With a sincere heart and unfeigned faith, in Our Presence, you abjure, curse, and detest, the said error and heresies' . . . We now declare that this miserable leaning tower" —he flattened the clay with his fist—"fall! Your turn, Blevyn." Was he angry at himself for playing the fool or for exposing his lack of talent?

"Oh, Aeneas, look what you've done!" Blevyn leaned over, touched him on the shoulder. "You're very naughty."

"You value what I disprize? Forgive me." When he turned around he was relieved to see a dimpling of her cheeks. She was not displeased with him, just saddened by him. "My turn," she said. He got up. She took his seat.

From the beginning she transformed his clay. First she mixed it with water. She drew wire through it. She kneaded it, opened it out, pulled it up, widened it, all the time kicking the foot-lever, sometimes dropping her thumbs down to shape the clay to even thickness, sometimes, forefingers atop middle fingers, bringing the vase to an ever more perfect proportion. When the piece was finished, she drew wire under it to loosen it from the wheel head.

"Elegant," he murmured over her warm shoulder.

"Would you like to have it?"

"I'd love to have it. Thanks!"

"I'll fire the kiln and send the vase parcel post in a couple of days."

"I'll leave you my home address. My *university* address," he corrected. "I'll loan the vase to my mother. If you give me your address, she will be writing to you."

"Thank you."

"Thank *you*." Aeneas moved to the window so that she couldn't see the tears. He really was still a boy, so impulsive and undisciplined, so easily touched by kindness. As once with Brandy, so now with Blevyn. He must never see her again. "All I can give you in return," he said, making it sound light, "is an old magnolia tree. That is, if you'd like to take a walk?"

"I'll put on a sweater and tell Archie." She sounded enthusiastic.

When they set out some minutes later, the afternoon sun was winter-low, filtered through pines. A chilling wind scattered leaves before their feet. At first he walked in front of Blevyn, conscious of keeping a distance. After a while they began to walk side by side, stride for stride, pausing now and then to watch squirrels chasing up and down trunks. Once they passed a roundeyed raccoon who studied them superciliously as if with a lorgnette before slinking off to its opera.

"He thinks we're beneath him," Blevyn laughed.

She reads my thoughts.

"By the way," he asked, "who bags the squirrels and rabbits that Flora makes into stew? Do you hunt, too?"

"Not I. She does it all. She can nail a rabbit's rump at three hundred feet. That is, unless she suddenly forgets what the gun is for." There was a pause. "I apologize about Flora," she said.

"Whatever for? I should apologize. I can't restrain myself from smiling when she forgets what a violin is or thinks her doll has stopped breathing."

"I don't mean," Blevyn pressed, "when she's a helpless baby. I mean, when she asked you if you are married. It's none of her business. Any man who comes to the house, though, like the game warden, she'll ask him the same question. She's like those religious types who stop you in the street and ask if you're saved. We have to be saved."

"Marriage is salvation?"

"Don't be silly."

Aeneas stopped walking. "I have nothing to hide. Things may be headed for a dead end. My wife is seeking a self-fulfillment that leaves me stranded. I can't say I blame her."

"Don't you think a wife should devote herself to her husband's happiness?"

"I used to think that," Aeneas said. "Now I think a woman's independence is too dearly earned to be surrendered to a man. I've been thinking lately: in love there is no superiority."

"I like that," Blevyn said. They resumed the walk. "I was married."

"Was?"

"He was killed."

"I'm sorry."

"I'm sorry, too. I'm sorry Hank was killed. I'm not sorry that the marriage ended. I was trapped. When he died, I was free to grow."

"Growth is hard," Aeneas said. "Let's find the tree."

They broke through prickly underbrush, weeds and wild pea-vines. Here and there he saw scatterings of mast of a kind once fed to razorback hogs. He wondered if he'd strayed off course. Soon the woods looked familiar. He recognized the old glade up ahead. Presently they stood under the magnolia tree. It was not as towering as he remembered it as being, but it still concealed mystery in its deep shade. "It's so beautiful!" Blevyn exclaimed.

"Hang on," he said. He removed his leather jacket, boots and socks, ducked under branches, and began to climb. When he finally stood upon Brandy's branch, he leaned into the trunk and stuck his hand into the old treasure hole. A mushy ooze of decayed stuff resisted his probing until he felt a prick, closed fingers, took out an object. He climbed down and held out to her in the palm of his hand a small chipped flintstone. "It's an arrowhead. It's for you." Just then a whir and whiz of birdwings above alerted him to the sky. Dusk was gathering. He sat on the ground, put socks and boots back on, stood up and grabbed jacket. "Let's go."

He had successfully resisted the impulse to hold her by the hand.

By the time they got back to the cabin a black and moonless night had closed in. A fog swirled in the air and in his heart. He dreaded the return trip to Poe's Hill. He felt sick with desire for a new—but impossible—life.

Candles were lit, the fire blazed, shadows played on walls. Archie and Flora were seated by the fireplace. Aeneas went and thanked them. "Don't get up. I want to remember you like this." Blevyn was standing by the bookshelves. Giving himself time for one last look, he said to himself *Yes her eyes are as blue as the sky*, and, aloud to her, "Good-bye."

Then he heard a noise like that of an oil drum overturned. The noise came from outside the back door in the kitchen.

"Archibald?" Flora was looking up from her knitting, eyebrows wrinkled. "I heard something. Sounds like them raccoons got into the garbage."

"Now, now, Mama. That happened a long time ago."

There were pounding knocks on the front and back doors. "Open up!" came a man's voice. "Special agents of the Federal Bureau of Investigation!" The pounding continued. "F. B. I.! Open up!"

Aeneas looked at Archie. "I'll get it," he said. "You get the back door."

When he opened the front door, he saw three tall men wearing double-breasted suits and snapbrim hats. They bore the stamp of law officers all right. "What's the problem?" The agents brushed him aside and entered; a fourth agent was following Archie in from the kitchen. At a nod from an agent with Viking eyes, two agents began ransacking the living room, sweeping books off shelves, pulling papers and what-nots from chests, drawers, and a closet. The fourth agent, who was chewing gum with his mouth open, went and glared at Blevyn, his arms akimbo. Viking Eyes finally spoke. "We have a Presidential warrant for the arrest of Mrs. Henry Hayakawa. Are you Mrs. Hayakawa?" He directed his steely glance at Blevyn.

"I am Blevyn Skye," she said evenly. She stood a foot shorter than Chews Gum with Mouth Open. "I was married to Henry Hayakawa."

"Her husband was killed," Aeneas said. Chews Gum with Mouth Open approached him and said, "Is that your vehicle outside, black '37 Ford sedan, N. C. license—"

"You get out of my house," Archie said in a trembling voice to Viking Eyes. "Blevyn's father was a brigadier general of the United States Army. There ain't no such thing as a goddamned Presidential warrant."

"Danger to the public peace and safety of the United States," Viking Eyes intoned. "Found anything?" He glanced at an agent just coming from the direction of the bedrooms. The agent held up a small Kodak camera. "We have contraband," said Viking Eyes. "Any pictures of the Emperor?"

"Negative."

Chews Gum with Mouth Open spun Aeneas around. "Put your hands over your head! Move!" Hands roughly patted Aeneas down. He could feel his wallet being removed from pants pocket. "You can turn around . . . Aeneas Caldwell?" Aeneas lowered arms, turned around. Chews Gum with Mouth Open handed him back the wallet. "Fraternizing with an enemy alien," he said.

"Let's move!" Viking Eyes shouted.

Blevyn's wrists had been handcuffed behind her back.

"Where are you taking her?" Aeneas's cry erupted when Blevyn threw him a terrified glance over her shoulder. The agent shoved her out the door. "Blevyn! I'll get you out of this, I swear! I'll—" A thought came to his whirling mind: Stimson, Uncle Doc's Stimson. "I'm calling the Secretary of War. Don't worry. Blevyn!" He ran onto the porch just as she was being shoved into a waiting car. Headlamps were switched on.

Viking Eyes came up from the parked car. "We don't like this any more than you do, Mr. Caldwell," he said in an unexpected professional tone. "German U-boats in coastal waters." He leaned in, lowered his voice. "Federal Building, Poe's Hill. Your I. D. will be checked. If you're clean, we'll call you." He strode to the waiting car, climbed in, slammed door. Started, reversed, braked, spun forward and around, the car cafroomed into the night.

18

Blevyn

"A MISTAKEN MARRIAGE EXPRESSES A NEED."

Thus Archie. Although Aeneas was accustomed to hearing sententious academicians moralize about topics as if they knew all the answers, he respected Archie, the retired insurance agent, for good sense based upon a long experience of human affairs. He had accordingly been listening intently for the past hour. It had taken them a while to tidy up the mess left behind by the F. B. I. agents. Archie tucked Flora into bed with her doll. Finally the two men had settled down in front of the fireplace, the rest of Aeneas's pint of Old Crow poured in two glasses. The question of Blevyn's marriage to Hank Hayakawa had been raised.

"It might be a need," Archie went on, "to be dominated or to be free, all forms of slavery. People who think they are free from society turn out to be free only to be themselves. That's a kind of slavery, too. What Blevyn needed from Hank Hayakawa was something he couldn't give her: Japanese-ness. She wanted to discover and to reconcile her dual heritage. She discovered she isn't Japanese."

"Third generation?" Aeneas offered.

"Something more," Archie nodded. "Because of this mixture, a rare one, between a second-generation Japanese American mother and a Euro-American father. Minnie, her mother, deliberately neglected to introduce Blevyn to the old language, the old customs, not from disrespect but from the practical standpoint of raisin' the child in the homogeneous American way. As often happens when you deny something to a child, she craves it. The story really begins with Tanaka."

"Who was?"

"Her grandfather." Archie paused to sip his whiskey. "From photographs he had the look of a samurai, a jet crew-cut settin' off a fair complexion as he stands straight as a bamboo tree and stares at the world with large, lustrous dark eyes. He had heard that residence in the States would allow him to escape conscription into Japan's military service. He wanted to come here, only it was almost impossible to obtain permission to travel. Somehow he ingratiated himself with U. S. naval cadets in Yokahama. In gratitude they smuggled him aboard their ship and brought him to Seattle in 1875, or thereabouts. What did he find? Stoop labor and hatred. The stoop labor, he didn't much mind. The skimpy wages were a darn sight more than what he had been accustomed to earn. He never intended to stay, anyway. He worked hard, saved his money, stashed it in a bank, later transferred it to the Furuya Bank in Seattle. The hatred, though, was a shock. There was lots of anti-Japanese feeling on the West Coast, then as now. Tanaka was routinely insulted, called 'yellow belly' and the like. He had trusted *hakujin*, white people. They treated him like the scum of the earth. But he stayed on. Then according to custom his parents arranged a marriage for him and sent him a Japanese bride.'

"Sir, a good Japanese wife is supposed to be quiet, reserved, somewhat subservient. Tanaka's wife was good all right. She had sass, too. I'm coming to that . . . Tanaka's wife married him out of duty, not of love in our sense. She dutifully gave birth to a most beautiful daughter, our Minnie. The thing was, Tanaka was strictly a man of tradition, a kind of feudal lord in family affairs, and he had an old debt to pay off to a friend in Japan, a debt he couldn't pay off except in one way: to give Minnie to his friend."

"Give?" Aeneas queried. "As a bride? A mistress? A member of the family?"

"The latter," Archie replied. "It was honorable. So when Minnie was sixteen-years-old, Tanaka sent her with her mother back to Japan. But without telling them what lay in store for the girl. They believed they were just taking a vacation. Only when they arrived in Japan did they learn of the arrangement. As Tanaka's friend and his parents were on hand to enforce it, Minnie had no choice but to stay. Tanaka's wife was so infuriated by his deceptiveness, she decided to remain in Japan. She never returned to the United States.'

"A couple of years went by. Although Minnie learned to speak and read some Japanese, she was already, so to say, an American. She realized she would never fit in over there. She started thinking how to escape. Tanaka, she remembered, had been smuggled out on an American vessel . . . Well, Minnie knew that visiting Americans liked to be entertained by *geishas*—girls trained to provide singing, dancing, and amusing conversation. Her English could be a great asset if she became a *geisha*. She persuaded her mother and Tanaka's friend to set her up in that line of work. In 1899, when she was twenty years old, her opportunity to escape arrived.'

"One of our naval vessels was bringing soldiers home from the Philippines campaign. It put into port. My son, then Lieutenant Hampton Bygie Skye, was one of the officers. They went ashore, went to a teahouse. Who should come along but the prettiest gal Bygie had ever seen—Minnie! She slips him a note which reads, 'I am not a Japanese *geisha*. I am an American citizen born in Seattle and being held in Japan against my will. Please help me to return to the United States'. Well, Bygie was a chivalrous Southern boy from the top of his head to the bottom of his shoes, and he could get what he wanted from superior officers on the warship. He looks at Minnie, meaningfully nods his head, and whispers in her ear. The next evening he and his fellow officers return to the teahouse. With them they bring a sailor's outfit and a box of Red Cross bandages. You see, as soon as Minnie has given her performance and is alone, she discards her costume, shears off most of her hair, dons the sailor suit and wraps her face and hands in the bandages! That evening all anybody sees down at dockside is a bunch of boisterous American boys holdin' up a considerably beaten-up sailorboy who is seemingly very drunk and full of American cuss words.'

"Bygie and Minnie stopped over in Honolulu and got married. It was a good marriage and a popular one. Minnie always helped Bygie to advance his career wherever they went. They went everywhere, one post after another, one promotion after another. He was already a major in artillery by the time they settled for a while at a camp near Columbia. We learned to know and love Minnie at that time. We were present when Blevyn was born in 1911. She's really a Southern belle, bred in the bone . . . Curious about her name?"

"I was going to ask," Aeneas said.

"It's Welsh. We Scotch-Irish folks have a soft spot for the Welsh. They're fiercely independent and they love their language and they think people who try to subdue them are just pigtracks . . . I'm not worried about Blevyn's arrest. The Welsh name rubbed off on her. She can take whatever's dished out. Besides, her only crime is that bad marriage."

The fire had warmed Aeneas's glass. He finished the drink, put the glass down. "Crime? Was Hank Hayakawa identified as some sort of threat? Did he have a record? Or was the Japanese name sufficient to put the F. B. I. on his tail?"

"We never knew much about Hank." Archie's face was clouding over. "He was political. Joined the Communist Party. That got him into trouble . . . We'll talk about Hank right smart.'

"Blevyn was still a little girl when Bygie died of the swine flu in San Francisco. She had hardly known her daddy. He'd been in France during the Great War. He was home only a couple years before he passed away. It was tough on the ladies. Minnie moved into a Japanese section of Los Angeles. She sent Blevyn to a non-Japanese school. The boys and girls Blevyn went swimming and dancing with, went to big-band dances with and picnics, they were none of them Japanese. So you have to imagine what it was like when one day old Tanaka turned up on Minnie's doorstep. He was dying of lung disease. Although Minnie had a grudge on him, she took him in. All those years, you see, he'd been living alone, wandering around the West, stamping ballast and maintaining rails, digging in the mines, doing blast-furnace work ten hours a day for two-bucks-fifty a day. As the man says, 'Home is the place where, when you have to go there, they have to take you in'. Minnie did that. Blevyn adored the old rogue. She adored him because he was so totally a stranger. She adored him because of the way he sustained a love for life in spite of adversity. She adored him for what she thought he represented, the working classes. He was to her a hero. Now comes the Hank Hayakawa part.'

"When Blevyn was eighteen she matriculated at California. That was in 1929. She graduated in 1933 and studied for another two years to complete her Master's and prepare herself for a career as schoolteacher. She was going to teach English and Art. You didn't know that, did you, unless she told you? She was also training as an artist. Watercolors . . . Anyway, in the spring of '35 she met Hank Hayakawa. He was a *Nisei*, a second-generation Japanese American from, I think, Sacramento, older than she and supposed to be finishing up a degree in engineering. He spent most of his time makin' speeches at rallies on behalf of the downtrodden masses, mimeographin' pamphlets that called for people to strike against the bosses: all that heady stuff. He had a chip on his shoulder bigger than the Golden Gate Bridge. To Blevyn, though, he was just an idealist. She eloped with the son of a bitch.'

"How could she have known that he was a gambler and a con, a little dictator with a violent temper? What did he see in her? An adoring female. A woman with money of her own. They got married. She managed to finish her degree. It wasn't long before he was stealing money from her. Soon he was slammin' her up against walls, batterin' her black and blue, threatenin' to kill her if she doesn't do exactly what he says. She stuck with him for two years. One day he disappeared from their Berkeley apartment. Later she learned he had hired on to work on the Parker Dam in Arizona. There was trouble there, just as there had been trouble during the construction of Boulder Dam where there were 70,000 violations of the eight-hour workday law. Hank organized protests. One day his body was found near a high-voltage power line. Electrocuted hisself, they said. That's pigtracks, of course.'

"Yes, sir, she had some money of her own. I neglected to mention, it came from old Tanaka. It happened this way. Here was the old rogue at Minnie's L. A. home, and ever'one thinks he ain't worth a plug nickel. Unknown to family he had hoarded his savings with the Furuya Bank in Seattle. Of course it went bust later in the Depression, but in the 'twenties Tanaka had about $30,000 there. Just before he died he transferred all of it to a L. A. bank—in Blevyn's name. That's how-come she had some little support to put her through college and later to keep her afloat when she was denied school employment on account of her ancestry.'

"Let me tell you, Aeneas. I'm as ready as the next man to avenge Pearl Harbor. There might could be a few disloyal Japanese on the West Coast. We're 3,000 miles from there. We're so far out in the woods you have to catch people to put shoes on 'em. To have our government following Blevyn's every move and busting in here with the half-assed idea she's an enemy alien is about as shameful as it gets."

Rising from his chair, Aeneas went to the bookshelf and picked up the broken framed photograph of Brigadier General Hampton Bygie Skye. "I wish I had known your son in France, sir," he said.

"He would have been pleasured to know you, sir," said Archie.

Letter from Aeneas Caldwell dated December 10, 1941, to Blevyn Skye

Dear Blevyn:

Every day now I spend much of my time at home waiting for a call from the Federal Building announcing your release from detention. I did put in a call to a friend in West Palm Beach. He has promised to send a telegram on your behalf to Secretary of War Stimson. He warns me not to expect quick results. Yesterday I joined a long queue at Selective Service. They told me bluntly I'm too old to enlist. I went to university, handed out my exams. About half of my students were absent. They are "joining up," I was informed.

Returning from Throstle's Nest the other night I found awaiting me an empty house. My wife, Trinc, and kids were gone, leaving me Roguey, a very anxious cocker spaniel. He had food and water for a couple of days. On the kitchen table I found a note from Trinc, dated the sixth.

She wants the children to appreciate "culture." First she is taking them to visit the Heartwell estates in Connecticut. Then she plans to rent an apartment in New York. The children will be enrolled in private, same-sex schools. She herself will be taking a "refresher course" in nursing and hopes to become a nurse in the Public Health Service. She says nothing about a separation leading to divorce.

Archie said something cogent to me: people who think they are free turn out only to be free to be themselves. It's just as much a form of slavery as to be locked-in to social conformity. I wish Trinc well in her quest for freedom. But she has earned my contempt. For that, I have to struggle with my pride. Perhaps the opposite of love is not hate but grief, a bereavement of the soul when a commitment rooted in old affection and long companionship is tossed aside, like a Kleenex.

They are surprised she speaks English so well and has degrees in English literature. They are surprised she cannot read, write, or speak Japanese. They are surprised she hasn't been to Japan or attended Japanese schools. They are surprised she is a baptized Christian and not a "disloyal" Buddhist.

They have mugged and fingerprinted her, put her in solitary confinement, and prohibited her from speaking to an attorney or from informing anyone where she is. They have interrogated her for days without discovering anything more incriminating than her marriage to a Nisei and a Communist. Most of all they are surprised that she doesn't look like an "enemy alien." One agent, while studying her body in a kind of patronizing smugness, confesses that her blue eyes astonish him and that he didn't expect her to be dressed western-style in a cashmere sweater, Levi's, cotton socks and tennis shoes.

What do they expect her to look like? A bride with face plastered white with rice powder? What do they expect her to wear? A blue silk kimono and scarlet cork-soled slippers? Whom is she expected to marry? A 300-pound sumo wrestler procured by a *baishaku-min*, a go-between?

In her cell late at night, amidst the clanking of steel doors and the sporadic caterwauling of invisible prisoners, she remembers old Tanaka's coming, dying, to L. A., old Tanaka, his face a mass of wrinkles, his arms and legs shriveled up, his lungs toasted by the effluvium of blast furnaces, his teeth missing or broken. She hears old Tanaka's voice talking the stories that Minnie translates. In the depths of old Tanaka's incomprehensible voice there is a collective voice, the voice of people who have spilled ashore like silkworms, bringing old codes. Now and then old Tanaka's English peeks through the gibberish, *oh lie* for all right, *sun kyu* for thank you. He repeats a phrase, *sonna koto wo shitara haji wo kaku*, translated as "Such actions will cause disgrace." The phrase resonates in the history of pride, graceful, austere, defiant and aloof, a wailing music attuned, though faintly, to her blood.

Minnie, to please old Tanaka, puts on a purple kimono patterned with golden chrysanthemums, a costume that sixteen-year-old Blevyn has never seen her wear before. The long length of Minnie's black hair has been coiled into a low thick bun at the nape of the neck, a coiffure Blevyn has never seen her exhibit before, and there is food she has not often eaten before, served in hand-painted, red-lacquered bowls. There are buckwheat noodles floating in chicken broth; there are bamboo shoots and kelp neatly rolled and tied and spicily flavored shrimp and salted herring roe soaked in soy sauce and vinegar-flavored rice wrapped like a jelly roll in sheets of seaweed.

"Would you like some fried soybean cake, Grandpa?" she asks, showing him the cake.

"*Sah.*" Meaning *please.* "*Sun kyu.*"

Their home is near Fifth Street east of Main. At dawn great trucks pour in from the Imperial Valley, from Riverside, and from the San Fernando Valley. Fresh fruits and vegetables are unloaded in the block-square Japanese wholesale market. The produce is artistically displayed.

Blevyn is not confined to a neighborhood. A bountiful land spreads out from L. A. in all directions in the clear, clean air. Beyond the vast flowering orange groves stretching eastward to San Bernardino, snow-capped mountains rise, inspiring her earliest paintings. The Yellow Car streetcar system at five cents a ride threads through the city, its passengers jabbering in tongues from a parliament of nations and races, sudden bursts of laughter or mortified mutterings mingled under a common sky.

Old Tanaka, too, is happy. Would he have preferred to return to Japan? Minnie asks. He shakes his head, grins toothlessly, "*Oh lie.*" With a shrug he says something that sounds like *shikata ga nai.* Minnie translates: "It could not be helped."

Viking Eyes called Aeneas at ten o'clock on the morning of the twelfth of December. Mrs. Hayakawa would be released at eleven o'clock.

A cold sleety drizzle was falling in downtown Poe's Hill. Salvation Army Santa Clauses were ringing bells with forlorn intensity. Christmas shoppers struggled to keep their umbrellas from collapsing in the wind. Here and there in the entrances to department stores bedraggled soldiers lit cigarettes in cupped hands and gawked at girls passing by.

Aeneas parked in front of the Federal Building at eleven sharp. The granite stones and iron-barred windows of the four-story building added their ominous touch to foul weather. Even the swoop and flutter of pigeons from rooftop to pavement and back were woebegone. No one could be seen going in or out of the revolving doors. He hopped out of the car and ran toward them, and just then one of them moved counter-clockwise. It was she, not seeing him as she bent head and folded arms in the cold.

"Hi." He rushed up to her. Her mouth parted in surprise before she gave him a small smile of recognition and brushed a strand of wet hair from her brow. "Hi," she said.

"Didn't they tell you to expect me?"

She shook her head. "They told me only half an hour ago they were letting me go. They didn't say anyone was meeting me. I wasn't allowed to call a cab . . . Thank you."

He took off his leather jacket and wrapped it around her shoulders. In her hand she held the Kodak, the famous contraband. "Take pictures during your vacation?"

"Lots," she deadpanned. "Lovely ceilings."

"You 0. K.?"

"Sure. And you?"

"Fine."

"Isn't this great!?" She lifted face, shut eyes.

"Liberty?"

"No, silly, the rain." She popped her eyes open, grinned on some self-command to guard her feelings.

"We aim to please," he said. "Let's dash for the car before our clothes begin to smell like ice cream sundaes made from mothballs." She slipped her arm under his arm as they walked rapidly. When they were seated in the car, she shook back her hair. "Did you say ice cream sundaes?"

"I said ice cream sundaes."

Blevyn heaved a big sigh. "I've been dreaming of hot fudge sundaes and banana splits. And a hot bath with perfumed soap. And new clothes. And the movies . . . A few nights in the calaboose and you discover things about yourself of great social import. For instance, all you need is ice cream, a bath, new clothes and make-believe. Don't you think, Aeneas?"

"I've never been in the calaboose. Your philosophy is a true danger to the public peace and safety of the United States. Walgreen's?"

"Walgreen's will be perfect."

"Blast!"

"What is it?"

"Where can I get you a hot bath? We could drive to my home. It's empty. But." He stopped, face hot. "Excuse me."

"No problem," she said. "I have a charge account at the Bright Leaf Hotel. I stay there when I'm in town. I'll just get a cut-rate room for an hour . . . Empty?"

"Slip of the tongue."

"No. Tell me."

"She packed up and left before I returned from Throstle's Nest. Took the kids to live with her in New York. No indication when she's coming back . . . What about your new clothes?"

"I have a charge account at Bell's. You're talking about your wife?"

He ignored the question. "Are we going to the movies? Do you have a charge account at the movies?"

"Goody," she said.

"Rialto, Criterion, Carolina or Bijou. Your pick."

"What's playing?"

"I'll buy a paper . . . Banana split with hot fudge, nuts, and a cherry on top? Save the cherry for last."

"My treat," Blevyn said.

"No way," he smiled. "They kidnapped you without your purse, don't you remember?"

"They didn't get my mad money."

"What's mad money?"

She pulled a ten-dollar bill out from under her sweater. "Mad money," she said. "It's money you take on a date in case the guy is a jerk. If you get mad at him, you have to find your way home without humiliation."

"Ah," he said. "Apart from a couple of dances at college, I never had a date. You'll have to bring me up to snuff on the procedures."

"You're doing fine," Blevyn said. "Start the engine."

WHEN THE LADY IN THE CHAPEL was only a projection of his poetic soul, unattainable and divine, he had been able to pour out to her with utter sincerity all his feelings of tenderness and desire, provided that she didn't manifest herself as someone real, in which event he knew he would be scared to death of her. But now that she was real or at least seemed to be real—for his desire for Blevyn Skye made reality and appearance more or less indistinguishable—love and fear were mingling with an awful intensity. One moment he wanted to throw caution to the winds and declare himself her devoted slave for life, whatever the consequences, and the next moment he wanted time and distance and clarity. Were he only in love with love, and not with her, he still had the sense to perceive his folly. But he cared for her, felt compassion for her, liked her, wanted to be her friend. It seemed only reasonable that he should try to control his desires. The most effective method that he knew for doing that was to talk about physics.

Her mouth was rather wonderfully crammed with bananas

and ice cream. The counter stools at Walgreen's drug store were rather wonderfully designed so that, whenever he caught himself in too prolonged an interest in her body, he had but to swivel himself around and watch the fountain-girl scooping ice cream for other customers, to cool the chain reaction.

"In quantum reality," he heard himself saying, "we do not inhabit a universe of subjects and objects. Common sense insists that we do. Common sense also insists that Time is real and has causes and effects. Let us suppose, though, that everything is connected. In that case Time does not exist in our usual sense, and the causes of things are not, as Newton believed, mechanical."

"The causes of things," Blevyn said, her mouth full, "must lie outside our observations."

He looked at her in wonderment. Why wasn't she bored? "Excellent," he said. "Except that I wouldn't say 'outside' but 'in the background'—an order behind appearances. For example, how does one person in one place communicate simultaneously with another person in another place? How does one person in one place have simultaneous knowledge of an event in another place without prior information about such an event? A coincidence that has meaning but no apparent cause would be timeless. Right? Such meaningful coincidences happen to people all the time. My wife, for instance, was living in Connecticut at a time when I was in New Mexico. Evidently at the very moment when I was being assaulted by a gang of thugs she envisioned the event. Terrifying, right? But if we accept the miraculous at face value, for the sake of argument, why not take a mental leap and propose a 'mind' in all things? In other words, everything in man and nature has a spiritual as well as a physical being. What we call the miraculous is then really built into the structure of the universe." He swiveled around to look at Blevyn. He swiveled around to look at the fountain-girl. "What do you think?" He swiveled around to look at Blevyn.

"I think," she said after wiping her mouth with a paper napkin, "that it isn't always mere coincidence when a man and a woman or close relatives experience things simultaneously. Even strangers from opposite ends of the earth may be connected in ways we don't know about."

"Mystical," Aeneas said without looking at her. "And mysticism is a dirty word to most scientists. Mind you, I was never top of my class in anything."

"Remember what Dostoevsky said about his hero, Alyosha? 'He was always one of the best in the class but was never first'."

Aeneas took a quick look. She was smiling, warmly. He said, "Were you never first, too?"

She clapped a hand over mouth. "Oh!" she exclaimed, "I was always first!"

"A woman who has body and sex and mind and heart and talent and a sense of humor frightens the pluperfect daylights out of most men."

"Do I frighten you?" Why was she leaning on her elbow on the counter, her breasts unsloped in the cashmere?

"You scare me to death," he said.

Even he laughed.

When she finished her banana split, they crossed the street to Bell's department store. Rain stung their faces. The *beep-beep* of cars mingled with the *tinkle-tinkle* of Salvation Army Santa Claus bells.

For once, the perfumed air of the store acted on his nerves as an aphrodisiac. Shopping with Trinc had been an ordeal. She bought cheap, inferior goods as if to remind him that she was forcing herself to live on his small income. Ironically, now that she was footing her own bills, she would probably become extravagant and enjoy herself—exactly what he wanted. But why blame her for his own faults? One look in the mirror over the perfume counter informed him that, because of the rain, he'd been wearing Calhoun's battered old hat. He hadn't remembered to tip his hat to Blevyn at the Federal Building, and he hadn't removed it at Walgreen's. He reached a sudden resolve, took off the hat, and showed it to Blevyn. "See this? It was my father's. I wore it at Harvard. I took it to Europe. I've been plunking it on my head for decades. I don't need this hat. I refuse to be haunted by my father. I'm not Henry Fonda in *The Grapes of Wrath*. It looks like the bleached and speckled underbelly of a drowned mouse. I shall wear no hat in future. While you are in the ladies' department, I shall be in the men's department getting myself transformed from a rumpled professor to Joltin' Joe Dimaggio. I shall blow us to the purchase of an umbrella."

"Not, I hope," Blevyn said, "a Madama Butterfly parasol?"

"If I can start a new life," he said, "so can you."

An hour later he was wearing a dark blue double-breasted suit, a pink button-down oxford-weave shirt with silver cufflinks, a red silk necktie and stiff new shoes, brown. An English "brolly" was in one hand, a box with the old clothes in the other. He had left his father's hat with the sales clerk with instructions to give it a decent burial. He went to find Blevyn in the ladies' department. She was having her purchases boxed.

"Get a load of this," he said. "Wall Street tycoon? Duke of Windsor? or just a gigolo?"

"Handsome," she said.

Under the umbrella they walked to the Bright Leaf Hotel. When she disappeared in an elevator, he sat in the lobby for an hour and read newspapers. A glass chandelier cast a pale light over tile floors and brass spittoons. Groups of men talked excitedly as if they had received shots of a mind-altering drug. The war? The stock market? The weather? Duke's Rose Bowl-bound football team? Whatever it was the men were discussing, he himself felt as if he were observing the passing parade with the serenity of a bodhisattva. He was flowing in the stream of a new life. Whatever happened, let it happen. When Blevyn emerged from an elevator, followed by a redcap with boxes, she stunned him, so radiant she appeared in clothes of elegant simplicity. The ankle-length dress was a robin's egg-blue, worn just off-shoulder. A pearl necklace at the throat. White kid gloves.

On her arm a tweed overcoat. Her hair full and soft and dark, make-up almost imperceptible in the fresh blush of cheeks.

"Lovely," he said, standing up and clearing throat. "I've been studying the paper. We have Gary Cooper in *Sergeant York*, Irene Dunne and Cary Grant in *My Favorite Wife*, and a Welsh mining saga called *How Green Was My Valley*."

"Wouldn't you like to see *Sergeant York*?"

"I hope I never again see a German machine-gunner at the moment when he realizes he's going to be shot."

"*My Favorite Wife*?"

"There's something off-putting about that word 'wife'."

"That leaves *How Green Was My Valley*," she said. "Coal-mining stories are my passion."

"My treat. 50¢," he said. "You may need your mad money."

"I'm having fun," she said.

He helped her put on the overcoat. Just then he recognized a man who was entering the lobby from the street and folding an umbrella. "Don't look now," he whispered aside to Blevyn, "but there's a college administrator heading our way. He will smile and speak heartily but, if you listen carefully, you'll hear a sound like something being strained through a sieve. That's the knife he is sharpening in order to stab you in the back . . ." Aeneas squared shoulders and hailed the Dean of the School of Divinity. "Hello there, Perry!"

Peregrine Pinker blinked eyes, rushed forward to shake hands, plump red face beaming as if his cup had not run over until that moment. "Aeneas, my boy! Splendid, perfectly splendid! Spot of weather? So—so London!"

"This is Miss Skye," Aeneas said. "She works with the F.B.I."

Perry made a short bow, took Blevyn's hand with two beefy hands, pumped it. "A very great pleasure indeed. What sort of work do you do with the F. B. I., Miss Skye?"

"I assist with kidnapping," Blevyn said.

"I seeeee." Perry nodded slowly. His smile faded. "Well. Must toddle off. Wedding reception . . . Join us for a bit of bubbly?"

"Thank you, no, Perry," Aeneas said. "We can't keep J. Edgar waiting."

"Jolly good . . . And how is your smashing wife?"

"Smashing, Perry, smashing." Aeneas almost added, "our marriage."

"Ta-ta." Peregrine Pinker waved and went.

"Whew," Aeneas sighed. "My short happy life as a moral paragon has come to a sticky end. He was the one who saw me in *Watch on the Rhine* and put me in the pulpit."

"He did a good deed in a naughty world so that I could see you and get a crush."

"So that's what it was. I saw you surrounded by light. Time didn't exist—"

"—in the usual sense," she finished for him.

"I wrote you a letter," he said.

"I never received it."

"I never sent it," he said. "Or the other letters. This was before you were you."

"And now? Will you send them to me now?"

He said nothing.

"Aeneas?"

"Well, I—"

"What do you mean, before I was I?"

"It's hard to explain."

"I thought you liked me," she said.

"Of course I like you." Aeneas paused to catch his breath. "I want to see you again. Would you like to go to dinner next weekend at the Carolina Inn?"

"I'd love that," she said, "but there's something I have to tell you. The F. B. I. has threatened to have me arrested unless I leave the States that are under the jurisdiction of the Eastern Defense Command."

His heart went cold. "Yes?"

"I'm going to L. A.." She glanced away. "Minnie will need me."

"For good?"

"I don't know. After L. A., I'll probably look for a teaching job in Chicago, or in some small town in the Midwest. I'm sorry. It was selfish of me to ask for the letters."

"No," he said. "I was the one who mentioned them."

"I wanted them to remember you by: the play, the Chapel, the magnolia. Oh, and I didn't thank you for the arrowhead. I'm going to make it into a pendant."

"All right," Aeneas said.

"All right what?"

"I'll send the letters."

"Thank you," she said. "Promise?"

"Promise." He picked up the packages. "Shall we go?"

RETURNING TO THE PARKED CAR after the movie, huddling together under the umbrella, they said nothing, but as she was about to get in, she kissed him quickly on the lips. "Thank you for a lovely time, and for all your support." Before he started the engine a few minutes later, they exchanged addresses and telephone numbers. One of these was for Mrs. H. B. Skye, Los Angeles.

"How are you planning to go?" Aeneas asked. "According to the papers, there's panic on the West Coast, but it's 3,000 miles from us here."

"I'll take my pickup."

"Alone?"

"I've done it before."

He was about to say he would come with her but remembered with bitter irony he was supposed to be serenely uninvolved in fateful happenings. "Telephone me along the way," he said instead.

"I'll change my mad money into dimes and quarters."

As they left town they had an animated conversation about the movie, laughed about the encounter with Peregrine Pinker, and remarked upon the beautiful devotion of the Skyes. They fell silent, knowing without further speech that the record of remembering Time had already been inscribed for them. When they arrived at Throstle's Nest there was a cruel display of romantic landscape: a light snow had fallen and everything was freshly sparkling beneath a brilliant moon.

"Goodbye," she said swiftly. She picked up her packages, leaving behind the one with his leather jacket, climbed out of the car, ran to the porch and entered the cabin without looking back. Hot tears lurched into his eyes. He felt about ninety years old. Just as he was reversing the car, however, a lantern appeared in a window. The door was opened. Blevyn came and stood on the porch, a flood of light behind her.

Impelled to defy all finalities, he sprang from the car and ran to her. She fell into his arms.

He kissed her mouth wildly, then gently. Her cheeks were wet to his touch.

"I love you," he blurted out even as his heart was sinking.

Lifting her hands to his face and beseeching with her eyes, "I love you, too," she said.

Then broke from the embrace, fled, and closed the door.

"Hello? Ma-Betty?"

"That you, son?"

"Merry Christmas."

"Same to you. How's the family?"

"They're in New York."

"Oh?"

"Yeah." Aeneas bent close to the telephone even though his house was empty save for himself and Roguey. "Trinc wanted to get away for a while. I wrote you all about it . . . Look. I need advice. I met a young woman. I'm in love with her. I doubt it'll ever work out. I made her a promise."

"Promise? You didn't promise marriage?"

"No, nothing like that, Mom. Until this thing with Trinc is

settled, I wouldn't ask someone to wait for me in the wings . . . I promised to send her some letters. If I send the letters, I run the risk of toying with her affections. If I don't, she'll feel betrayed. She needs support. Do you understand what I'm saying?"

"Yes," said Ma-Betty. "You're saying you're an adult."

"I gave my word."

"Then you have to keep your word."

"Thought so."

"Son, when I find the recipe for grasshopper molasses, I'll see to it you get a lifetime supply . . . What's the name of this person you're in love with?"

"Blevyn. Blevyn Skye. Look . . . Right now she's en route to L. A. with her grandparents. I told her to call you. 0. K.? She's an artist. Will you help her?"

"Leave her to me," Ma-Betty said.

PART III

The Planetary Imperative

19

Promise Land

Entries from the "Diary" of Blevyn Skye:

Los Angeles, January 10, 1942

PROFESSOR CALDWELL'S LETTERS HAVE ARRIVED. There are twenty of them, beginning last November with his vision of "me" in the S. A. U. Chapel and closing with a brief note saying how happy he was to hear from Ma-Betty that we visited at her home in Taos before we continued our journey to Los Angeles. Greatly as I am tempted to respond to him with sentiments commensurate to his own, I must bear myself toward him as an affectionate but somewhat distant friend.

He seems to have a powerfully developed desire for affiliation with humanity, an attachment that assumes the form of a self-induced participation in a superior Being. Yet I am only an inferior representation of that Being, perhaps his guide to it, no more. Is it not somehow inevitable that he will sacrifice his love for me if he is to pass on to his proper end? He has come to happiness through perception of Light. Accordingly he finds perfections in me which I have not.

All this I could wish otherwise.

Los Angeles, May 5, 1942

Everything blacked out as a precaution against extraordinarily unlikely Japanese air raids. Dim shapes of cars pass down our streets: police. The hills have pitched their black tents for the night of dinosaurs. I have moved from my third-story window back to bed. I will try to write tonight with my head covered by a blanket, using a flashlight. Will I be strong enough to cope? My hand still trembles. It has trembled for three days and nights. I must not listen to the voice of shame. It whispers in my ears that I deserve to be hated, humiliated, disgraced. I must not listen to that other voice either, rage. Remember Aeneas. Write swiftly, purge memory, forgive.

It is five o'clock in the morning, *that* morning. Curfew does not end until six o'clock. I am awake. As usual nowadays it is so strange to wake up in the morning and know that for the rest of the day until eight o'clock at night I will see very few people who are not Japanese. Soon all up and down our streets there will be raucous laughter and old men reading aloud from Japanese newspapers as if reciting from a play. There will be lottery tickets torn up and strewn in dirty gutters. There will be savory odors of oriental food in grocery stores. There will be families who are forced to sell their homes and household goods for 15¢ on the dollar and others who will be out in gardens breaking and burning phonograph records and books, golf clubs and baseball bats. Lifetimes of labor have already been lost, livelihoods, all hopes and plans. There will be rumors. We are all being deported to Japan. We will all be exchanged for American POWs. We will all be killed as hostages in reprisal for atrocities committed by Japanese soldiers. Or we will all have our freedom restored as soon as we are relocated out of the military zone. Anything is possible.

Now it is the twilight of morning when fog-fingers grope around telegraph poles where notices of our evacuation have been tacked up for a week. Out in the street a milk truck rattles to a stop. The woman on the third floor of the pink clapboard house in Little Tokyo hears it and rises. She is going to collect from the front porch the final delivery, two quart bottles of milk, and to thank for his services the milkman, a thick-set white-uniformed man with tufts of anthropoid black hair protruding from his shirt. A small woman about five feet two inches, she puts on a robe and dashes barefooted to the staircase. On the second floor she peeps in her mother's bedroom. Her mother is sleeping soundly. There is evidence in the room of last-minute preparations for E-day—evacuation day. The future life of mother and daughter will in part be determined by what little of the old life can be stuffed into a dufflebag and two suitcases. The daughter imagines that the promised "haven of refuge" will be a camp deep in an American Siberia. She has laid out on the floor, ready for packing, heavy winter overcoats, sweaters, woolen slacks, flannel pajamas and bottles of vitamins. She has already packed her watercolor set. The mother, who up until a few days ago has believed that someone will intervene for her, has only begun to sort out bed linens, toilet articles, and eating utensils from the framed photographs, bottles of soy sauce, jewels and evening gowns that must be left behind.

On the ground floor the woman pauses to peep into the bedroom currently occupied by her old grandparents. There is an implication in the orderliness of the room that they will be staying for a long time to take care of the house and the family belongings. The shotgun next to the grandmother's bed implies that, old and sick as she is, she is not to be trifled with. The grandmother sits up in bed, blinks her eyes. Formerly a concert violinist she is acutely sensitive to sounds and must have heard the milkman's truck rattling a block away. The woman puts a finger to her lips, turns and goes to a vestibule, unbolts the front door and steps out on the porch. A pale dawn light surrounds her.

My cam-eye reveals that the porch, floor to ceiling, is about ten feet high and that there is a large eye-hook screwed into the ceiling for the purpose of hanging a heavy flower pot. My cam-eye moves to milk bottles at the woman's bare feet. She bends slightly, picks them up, looks around for the milkman. Suddenly the bottles slip from her grasp and smash against the floor. At the same time a sharp and agonized gasp of breath can be heard, followed by a muffled scream. Several quick camera frames establish the scene. The woman has been gagged by a rag. A man's hairy hands are busy with binding her wrists behind her back. She tries to kick him but ends up sprawling upon the floor. Her face is gashed by broken glass. Blood soaks into a Welcome mat.

A cam-eye close-up reveals the noose that is being slipped around the woman's neck. The camera pans, following the rope up to the ceiling where an ape in white uniform—he stands on a table—is pulling the rope through the eye-hook. In the next sequence he is pulling the rope hand over hand like a sailor weighing anchor. Bare feet are yanked from the floor. There is a tight shot of the woman's face, her quivering, bleeding cheeks and bulging eyes. Sounds accumulate: retreating footsteps, rattle of a milk truck, moans and gargles of strangulation.

Although everything on the porch has been happening with chilling and methodical speed, with no words spoken, no venomous, hissing cries of execration, it is of the utmost importance for the audience to be treated to a slow sequence of sights and sounds. One sees the woman's feet kicking, twitching, then drooping almost motionlessly. One hears the single blast of a shotgun. One sees and hears the thump of a body as it hits the floor like a lifeless sack—except that the woman's eyes are blinking. The cam-eye is jerked up. There in the doorway a wrinkled-faced old woman in a thin nightgown is lowering a shotgun. Her eyes reflect horror and fury and amazement as if at the very moment of saving her granddaughter's life she is beginning to forget what she has witnessed, what she is doing.

The picture show is over. The lights come on. The audience moves toward the exit. Collectively it is thinking: What if Flora had not heard the shattering of the bottles? What if Flora had not, sensing danger, grabbed the shotgun? What if Flora had forgotten how to operate the shotgun? What if she had not had the presence of mind and the skill to sever a lynchingman's rope with a single blast aimed six inches below the eye-hook? As the audience files into the street, relaxes into chit-chat and puffs cigarettes, it feels collectively disappointed, even sickened. The film has produced no catharsis. Why didn't the woman stagger into the house and call the police? One supposes that a Jap is a Jap, submissive. Or one supposes that calling the police will accomplish nothing.

Poor woman . . . How about a drink for the road?

Extracts from a letter from Blevyn Skye, dated June 15, 1942, from the Tule Lake, California, Relocation Center, to Aeneas Caldwell, Poe's Hill, North Carolina

. . . Six months ago, in spite of having been suspected of being an enemy alien, I never believed I would be sent to a concentration camp. As recently as two months ago what seemed a remote possibility did not yet loom large as a very real eventuality. They do things like that in Nazi Germany and the Soviet Union, I thought. This is America. This is the Promised Land even though for some of us such as my grandfather, Tanaka, it is also an ambiguous Promise Land, a sort of confidence game based upon faith in democracy. But five days ago, having been held with Minnie in a detention camp for five weeks, we along with others were herded like cattle into an ancient train and taken under armed guard to a bleak desert location near the Oregon border. Officially a "relocation center," it is, as everyone knows, a concentration camp. My conscience keeps trying to find an explanation for our fate consistent with faith in the workings of democracy.

Back in Throstle's Nest in December, Archie suggested that I could meet the requirements of the Eastern Defense Command by moving only as far as the Midwest. As you know, I had already considered this plan. The idea was, drive to L. A., find a caretaker for Minnie's house, and then return with her to a Midwestern city. Archie objected. It was "mad" to drive 3,000 miles alone at a time when, according to the broadcasts, people on the West Coast feared an imminent invasion by Japan and were inclined to think of Japanese American citizens as potential traitors and saboteurs. Although I protested that I could look after myself and that, should the Japanese invade, I would help to man the barricades, he said, "Pigtracks!" He and Flora would accompany me on the trip. It would be an adventure for her. Except for one concert performance in Baltimore, she had never set foot outside of the Carolinas. She longed to see Bygie's Minnie again. Besides, she could receive proper medical treatment in L. A. Soon I consented to Archie's plan.

We spent a week preparing for departure. Archie found some neighbors to take care of Throstle's Nest during his absence. I fired and glazed your vase and posted it from Rollins along with that note telling you of our revised plans and asking you not to worry if I didn't telephone regularly. The day before we left, Archie loaded my pickup truck with enough goods for an expedition to Timbucktoo. There were spare tires, snow chains, extra fan belts, five-gallon drums filled with gasoline, a canvas water bag to sling in front of the radiator as a cooling device, a canvas tent, a mattress, bed rolls, jugs of drinking water, Mason jars of preserved fruits and vegetables and a shotgun. He also loaded a First Aid kit with Red Cross bandages and an old Citadel cadet's uniform, explaining that, if we ran into trouble, I was to disguise myself as a wounded U. S. Marine! Here I'd been thinking of my old grandfather as a retired insurance agent only. It turns out he could have been quartermaster for Lewis and Clark or a producer for the Elizabethan stage. I couldn't imagine our having use for all of the impedimenta. By the time we arrived in L. A., however, more than two weeks later, we had had need of everything. We had experienced three blowouts, a blizzard in the Sangre de Cristo Mountains, a busted fan belt and overheating radiator in the Mojave Desert, and on several occasions in Arizona and in California, when my features fitted someone's profile of a Japanese person, we were denied gasoline at filling stations, food at restaurants, and lodging at hotels. Once in the Painted Desert, too, Flora shot a jack-rabbit. She cooked her rabbit stew in a pot suspended from a trivet over a campfire. Archie had packed those items. As for the Red Cross bandages and Citadel cadet's uniform, more later.

Something else. Always since I was little my ambition has been to be an artist. Even while I was studying literature at Berkeley, I attended night school at an arts institute. I've dabbled in watercolors ever since. Because we would be stopping at intervals during our trip and I would have time for sketching, I packed my easel, tubes of Windsor & Newton paint, sable brushes and a block of Movlin à Papier d'Arches—French watercolor paper I had purchased in New York.

We departed in high spirits on the 20th of December. When the time came to leave Throstle's Nest, I felt filled with sadness. I had been happy there and free. Now the freedom I had always taken for granted was assuming deep meaning because I was deprived of it. I touched the arrowhead which I was wearing as a pendant and thought fondly of your magnolia tree. There was no time for moping. We stopped in Columbia for lunch and made it to Augusta just before dark. A gray evening was spread out against the sky "like a patient etherized upon a table." Wherever I looked in that still-defeated Southern city I seemed to see wraiths of yesterday dwelling in the shadows. That night in our shabby-genteel hotel I took out my paints and tried to convey this impression to paper.

Of course I should have called you that night or at some time during the next five nights. I confess: I dread the telephone. It does not respect space. It shatters sentiments into fragments.

When I answer a telephone, there is a moment of apprehension during which I feel as chilled as if I were breathing the fetid air of a suddenly opened catacomb. If a friend speaks, I am delighted; like as not, though, the speaker is someone with whom I am but slightly acquainted or not acquainted at all. I do not understand this urge to speak with strangers. I want health, a few friends, good books, music, my paints, solitude. Once in Berkeley I took in a stray dog. When he heard Hank's voice over the telephone, he cocked his head sideways, once, and vomited.

Days came and went, with them, cities: Atlanta, Birmingham, Memphis, Little Rock, Oklahoma City, Amarillo, Albuquerque. As the confinements of people and history dropped eastward behind us, the land opened up vast promise. How superficial and destructive, I realized, is the notion that man must increase and multiply and subdue the earth! Before one's very eyes, as you, yourself, know so well, there expands the ineluctable and gravid beauty of Being of a world which exists beyond our lone beginning and our oblivious sleep. I painted several pictures that attempt to convey this realization: the sun pouring liquid gold where horizon meets blue infinity; clumps of mesquite and sagebrush in a blue valley nakedly and tenderly ravished by moonsmoothness; mountains with wrinkled skin like that of old Indians.

I was so glad I called you on Christmas Day! Trust you to have spoken already to your Ma-Betty. She invited us to come to Taos for a few days. Here we were, the outcasts of Route 66, two old folks (one with a rubber doll over which she weeps from time to time) and a fugitive from the F. B. I., our Grapes-of-Wrathy truck covered with mud and buffeted by storms. Here we were in the middle of New Mexico, only now and then cheered by pinpricks of electric light in far-off towns and ranches. And we are invited to sanctuary. A stranger in Taos, one Elizabeth Blumberg alias Ma-Betty, makes expansively generous gestures toward us as if consciousness itself has been widened through relationship with the land.

By way of gratitude I return to you some scenery you must have cherished as a boy.

There is a good place away and above the world, a place I love. Go there, go north from Albuquerque more than 150 miles along roads engineered by humorous goats. Go the full day's drive, a precarious one, through the small provincial capital of Santa Fe, through tiny villages of flat-topped adobe houses built around a church and a plaza. Go up narrow, steep dirt roads where a 400-foot drop to the Rio Grande awaits the unfooted burro loaded down with wood. Go to a vast tawny plateau enclosed on three sides by a towering mountain range with shining peaks. And there you will find that good place: Taos. The air there is thin and clean, the light intense—we have come through the blizzard—and smoke is rising in straight plumes from adobe houses in a far-off, struggling vista. We come closer. Flocks of sheep are moving in slow white patterns across whimsical little gulches and bottom lands. Willows are letting their stringy, long winter hair down to sundazzled streams. A wooden-wheeled wagon drawn by a pair of horses creaks past adobe walls, past the snowmelt tumbling from weathered, protruding *vigas*, past blue doors and blue windowsills bearing the beams of the setting sun. Breathe deeply now the odors of cedar, sage, and piñon. See the Christmastide *luminarias* of pitchwood, the *camposanto* with fresh-cut flowers on gravestones, the narrow, nameless, crooked streets, the horses tied to hitching posts in the plaza.

Por favor, where is the home of Phillips and Elizabeth Blumberg, the famous artists?

A glissade of giggles. Eager, brown young faces.

There, Señora, there where the shapes of pyramids arise in rosy glow.

No, no, *compadre*. Cristo Rey! It is over there on the mesa far from the sacred mountain.

A thousand pardons, Señora! It is there where the rainbow touches the earth . . .

Ma-Betty told me later about the New York artist whose first experience of Taos "hit him like Saul's vision on the road to Damascus."

I entered the deep gloom of La Fonda Hotel, took a breath, and telephoned the Blumberg residence. Half an hour later I observed two magnificent bay horses come trotting into the plaza. Astride one of them was a man with long flowing white hair poking from his Stetson; in his gray shirt and Levi's he looked like one of the outlaws of Poker Flat. Astride the other horse, looking regal in her black dress with silver belt, riding boots, shawl and a flaring hat that Rembrandt would have envied, was a plumply lovely lady of about seventy who alighted from the saddle on fairy feet and saluted us with a friendly grin.

"Ma-Betty," she said.

I introduced us and apologized for not being able to find her house.

"Grasshopper molasses!" she bellowed. "You artists are welcome here, not treated like cockroaches as they are everywhere else in the land of Philistia! 'Sides, sneeze before you eat, company before you sleep. Phillips here has been sneezing. Get in that tin horse of yours and, if the tires stick in mud, remember that a walk in the snow is the best cure for chilblains."

What, Aeneas, had you been telling your mother? I had never before been greeted as an "artist." I felt as if I had been levitated to a height about two feet off the ground.

We followed their horses for a couple of miles out of town until we came to a plateau from which we could see the entire Taos Valley from Wheeler Peak to the Rio Grande. The rutted, snowpacked trail, bordered by enormous ghost-gray cottonwoods, eventually led us to Blumberg Heaven, the sprawling adobe house, the log barn and stables surrounded by an adobe wall and nestled in a thicket of cottonwoods, aspens, and Russian olive trees. The lights of the house, powered by a generator happily humming like a god of the hearth, printed colored parallelograms on the snowwhitened courtyard. All this you know.

But permit me memory. Understand that as I write in a 20'x 10' barracks room, I look out the single, dirty window and see floodlights illuminating a high barbed-wire fence and, at intervals along the fence, tall watchtowers manned by guards with machine guns. Permit memory, then, as I revisit the house, see again the low-ceilinged rooms, their varnished *vigas* gleaming in firelight, their whitewashed walls covered gloriously with original paintings by your parents as well as by Dasburg, Gaspard, O'Keeffe, Marin and Fechin, all those scenes of Indians on horseback, "squaws" with *ollas* above shawls, adobe houses sheltered by cottonwoods alongside a river, the pyramids of the pueblo, the clouds tearing against the peaks— all that semibarbaric splendor of cobalt blues accentuated by burnt umber and vermillion. Permit me after a dinner of what is known in the concentration camp as "edible offal" to recall the dining room with its long French windows. I sit again in a studded leather chair at the heavy oak table. I contemplate by firelight and candlelight Felicidad's mouth-watering platters of mesquite-broiled sirloin steak, blue-corn tortillas and white-corn posole smothered in green chile peppers, the crocks of churned butter, the chokecherry jam, the paté de foie gras, the cheeses and wines of France, the Brazilian coffee with brandy.

"If a storm threatens during harvest time here," I hear Ma-Betty saying again, "a virgin runs toward it, her hands filled with salt. When she reaches the crest of a hill her arms widen in the sign of the cross, and the salt sifts out. Dark clouds will gather, but there is no rain or hail." I hear this story, and I know it must be true for those who live in harmony with nature. I believe that art should be rooted in nature. Here in the concentration camp we are forbidden to have cameras, but, so far, nobody has confiscated my brushes, colors, and paper or the sketches I am making of desert winds flinging clouds of dust against our ugly tar-papered barracks while, in the distance, Mount Shasta looks down with serene indifference upon the Land of the Free.

One morning after breakfast—*huevos rancheros* swimming in pinto beans and green chile!—Ma-Betty took out old photograph albums to show us what Throstle's Nest was like at the turn of the century. You were right. Little has changed. I even recognized some of "our" furniture. She also showed us one A. Caldwell in his metamorphoses, cowboy, soldier, actor, scholar, bridegroom, pipe-smoking pater-familias, academician receiving honorary degree.

"Born grown up," Ma-Betty said of you proudly.

"What's that?" I asked when she opened an album to a page showing early Kodak pictures of Taos. I pointed to a Christmas-card scene. Silhouetted in clean flowing lines against a backdrop of Wheeler Peak and El Cuchillo was an elongated, flat-topped adobe with thick, capriciously molded buttresses and a primitive wooden cupola with cross atop. Hugging the very earth it was made from, it bore a closer resemblance to an overturned ark than to a Christian church.

"The *morada* of Los Remedios," was her reply. "It was abandoned by the brotherhood of Los Penitentes long before we arrived in 1906. My former husband purchased it for a song. Aeneas and I lived in it for a couple of years; then I lived in it alone until I met Phillips in 1916. As the British say, I used to live in an 'ouse and now I live in an 'all."

"It looks magical!" I blurted out.

"Then let's go see it," she cried, clapping hands. "Felicidad will fix us sandwiches, and we'll hitch up the buggy and go and have a picnic. Only, we want to be there before noon so we can hear the church bells ringing in the villages roundabouts. It's about five miles yonder to Hondo rim. Rain, rain, go away, little Betty wants to play!"

We went, leaving Archie and Flora to stay warm by the fire. I had my first buggy-ride as Ma-Betty held forth on various subjects, including *Los Penitentes* and art.

"Although it seems rather barbarous and scandalous before modern society that the brotherhood flogged themselves to atone for the blood shed by Christ, the members that lived according to the brotherhood's rule and renounced all evil practices were and are the best and most sincerely religious people. When you see inside the *morada* where the *latillas* of the ceiling are stained with dark blood, you have only to use your imagination to hear men moaning dirges and chanting prayers as they flagellate their bodies. With a little more imagination you can watch them shouldering a red-robed likeness of Christ that is mounted on a platform within a flower-decorated wooden frame. They carry it outside and in to a bitter wind and the sting of snowflakes . . . No one who has not heard the anguished cry of humanity is apt to make art that inspires awe."

"What do you mean by that, Ma-Betty?"

"Giddap, Hark, or I'll take a hair from your tail and tie it around your dingdong! Hee-yah! What did you say, Blevyn? . . . Yes. The artist is religious, too, in his or her own way. The artist is like the good men who met secretly in the *morada*, both innocent and violent. You have to suffer. I mean you suffer in yourself. And because you suffer, even though you may not know why your suffering is so painfully acute, you suffer with other people, *all* people. You know what's going on inside them. You feel their souls, and a strange joy is born inside you. When all is said and done, whether you paint or teach or write or compose or dance or act, what matters is not the ease or facility or cleverness or manipulative technique but the joy and the agony of your toil in the human mystery. Stick a pin in a painting by a Master and it will bleed to the prick."

We arrived at the *morada* in time to hear the pealing of bells from churches in Arroyo Hondo and Arroyo Seco.

"We put fresh mud on the walls every few years. We have the chimneys swept. We generate our own electricity. The well water is pumped into the house. We do keep, though, a foot in the Middle Ages. You still have to use the two-holer outside, and you can't have a telephone."

"Perfect," I said. I was feasting my eyes on everything, the

Navajo rugs, the *kiva* fireplaces, the bookshelves, the niches with *kachina* dolls carved out of cottonwood roots, the pictures of saints in tin and glass frames. "I think anyone would be happy living in your Middle Ages, Ma-Betty," I said, "just listening to the bells."

"Would you like to live here, Blevyn?"

"I just said."

She looked me in the eye. "I mean that you and your mother can come here to live. No rent, no obligation. We like to have the place occupied. It's a perfect studio. Stay until the war's over. Stay forever."

When I protested, she cut me short. "We have our reasons, Phillips and I. We've studied your sketches and the vase Aeneas sent and we've come to the conclusion you've more talent than anybody who has come this way since that flinty dame, Georgia O'Keeffe, over there in the Chama Valley. But. . . you have a long way to go. You have to paint in oils, child, or those rascals in New York will put you down for a 'primitive' or a 'regionalist' or some sort of hifalutin nonsense. We'll show you what we know. See a pin and pick it up, all that day you'll have good luck . . . See that door?" She pointed. "No metal hinges. It swings on those curved wooden extensions that are socketed in the frames. As soon as you and your ma come to live here, I suppose you'll be wanting a door that shuts properly. Am I right?"

"I like my doors open," I said.

"Hoo-rah for you!" she exclaimed with a lovely smile. "Exactly what Aeneas would have said. But . . . let's understand each other. If you worship at the altar of art, you'll have to make sacrifice. You'll have to sacrifice marriage, having children, and all that. If you have it to do, getting married, for instance, then so much the less your dedication to art. Now, you'll say, I'm married to Phillips. But you've probably noticed that he rarely says anything. That's because he's painting even when he's not painting. I'm much the same, except I talk too much. We're made for each other. Marriage to anyone else would be a disaster. Our life is in art. Are you ready for that?"

I ran and gave her a hug.

No churchbells now.

Sirens call us. Roll calls, meals, everything.

You stir in the black barracks. You grab towel and toothbrush, go out, cross the firebreak, enter the "latrine." You don't want a shower because there is no privacy. The water is cold anyway. You pull your eyes up and over the barbed-wire fence. Perhaps Mount Shasta is a beacon of promise, but the world outside, which by rights is your world, is hostile. We have nowhere to turn. At times we begin to lose faith in ourselves and in our ability to take it.

Ma-Betty inspired me. I paint, paint, paint. I forget the world.

There are rumors that all letters are to be censored. This letter must be finished and sent before it is scissored to pieces.

Speaking of scissors. Yesterday the guards ordered a crackdown on "weapons" and went from family to family collecting anything they considered dangerous. Poor Minnie. In her last-minute haste to meet the deadline for evacuation from L. A., she packed three pairs of scissors and two knitting needles. The guards took them all.

When we left Taos, I felt confident we would soon be returning to live in the *morada*. It didn't occur to me that once we entered California we wouldn't be permitted to leave it.

The trouble with gas stations, restaurants, and hotels began in Arizona. One sign read: "This restaurant poisons both rats and Japs." We camped in the desert regularly, slept by day, traveled by night. It was at this time that I wrapped my head with bandages and put on the cadet's uniform.

Situated on the California side of what's left, after dams, of the once great Colorado River, there lies the town of Needles. Steinbeck had Pa Joad die there, never to enter the Promise(d) Land. Not far away my husband was killed at Parker Dam. With such heartwarming associations in mind the night we crossed the bridge into Needles, I was not entirely surprised to find the road blocked. Floodlights bathed with cinematic eeriness the ghostly figures of armed policemen. Why ghostly? A fierce wind was coming in from the Mojave, blowing soft alkaline dust in suffocating clouds. Anyone not sheltered looked as if he had fallen into a flour barrel.

One armed ghost signaled for Archie to pull over and shoved a flashlight in our faces, asking about our destination.

"L. A.," Archie shouted into the wind. "We're taking this Marine to his duty station. Anything the matter, buddy?"

"Seen any Japs, sir?"

"Not since Texas," Archie replied. "Other side of Amarillo. You know, that Jap Reservation." Archie paused. I was amazed to have a grandfather who can invent stories impromptu. "Some of them yeller-bellies escaped," Archie went on. "They was injecting drugs into hogs and cattle. Fixin' to take control of the Gulf of Mexico. We had to call in the Marines to save our women and children."

A wound opened on the officer's paste-white face. It was his mouth. "You don't say, sir."

"Hey, buddy," Archie went on shouting, "the guv'ment don't tell us poor folks shit . . . That's a good job you're doing, buddy. O. K. to pass?"

"Have a good trip, sir."

Archie didn't say anything until we were out of Needles. He stopped the truck at the edge of the desert. "A deputy out here wouldn't know a Marine from a mermaid. Or his hole from an ass in the ground."

"Archibald," Flora scolded, "you ought to be ashamed of yourself, telling lies and cussing."

"Now, now, Mama, you have to talk their language."

"What about the Indians?"

"What Indians?"

"The reservation. You said."

"Mama," Archie soothed, "we don't have to worry about Indians. We have to worry about pigtracks. . . Say! Look at those poor guys."

On the other side of the road two trucks had been parked. Furniture and suitcases were lashed to their sides with rope. Families of small Japanese were running around in the duststorm in a dazed and distraught manner.

We arrived in Los Angeles on January 4th.

From January to April nothing much happened. Voluntary relocation from coastal regions was announced, but after what we had seen in Needles and elsewhere, with Japanese American citizens turned back at the border yet having no home to which to return, it seemed better to stay where we were. As usual, Archie was the prudent one. He not only secured Minnie's power of attorney but also arranged to look after her house in the event of an evacuation. When in fact the day came when Minnie and I were forcibly relocated, we realized what a bulwark against disaster the little old insurance agent had erected. While other families lost their homes and lifetime savings, Minnie was protected.

E-day came. We had already been through the hassle of getting innoculated against typhoid; we had already been reduced from personal citizenship to an impersonal family number, a piece of white pasteboard which we were required to wear attached to our clothing. Archie drove us to an assembly point. Hundreds of silent, well-dressed people were standing among their dufflebags and suitcases. When Greyhound buses arrived that were to take us to an assembly center, most of the people were for the first time brutally awakened to reality: having been promised safe passage and having submitted to authority as proof of their loyalty to the United States, they suddenly saw emerging from each of the buses a soldier with rifle in hand. The soldiers stared at us impassively. It was clear we were all, including many small children, prisoners of war.

We were taken to a racetrack and assigned to whitewashed horse stalls in which the only item of furniture was a folded spring cot. We sat down on ours. A woman was crying in the next stall. We stayed at the racetrack for five weeks before we received notice we were being sent to a permanent camp in the northern part of the state.

Imagine some creaky old railroad coaches with all the shades drawn, and imagine yourself riding in one of those coaches for a day and a night while a MP is watching you with feral eyes, his bayonet unsheathed. It is dark at night because the lights fail to function. Train-sick children are puking. Once, the engine hisses and chugs to a stop, and you are allowed to step outside the coach for a breath of air. What do you see but a barbed-wire fence, erected in the middle of high, empty desert country and patroled by soldiers with rifles at the ready?

Promise Land.

During this trip Minnie got very upset with me. "You're not *Nisei* and you're only half Japanese. You're exempt. I don't like your making a sacrifice for me."

I tried to make her laugh. "Let you have all the fun? I need to study anatomy. I'm taking this opportunity to use you as my model —in the nude, Minnie, in the nude."

Minnie is a doll. Usually she is quiet and reserved, the dignified widow of a brigadier general and unaccustomed to being indecorously teased. On this occasion she buried her face with tiny hands and began to rock with silent laughter until tears filled her eyes.

Upon arrival here at Tule Lake we were all herded to an assembly area for a flag ceremony. We were ordered to "sing along" as Kate Smith's recorded rendition of "God Bless America" was blatted out of the throats of loudspeakers perched up on the guard towers.

God bless America, land that I love . . .

Of the thousand or more POWs who were supposed to sing, some didn't speak English, others were aware of a certain incongruity in the proceedings. A feeble noise arose half a bar behind Kate Smith's great-hearted jingoism. When my gaze lifted to a watchtower and I stared into the barrel of a machine gun, I began to sing inaudibly, then louder and louder until I hit the last line with the mindless euphoria of a cheerleader at a football game:

"... *MY HOME SWEET HOME!*"

People turned to stare at me. Never in my life have I felt so embarrassed and self-conscious. Then a few people nervously giggled. The giggles rippled through the crowd. Finally everyone was laughing a side-splitting laughter. I realized that they weren't laughing at me but at tyranny, itself.

I have by heart what Thomas Jefferson wrote in a letter to Dr. Benjamin Rush: *I have sworn upon the altar of God, eternal hostility against every form of tyranny over the mind of man.*

Jefferson, thou shouldst be living at this hour!

Love,

Blevyn

P.S. I've asked Ma-Betty for a raincheck on her invitation to come and live in the *morada*. I also asked her please to send me oil paints, brushes, and canvas. She doesn't have to send me paint rags. I'm wearing them.

20

Shoes

AS A LITTLE GIRL IN THE EARLY YEARS of the twentieth century, Trinc believed she was perfectly fitted into her family names. To have been born and named Susan Heartwell DeRoman was not only to have the silver spoon but also to be confined as in a magical pair of shoes of the kind preferred by Prince Charming. Her mother, the Heartwell, had belonged to a self-styled aristocracy in Connecticut, the family having acquired fame and wealth during one hundred years of operating Heartwell Brothers Mills. Her father, Gayle DeRoman, was a rich Wall Street lawyer from New Orleans who claimed descent from Charlemagne.

When she was fourteen, the year being 1912, the DeRoman name began to pinch her. Because that amiable gentleman wanted his Heartwell wife to provide him with a male heir, he deserted the family. In 1916, after the divorce was finalized, he married his tubercular mistress and not long afterwards begat his only son and named him after himself. She became aware that Heartwell pelf had been accumulated off the sweat of immigrant laborers. When, in that same year of 1916, her one night of glorious sexual intercourse with a penniless pauper named Dr. Aeneas Caldwell became known to the family, her grandfather paid thugs to castrate that so-called

- 355 -

"insolent intellectual social climbing seducer." Although her lover survived the assault with sex in working order, Trinc determined to do everything in her power—which, *as* woman, amounted to very little—to be a barefoot Cinderella. She could still fit her identity into the family names while refusing to let them tie her up in laces.

Leaving behind Orford Parish and the impertinent life of debutante and Junior Leaguer, she went unchaperoned to New York, put herself through a strenuously proletarian course of nurses' training, graduated R.N. with coveted Nightingale Pin, and for a time earned the wages of authenticity by emptying slops of Manhattan princesses in an insane asylum. The experience toughened her spirit into a leathery one. She had married her Aeneas Caldwell, followed this Doctor of Philosophy and Professor of Physics to the boonies of Poe's Hill, North Carolina, and agreed to live off his salary of $2,000 that a university there was willing to bestow upon him. They had two children, Diana and Billy, the boy named after Dr. William Knight, the uncle who had served as her surrogate father after the DeRoman decampment. She sent the children to public schools. She drove one car, her husband's, first a Model-T, then a 1936 "Thrifty Sixty" Ford. She created a fairy-tale castle out of a green-moldy brick duplex on the wrong side of the railroad tracks, did all the chores herself even though she could have a hired a servant during the Depression for a dollar a day, and quit smoking in order to avoid paying 25¢ for a pack of Old Gold cigarettes. Faculty wives avoided her because word got around that she was a Heartwell. Although she loved her husband too much to surrender the down-at-the-heel clogs of soulmate, cook, laundress, scullion and mother, who could blame her if, sometimes, she dreamed of returning to the New York she remembered from the Jazz Age? She had actually met F. Scott Fitzgerald, Edmund Wilson, Donald Ogden Stewart and Edna St. Vincent Millay. She was, unfortunately, happy. And still had no antipathy to virtue.

She also had or seemed to have the cakes and ale. After deserting wife and child, DeRoman had established a Trust Fund for Trinc, the capital of which she could invade whenever she wished even though he warned her, as later he never did his son, to expect nothing more from him, no gifts, no loans, no inheritance. The market value of this Trust was increased by tenfold until 1929 but was then decreased by 80% on one black day on Wall Street. Her Heartwell mother and grandmother had bequeathed to Trinc oodles of stock in the family's corporation, but Heartwell Brothers Mills had gone into bankruptcy in 1940, its machinery transported to a competitor's mills in Alabama, its acres of nineteenth-century brick factories now as empty, silent, and forlorn as Roman ruins. The stock was worthless.

In short, Trinc was assumed by everyone to be rich when in fact she barely had enough capital left to provide for old age, not counting wages from a nursing career once the children were grown up, and not counting Social Security.

Still, she revealed nothing of her predicament to the family, especially not to a father who would scorn her as a failure, a stupid female, an heiress *manqué*. Throughout the Depression years and now into the years of the Second World War, she drew upon capital little by little and explained occasional extravagances as windfalls from Lady Bountiful. Even though her father sometimes inquired by letter about her circumstances as if to hint he would entertain requests for money, she wanted him of his own accord to recognize her as worthy to fill a DeRoman's shoes.

Gayle DeRoman, appearances to the contrary, was not in her opinion a typical egotist. He had formed lasting friendships, had loved his second wife and deeply mourned her early death, had distinguished himself at the bar for probity and good sense, and had a charm admired in the board rooms and full-dress balls of fellow solipsists. He was, however, an exhibitionist. He bragged about himself incessantly, about his great exploits as a Yale football player of the Walter Camp era, about his great cronies in the Skull & Bones "crowd," about his great success on the stock market, about his great adventures during the First World War when he served as a Judge Advocate on General Pershing's staff, and about his great son, Gayle DeRoman, Jr. After that war he insisted upon being called "Colonel." Trinc could see from a distance how her father's desire to make a son in his own image had produced in Gayle, Jr., an alcoholic and a gambler, a failure at private schools and colleges, and twice in marriages to Hollywood starlets, ever the one to beg from Colonel—and get—bailout sums just before litigious ex-wives or the Mafia closed in for the literal kill. As for Charlemagne, Colonel had paid a genealogist handsomely to inscribe on a vellum scroll the name of that ninth-century Frankish emperor of the Romans at the root of the family tree, there then being a inexplicable gap of 500 years before Charlemagne's alleged genes somehow popped up in a gypsy bogtrotter in Camargue.

In September of 1943 three events had brought Trinc's conscience into conflict with necessity.

In 1941 Colonel had opened the door to his Will just a crack. Attending Trinc's forty-third birthday party were visitors to Poe's Hill, Uncle Doc and Colonel, the former giving her a mink coat from Sak's Fifth Avenue, the latter, who was drunk, nothing—nothing until the moment he aimed a bitter glance at Uncle Doc and announced that in his Will the estate would go to Gayle, Jr., with Yale University as contingent beneficiary, "provided, however, that Trinc get a Court Order legally changing my grandson's name from William Knight Caldwell to Gayle DeRoman Caldwell, in which case, should Gayle Junior predecease Trinc, she will inherit my estate, Yale, as before, contingent. . ."

Second, on December 6, 1941, the day before the bombing of Pearl Harbor, Trinc had left Aeneas in Poe's Hill and taken Diana and Billy to live with her in a furnished apartment in New York, her reasoning at the time being that Aeneas had become so preoccupied with secret research at his university that he no longer cared for wife and children, but if he truly loved them more than quantum mechanics, she had somehow believed, he would come clinging to her knees. In the meantime she would and did take a refresher course in nursing, qualify for jobs in public health, pick up tennis lessons from a pro, blow the culture-deprived children to the expense of concert and theater binges, and send Billy to a private school where he could be prepared for later admission to Phillips Academy and to Yale.

"Why can't I go to private school?" Diana's complaint caught Trinc by surprise. It had seemed natural to her that money withdrawn from capital should be used to further the education of boys. "Because, dear," Trinc had replied disingenuously, because two private tuitions could mean penury, "you're already being prepared for your future role as wife and mother."

"And divorcée, too, I suppose?"

"Your father requested a divorce and I refused him."

What Trinc didn't know until Aeneas wrote her after Pearl Harbor was this: he had met a young woman of Japanese American descent with whom he had fallen in love "even though I know I'm too old for her and in any event, due to the secrecy of my work, I can't see her again or communicate with her because she has been interned in a concentration camp in California." She was appalled to learn that concentration camps even existed in the United States but relieved that Aeneas's "mid-life crisis" had been thwarted by one of them.

So much, as Trinc realized, for the he'll-come-clinging-to-my-knees theory. Women did the clinging. Evidently men did not cling except in movies starring the hand-on-heart courtliness of Fred Astaire.

In April Aeneas had gone to New Mexico to continue his work and was living forty miles from Santa Fe in a place called Los Alamos in the remote Jémez Mountains. In July Trinc had moved herself and children to Santa Fe, purchased an adobe house on East Palace, hired a gardener and factotum named

Policarpio and a cook and maid named Aida, bought a pre-war English Daimler and a Harley-Davidson motorcycle, secured employment as a public health nurse in a military hospital at Los Alamos, was seeing Aeneas there almost every day for lunch at Fuller Lodge, and on Sundays, when he came to take the children out for hiking and fishing expeditions, she was demonstrating to him an Odysseus and Penelope duality.

Third, Gayle, Jr., had been killed in action just last month, in August. Having enlisted in the Navy early in 1942, he had recovered from alcoholism and as a fighter pilot had been credited with shooting down three Zeros. He, himself, had been shot down "somewhere over the Pacific," the body never found. Trinc wrote Colonel offering condolences, the anguish for the loss of a half-brother sincerely felt because he had converted himself from a scapegrace to a true DeRoman. Colonel wrote her that he was "heartbroken" and "ready to die." Did she remember the "conversation" at her birthday party? Trinc sent a telegram to Colonel, who had retired to the New Haven Lawn Club at 193 Whitney Avenue, saying she was obtaining a Court Order changing Billy's name to his, should Colonel truly wish to immortalize himself outside the kennels of the Yale bulldog. Colonel sent his telegram in reply: DYING. URGENT YOU COME. WILL PAY FOR TAFT HOTEL ROOM AND MEALS. BRING COURT ORDER AND TENNIS RACQUET. SHE HATES ME THAT WOULD UPON THE RACK OF THIS TOUGH WORLD STRETCH ME OUT LONGER. DADDY.

Daddy? *King Lear*?

TRAVELING FROM LAMY, NEW MEXICO, on the "Santa Fe Chieftain" to Chicago and from there to Pennsylvania Station, Trinc dressed as if caught between two worlds, belonging to neither. The organdy dress, the elbow-length white Parisian gloves, the worn and tacky fur coat and the hat that looked like a diaphragm with a hummingbird pinned to it projected an image of herself as at a cocktail party with Scott Fitzgerald, whereas the cowboy boots or, as she loved to call them, "shitkickers" were defiantly déclassé and tawdry. Although she could have been booked for Pullman cars and could have been feasting in dining cars, she miserably sat and fitfully dozed in hot, smoky, unventilated coaches crammed with beardless soldiers and sailors and other huddled masses. Her table d'hôte consisted of her own paper bag filled with greasepaper-wrapped peanut butter sandwiches, boiled eggs, apples, Baby Ruth candy bars, and 12-ounce bottles of warm Pepsi. She had the figure of a twenty-year-old ingénue, but, if any G.I. tried to get fresh with her, the gloves from the Marcel Proust era served to convey the message that a necking party with her would prove a strenuous affair, like running an obstacle course in Basic Training.

The exhaustion she felt upon arrival in New York she had earned as a badge of accomplishment and paltry gesture of solidarity with the millions who had gone and were going to war. Expecting autumnal weather, she brought the fur coat but found a city sweltering in humid heat, air stifling and poisonous, the nuisance of carrying a small suitcase and tennis racquet so irritating that she almost hailed a cab to take her the few miles to Grand Central. Instead, she walked. Her silk-stockinged feet were blistering inside the shitkickers. Strands of her long, slightly graying auburn hair stuck to perspiration on her brow. Once in Grand Central she hurried to the concourse, found her train to New Haven just in time, and boarded the nearest coach in order to avoid having to tip a porter for a minute's help with the suitcase she had already lugged competently on a journey of 2,000 miles. She was pleased to find that her coach contained a few gentlemen in dark suits and neckties who studied the *Times* and *Wall Street Journal*, albeit most travelers were G.I.s sprawled asleep in the aisle and even in the baggage racks. All seats were taken. She slipped off coat and imagined herself as—for a mere couple of self-sacrificing hours—one of those refugees on Pathe News, fleeing Nazis on a last train out of Paris.

"Ma'am?"

He was tall, middle-aged, Gary Cooperishly handsome and shy of voice, a compatriot from the lost world of courtesy. Standing up from a window seat he tipped to her his yachtsman's cap. "Please take my seat. I'm just going to Greenwich by way of Stamford." The seat next to his was overflowing with an extraordinarily fat young woman with a nasty black eye, peroxided yellow hair, and a thigh-sized arm wrapped around a tiny baby in diapers. The gentleman, taking care to avoid stepping on this obviously abused woman's squashed moccasins, wriggled his way into the aisle, nodded to Trinc on a half smile, and made for the exit to the next coach. After Trinc, leaning, had coat, suitcase, and racquet placed in the baggage rack next to the unpolished but noble leather boots of a soldier stretched out there, she squeezed past the Wagnerian-opera-qualified woman and, flopping down, smiled and said to her, "Cute . . . What's her name?"

"Scarlett," the woman replied with the obligatory meltdown of features. "From the movie."

Trinc imagined a brute of a husband blackening the woman's eye and beginning a sentence with *"Frankly, my dear . . ."*

She removed gloves, fumbled in purse for an Old Gold and matches, and was presently smoking the forty-third cigarette she had lit up since leaving Lamy—since in fact she had been in nurses' training. The window mirrored her face. Why did she think she looked tired and careworn? Still tanned lightly as the leather of her shitkickers, why did she look as ghostly pale as an x-ray? At least the luridly phosphorescent coachlight reflected in her soft brown eyes some of the wildness that had entered her soul from sights of endless plains and towering mountains. She had been riding her motorcycle daily on the 80-mile roundtrip between Santa Fe and Los Alamos. She was indeed wind-lashed and sun-dried enough to be shoe-leathery. She had exchanged the steel and concrete, penile sky-rapers of New York for the Earth Mother of New Mexico, for a house made of mud and for floortiles so warm to the touch she often took off shoes and danced, alone and barefooted, upon them. She turned from the window, crushed cigarette under heel, pulled off shitkickers and relished the rude rapture of hot and smelly feet released as if from a lifetime of confinement.

"All a-bawd!"

The familiar accent of a conductor on the platform reassured her that she was, after all, a Yankee, self-reliant, stoic, conscientious and anglophile. A nervous upward gaze at the suitcase reminded her, however, of an old-fashioned American inheritance that she was about to repudiate: rectitude. The Court Order changing Billy's name to Gayle DeRoman Caldwell was in the suitcase, thanks to a greedy attorney in Santa Fe who had introduced her to a corrupt judge who had not required Billy's consent to the procedure and in effect waived Billy's rights to his own identity. Not to worry of course. Billy would always be Billy, and Colonel's bribery would always be the exhibitionism of a Let's Pretend Charlemagne of that charmingly disguised, biblical empire of Misogyny.

Whistleblast.

A locomotive jolted the train forward. It lurched, screeched, snaked through black tunnels dotted with bleak little lightbulbs that she immediately *un-saw* in order to bring to mind New Mexican nights, stars to which all living things were mysteriously related. Perhaps, had she not fallen in love with a star-gazing physicist, she might have married that Gary Cooperish yachtsman, lived near the New York, New Haven & Hartford Railroad, and committed adultery: Madame Bovary, Yonville-l'Abbaye-on-Long-Island-Sound. As the train emerged into soiled sunlight near 125th Street, Scarlett's scream— "Yeeeeee!"—detonated professional adrenalin in Trinc as if it were the yelp of a dog with tail caught in blades of a lawn mower. Poor baby. Face crumpled and blowzy. Snot ballooning from nostrils. Stool like orange Jello gelatin oozing from diapers.

"Yeeeeee!"

"Shaddap! Gonna whupass ya!" Thus great white whale. Perhaps her name *was* Moby and she was married to a man named Dick. Who would name a beautiful child Scarlett Dick? *I've got to stop inventing names for people.* Would it be proper etiquette for a nurse and fellow mother to propose an exodus through the dry patches of a sea of gently shaking meat to the promised land of the washroom? Trinc made a lovey-dovey oo-y coo-y noise in her throat. Scarlett stopped crying, opened a wee, toothless Metropolitan Opera Company soprano's mouth. Trinc gazed out the window at old men like blimpish colonels on fire escapes and at a rooftop billboard inscribed REPUTATION IS WHAT MEN THINK YOU ARE, CHARACTER IS WHAT GOD AND THE ANGELS KNOW YOU ARE.

"I know what you're thinking."

Moby's voice startled her. "Really?" Trinc turned to see a look of resentment registered on her neighbor's face. "I was just thinking," Trinc said with an effort at humor, "I blew it with God and the angels."

"You're thinking my black eye, my husband must of beat shit out of me."

"Point," said Trinc.

"We had an accident, me, Charlie, and the little one."

"I'm so sorry."

"It weren't no fault of Charlie. He was driving under the limit." Moby nodded her head as if to affirm the accuracy of her memory.

"So you got the black eye in the accident? How painful!"

Moby opened palms of surprisingly small but prehensile fins. "Charlie's in hospital, broke leg . . . The other man was in the wrong lane, goin' like a house a-fire. Killed hisself . . . Our car's a write-off."

"Really," said Trinc in a murmur, trying to think of a cliché she could offer with a theatrical sigh. "In the midst of life." She stopped, exhaled. "Your husband in hospital. No car. What can you do?"

"No big deal," Charlie's wife said, opening palms. "The dead man is paying."

"Excuse me for intruding. I'd be happy to help you change Scarlett's diapers. I'm a nurse. Your shit, as they say, is my bread and butter."

"She's a good baby."

"I didn't mean—"

"She'll last until Hartford."

"You're going to Hartford?"

"My folks live near there."

"I used to live near Hartford, too. Orford Parish."

Charlie's wife rolled her eyes. "Wow! Like small worldsville! Like my hometown. Imagine . . . Who was your folks?"

"Heartwell. On my mother's side. I'm Mrs. Caldwell. From New Mexico now . . ." Trinc stopped herself again. Charlie's wife's eyes had narrowed to slits, the face as dark as it had been bright the moment before. "I could tell you was a Heartwell," Charlie's wife said, dropped glance to floor, and stared at the shitkickers for a few moments as if pondering some mystery laced in them. "Nice boots," she said. Since the tone of the remark did not seem to Trinc intended as complimentary, she turned back to the window. *Stupid stupid*. She had only meant to be friendly. Had the mere mention of a name from a bygone era harpooned the poor woman? *Why can't I fit perfectly into myself without names?* She wasn't one of those poised, always chirpy, always smiling blobs on the new gadget called television she had seen when she lived in New York.

"I guess you need a passport if you live in New Mexico, huh?"

Trinc didn't respond. Long ago she had disciplined herself to un-see the mauled stump of arm of the girl who tried to pet a bear at the Bronx Zoo, to un-smell cadavers in the morgue, to un-hear the screams of children with third-degree burns. Now there rose in memory the Mexican who had come to her house to clean out the septic tank. He had painted a sign on the door of his beaten-up pickup truck: YOUR SHIT IS MY BREAD AND BUTTER. He had explained: "*Perro que no ladra, no encuentra hueso.*" "The dog who doesn't bark doesn't get the bone." She had learned enough Spanish lately to translate that proverb.

Rhythmic rocking must have lulled her to sleep. Her muscles had adjusted to heaves and bends without effort on her part. She was jolted into consciousness when a metal door was slammed open, letting in a wave of journey-noise, the wailing of a locomotive's whistle. As the train was slowing down, she sat up quickly. Moby Dick and Scarlett were gone, as were the gentlemen who had been folding newspapers in order to study the Dow Jones and other batting averages. Gone, too, were some of the soldiers, though some remained in the baggage racks, their faces gray and creased and lumpy as dough. She must, she swore to herself, make an effort with Colonel. No Court Order would lift him from the rack of the tough world— but his flesh-and-blood daughter's love might.

"New HAVEN! NEW Haven!" A conductor was hurrying down the now-cleared aisle. She bent down to put her boots on.

They, too, were gone.

Mother of God. Trinc felt so disinherited by the theft that she threw back her head and laughed. If the whale tried to stuff flukes into *them* slippers, Prince Charming was bound to be disappointed.

She stood, retrieved coat and racquet and suitcase—still there!—from the rack. She snapped open the suitcase, found her worn-out tennis shoes, and put them on. As the train crawled past a platform, she scanned a waiting crowd and, feeling impelled by an excitement she had not expected, recognized Colonel not a hundred feet away wearing a battered fedora, a baggy brown suit, and a pair of spit-and-polished, calf-length First World War officer's boots. "Trinc" was the name of the only person he was waiting for. He had nicknamed her when, as a child, she had opened his bottle of French wine and tried to say "Drink." He had probably believed that all little girls grew up to be lusty, inebriated wenches with ample cleavage.

"MIND IF I SMOKE MY CIGAR?"

Superfluous the courtesy: Colonel had already lit the big black cigar, already extinguished the match with practiced flick of beefy hand. The tone of his voice seemed weirdly deferential. About the first thing he had said on the trolley-car ride from the station was to the effect he *had* changed his Will, making her his heir as soon as it could be signed tomorrow. She had to give him the palm for suddenly accepting a female as a worthy DeRoman. Seated on ladder-back chairs in his bed-sitter at the Lawn Club where females were strictly vetted, they were sharing the powers and privileges of the masculine hegemony.

"I love the aroma," she lied, yearning for a cigarette but fearful lest he perceive her nervousness.

"Havana." Drawing smoke until his sagging cheeks were sucked in, he exhaled with an expression of pure pleasure. "One of my Bones crowd got me a box of Havanas on the black market in New York."

"Lucky." Trinc had already surmised after a luncheon of filet mignon with Tabasco, french fries, cheese cake and sorbet in an exclusive male club that Colonel had no problem with wartime rationing. She herself was lucky to obtain a stick of butter per week, a tin of Spam in place of beef. The image of a Skull & Bones spook dealing on the black market struck her imagination as an emblem for her own loss of rectitude: a Gray Eminence standing behind the President of the United States, stepping out of an armored truck, and handing dollars over to a thickly mustachio'd Cuban in dark pin-striped suit, white tie, white shoes and the mandatory *sombrero de fieltro*. "You don't have to worry about a lack of shoes, stockings, bath towels, film, Coke, tires and soap flakes. I have to scrape away at a bar of

Ivory just to have flakes to use in the washing machine."

"We all make our sacrifices." Colonel peered over his sack of a belly and down at his boots.

"I wasn't complaining," she said, fearful he was alluding to Gayle, Jr.. She changed the subject to Santa Fe, how she had been welcomed at a "place" called P.O. Box 1663, how she had bought her house and hired Policarpio and Aida and purchased a car and motorcycle.

"It's about time," he remarked, "you spent some of your wealth on yourself and have servants with charming names and your first motor car. Tell me about the car."

It was also about time she told a story, DeRoman fashion, even though the joke was on her.

Civilians and military personnel were pouring in to work on the Hill. When she arrived in Santa Fe she discovered that most of the used cars had already been snapped up. She hoped she could find a luxury car that nobody else could afford or that the owner could not operate with only an A-ration card. "I placed an ad in *The New Mexican*," she said, warming to the story. "'Top dollar late model sedan', etc., and, presto, a movie producer in L. A. called to say that his girl friend in Santa Fe had a used Daimler she wanted to get rid of because she didn't like right-wheel drive; he gave me her number and her name, Theodosia Bird. I called her and said, 'Theodosia, I understand you are so-and-so's girl friend and want to sell your Daimler', and she said, 'I'm not his girl friend, I'm his piece of ass', and I said, 'Let's meet at La Fonda Hotel for cocktails', and we did. I expected Theodosia to be an old showgirl with peroxided hair and a Mae West snarl. But she was lovely, young, about twenty-five. She's not interested in getting married. She calls herself 'liberated'. Once a month the movie producer flies to Albuquerque in his private plane and they, you know . . . She studies law at the University of New Mexico but lives in Santa Fe during the summer—"

"Trinc!" Colonel erupted. "The Daimler! You go on as if you haven't spoken to anyone in a long time. You bought it?"

"Yes. It's silver-gray."

"British cars are hard to maintain in wartime. How much did you pay?"

"Five hundred cash," she said. "Theodosia was very nice."

"A good car?"

"It drove very well when Theodosia took me out for a spin."

"And?"

"After I bought it, I had Policarpio look it over."

"And?"

"He said it was a fixer-upper."

"A lemon?"

"Well," she said, "I don't know anything about cars. The whatyacallit, the carburetor needs replacement, and the radiator was full of oatmeal. Anyway, I'm storing it in the garage until the war's over."

Colonel cleared his throat. "Of course you informed this, er, whore, this Theodosia, about the mechanical difficulty?"

"Oh yes," Trinc said. "She was profusely apologetic. She said it was the movie producer's fault, giving her a car like that instead of cash. Anyway she thinks I'm pathetic to be chasing after a man when I could be, she said, 'living it up', and I should 'change my image'. 'Trinc', she said, 'I'm going to do you a favor'. And she did. She gave me her motorcycle."

"Her motorcycle."

"A Harley-Davidson. I told you I go to work on it."

"You live in a mansionhouse and go to work on a motorcycle?"

"Liberating."

"No more questions," Colonel said. He reached over and patted Trinc on the head. "*Toujours gai*, that's the spirit . . . I wasn't home to teach my little girl about the world. It might have been better to purchase a Studebaker wagon and a pair of mules than a Daimler, but . . . go like the wind on your motorcycle. Harvard may fight to the end but Yale will win! . . . Now tell me about Aeneas. Pretend I'm your lawyer."

Half an hour later they were still in his smoke-filled room. He still wore his polished boots.

If one un-remembered his vanities and prejudices, he really was a boy, her father, a boy with an affectionate nature and a desire to please. He was at heart a good soul who had served his country, as once his Wall Street clients, well. He had a right to call himself Colonel. He had a right to wear the Croix de Guerre and the Distinguished Service Cross. He was wearing them now on the breast of his brown jacket. But, Trinc realized with a pang, this boy, though only seventy, was old, old and heartbroken. She had noticed as he approached her at the station that he walked pigeon-footed with his body tilted forward as if he leaned into a wind. He still had the thick neck, beefy hands, and robust chest of a football player. The head, bald as the bust of a Roman emperor, was shrinking back against the skull; jowls resembled the gizzard of a buzzard.

His room was furnished simply. He had a roll-top desk, the ladder-back chairs, and what looked to be a Salvation Army bed. On one wall was hung a Confederate flag, a blue Yale pennant, and a framed medieval etching of Satan as a woman; on other walls were framed photographs, footballers with handlebar mustaches and hair parted down the middle, General Pershing (autographed), Marshal Foch (autographed), Gayle, Jr., in the uniform of a Navy fighter pilot, and she, herself, in a nurse's uniform looking as jaunty as Amelia Earhart.

"I'm not sure I agree," Colonel said. He had been standing at a window, listening to her with his hands linked behind his back. He turned about and hooked thumbs in vest pockets. "You tell me he's in love with a Japanese American girl. That could get him in a lot of trouble. But I like a man who is faithful to his feelings. Point in his favor. The other point in his favor is, he doesn't have my prejudices. I confess it to my chagrin: I don't mingle well with persons whose color and culture may differ from my own, and I believe that a woman's place is in the home.'

"Another thing. You say you refused him your bed because he was coming home late from the laboratory. You say he made his bed in the attic. You say he went on a camping trip even though you warned him of the consequences, namely, you and the children might be gone when he returned. So you up and deserted him the day before Pearl Harbor, and for over two years the two of you have led separate lives. My dear young lady." Colonel peered at her through red, rheumy eyes. "As a lawyer I would naturally refrain from finding fault with my client. As your father I must tell you your credibility is cuckoo. In fact, you've been bitchy. I don't know of any husband so misanthropic or so vindictive he would make his bed in the attic unless he truly believed his wife had banished him from her affections. I think you've developed the rather nasty habit of failing to put yourself in another person's shoes. Now that you've moved to Santa Fe to effect a reconciliation with Aeneas, you might consider offering him an apology . . . Has he committed adultery?"

"Aeneas?"

"Historical evidence to the contrary, namely my desertion of the family for another woman, I'm a great believer in fidelity. If Aeneas has been faithful to you, a reconciliation may be possible."

The question made her smile. "His penis is his bond," she said. "A few minutes of fun and he is committed for life. He would have to marry every woman he sleeps with, and Brigham Young he isn't."

"Have *you* committed adultery?"

"I?" She drew herself up. "I may be a bitch but I lead the lonely life of a *nice* bitch."

"Good," he nodded, still the lawyer. "Loneliness is a facilitator of accommodation. If you are willing to recommit yourself to love, and if you are contrite—I say 'contrite' instead of 'guilty' because guilt is a burden of self-absorption—Aeneas may feel inclined to forgiveness . . . Let me get this straight. Two responsible people keep themselves chaste for eight years, marry, have children, remain faithful, are blessed with good health and rewarding work and have money, with more money on the way. Why would the marriage be breaking down?"

"It needs a tune-up," Trinc said. She was still smarting from the accusation—from Colonel of all people!—that she had failed to put herself in another person's shoes. True, though, she had failed Aeneas.

"Like your Daimler, no doubt . . . Did the two of you become friends before you married? Your mother and I made that mistake. We married without becoming friends. It seems to me you and Aeneas understand one another and are able to communicate. He has fallen in love with another woman. He has the sand to confess as much. Your response? You tell him divorce is out of the question. Why do you oppose his freedom?"

"I don't oppose his freedom," she thought and said. "I support his genius . . . Can you think for a moment of anyone in the family, any DeRoman, any Heartwell, who will be remembered? Heartwell Brothers is already forgotten. You are not going to be remembered. You were a Wall Street lawyer. Nobody remembers Wall Street lawyers. Dr. Aeneas Caldwell is going to be remembered, to the rear of his betters, but remembered. I intend that he be accorded his place in history."

"This is new." Colonel cracked a weary smile. "If one as humbled before history as I may venture to express an opinion, there may be much in what you say. The century began with Einstein. By the end of the century these atomic physicists may well come to be regarded as in the vanguard of civilization. Push your man to great achievement! Good! I hadn't thought you would sacrifice yourself so much. I thought you wanted my money not because you need it but because it's *mine*. Now that you're going to get it, I'm delighted you have found a noble cause."

Trinc shifted in her seat. She heard in the distance the clanging of one of New Haven's antique, open-sided trolley-cars, the sound like that of a bell buoy to someone aboard a foundering ship. She had drifted from her moorings, had listened to the siren-song of a woman who mocked and hated—and still depended upon—men. At first Theodosia had seemed persuasive. Over cocktails at La

Fonda she had adroitly made Trinc, not the Daimler, the topic of conversation, made Trinc feel guilty for only pretending to play at a woman's need for self-fulfillment instead of committing herself to the Struggle, to defiance of spurious laws of thunder-gods whereby men subjected half the population of the globe. "Men," Theodosia had said, "should be our Pullman-car beds, pulled down for service at night and stuffed back in the walls during the day." Trinc had at another time accepted the Harley as demonstration of eagerness for revolution. Now this boy-father of hers who had once ridiculed suffragettes and perhaps still believed in the formula that Eve-ate-apple-equals-original-sin was applauding her spur-of-the-moment remark about using wealth to support genius. It was hardly a revolutionary cause. It was none the less a safe harbor. Trinc sensed a new vocation: a woman of eminence, a rich and powerful promoter of a husband with clay feet inside worn-out shoes, a force of destiny.

These reflections, which took but a moment, left a hollowness in the pit of her stomach. Colonel liked to play games. His part of the bargain had been to change his Will. Trinc's part was to present him with the Court Order changing Billy's name. *The dead man is paying.* She bit down on her lip and stood up. Blood rushed from her head.

"I've got cold feet," she managed to say in a voice above a whisper.

"Take off your tennis shoes. Let me get you a hot-water bottle."

She looked at him sharply. He wasn't mocking her. He seemed genuinely concerned. He was still standing in his lawyerly pose, still judging her as a witness of dubious credibility. There was tenderness in his wet eyes. "I mean," she said, "I don't like to play games."

"You've taught Aeneas to despise you, Trinc. Are you afraid you won't win him back?"

"That's not it at all. I despise myself."

"Then divorce him, let him go," Colonel said. "His alleged genius may require more than money to be accorded a place in history."

"The point is," Trinc began, stopped, and began again as her voice relaxed. "I've been impersonating the real owner of my life. I've allowed myself to become like one of those blobs on that new machine they call television—an image of someone inseparable from her role . . . I've brought you the Court Order."

She went and took the Order from her purse, transferred there when she had unpacked her suitcase at the Taft Hotel. "You are right. I've wanted your money because it's yours. I've wanted to prove that I'm as worthy of you as a son. But I want you to change your Will again. Now I want you to leave your money as you truly wish. I can't convert Billy into your namesake. I ask that you take this Court Order and tear it to pieces. I ask that you forgive me for tempting you. I don't want a benefit from your death. I want you alive, and for a long time."

"Forgive *me*," Colonel said, took the Order from her hand and without looking at it tore it into four pieces. "It won't be necessary to change my Will again. It's all drawn up at Pringle & Pringle, only awaiting my signature tomorrow to prevent my money from going to Yale . . . May I propose a plan for the rest of the afternoon in the company of my charming daughter, the last of the DeRomans?"

SHE RETURNED TO THE TAFT FOR A SNACK and nap. At four o'clock, as agreed upon, she brought her tennis things to the Lawn Club, left them there, and went with Colonel by trolley to the Green at Elm Street. With Yale occupied by the military, there was a Retreat ceremony every afternoon on the Green. Colonel had explained that he liked to go to it every day. They mingled in a large crowd as a column of more than a thousand men marched briskly out of the Old Campus, singing about the wild blue yonder, and assembled before a flagpole.

Colonel drew a small paper bag from his pocket. She thought he was going to scatter seeds to pigeons in the manner of lonely bums in Central Park. Instead, he stepped in front of the crowd and, removing from the bag a pair of baby shoes, kneeled in order to place them in a line-up of other shoes, men's military boots, already positioned. He came and stood rigidly by her side. As a military band began to play "The Star Spangled Banner," he held fedora over heart and moved lips soundlessly.

Trinc looked across the sunny Green, past the colonial church, past elms whose leaves were turning yellow and to the fortress-like walls of the Old Campus. Even though Yale had denied Gayle, Jr.'s application for admission, Colonel's Antigone-gesture, she now realized, made his son a part of tradition. Her gaze came down to the line of empty shoes as a bugler sounded the haunting notes of "Taps." The flag was inched down and furled. When Colonel had collected Gayle, Jr.'s baby shoes, tears glistened on his cheeks. He offered Trinc his arm. They decided to walk along Whitney Avenue.

"See there?" Colonel pointed. "The tops of street lamps are painted black so that no glow can shine upward. Of course we don't expect an air raid anymore."

"You haven't, have you, covered your heart so that no glow can shine upward?" she said in teasing tone. She hugged his arm, the jacket flavored with old-man odor and the residual effluvium of cigars. "Before the war," she said, "Aeneas spoke of the possibility of a bomb that can destroy an entire city in an instant. I think, but don't know, that's what he does on the Hill, making a bomb to end the war. It would be unprecedented in human history. If I hadn't been so stupid stupid stupid, I would have realized earlier why he was being so secretive and so distant from the family . . . Walk slowly . . . I'll tell you a story. Aeneas works, as I do, every day but Sunday at this secret place we call the Hill. A few weeks ago he drove to Santa Fe and picked up the children to take them fishing . . ."

She began the story as the children had told it to her.

It had been a hot cloudless summer morning, one of those New Mexican mornings when one can see clearly for a hundred miles, the last trapezoid patches of snow on the Truchas Peaks shining like polished silver platters set out for gods and goddesses. After driving the Ford into the mountains Aeneas had parked by a lake that was a blue eye in a green Cyclops. The canoe he had rented from a Santa Fe sporting goods store awaited them. They paddled it to the middle of the lake, dropped fishing lines. Somehow they had paid little attention to the crack of thunder and the swift blackening of the sky. Suddenly lightning daggered down to a distant peak. Rain fell, pitter-patter on water that had been glass, followed by a fierce wind that had aspens on the shore violently convulsed. Hailstones rattled the canoe with the rapid drumfire of a waterfall, hailstones big as golf balls. The canoe had begun to sink.

"They swim for their lives," Trinc continued. "The water is icy cold. It numbs their bodies. Their teeth are chattering. But they are all good swimmers. They reach shore and run shivering to the car. Later, when they get home, Billy is feverish. His cheeks are burning hot. His eyes are glazed, his speech is slurred. Policarpio lifts him up and carries him to my bed in the master bedroom. I take Billy's temp. 1-0-4. Pneumonia, I think. Aeneas goes to look for a doctor."

They paused on the curb. She took his elbow, and he allowed her to guide him across the avenue. She resumed her story.

"He couldn't find a doctor. What does he do, the big oaf? He goes to the Governor's Palace where Indians squat on the portico bricks and sell silver and turquoise trinkets to tourists. He asks for a *curandera*, a medicine woman, one of those witches who are supposed to keep owls. The great physicist, you see, believes in nonrational healing. The Indians tell him there's an old Pojoaque woman named Tonantzin who has, they say, 'the power'. She is in the plaza.'

"I hear the car. I rush to open the door. Aeneas is there with this old Pojoaque woman wrapped in a black *rebozo*. Her skin is as wrinkled as that of a sea-turtle at the Aquarium. Her unfathomably black eyes glitter like obsidian. While Aeneas is explaining things, Tonantzin brushes past me. I am in a kind of trance. I go and stand by the bedroom door and watch this tiny woman caress Billy's face and chest and limbs with hands like the talons of eagles. She takes some dried corn out of a pouch and sprinkles it in four directions leading from the bed. She begins to chant in a low and unintelligible voice that makes my sinuses vibrate. After a while Tonantzin approaches Aida, mutters something in Spanish, gives her some herbs. When Aida returns from the kitchen with a bowl of tea that looks like chewing tobacco, Tonantzin pours the concoction down Billy's throat. His body jerks as if he has stuck his finger in an electric socket. He becomes rigid and stares at the *vigas* over his head.'

"I am, as I said, in a kind of trance. When Tonantzin gives instructions in Spanish to Policarpio and he passes them along in English to me, I just nod my head. No one is to come near the bed until the moon has risen to its highest point in the firmament. The window must be left open. The electricity must be turned off. Clocks and wristwatches must be collected and stored in the pantry. All this was done. Aeneas, Diana, and I, and the servants, we sit with our backs against the walls of the bedroom and wait until moonlight floods the room with a soft blue glow. We hear a strange voice from outside the house, below the open window. Old Tonantzin is crooning softly. There is no other sound but this one. I have a sensation as if feathers are gliding over my nerves and simplifying the almost infinite complexity of the soul. How long this procedure continues, I do not know, having no watch, but suddenly the singing stops. It leaves a hollow space in the pit of my stomach.'

"Billy sat up in bed. 'Where's Grandpa Gayle?' he asked in a plaintive voice. 'Where's Grandpa Gayle? We didn't say we love him.'" Trinc paused to look her father in the eye. "He had been frightened of you two years ago when you got drunk at my birthday party and left the house without saying good-bye. Yet in the critical moment he was worried about you. I dared not approach the bed until I made sure the moon had risen to its highest point in the firmament. I went outside. The Sangre de Cristos bulged in the wash of light. Tonantzin was gone.'

"When I returned to the bedroom, Aeneas, barefooted, was already hugging and kissing Billy. 'The fever's gone', Aeneas said to me. He put his arms around me for the first time in years and spoke the words of a hymn:

> "Send down Thy peace, O Lord;
> Earth's bitter voices drown
> In one deep ocean of accord,
> Thy peace, O God, send down."

They paused at the entrance to the Lawn Club. Colonel cleared throat. "You made that up," he said with a nervous twitch of lips.

"I didn't make it up, Daddy," she gasped. Through the agency of Billy's very words she had confessed that she loved him, and yet in the Cordelia moment she had not only failed to heave her heart into her mouth but also come across as dishonest.

"I want you to have Gayle's shoes," he said.

"Thanks very much," she declared with ill-concealed sarcasm. "I don't think they're quite large enough to replace my shitkickers."

"I want you to take them now, goddamnit, now, and keep them!" He thrust the paper bag into her hands. His face was almost apoplectic in its redness, visibly shaken by a wrath for which her jealousy of a brother, hitherto unacknowledged by herself, was responsible.

"O.K., Daddy," she said. "I understand you now."

"LOVE FORTY." HE WAS CALLING from his side of the net for a time-out. He waddled to the chain-link fence that had caged them in the tennis court for almost an hour. He toweled his face off, leaned over, extracted a cigar from a box, stuck it unlighted in his mouth and sashayed back to baseline in an exhibition of cockiness.

She had never played such a terrible game of tennis before. On service she was tossing the ball as if it were made of cast iron, hacking at it without follow-through, pooping it into the net. She had double-faulted so often that Colonel merely stood with racquet at side. He himself served flat-footed, pulling the racquet in front of his face and dinking the ball so gently that it seemed to fall over the net out of weariness. Somehow he served aces. When she gathered anchored feet in order to swipe at one of his patty-cake bloopers, she seemed to have the athleticism of an Emily Dickinson. Trinc hadn't won a single point. He led five games to zero, and she was losing service at love forty.

Colonel removed the cigar. "Let's call it a draw and retire to the clubhouse for martinis," he called out.

Trinc stared at her racquet. "I don't understand what happened to my game."

"Call Tonantzin," he said, "for some power."

"I need a cigar," she said.

"Ladies at the Club are not allowed to smoke cigars."

"I won't smoke it. It will just be a phallic symbol."

"I'm down to my last cigar," he grumbled, but he sauntered over to the fence and took a cigar from his box of black-market Havanas.

She could play singles for five sets followed by doubles for three. She had a service, American twist, that left her opponents' bodies stumbling and crashing unfooted to the court. Her volleys exploded off her racquet with the force of something useful for military ordnance. Her forehand passing shots caused players to mutter curses. Her backhand slices, like a baseball pitcher's sinkerballs, could make a player's racquet into a flyswatter with a hole in it.

Approaching the net, he held out a cigar, hesitantly. "I won't accept it," she said, also approaching the net, "if you're going to be petulant."

"I won't need it. I'm going to die."

"Don't try to psych me out," she said. "With one point remaining to be played? Pull yourself together and take victory like a man . . . Are you going to die right now?"

He patted his chest. "It's my heart."

"Have you seen a doctor?"

"What good would it do?"

"Shall I take your blood pressure?"

"It's the aloneness of it all," he said. "When you told me I'll be forgotten, you only said what everybody thinks about Wall Street lawyers."

"You're my father, not my lawyer," Trinc snapped. "I'll remember you . . . Did you smoke a cigar when I was born?"

"What difference does it make?"

"Lots, if you were so disappointed about having a daughter that you couldn't celebrate. At least Abraham waited for his 90-year-old bride to deliver the goods. Shall we finish the set? We all have to die sooner or later . . . Now give me the darned cigar."

He passed it over the net. His own cigar he again had stuck, at an aggressive angle and wet with saliva, between his teeth. "Remember, Colonel DeRoman was a man."

"You shouldn't have reminded me," she said. She stuck *her* cigar between her teeth, turned her back, marched to baseline. Acting upon a sudden inspiration, she took off her shoes and socks. She hitched up skirt. She plucked linen shirt away from bra. She clawed hair away from eyes. She ran in place, feet happy on grass, knees like pistons. She shook out her arms, snarled at the sun, clamped down on the cigar. She muttered to herself, "That good for nothing, double-dealing galoot! 'Y' stands for Yellow!" Ready at last, she gripped racquet, rocked on feet, bounced the ball in left hand three times, tossed it high, gathered bare feet under her, arched back and swung the racquet.

ping THWOP!

A puff of dust rose from the grass in front of Colonel.

"I wasn't ready," he said.

"Bull," she said. "Fifteen forty." She returned to baseline, again prepared herself and tossed the ball. She met it at the furthest extension of her arm: *ping* THWOP! The ball left him standing motionlessly in his shoes. The cigar had dropped from his mouth.

"Ace," she said.

"Out," he said. "Second serve."

"You never saw it," she protested.

He picked up cigar, clamped it. "Out."

"Cheat," she said. "This one's for Mother. You cheated on her, too." As she prepared to serve, she noticed that he was crouching inside his baseline, expecting her to give him something soft, something he could kill. She decided to slam the ball with spin enough to kick it into his solar plexus. She tossed the ball, swung: *ping* THWOP! It was a slow-motion movie, Colonel back-pedaling with what looked like a peeled brown banana smashed against his mouth. She had scored a direct hit on his cigar. She approached the net, tossed him her cigar. "It's the General Staff," she said. "It's the Empire State Building. Thirty forty."

She returned to baseline. "This one's for the Indians," she said.

"What Indians?"

"Custer's Last Stand."

"I don't see any Indians."

"That's what *he* said."

ping THWOP!

"Deuce."

He retreated to the fence, glared at her. She decided to take everything off her next serve, curl him a chopper over the net. "This one's for God, for country, and for Yale," she said.

"Leave Yale out of it," he said.

"That's the idea," she said. "Thanks for changing your Will."

ping zzz flop.

"My advantage," she said as he picked himself up from the

grass. She decided to dink him one of his own kind of itty-bitty patty-cake bloopers and volley his return. "This one's for equal rights for women," she said.

"What have women got to do with tennis?"

"If all you score is love, you got nothing."

ping pop GA-SWOP!

Her volley had knocked the racquet out of his hand. "You're trying to kill me," he said.

"I'm taking you in live for the necktie party," she said. "Your serve."

His side of the court now looked as big as Kansas. At the net she would spook the Skull & Bones spook out of him. Sure enough, after three double faults he just managed to lob the ball over the net. She took it on the high bounce and crunched it with her overhead slam. It bounced over the fence, off an elm tree, and across a garden before it came to rest by a lamp post, the top of which had been painted black as a precaution against such air raids.

Twenty minutes later she was serving for the break at five games to five, forty love. Colonel was walking hunched over, like Quasimodo. He waved for time-out. Dripping with sweat and panting heavily, he took the cigar from his mouth. "You'll never get the crown jewels," he taunted and added, "Private DeRoman."

"You shouldn't have told me," Trinc said. Off in the distance a motorman was beating a steady clang on his trolley's resonant floor-gong. Safe harbor was close.

He hunkered down and covered crotch with racquet.

High, high went the toss.

Back, back went her arch.

The ball seemed to hang overhead in space-time, a Mother Earth spinning in equilibrium with the Sun.

ping THWOP!

Low, low sailed the ball over net. High, high over baseline flew her soiled feet.

"A-yeeee!"

His scream reminded her of Scarlett. Now he was a letter "X," legs spraddled sideways, racquet dropped, arms down, hands over crotch and eyes squeezed shut in the attitude of an impotent mythology. She leapt over the net as he made gurgling noises in his throat and clawed at the air.

Then he bounced to his feet, laughing. "Heh-heh-heh." The cigar he dropped to the grass was only a damp firecracker. "You missed."

"Exhibitionist," she said. She had a sensation of enormous relief. "We'll call it a draw."

Redfaced and chortling he came and laid a heavy arm on her shoulder in a fraternal gesture. "Did I ever tell you, Colonel Caldwell," he said, "that the boots I wore today are the same pair I was wearing when Black Jack Pershing presented to me at a formal ceremony the DSC? Well, I want you to have them."

"Do I get a 'goddamnit' with my promotion, Daddy?"

He picked up his racquet, went to the fence and returned with towel, cigar box, and can of tennis balls.

There were no enemy aircraft in the sky, only stars invisible in daylight. She knew they were there, knew she fitted into them as they into her. "Have I told you," she said, "about the Mexican who cleaned out my septic tank and said, 'The dog who doesn't bark doesn't get the bone'? Martini time."

When she lowered her gaze, he was meeting it. "Goddamnit, General DeRoman," he said quietly and gently, "goddamnit." He beamed upon her a beautifully warm smile before his face crumpled like little Scarlett's. He dropped the items in his hands and reached to clutch his chest and pitched forward upon the grass. She ran and knelt over him to feel for his pulse. She could not suppress the unprofessional Florence Nightingale gasp of horror. He was no longer pretending.

For the next few days she would be as much as possible *un*feeling the grief that would let go of her only at death. She called the ambulance and it came. She called Pringle & Pringle and next day went to see one of their lawyers in his office after she had stayed awake half the first night at the Taft Hotel, resisting the urge to smoke a cigarette but not to weep. Colonel's Will was, as she believed it would be, unsigned, the former Will giving the estate to Yale incontestable and ready for probate. It surprised her that Colonel wished to be cremated, his ashes left unburied and unsung, no memorial service, no reading of the record, no monument. Again she had a sensation of enormous relief. She even laughed to herself, knowing Colonel, the *great* lawyer, would have been first to grasp the irony and accept the mockery of his failure to sign his own Will. It took her only an afternoon to return his curiously Spartan room to its original state, an empty and powerless and nameless ruin. She tagged the furniture for delivery to Salvation Army. She boxed books and papers for delivery to Sterling Memorial Library. The Yale pennant, the Confederate flag, and the etching of Satan as a woman she put in a small box labeled FROM GENERAL DEROMAN TO SPOOKS, SKULL & BONES, YALE STATION. She boxed and addressed to herself in Santa Fe the medals, Gayle, Jr.'s baby shoes, and a vellum scroll showing a family tree from which the name of Charlemagne had been so removed that only she would have known it had ever been there. She had scissored it out, separated the emperor from greatness, and stuffed two pieces of leftover, wadded-up parchment into the toe-ends of Colonel's boots. Having saved herself the expense of buying Dr. Scholls's inserts at a drugstore, she wriggled her toes inside the boots and discovered in them a perfect fit.

The morning she stood on the platform waiting for the train that would take her to New York and Points West—to the husband whose love and honor and sacrifice she understood and cherished as never before—she might have been observed wearing a pair of spit-and-polished, calf-length First World War officer's boots, her shoes now, General DeRoman's shoes. They were not exactly the bone she had barked for. They were none the less a bone.

21

The Undoing of the Wild

A lone gray wolf had been for many years roaming the Jémez Mountains and the valley of the Rio Grande. In the higher elevations where there were no man-made marks in applegreen meadows and blue forests of spruce, aspen, and ponderosa he had howled unmolested at many moons with bones in their teeth. Free, he had looked down thousands of feet from rocky promontories to ancient Indian pueblos and Spanish villages. He had hunted for rabbits and wild turkey in the deep-cut, golden-streaked canyons and arroyos of the Pajarito Plateau where the Old Ones had built and abandoned their pueblecitos a thousand years ago. Even when the lodge and log cabins and water tower of the Los Alamos Ranch School intruded upon his sanctuary, he seemed to have nothing to fear. He believed in the principle of eminent domain.

So he had grown bold.

About the time when brilliant Canopus skimmed the southern horizon with her red, blue, and yellow feathers, about the time snow whirled and drifted to a depth over his head, he followed a narrow, winding, precipitous dirt road down to the valley and sacrificed chickens, sheep, and goats. As he licked the bones he listened to what Brother Eagle or

Brother Deer might have to say to him about the farmers with thundersticks; he had developed some acquaintance with their whine and, occasionally, sting. About the time when winds dried the earth to a parched khaki color and walls of coffee-colored water hurtled down from the mountains to the river, he always returned to the wilds of immeasurable America.

Suddenly huge yellow caterpillars churned dust, leveled trees, tore down hills. Applegreen barracks and factories sprouted where meadows should have been. Fencing appeared, miles and miles of it, chain-link fences seven feet high with barbed wire coiled atop. Armed men patroled the mesa on horseback. Sirens wailed. The air was full of black smoke. Jeeps and trucks and tractors crawled into the mountains. In the past year there had been many ear-splitting explosions. Thousands of trees lay flattened as if smacked by the hand of a wanton god. Game grew scarce. Streams and puddles stank.

The old wolf grew sick. Slowly and painfully his life was ebbing away . . .

JUST BEFORE DAWN ONE DAY IN APRIL, 1945, Aeneas emerged from a laboratory in remote Omega Canyon and lit his pipe. For weeks he had been assisting Otto Frisch and his group with an experiment that Dick Feynman had likened to tickling the tail of a sleeping dragon: split-second atomic explosions. The group had erected a ten-foot iron frame, a "guillotine" that supported upright aluminum guides, these being surrounded at table level with blocks of uranium hydride. To the top of the guillotine the experimenters raised a hydride core slug about two by six inches in size. It would fall under the influence of gravity, accelerating at 32 feet per second/per second, and when it passed between the blocks it would momentarily form a critical mass. Even though the U-235 reacted slowly due to its having been mixed with hydride, the Dragon *did* stir. The experimenters had come as near as possible to direct evidence of an explosive chain reaction without blowing up the lab and its weary inhabitants— or the world.

Like Frisch, Aeneas had worked about seventeen hours a day and allowed only the period from dawn to mid-morning for sleep. He had never felt so exhausted in his life. Between his actions and his consciousness a chasm had been widening for years, like a permanent fault in the geography of his mind.

His hand trembled as he lit the pipe. Stress-pain, as it had for years, gnawed at cranial nerves. Eyeballs felt as if a cat had been scratching them. Perhaps there was something more to his symptoms than fatigue and stress, something insidious. No one knew what acceptable levels of radioactivity were. No one knew how many years, weeks, or days might pass before the Dragon's bite produced a fatal proliferation of leukocytes.

That he was suffering from moral asphyxia, he had no doubt. The work at Los Alamos had been difficult and exciting, the culmination of three centuries of physics, work that should have been accompanied by a feeling of exaltation commensurate with the discovery in secret places of the ticking of the universe. Although he was only a small vessel in a flotilla surrounding such battleships as Bohr, Fermi, Teller, Segré, Bethe, Frisch, Director J. Robert Oppenheimer and others, he had made his contribution to the building of the Bomb. He had assembled particles so that they would interact with each other, hit each other, scatter, sometimes give rise to new particles. As one of the seniors associated with the project—he was fifty-five, five years younger than Bohr but fourteen years older than Oppenheimer and more than twice the age of the majority of the assembled scientists—he had sometimes been consulted about matters for which the very young, locked-in to their specializations and cowed by authority, might have limited discernment. But to suffer a loss of moral consciousness and at the same time to be aware of that loss was a disturbance bordering on schizophrenia. It was as if he could permit himself only a small dose of remorse of conscience. Once he started *thinking*, he exposed himself to the contamination of guilt.

Puffing on pipe he had the sensation that he was being watched. He scanned the rim of the canyon. Probably some of General Groves's ubiquitous security agents were prowling around up there, sniffing for treason. Indeed, now, something on a rocky ledge outside the chain-link fence had just moved. A shadow, a gray blur. An animal of some kind, a large animal, larger than a coyote. It was a wolf. It was hunkered down on the ledge and was staring, it seemed, at him, staring with eyes that mirrored the slate-gray birth of billions of years of dawn.

For a moment Aeneas knew the atavistic fear of the Paleolithic hunter. His viscera tightened. Then he relaxed. There was less and less mystery about Leviathan, at least where nuclear reactions were concerned. When the Dragon stirred, it produced little wonder. But this majestic wolf—why, it was mysterious and wonderful!

Still it stared at him. Aeneas gave the wolf a hand-salute of recognition, knocked ashes from pipe, and returned to the lab. Some men were already stretched out on cots, sleeping the instant, dreamless sleep at the limit of endurance. A nauseating odor of unwashed bodies mingled with that of scorched metal. A cotton-woolly fog of drowsiness was gathering in his brain. As he sat on a cot and prepared to sleep with his boots and field jacket on, he thought he heard the howling of the wolf. The sound shivered through him. Again there came the cry of the wolf, a hauntingly melancholy song that awakened in his soul long memories of its own ancestral wildness.

He kept by his cot a pair of binoculars with which to observe the eagles and hawks and bluejays of the Pajarito Plateau. He grabbed the binoculars and went outside. The wolf was still on the rocky ledge outside the chain-link fence. Focusing the binoculars, Aeneas could see that the wolf was scratching himself. And then he saw a sight that he would hope never to meet again in dreams, a sight he had seen before, seen only six months ago when Roguey, who had been running loose near the Tech Area ever since Aeneas had arrived in Los Alamos two years ago, exhibited a suppurating jaw and swollen tongue and patches where hair had fallen out. He had to have a vet put down the cocker spaniel. The wolf, as had happened to Roguey, was dying of radiation contamination.

He lowered the binoculars. He had not permitted himself a grieving for the loss of his dog except for a feeling that had passed through his heart like a slug accelerated by gravity. Now the sight of the wolf undid him with the unspeakable realization of the undoing of the wild. Tears rolled down his cheeks in the acid-cold air.

THE WOLF HAD CLOSED THE CHASM in his mind. Whether it was he had always mystically perceived a bridge between mind and matter, or whether he had never quite lost his innocence, from the moment he saw the dying wolf his faith flooded back. He was once again intensely aware of the interconnectedness of all life, once again filled with awe and reverence, with compassion. Surely the primal consciousness of a creative spirit in the universe had never been wrong. Science affirmed it. One had but to lift the mask of the obstructing self in order to participate in a dance of light and feel humbled in relationships of every kind, including relationship with a dispossessed and heedlessly sacrificed wolf.

Frisch of the British Mission made his report about the Dragon experiments, and the group disbanded. Aeneas returned from Omega Canyon to his "normal" life, kept office hours in the Tech Area, filed classified documents in his safe, attended Oppenheimer's colloquia, dined at Fuller Lodge, and slept in the snug chinked-log cabin which had been his "bachelor" quarters. He was *thinking* again. Like everyone else who knew the purpose of the secret project on the Hill, he had chosen to surrender authority in the matter of the atomic bomb to a separate, secret state, an elite presided over by President Roosevelt. The choice had been justified by the need to race against time as the German Reich made itself invulnerable and dominated the planet through possession of atomic bombs. But with the liberation of Paris by Allied troops came the news that Germany's uranium project had failed, perhaps sabotaged by Heisenberg. The "Lost Almosts," as wags among scientists and their families called themselves, were proceeding to build the Bomb even though it would, Aeneas hoped, not be used.

Now Roosevelt had died. Suddenly, it seemed, the secret state and the public state might be combined as a single sovereignty to which alone the scientists and other independent-minded investigators would become subservient, no longer hierophants of the mystery and wonder of the universe but mere pawns of coercive government.

Aeneas realized how empty his life had become. He could live it no longer alone, separated from Trinc and the kids.

Recently he had had a dream. In the dream he was sitting on the back porch of a small apartment building in Brooklyn Heights with a view of New York harbor from the Statue of Liberty to the skyscrapers of lower Manhattan.

The place, he recognized. In the old days he had often strolled across Brooklyn Bridge to visit a Harvard classmate who lived in the Heights in precisely that apartment. The two of them would talk and drink beer for hours and contemplate the view, tugboats escorting an ocean liner toward the Narrows, the Statue lifting her lamp beside the golden door, the skyscrapers trying like blind periscopes to subjugate the sky. Although these images presented themselves in the dream, its focus was upon the tens of thousands of lights in a checkerboard pattern upon the skyscrapers. They horrified him. Turn off the lights! Go home before it's too late! It's all useless, useless, useless! He silently shouted. As if in response to him windows in the skyscrapers were flung open. An old woman appeared in one of the windows. She had a cloth wrapped around her head and in her hands she carried a mop. She squeezed and shook the mop. She closed the window. Other tiny figures appeared at windows, all of them women, all squeezing and shaking mops in a synchronized performance like that of the Rockettes at Radio City. Then all the mops were pulled in, all the windows closed.

Save two. In the two open windows, darkly silhouetted against a background of gold like that in a Byzantine painting, two mopless women appeared, their oval-eyed faces shining upon him: Trinc and Blevyn.

When he woke from the dream, he not only recalled it but also was able to interpret it. The scrubwomen were indifferent to his apocalypse-crisis. While the clerks and the secretaries and the executive officers and sundry others who crawled over these antheaps in the daytime had gone home, legions of women occupied them by night, unacknowledged legislators, like Shelley's poets, tidying up the accumulated debris left behind by the violent and clandestine patriarchs. Trinc and Blevyn, although they were not scrubbing floors, were aligned with women throughout the ages. In the dream—in the spiritual dimension—they were one and the same person manifesting the ineradicable human need for survival.

Beyond the dream there was the dimension of time. When, in it, he contemplated Trinc and Blevyn, bringing them before the bar of fate and considering his love for them from the perspective of growth, he recognized and accepted what he had become: a scarecrow. In the dream, Trinc had been young, but her youthfulness, including the power to inflict pain, had not irritated him. Blevyn's youthfulness, on the other hand, had, and he discovered that he pitied her. It was not a patronizing pity. It was a father's pity for a daughter, the adoring mirror which has yet to be put to the test of life and possibly shattered. And he already had a daughter, Diana, almost a woman of the same age, eighteen, as Trinc had been in Poughkeepsie, Diana now a slender, peerless beauty with Trinc's auburn hair and large, soft brown eyes, Diana chaste as her name.

With these reflections he sacrificed Blevyn. He had actually sacrificed her from the beginning. In January, 1942, more than three years ago, he had taken Ma-Betty's advice and kept his promise to send Blevyn his letters. Had he been trying to prove to himself the reality of an impossible love? And when he asked Trinc if she wanted a divorce, had he been trying to stifle his doubts about a marriage with Blevyn?

He needed Trinc now as never before. She was the only wife, the only lover, he had ever really wanted.

She had been a "poor little rich girl," but from the time he had met her in 1916 to the time he had married her in 1924 to the time of their separation, Pearl Harbor Day to the present, he had not wanted her money. It had been until recently his rival. She had, he had believed, DeRoman's original endowment plus an inheritance from Ednah Heartwell and from Hen; she had, he had until recently assumed, inherited five-million dollars from Colonel following his death from a heart attack in New Haven in September, 1943. She was independent. Good. She desired fulfillment. Good. She had employment as a nurse. Good. But if she didn't need his love, what part could he act except that of an old friend, loyal, helpful, and reserved, glad to be of service but careful not to get too involved? And what if she spurned him when he renewed the courtship? Would he then succumb to fantasies about a New Life with Blevyn? She had been sacrificed and a chain reaction of affections had followed. He reviewed the situation over and over. First, he had called Ma-Betty to the rescue. Second, Ma-Betty had discovered for herself Blevyn's artistic talent and vocation. Third, Ma-Betty had persuaded a New York magazine to publish Blevyn's sketches in an article about Japanese American life in an internment camp. Fourth, late in 1944, Ma-Betty had secured Blevyn's release from Tule Lake, escorted her to New York, and introduced her to the art world's cognoscenti. Fifth and finally and only last month, Ma-Betty had set Blevyn up in the *morada* of Los Remedios.

Remedies indeed! Although Ma-Betty had not been one of the goddess-like ladies in his dream, she had been mopping up her romantic boy's mistakes—a Venus ex machina.

Oppenheimer was giving a memorial tribute to Roosevelt on Sunday, April 15. Aeneas had asked Trinc and Diana to drive up from Santa Fe for the occasion and to stay overnight as his guests at Fuller Lodge. Trinc responded enthusiastically to the invitation.

ONE CHILLY AFTERNOON TWO YEARS AGO he had been grading papers at home in Poe's Hill when there was a knock on the door. Out on the stoop, rubbing his hands and looking nervously about, stood a little man in a baggy suit, a porkpie hat pulled down to his eyebrows. He recognized Jack Lehman, a fast-neutron physicist for whose doctoral thesis Aeneas had served in the capacity of outside examiner.

"Jack!" he exclaimed in surprise as he opened the door. "You act as if you're being followed . . . Come in, for crying out loud, and have a hot toddy."

"Is anyone here?" Jack said in stage whisper.

"Just me and the dog." Aeneas explained that the rest of the family was in New York so that the children could have private schooling. Jack came in, removed his hat, and, without a word to Aeneas who was following him, went through the house, inspected closets, drawing blinds, and closing and locking doors. As he seemed to be burning with an inner fire, Aeneas said nothing until they were sitting in the living room. "How about that toddy, old man?" He rose.

"Sit down," Jack said. "No matter what you do for the rest of your life, nothing will be as important to the future of the world as your work on the project I am here to tell you about."

Half an hour later the "project" still remained a matter of high-sounding words such as "honor," "duty," "fate of civilization" and mysterious references to "a Shangri-la in the Jémez Mountains" and to "P. 0. Box 1663, Santa Fe." The latter, it seemed, would be his only address. He would need to secure a leave of absence from the university and a security clearance from the government.

"When can you leave?" Jack asked after Aeneas had agreed to be recruited.

Aeneas said he could leave almost immediately. "I don't need persuasion to go to New Mexico," he added. "I lived there once, and my mother lives in Taos."

Jack frowned. "It is forbidden to leave Site Y except on Sundays and then only to stay in the immediate area. You will need special permission for your mother to come to live with you."

"Not to worry." Aeneas started to laugh at Jack's misinterpretation but refrained. Jack, like most physicists, came ill-equipped with a sense of humor. It seemed that he and his boss, Oppenheimer of Berkeley, had been recruiting some men too young to be parted from their mothers.

As soon as Jack left, Aeneas cried out, "Shangri-la, Roguey! If you weren't a security risk, I'd tell you we're probably going to develop a bomb in which energy will be released by a fast neutron action." The dog cocked his head. Aeneas was certain that this project would be the one he had foreseen as being inevitable after he heard Bohr and Fermi break the news of atomic fission. He had also already learned through scientific channels that Fermi, working in 1942 at a secret location at the University of Chicago, had established the feasibility of a chain reaction. Aeneas had needed no persuasion about the importance of the project. The truly astonishing thing was that the remote mountains of New Mexico had been selected as the center for a world-shaking event.

He was so excited he forgot that he was supposed to be on no speaking terms with Trinc. He called her in New York with his news. "Why don't you and the children come for a visit this summer?"

"Will we all fit into a P. O. Box?"

"It's out of the pages of Willa Cather's *Death Comes for the Archbishop*," he said, "dark coppery faces of Indians and so forth. The children will love it."

"And what will you be doing?"

"I'll be manufacturing the front ends of horses to be shipped to Washington for completion."

For the first time in years he heard her laugh. That fact plus the lure of one of her favorite novelists led to a deal: she and the children would come to Santa Fe in July, later in 1943.

In April he went. As he and Roguey crossed the country in the Ford he congratulated himself for breaking the ice. Perhaps Trinc, not just the children, would be enchanted with New Mexico. Upon arrival in Santa Fe, however, he had misgivings. Unlike Ma-Betty and Blevyn, Trinc could not possibly be enchanted by a city of 20,000 populated mostly by poor Mexicans and consisting mostly of adobe structures that looked as if they had been dropped from the sky during a rainstorm. When he reported for duty at 109 East Palace, a one-story building with a shabby screen door leading to an inner office, he received a warm greeting from a smiling, blue-eyed woman in her forties, Dorothy McKibbin, and imagined her as a friend for Trinc. But when Dottie gave him directions to Site Y about forty miles away—take the Taos highway to Pojoaque, turn left for ten miles on the washboard dirt road, cross the Rio Grande at Otowi and try not to get stuck in the mud on the way up to elevation 7,200 feet—he had a shock of recognition. This was no Shangri-la he was going to. It was Los Alamos, site of a dude-ranch school for boys in need of Spartan discipline. Ma-Betty had visited it to have lunch at the lodge and to ride trails that led to a hot spring. Surely Trinc would take one look at Los Alamos and head for the divorce courts.

After Dottie McKibbin cranked out for him a pass on a primitive machine, he followed her directions. The sky darkened, lightning flashed, thunder roared. As he negotiated hairpin turns on the way up to Pajarito Plateau, he appreciated her warning: several cars were stranded up to their hubcaps in mud, leaving their miserable drivers to curse in what seemed to be a variety of European languages. No, this was no country for Susan Heartwell DeRoman Caldwell even though memory contradicted this conviction. She had always likened herself to a water-fairy. Out of that element she materialized in Poughkeepsie. During the Cherry Grove hurricane of 1939 she had behaved with the fortitude of a duchess on the *Titanic*.

Later that first day he was the one who felt disenchanted. MPs in battle helmets met him at the East Gate, scrutinized his pass. Jack Lehman hadn't mentioned that the project was under military control. At the old pump house, a temporary security office, WACS photographed him and pressed his fingerprints on a permanent pass. At the housing office in an old wooden garage beside a water tower, he was assigned a room in the Big House, a two-story men's dormitory. Only through stubborn persistence was he able to get assignment to a small log cabin that had belonged to the boys' school and that was tucked away in a quiet stand of pines away from the military-style barracks, Quonset huts and trailers, away from the Tech Area under construction behind a Cyclone fence. That evening as he dined in Fuller Lodge, charmed as he was by the massive *vigas* that supported the cathedral ceiling, by the sight of great logs ablaze on the hearth, and by the breath-taking view through French doors of the Sangre de Cristo he had so loved in his youth, he had encountered Oppenheimer. Nervously swinging his limbs as he spoke in soft voice, the Director, cigarette in mouth, had no sooner introduced himself than he asked, apropos nothing, "Do you know what *Ahimsa* means, Dr. Caldwell?"

Aeneas vaguely remembered from a philosophy class at Harvard that *Ahimsa* was a Sanscrit word meaning "doing no harm." If this man who worried about harming people was responsible for building an atomic bomb, he had Aeneas's sympathy. "I'm not a sage, Dr. Oppenheimer," Aeneas said, "but

I recall what Shakespeare says in *Measure for Measure*: 'It is excellent to have a giant's strength, but it is tyrannous to use it like a giant'."

Oppenheimer had smiled slyly, then moved on to the next table and crushed his cigarette in an ashtray in a strange kind of tantrum, as if driven beyond endurance by his moral dilemma.

For months Aeneas had been helping Jack Lehman install, first, a cyclotron, then a long-tank Van de Graaf generator. When he was permitted to meet the "Santa Fe Chieftain" in Lamy, he was confronted by the three persons he had loved most dearly— though, it seemed, on another planet known to those on the Hill as Civilization. Diana flung her arms around his neck. Already affected by preppy decorum, Billy just shook hands but threw him sideways glances full of a shyly concealed admiration. Trinc herself, though she flinched when he kissed her on the cheek, made lively conversation about the trip, New York, the children's doings. It had been as if she had excused herself from a room in order to powder her nose and had returned to pick up life where she had left it. She had seemed more confident of herself than ever before and without hostility toward him or toward his new environment.

After they had stopped at East Palace to obtain temporary passes, Trinc announced unexpected plans. She was buying a house in Santa Fe, buying a car, sending Billy to Andover and Diana to the local high school and going to work as a nurse.

"I'm afraid you won't like it here."

"Dottie's going to help me to find a house. She believes there may be a job for me at your hospital on the Hill."

"My hospital on the Hill?" Was she proposing to sit on his tail? He was dumfounded, also thrilled. "They use Ranch School mercurochrome and iodine for everything. Linens used for surgery are sterilized in the kitchen oven. Dr. Nolan's main work is delivering babies born on the Hill."

"You mean born inside Box 1663, don't you?" Billy said.

Everyone laughed.

She had landed the job that afternoon.

He felt intensely proud of her. At the same time, however, he wondered whether she was a Lost Generation bird who, after beating her wings for a while against the twin cages of boredom and responsibility, would decide to take flight.

She became a familiar sight on the Hill, commuting from Santa Fe on her Harley and often arriving at the shack called a hospital with her goggles and outer garments splattered with mud. Why she didn't buy another car—he knew about the Daimler fiasco—he couldn't fathom, but eccentric behavior was her own business. He was glad she didn't exhibit it when she joined him for lunches at Fuller Lodge and rubbed elbows with Nobel Prize winners. Little by little he was discovering aspects of her character of which he had previously taken little notice. When on occasion he would drop in at the hospital and observe her performing her duties in a starched white uniform with Nightingale pin, he was struck by the goodness and happiness that glowed in her face. Hitherto he had believed her nursing to have been a contrivance for escaping from the Heartwells and for treading water until marriage and motherhood came along. Now he realized she had a vocation, a passion fueled by something more than a desire to prove competence. It was a vocation fueled by compassion.

One afternoon as he and Trinc were eating lunch together at the lodge, their table was approached by Captain DeSilva, the security officer, and by a man introduced as Dr. Troy Turner. Even before Turner spoke, Aeneas had instinctively disliked him. He was a big man about Aeneas's own height and age. Thinning hair was slicked back with pomade, and the purplish veins on cheeks and nose combined with fat jowls to reveal a seasoned alcoholic. It wasn't the outward appearance so much as the secretive smile and prepossessing air that stirred dislike, these and the fact that he and Trinc knew each other.

"Trinc?"

"Turner?"

"He said you were old friends, Mrs. Caldwell." Captain DeSilva bowed and left.

"This is my husband, Aeneas."

Neither Turner nor Aeneas offered to shake hands. Turner smiled with pursed lips. "I've heard about you," he said. "It's my new job to see to it that you ten-to-the-tenth boys don't try to escape to civilization."

"Oh? Are you here to keep me in or to keep the enemy out?"

"How have you been, Turner?" Trinc asked.

"Suffering, Trinc, suffering." He opened palms in mock despair.

"How's Dora?"

"Haven't the foggiest. We were divorced. I remarried and got divorced again. I suppose I've never understood love and marriage."

"How's Dr. Nicovich?"

"Nicky drank himself to death. And your roommate, the one you always regarded as best in your class?"

"Mallie Devine? I completely lost touch with her."

"Yes. Mallie. She went to China on a mission and got her throat slit during the rape of Nanking."

Trinc turned pale. "What on earth are you doing here?"

Turner blinked eyes. "Thanks to an old fart whom I learned is your uncle, Dr. Knight, I was asked to give up medical practice after I sawed off a patient's leg. It was the wrong leg. . . Easy come, easy go, that's what I always say. I moved to Washington and have made a new career in army intelligence. How does it feel, Trinc, to be one of the hoi polloi?" He looked at his wristwatch. "Do you still dance? Perhaps we'll be seeing you at the square dance some Saturday. Do you dance, Aeneas?"

Aeneas, though infuriated, nodded solemnly. "Indian dancing," he said. "I put on a breech-clout and submit to the power of the earth mother . . . Good afternoon, Dr. Turner."

After Turner had sauntered away, Trinc explained hastily, "He was once my instructor in surgery. We went dancing a couple of times. I discovered he's phony as a rubber check."

"Would you care to go dancing with me?"

"I'd love to." Trinc placed her hand over his. "Don't be jealous."

"Me jealous?" His clowning made her smile. He relaxed. "I've been thinking, Trinc. I've been a clot to have the car while you risk your life on a Harley. I'm swapping the car for your motorcycle. Deal?"

"Thank you," she said, again placing her hand over his. "I like it that you care about me."

"As for the dance, we'll put on our glad rags the way we used to. I'll wear my new Duke-of-Windsor outfit. You can wear your mother's 'little dress' or facsimile since it's probably still in mothballs back home. The house, I mean. All the ten-to-the-tenth boys, as your friend calls them, will be wearing dungarees or unpressed pants and open shirts, no ties, and unshined shoes, and their wives will be wearing shirtmaker dresses and Indian moccasins. Let's knock 'em out, Trinc!"

"May I ask a favor?"

"Shoot."

"May I bring Diana?"

"Great idea."

"She's having trouble making friends in the high school. She misses her daddy."

"Oedipus Complex?"

"Be serious," she said. "That was an old joke your mother didn't understand."

"Well," he said, "I'm tired of misunderstandings. For instance, did you have Billy's name changed?"

She glanced away on an expression of disdain, then turned and met his gaze. "At my request, Colonel tore the document into pieces. I'm truly sorry for having been so angry with you I lost control of myself."

"And I," he said, "apologize for saying I love another woman. I've also lost control of myself. I'm sick to death of the project here, but I'm buried in it so deeply I wonder if I'm human. We'll talk sometime, Mrs. Caldwell?"

"Deal," Trinc said.

She leaned over and kissed him on the cheek.

Among the secrets he had been keeping was one with little relation beyond coincidence to the war. Cousin Tubby's son, Karl Playfair, had arrived in Los Alamos as a member of Chadwick's British Mission. Although Aeneas had had as yet little time to cultivate the acquaintance, he was impressed by the boy's quiet, unassuming manners, gaiety of spirits, and true politeness based on simple sympathy and unpretentiousness. If he introduced Diana to Karl, he might make up for his years of parental neglect. "May I bring a young Anglo-American friend of mine to the dance? He's a brilliant Cambridge physicist."

"Thank you for caring about Diana," Trinc said.

Dances were still being held in the lodge on Saturday nights. He knew that Trinc and Diana would be in for a treat, especially when Willie Higinbotham let loose on his accordion, the one he called his "Stomach Steinway," and worked the crowd into a frenzy with his reels, waltzes, and polkas. The punch would be laced with grain alcohol from the Tech Area, and there was always the possibility that some future Nobel laureate would get drunk and smash lightbulbs or tear the faucets out of the men's room. Aeneas was in the mood for some hillbilly partying or almost anything that would upset the military police or send an earth-tremor through Oppenheimer's neat organizational charts.

A few days after that lunch with Trinc he had located Karl Playfair in the Tech Area and invited him to the dance. The tall, blond, blue-eyed boy stepped out of a labyrinth of pumps, meters, and intertwined wires, put a slide rule in a pocket of his tweed jacket, and grinned broadly. "I shall blow up this place proper, you know, if I fail to fall to this occasion," he said. "May I ah-ask what's square about this square dance, sir?"

"The scientists," Aeneas said. "They'll need some roughing up. Don't you play bagpipes?"

"That I do, sir."

"Bring the pipes, Karl."

"Rather," he said. "It's all very sad music. We can't afford much emotional content in Shangri-la."

"Emotional content, Karl, is exactly what we need."

"Then," Karl said, "I'll play a plaintive tune and recite a ballad from Yarrow Water, let the tears fall as they may . . ."

Aeneas's recollection of the dance a year ago had become blurred. He remembered the hilarity, the shouts of twirling dancers under the chandeliers. He remembered the lovely dresses of his women, the applause for Trinc as she executed an intricate Swedish reel. High on punch toward midnight, he had listened to the languid screech of Karl's bagpipes. He remembered Karl's heartfelt recital of "The Douglas Tragedy" as having a personal meaning for him:

> *And they twa met, and they twa plat,*
> *And fain they wad be near;*
> *And a' the world might ken right weel,*
> *They were twa lovers dear.*

As Karl was reciting, Trinc held one of Aeneas's hands and Diana the other. He noticed that Karl couldn't take his eyes off Diana. And he remembered how, at the end of the evening, the four of them went upstairs to get the view from a balcony of that sky filled with stars.

"Mrs. Caldwell?" Karl gave her an envelope. "Mum asked me to give you this and to tell you sincerely, had it not been for you, she and I might have starved to death in New York . . . Do open it, Mrs. Caldwell."

"I know what it is," Trinc said. "I'd forgotten all about it."

"What is it, Mom?" Diana said.

"I'll answer," Karl said. "It's a money order for $5,000. Mum is sorry she took so long to repay you, but when she heard we would all be together here, she got cracking."

"It will come in handy." Trinc gave Karl a hug. "You all might as well know I've quit my job at the hospital here and taken another one in Santa Fe."

If happiness had blurred memory, misery lit it up. Aeneas was thinking, *The bird has flown.* So he had backed off. He had seen Trinc briefly in the summer when he and Karl borrowed a jeep and took everyone to Valle Grande for a picnic or for a hike around Truchas Peaks or for dinner with Ma-Betty in Taos. Once, when Trinc stayed in Santa Fe, he and Karl and Diana had driven to Taos. There he had had another awakening.

It was the end of September. Aspen flames buttered the blue mountains. He and Ma-Betty were seated in the patio garden, gazing across a long green and yellow sea of sagebrush and sunflowers toward the Jémez Mountains. About a mile away Diana and Karl were strolling hand in hand.

"Those two seem meant for each other," Ma-Betty had remarked. "I suppose it's no skin off your nose that they're cousins?"

"Second cousins," he amended. "I hope you won't interfere."

"Me interfere?" She rolled her eyes. "I never interfere with people. I just open their eyes to what they have to do. If you weren't so stubborn, I could tell you a thing or two."

He rose from his chair and stood by the adobe wall. "I'm listening."

"All right," she said in a decided tone. "I can understand a woman's feelings if her husband is married to his work. I can understand a husband's feelings if his wife has things to do other than to be a housekeeper. But this separation between you two is ridiculous. You need to give her some heart. How can you do that when you haven't a clue about her predicament?"

"Hold it," Aeneas snapped. "You used to complain that Trinc didn't work. I didn't complain. When she gets a job and flourishes and *then* quits, I come smack-dab up against an old problem: she's rich."

"Oh," Ma-Betty groaned, "grasshopper molasses! She's

not rich. She's just too proud to tell you she has lost almost everything."

Aeneas whistled after a pause. "But she has—"

"Had, son, had. Most of it was lost in the Crash. The inheritance from her mother and grandmother proved to be worthless stock. And her father neglected to sign his new Will, leaving everything to Trinc, so that the old Will took effect, leaving everything to Yale."

"How do you know all this?"

"Because Diana told me. She wasn't supposed to, because Trinc made her promise to tell no one."

"I'll be damned." He whistled again.

"0. K.," Ma-Betty went on, "I exaggerated a little. She still gets trickle from her trust account . . . But she has to work for a living. She quit her job on the Hill because she found a job with the Public Health Service that would pay better. You—you're so off in the clouds, you believe she quit and has been having it easy . . . Do you think she wanted to quit the job on the Hill? Of course not. The two of you were beginning to see one another again on a regular basis. She had to quit just to get enough money to pay Billy's tuitions. Wouldn't you like to know where she works?"

He felt his cheeks burning. He looked at his feet, nodded silently.

"She works at the Santa Fe Detention Center, in the hospital."

He took a deep breath, let it out slowly. "You mean she's nursing POWS?"

"They're not POWS. They're Japanese civilians, some of them Americans but lots of them Peruvians who've been kidnapped to this country even though Peru is not at war. Don't ask me to figure it all out. How would you like to try being a nurse to a couple of thousand lonely men including simple fishermen from Callao or small businessmen from Lima, people arrested and plundered by their own compatriots and shipped here like slaves? I'll tell you another secret: Trinc loves these people."

Aeneas leaned elbows on the wall and watched as the last purplish-red rays of the sun ignited clouds. The sky, at once warmly promising and darkly empty, seemed to reflect the dual possibilities of his own soul. Further to the west in Chaco Canyon lay the bleached bones of his father. Always Calhoun's suicide had prompted him to serve a high purpose or suffer self-contempt. But though he envisioned a new world in which all peoples gradually would come to understand the scientific basis for one humanity, the work he was doing might lead to his father's world writ large: self-destroyed. Was it his task to serve an empire at the price of freedom? Was it his duty to wrap the planet in a shroud? Or to begin a process of history that would evolve to a universal conscience? He, not Trinc, had erected barriers to the flow of life. He had duplicated his father's denial of love. As the sun threw into relief and cast in a rosy glow the darkening carpet of the desert, he felt there was hope for him yet.

He swung about. "I'll go back to her if she'll have me."

22

New World

So the wolf had made him whole again.

He wasted no time in developing a plan for Sunday, April 15. As soon as Oppenheimer's memorial tribute to Roosevelt had been delivered, he would rent mounts from the Army and ride with Trinc to Valle Grande, an ancient volcanic cone high in the Jémez Mountains. In the seclusion of a hot spring he would have the long-delayed heart-to-heart talk with her. As few people seemed to know about the spring, he had already received from Ma-Betty, who had once known it well, detailed directions. He contacted Karl in hopes that he would be available that day for keeping Diana entertained. As it turned out, Karl was spending almost every weekend in Santa Fe putting Trinc's Daimler into working order; he would drive Trinc and Diana up to Los Alamos in the Ford.

Sunday morning the mesa was deep in snow. A bright sun shone, casting blue shadows behind the walls of silent buildings. He was hopeful there would be enough snowmelt by noon to proceed with his plans.

Everyone arrived on time to join the crowd in the theater. He and Trinc sat next to the Tellers and the Ulams. It worried Aeneas that Ed Teller and Stan Ulam were already working on a Superbomb that would be a many times more powerful than the atomic bomb. Niels Bohr had been warning scientists and politicians about the absolute necessity, prior to new research, of placing so-called "weapons" under international control.

Oppenheimer, as usual, looked ghastly. Pale skin was drawn tightly over the bones. The burning intensity of his eyes was more than ever accentuated by the glossy black eyebrows.

"When, three days ago," Oppenheimer began, "the world had word of the death of President Roosevelt . . ." Aeneas heard, "We have been living through years of great evil, and of great terror. Roosevelt has been our President, our Commander-in-Chief, and, in an old and unperverted sense, our leader. All over the world men have looked to him for guidance, and have seen symbolized in him their hope that the evils of this time would not be repeated; that the terrible sacrifices which have been made, and those that are still to be made, would lead to a world more fit for human habitation . . ."

Aeneas's mind wandered. What was a world more fit for human habitation than one without nuclear bombs? And why were the good and gentle scientists gathered in the theater not yet ready to identify with humanity, itself?

". . . For this reason it is possible to maintain the hope, for this reason it is right that we should dedicate ourselves to the hope, that his good works will not have ended with his death."

The speech concluded, Aeneas held Trinc's hand in his and sat silently for a few moments. The speech had been moving, fitting, and eloquent. But what did those phrases mean, "possible to maintain the hope" and "dedicate ourselves to the hope"? Did the "good works" of the President continue to include a Bomb no longer, now Japan was beaten, militarily necessary? Aeneas again perceived Oppenheimer's dilemma: *Ahimsa* conscience was gnawing at him even while his appointed destiny drove him onward. He was someone very like Aeneas himself.

As they were leaving the theater with the subdued crowd, Dr. Troy Turner of G-2 approached them. Many years ago, when Turner had been a clumsy surgeon at the hospital where Trinc was training for her career in nursing, she had repulsed his advances. Now that he had attained unlimited, Gestapo-like powers, he seemed, to Aeneas and Trinc, fixated on a personal vendetta. Turner's face was tomato-red beneath a fedora askew. Aeneas could smell his sour breath from a yard away. "You going intr'duce me your pretty daughter?"

Aeneas read an appeal to him in Trinc's eyes. "You're drunk, Turner," he said coldly. "Please don't intrude where you're not wanted."

"Oh?" Turner's smirk faded. "The ten to the tenths shaying things they'll regret . . . Don't jeopardize shance of salvation or you'll be blacklisted." After pushing up his fedora Turner about-faced. He staggered to the street and climbed into an olive-drab truck marked "U. S. Army Corps of Engineers."

"Well, you guys," Trinc addressed Diana and Karl, "what are you going to do?"

"We're popping off to the ski slopes," Karl replied.

"And what are *you* guys going to do?" Diana asked a bit too brightly.

"Your mother and I are thinking about getting married," Aeneas said.

Diana blushed. "Da-aaad," she grimaced.

THEY RODE BLACK HORSES up a winding dirt road from shadowy depths. Shafts of sunlight pierced snow-laden trees. Aeneas and Trinc paused to survey the great valley. The powdery snow had settled everything into a pure and pristine composure. Nothing stirred save a hovering hawk in the wind and a jackrabbit which poked elongated ears above a mass of yellow sagebrush. Up ahead, shining in naked splendor at one end of Valle Grande, steep cliffs rose. From a narrow canyon an ice-rimmed stream printed its tumbling passage on boulders with a meandering gleam. They spurred their mounts toward the canyon. Having reached it, they followed a bridle path that wound upwards along the roaring stream. After half an hour they came to its end. Tethering the horses to aspens, they climbed for fifty feet up a palisade of red rocks until they reached a level shelf of rock in a forested glade. And there it was: a bowl in the rock nearly fifteen feet across and filled with steaming hot water. Of the spring itself, there was no sign, for it seeped slowly, without a bubble, up through a white sand floor.

Aeneas opened his knapsack. Soon he and Trinc were warming their bellies with hot black coffee mixed half and half in the thermos bottle with scotch. Hungrily they devoured the Spam-and-cheese sandwiches he had purchased from the mess hall. Trinc held out her hand. He took it, pulled her into his arms. They kissed contented murmurs in their mouths.

"I love you," he said.

"I love you, too," she said.

They sat side by side. Aeneas finally spoke.

"There is a time for everything, and the time has come for me to reveal what I've been doing. I am sworn to secrecy, but it has almost destroyed your trust in me—and my peace of mind. I need your advice and support . . . We are on the Hill and elsewhere engaged in what is undeniably the most far-reaching and significant project in the history of man, a project that may well be the determining factor in the continued existence of life on the planet. But though we will be held responsible for the project, those of us who are most experienced in its various phases have little authority. Ed Teller, Hans Bethe and others have already tried to have decisions fully placed in our hands, and they failed. Still, we will eventually be held responsible, both by the public and by our own consciences, for facing the world with the existence of new, world-destroying powers. Actually, the things we are working on are so terrible that no amount of protesting will serve to save our souls. For men to choose to kill the innocent as a means to their ends is always murder. So what can I do? I cannot clear my conscience. All I can do is hope to preserve it. Even a bad conscience is better than none at all."

"It's a weapon," Trinc said.

"They like to call it a weapon," he replied, ruefully shaking his head, "but in the scale of things it's not really a weapon so much as it is an instrument of mass annihilation. We have usurped the power of the sun to make this instrument. We may use it to end the war; if we so use it, we will rejoice. But that will not be the end of it. Nick Baker—that's the code name for my old mentor, Niels Bohr—believes that a world resurrection must come from horror, and that in the long run all nations must possess our secret and work together to control it. Either we abolish all weapons of this kind, and change the bad habits of human culture, or the planet itself is doomed. I don't know whether humanity is up to the task. I do know, however, that we need the circles of compassion to expand, like the ever-widening ripples on a pond, to include the mutual humanity of all the other selves here and now and to come. That's the only new world worth the creation. As an expression of culture, war no longer functions as either divine or just. Given patience and fortitude to persevere and vigilance to protect our fragile planet from the last trumpets of our own folly, we may prevail. In the meantime—let me ask you—would it do any good, any good at all, so to act, that our children and their children's children knew that at such and such a time some people existed who cared about them and sacrificed themselves for their welfare?"

Her eyes opened wide.

"Does the instrument, we'll call it, work?" she asked.

"At first, lots of us, including the president of Harvard, Conant, who's overlording things in Washington, hoped it wouldn't work. If it failed, that would mean the Germans also failed. Now we've progressed too far to anticipate failure. The gadget will work. We'll be testing it soon."

"Have you discussed your feelings with Oppenheimer?"

"No," Aeneas sighed, "but it's a good idea."

"Suppose you quit the project? What are the consequences?"

Aeneas thought, then said, "Ed Congdon quit early, and

nothing happened to him that I know of. On the other hand, Leo Szilard, who invented the instrument, now repudiates using it. He has hassled the government so much there was talk he'd be interned for the duration of the war. He hasn't been interned, but agents shadow his every step . . . Me, I'm a minnow in this pond. Perhaps everyone would be delighted to get rid of me—one less person with whom to share the glory, so to speak. As I've said, I cannot clear my conscience, not even by violating security regulations by spilling secrets to you. I could make a stand, a small one that will do absolutely no good, but a stand."

"I'll stand with you," Trinc said.

At this moment, as never before, Aeneas and Trinc stood together before the bar of fate and inscribed their souls in the record of remembering Time.

He looked at her sharply. In the new world the old excessively masculine codes would be as outmoded as the Books in which they had been authorized. With Trinc standing with him, he would not flinch from the tasks ahead. In spite of her patrician background she had come the hard way up, after all, just as he had himself. "You've given me all I wanted," he said. "Let's swim."

They flung all their clothes onto the snow. She stepped into the spring until water came up to her breasts. "God! I feel alive!" she laughed. He, too, laughed after bellyflopping into the spring. He paddled over to her and they kissed. "I have a hard-on the shape of Florida," he murmured in her ear.

"Let's be glad it's only the shape, dear," she murmured back.

A FEW DAYS AFTER THE GERMAN SURRENDER in May there was a newspaper photograph of a blindfolded American POW about to be beheaded by a Japanese officer. Nagoya, Japan's third largest industrial city, was hit by 500 B-29s with the greatest concentration of fire bombs in history. Sixteen square miles of Tokyo were obliterated. American casualties at Iwo Jima and Okinawa and in the Pacific fleet had been so large that, it was speculated, tens of thousands of lives would have to be sacrificed in order to subdue the Japanese in their home islands. Yet Aeneas still believed that the war would soon come to an end without an invasion of Japan and without use of the atomic bomb. Not only were the Japanese beaten, but also if they were promised protection for their emperor, they would surrender. It was necessary, he believed, that the United States have possession of the Bomb. But it was also necessary that it not be used unless the conditions of the Pauline principle were met, namely that there was no intention or desire for deaths of the innocent masses. Could they be? Until recently even he had been morally asphyxiated.

He spent weekends with Trinc in Santa Fe. The idea of standing in solidarity with humanity was more than a rational hypothesis and comforting sentiment. It was the planetary imperative.

One evening he noticed that she kept her old Colt .44-caliber revolver suspended in a dried leather holster above the *kiva* fireplace in her living room.

"Mind if I have a look?"

"It's loaded."

"Unlike the first time." He was reminding her of the stormy night in Poughkeepsie thirty years ago. He lifted the holster off a hook, slipped the revolver into his hand, felt its weight, spun the chamber. He put the holstered revolver back on the hook. "Why do you keep it?"

"Uncle Doc gave it to me. God created men and women, but Colonel Colt made them equal."

"You don't use it except to relieve a shark of its suffering?"

"You learned about that, did you?" She looked at him oddly. "No, I don't use it except as a precaution. What if someone followed me home from the Detention Center? There are plenty of people on this side of the fence who seek revenge for the Bataan Death March in which New Mexicans, including many Indians and Hispanics, lost their lives."

Early in July, Ralph Lapp of the University of Chicago Met Lab showed up in Los Alamos with a petition from Leo Szilard to President Truman. It would be a crime, the petition argued, to use the Bomb. The world of the future would condemn its use and associate the United States with horror.

Aeneas signed the petition and went next morning to talk with Oppenheimer in his office.

After Aeneas had explained his support for the Szilard petition, Oppenheimer put down his pipe and said in soft voice, "You want society to be judged by the highest possible standards and to adhere in international affairs to a strict moral code. That is your position, and I can sympathize with it. But it is improper for a scientist to use his prestige as a platform for political pronouncements."

Recovering from chicken pox the Director looked a wreck. His dungarees, tightened by a silver-buckled belt, seemed hardly to be in contact with flesh.

"Does a political elite," Aeneas pressed, "deserve a monopoly on what could become the ultimate issue of human survival? It is in the *present* phase of the war, now Germany is defeated, that I am opposed on moral grounds to the use of these bombs. When there is no one to listen, opposition does not constitute a platform. So if scientists are helpless to affect events, all that remains for us to do is to go clearly and unmistakably on record that we are against the use of these bombs. A man who acts in the right spirit is not held to blame even though he has heretofore done what objectively he should not."

Oppenheimer's mouth twitched. "The atomic bomb is shit," he said. "It will make a very big bang—but it is not a weapon that is useful in war."

"In other words," Aeneas said, "machines are ahead of morals. When morals finally catch up with machines, there will be no reason for such creations. Meanwhile, what happens to your *Ahimsa*? You know better than I that *Ahimsa* means doing no harm. Agents cannot annul their agency. When we do harm, where is nobility?"

Oppenheimer spoke in a kind of whisper: "Nobility is giving permission to the sinners to wash their hands."

Aeneas rose to leave. "Thank you for your time." He had evidently come across to the Director as smug and self-righteous. "I suppose that boats in any weather are best left unrocked."

He went outside the Tech Area to smoke his own pipe. A squeaking, buzzing noise alerted him to the presence of hummingbirds. Half a dozen of them were performing loops and barrel rolls and dive-bombings and hoverings and flyovers in the sheer bliss of representing the Lilliputian Air Corps. What if some deeply thoughtful hummingbirds took command, right now, of their evolution? Would they try to find an ideal world of the inner life above the actuality of incessant aggression?

He returned to his office in the Tech Area. There was no longer much to do. The testing of the Bomb was scheduled for mid-July at a site code-named Trinity in southern New Mexico about a six hours' drive away. He had done his duty. He wasn't needed anymore. Why didn't he resign from the project while he was in Oppenheimer's office? Was his opposition to the Bomb mere petulance? Or was dishonesty in the name of national security an occupational hazard he was going to accept?

There was a knock on the door. Before Aeneas could rise to open it, Turner strolled in without a word, pulled up a chair and sat down. He had a briefcase in one hand and wore a rumpled seersucker suit. The fly of the trousers was unzipped.

"Let me see," Turner said while his gaze was still roaming about the room. "Aeneas Caldwell. Born 1890, Columbia, South Carolina, to Calhoun and Elizabeth, née Van Dyke, Caldwell . . . You must be one of the few Gentiles among our ten to the tenths . . . Harvard. Service in France. Post-doc Cambridge. Married to Susan Heartwell DeRoman, a. k. a. Trinc. Two children: Diana, William. Professor of Physics, South Atlantic University. Why are you quitting the project, Aeneas?" he asked suddenly and brought his gaze around.

"News travels fast," Aeneas said on a rising emphasis. Someone, he speculated, must have bugged the Director's office. Oppenheimer himself would never have betrayed a confidence or stooped to skullduggery.

"You *are* quitting?"

"I've signed a petition."

"Aeneas." Turner shook his head in mock disbelief. "The people likely to benefit from your position are not yet even born. Why do damage to the nation's respect for its men of learning? The Bomb will end the war. Enjoy."

"One has duties to others," Aeneas said, "not just to authorities."

"By 'others' you evidently mean the Japanese. It is impolitic to pay the slightest respect to the enemy . . . Ah! Don't be angry! Let's put it this way. You want to build a record against the United States so that you can make a stink after the war."

"Control yourself," Aeneas said to himself. Aloud he said, "I don't have to defend my love of country, and I don't have to listen to this crap. The only pronouncement I have to make is that science must be free. I'm as anxious as anybody else to see the end of the war by every possible means—every moral means. I hold my colleagues in absolute respect. What do you want?"

"I want to protect you from yourself," Turner said. "The sanctity of the doer counts more than the deed. I sit before you. I kneel down, as it were, before you. I have only zeal for the salvation of your soul. Therefore I must censure you for your faults. You have no position."

"The Bomb might end the war," Aeneas retorted, taking care to avoid responding to Turner's religiosity, "but it might also lead to a new war that will make the previous one meaningless and take the lives of hundreds of millions of people."

"Well," Turner said, "that's true." He placed the briefcase on his knees and opened it at an angle so that Aeneas could not see into its contents. He took out a pair of steel-rimmed glasses and placed them on his nose. "I'm just a poor doctor without a rich wife. A slob. I don't have your liberal mind. I do have some information that will interest you . . . Let's read from the record . . . 'Subject was court-martialed for cowardice in the face of the enemy'. Comment?"

"Acquitted," Aeneas said. His face felt hot.

"As you say: acquitted. Let's move on." Turner licked an index finger, turned a page. "Here's one. 'Subject was present at the Moore County, N. C., home of one Archibald Skye during arrest of enemy alien Mrs. B. S. Hayakawa on a Presidential warrant, 2030 hours, December 8, 1941. Subject hindered Federal authorities in performance of duty'. Comment?"

"Whom do I thank for lying?" Aeneas said. "Viking Eyes or Chews Gum with Mouth Open?"

"Aiding and abetting the enemy, Aeneas? Surely you don't believe in the overthrow of the government?"

"All Americans believe in the peaceful overthrow of the government," Aeneas said. "It's called democracy. Perhaps you've heard of it."

Again Turner licked an index finger, turned a page. "Here's more on the Jap," he said. "'Mrs. B. S. Hayakawa registered at the Bright Leaf Hotel, Poe's Hill, N. C., at 1640 hours, December 12, 1941, and checked out at 1730 hours, same day, at which time she was observed by a reliable sourceperson in subject's company. Subject falsely stated that said enemy alien was working with the F. B. I.' Adultery and perjury? Never mind."

"I mind," Aeneas said. "I remained in the lobby while she took a room for an hour or so to change clothes. I see that my back-stabbing friend, Dean Peregrine Pinker, has given your spies information of great national import."

Turner sighed heavily. "In an affidavit signed by Mrs. B. S. Hayakawa at such and such a time in such and such a place, she deposes that subject forced himself into her room at the Bright Leaf Hotel on December 12, 1941, et cetera, unzipped his trousers and demanded nonconsensual intercourse."

Aeneas said nothing.

"Of course," Turner smiled, "the affidavit does not exist. But if I *say* it exists, no one will ask to see it. The allegation will suffice. It will have a life of its own." Turner again let his gaze wander about the room. He removed glasses, closed briefcase. "If you return to civilization, your colleagues will give you a cold shoulder. You'll be blacklisted at every university in the country . . . As a matter of fact our sourceperson informs me that your tenure at South Atlantic University is subject to review. So—enjoy." Turner stood, moved to the door, about-faced. "You're screwed, Aeneas. Take it from I."

"You need to work on your pronouns," Aeneas said. "Speaking of zipping up, shall I inform General Groves that a reliable sourceperson, I, observed subject, you, with his pants unzipped? Shall one say, subject forcibly entered sourceperson's office with his pants unzipped and demanded nonconsensual intercourse and a copy of Carnegie's *How to Win Friends and Influence People*?"

Turner looked down at his pants, then at Aeneas. Aeneas smiled. When Turner had gone, Aeneas made a fist and muttered through clenched teeth, "Control yourself, control yourself," several times until his rage subsided.

SUNDAY THE EIGHTH OF JULY had been marked for a month on the family calendar: he and the children had been granted permission by the Immigration and Naturalization Service to visit the Santa Fe Detention Center for performance of a play. The players were Japanese American professional actors from Hollywood, interned for the duration of the war. The guests of honor were five Public Health nurses who had worked in the camp's TB ward or 74-bed hospital. One of the nurses was Trinc.

Now that Blevyn had been released from Tule Lake and had come to live in the *morada* at Los Remedios, Aeneas, through telephone conversations with Ma-Betty, had learned quite a bit about the camps in which over 100,000 citizens were interned.

The worst of the camps was undoubtedly Tule Lake because in it there were actually a few thousand Japanese disloyal to the United States. By contrast, the Santa Fe camp where Trinc was employed was not a concentration camp but a detention center run by the Justice Department for some 2,000 male internees. Still, there was a catch: some of these internees were Peruvians. Occupying an abandoned CCC camp on an eighty-acre tract about two miles from the Santa Fe plaza, these internees grew some of their own food, organized many of their own affairs, entertained themselves with baseball games and theatricals and were generally appreciative of an administration's humane efforts to tend to their welfare. It just made no sense that millionaire truck gardeners from California had been herded together with fishermen from Peru, no matter the angle from which Aeneas tried to look.

One thing seemed certain: fence-building had become a national pastime. Or was the ten-foot barbed-wire fence surrounding the thinly guarded Santa Fe camp a form of protection? Trinc was right: news of the Bataan Death March and other atrocities might incite some New Mexicans to a riot against the camp. Then, again, the real danger lay within the camp itself. Militant pro-Japanese internees had been transferred to Santa Fe from Tule Lake. After these Tuleans were ordered to turn over to authorities their sweat shirts with rising-sun emblems, a crowd of several hundred of them had gathered at the gate near the headquarters building and confronted fifteen patrol inspectors. When the crowd hurled rocks, the guards fired tear-gas grenades. The patrol inspectors, armed only with billies and gas grenades, entered through the confrontation gate, charged the crowd, and dispersed it after a series of scuffles. Once the trouble-makers had been segregated in a wire-enclosed stockade, the rest of the internees returned to submissive ways.

Their respect for the nurses, moreover, was absolute. The internees had been separated from their wives and families, the Latins from their native lands. The presence of women like Trinc had been a godsend.

Seldom before had Aeneas felt so intensely proud of her.

On that Sunday afternoon he, Trinc, Diana and Billy entered the camp and were escorted to folding chairs set in front of a jerry-built outdoor stage. "*¿Cómo está?*" grinned and bowed a little man with Three Flowers pomade on his black hair. "Honorable." With a grandiose gesture of his handkerchief he flicked imaginary dust from a chair and invited Aeneas to be seated. With repeated "Honorables" he did the same thing for others, and when all of the audience, mostly internees wearing surplus U. S. Army issue of a World War I type, had been seated, a grinning man with a pot belly and a gray mustache leapt upon the stage and motioned for quiet.

"That's Tommy Ishibashi, the cook," Trinc whispered. "He could have been released last year to go to the free zone east of California, but he wouldn't go. 'Nobody to do cooking', he told me."

"*Sun kyu*, everbody," said Tommy Ishibashi. "Acting company no do usual six-hour drama. Very boring. They do little play. We happy here. No worry, good food. Want work, 0. K., no want work, 0. K. too. Many good things . . . Please, nurses, to stand. Everbody applause, please."

Trinc and the other uniformed nurses stood up and acknowledged applause and whistles before they sat down.

"*Sun kyu* . . . Japanese Peruvians think nurses so kind they even put out food at night for the *cucarachas*!"

Tommy Ishibashi waited until laughter subsided. "They don't know we poison cockroaches!"

That brought the house down.

"Nurses, we say *sun kyu, sun kyu* for all your kind words and deeds. We say *sun kyu* for the smiles you have for each of us. We show now Japanese laugh for you."

Aeneas wondered how many in the audience had understood these words in English or how many would understand the actors when they spoke in Japanese. So far, communication was transcending language barriers. The play began. It was a farce with men playing women's roles, costumes, rice-powdered faces, and fans. The war has ended. Two men are returning from an internment camp, lugging heavy valises. Their wives receive them with shouts of joy that become even more jubilant when they learn that the valises are filled with presents for them. When the valises are opened, they contain nothing but rocks that the husbands have collected during internment. As the disgusted wives pelt the men with the rocks, the curtain is drawn.

There was wild applause. Aeneas figured that the play concealed an apology for the behavior of the Tuleans who had hurled rocks at the prison guards.

A thin young boy with a sickly pallor in his face approached Trinc, bowed, and presented her with a bouquet of wild flowers. "*Muchas gracias, Octavio*," she said. "*Permíteme presentarte a mi familia*. Octavio Nishimoto from Lima. He had a carcinoma removed . . . Octavio, *quisiera, con tu permiso, contarle a mi familia tus peripecias y las de tus padres. Cuando termine la guerra, será un verdadero privilegio para nosotros conocerles y acogerles . . . Mi casa es tu casa. Acércate y dame un abrazo*." She hugged Octavio. "*Amoroso*," she said.

Octavio bowed and went.

"Wow, Mom." Billy whistled under his breath. "Cool."

"Mentholated mama," Trinc said. "You are also *amoroso*."

"What did you tell him? He got tears in his eyes."

"Oh," Trinc said, "I asked his permission to tell you about his family and said that after the war we will be honored to know them personally."

As they walked through the crowd she told Octavio's story.

In March, 1944, long after Japanese Peruvians could conceivably have been a threat to the security of the Americas, and long after the American "program" was supposed to be ended, Octavio was arrested by Peruvian police and herded with his family and hundreds of others onto a waiting ship. He was sixteen. For three weeks he was confined in a cramped cabin with his father, his four sisters, and their mother, who was eight months pregnant. Rumor had it they were being taken to the Amazon jungle. Instead, they were shipped to a New Orleans holding cell. There they were told they were entering the United States without passports and would have to be interned by the INS. They boarded an eighteen-car, blacked-out train; in the rear of their car sat an armed guard who was fingering a rope. Taken to a camp in Texas, Octavio, very ill, was separated from his family and sent to Santa Fe. "The only good part of the story," Trinc said, "is that we were able to diagnose his lung cancer and have him treated. The cancer seems to be in remission . . . His family was prosperous in Peru. Everything they owned there was taken from them. Here they are held as illegal aliens to be exchanged for our citizens held in Japan."

"Brave new world," Billy said. Aeneas could not resist a smile. Only yesterday, it seemed, he and his little boy had tossed a football around and played "Whiskey-Wow-Wow" in ocean waves and gone fishing. Billy was over six feet tall, dark-haired and green-eyed, and showing off his prep-schooler's literary education.

Trinc gave everyone a tour of the hospital, introducing the family to various patients including one of the Tuleans whose head had been beaten with a billyclub during the brief riot. "The really serious cases," she explained, "like Octavio's, are taken to Bruns Hospital and treated by local physicians."

They went to La Fonda Hotel for late lunch. Under honey-colored *vigas* turning chocolate brown with age, they were just ordering combination plates of enchiladas and burritos when, in dim light in a far corner of the dining room, a couple stood up from a table and with their arms around one another's waists went laughing and giggling down a corridor and out of sight.

"Did you see that?" Aeneas said to Trinc. "Turner and some girl half his age."

Trinc's eyes had widened. "That's Theodosia, the one I told

you about who sold me the Daimler and gave me the Harley. She believes that men should be Pullman beds, used by night and stuffed back by day. Probably Turner is one of her Pullman beds."

"Maybe he's working on wife number three?"

"I don't know. She's not interested in marriage. She likes to live it up."

"Dangerously," he said. "Look, I have to tell you something. Turner has threatened to have me blacklisted at every university in the country. He has a libellous file on me and claims he can have me fired from South Atlantic if I quit the project. But my mind is made up. To hell with him."

She reached over, squeezed his hand, and said, "Don't let him get you down. He doesn't know what he's doing, and he doesn't care. I doubt he has power to have you blacklisted, even though there's darkness beneath his sentimentality."

After they returned to Trinc's house on East Palace later that afternoon, Diana and Billy went for a drive in the Daimler that Karl Playfair had somehow repaired. Alone with Trinc in the master bedroom, Aeneas lay beside her on the bed and spoke in low voice. "I'm leaving next Sunday for Trinity, that instrument test we talked about."

"What might happen?"

"We ourselves are not absolutely sure what will happen. In spite of calculations we are going into the unknown. We know there are three possibilities. One, that we all may be blown to bits if the instrument is more powerful than we expect. Two, it may be a complete dud. Three, as many hope, it may be a success, we pray without loss of any lives . . . I'm leaving the project as soon as the test is over, presumably on Monday morning early the sixteenth. I'll be coming home, here, to stay. Will I need a door key?"

She explained that the kitchen door was always kept open. Although Billy would be taking the bus to Taos for a visit with Ma-Betty, Diana would probably be home on Monday afternoon.

She had to make up her mind whether to attend the University of New Mexico in the fall or to stay in Santa Fe to be near to Karl. The cook, Aida, would also be home. She herself got off work at seven in the evening. "Why don't I take the day off, now my prince is coming home from his wanderings?"

"But maybe," he said, "you'd better work to keep from getting worried."

"A funny thing happened the other day," she said. "When I came home from work about 7:30 in the evening, a car painted olive-drab with 'U. S. Corps of Engineers' stenciled on its door was parked in the driveway in front of the garage. Three men stepped out. They wore identical short-sleeve shirts and panamas. They said they were F. B. I., but I did what you've always told me to do, saying they would have to speak with Dottie McKibbin down the street if they wanted information. They insisted that I let them into the house. So I did. They snooped around some, never giving any explanation for what they were seeking, and then they asked me about Aida and Policarpio and the kids, and about me and my working hours. Then they left. I think they were expecting to find you at home without permission for leaving the Hill. What do you think?"

"Just harassment," he said. "We have to start thinking seriously about the future. We have two houses. My annuities won't be any good for another ten years. If I can't find employment east of this garden of Eden, we're in for a struggle."

"I can always find work as a nurse," she said. "There's a letter from Uncle Doc that I want you to read. I wrote him to apologize for bitchy behavior and to ask if he had any information about Turner. You are right. He *is* dangerous. Uncle Doc says he is leaving me something in his will, what he calls 'a little windfall necessary for retirement . . .'

"Let's not worry." She turned, kissed him on the lips, left the bed and went toward the bathroom. "I still have the Toujours Moi you gave me for my birthday. Shall I put some of it on while you slip between the covers?"

LETTER FROM DR. WILLIAM NATHANIEL KNIGHT dated July 3, 1945, from New York to Mrs. Susan Caldwell, Santa Fe

My dear Trinc,

What an absolute delight to receive your letter!

Rest assured, you were forgiven by me a long time ago. I simply neglected to tell you. I've had a couple of minor strokes and get fuzzy-minded.

Of course I'm delighted William still bears my name and that he is flourishing at Phillips Academy. I'm sure if he sets his sights on becoming a writer, he will someday do so.

I was saddened to hear of the death of your father. I'm flabbergasted that Gayle, always the meticulous lawyer, neglected to sign his will leaving everything to you. When I'm gone, I'm leaving you a little windfall necessary for retirement. It ain't much, but it will sweeten the pot.

And tell Aeneas that I was glad to be of service, via Stimson, in getting that lady released from the clutches of the F. B. I.

I mentioned strokes. Day in day out I'm supervised by a couple of buzzard-pissin' nurses who perform indignities for which your profession is famous. When they're through with lifting me into the bathtub, they dump me in a wheelchair in order to torture my spine. Of course, if I could have you to come take care of this old carcass, I'd be tearing up the pea patch. Alas, it sounds as though you've got your hands full in Santa Fe. You like it there. I, myself, sure did forty-some years ago when I passed through there after wolf-hunting with Teddy in Oklahoma; we were on our way to the Rough Riders' reunion in San Antonio.

Remember my chauffeur from California, Jun Takamatsu, the one I was going to put through Cornell Medical School? Well, his is quite a story.

Even though he was over thirty years old he volunteered as a private in the *Nisei* 442nd Regimental Combat Team. After training in Mississippi, he shipped out as a buck sergeant from Newport News in May of last year. He was immediately involved in terrible fighting near the Anzio beachhead. Later he received a battlefield commission and led his men in the thick of fighting in the Vosges Mountains. Wounded in stomach and leg, he recuperated in time to re-join the 442nd in the last, recent battles in northern Italy before the German surrender. He was wounded again in the leg and is currently holed up in Florence awaiting his chance to ship out for home.

It eventually took 12,000 men to fill the 4,500 original places in his regiment. That gives you some measure of the loyalty and fighting spirit of the Japanese Americans.

Those damned nurses, they just stuck a thermometer up my rectum and told me to go to bed. Well, I'm going to copy out for you a passage from Jun's recent letter from Florence.

"Up a mountain, down a mountain into marshy vales, and up another mountain, sometimes marching, often running, hitting the ground, firing, running some more, hitting the ground again, firing some more, marching some more: we did this continuously for weeks. We put our minds on automatic. Everything we did, we had to do it instinctively. It was as though we stayed alive only by summoning a sense of purpose out of an eerie fog of mind from which had been forever removed the spiritual nourishment of the sun. Sometimes it was pretty sickening. Once we were crossing a field, keeping to the ditches and walking carefully to avoid old landmines on either side of them, and we were met by an almost unbearable stench of flyblown cattle carcasses and dead Germans. After that experience I led my men in directions away from such scenes. Always we moved forward. Machine gun bullets went *ack ack ack* and spewed the very ground in front of our boots. Quick-firing A. A. guns went *room room room* until the air rumbled. 88s went *crrrump* and shell bursts winked in the night sky like obscene meteorites. Big shells passed overhead with a whispering sound like the rustle of birds' wings.'

"And all this time it was spring in Italy. Wild larkspur, tight-packed flower buds just turning blue, sprouted from the ruins of an ancient village. Once while mortar shells were exploding all around us, I heard the lovely, varied, serene warbling of a nightingale while I was sprawled on jumping earth, my ears ringing and soil rattling down on my helmet. Once, too, as we were stalking along the bank of a canal, we heard birds in the marsh, bitterns perhaps, that sounded like people talking quietly. The sound stopped us every time, our fingers on triggers.'

"One morning we assaulted defenses anchored to a mountain ridge. A German suddenly stood up waist-high in a bunker and aimed a rifle grenade at my face at a range of ten yards. I had a hand grenade ready for throwing, its pin pulled, but with only seconds to live I couldn't move my arm. Hours, whole days, seemed to pass before my eyes in a spectral pageant of a life I would never have. Nausea gripped my stomach, paralysis my limbs. The German fired. The rifle grenade went *t-hiss* as it grazed my shoulder harmlessly. I fell forward, counted one/two/three, and threw my grenade. It exploded in the German's face and brought a machine gun crew staggering out of the bunker. I cut them down with my tommy gun."

You inquired about Dr. Troy Turner. I never much cared for him—a queer fella, shifty-eyed and withdrawn and not worth buzzard piss as a teacher. His surgical skills were O. K. to start with. Then he took up with Nicovich and began heavy drinking. When he botched an amputation, I had him kicked out of the hospital and his license revoked. Now you say he's an officer in army intelligence. Well, I asked an old friend in the New York Police Department if there is a file on Turner. You bet there is. He was charged in 1935 with raping a girl in his apartment. Turner, my friend informs me, would have been found guilty, but the girl dropped charges, fearing retaliation, I suppose. The case never came to trial.

Steer clear of this man. He has an old grudge against me and might try to take it out on you.

With all my love to you and yours,

Uncle Doc

23

Arma Virumque Cano

WOULD THE EARTH DISAPPEAR IN THE EXPLOSION? It was the most agonizing question in human history. Aeneas had been pondering it for years. During the hurricane of 1939 he had developed a theory.

According to calculations the extreme pressures and temperatures reached in the interior of the atomic bomb would not be high enough to fuse hydrogen with either nitrogen or helium in a self-sustaining nuclear reaction. One would have to take an incredibly enormous mass of water or air and raise it to a temperature of many millions of degrees before ignition of the atmosphere would even be possible. Although science had long been a story of accidents and miscalculations prior to Eureka-moments of discovery, in this instance where the explosion of the Bomb was concerned there must be no such thing as a margin of error. It was all or nothing. The nothing was too dreadful to contemplate. The *all*—a successful testing—meant that man, a stranger in the cosmos, had assumed god-like powers.

When he woke at five o'clock on the morning of July 15, he felt weighed down by the burden of destiny. Perhaps only he and a few other men could fully appreciate, while it lasted, the joyous aliveness of the day. It was like a waft of love irradiating the universe. He had never lost his faith that the future of mankind lay in the evolution of consciousness, synonymous with conscience. The book of his dreams, "The New Physics and the Coming World of Conscience," was already, though as yet unwritten, taking shape in his mind. Today, however, he could not steadily envision a bouncing-back from the abyss of annihilation.

He dressed for desert heat, putting on dungarees, fatigue shirt and boots. He cleaned out the log cabin, strapped a bag containing his belongings to the Harley, breakfasted in the mess hall and went to the Tech Area for the last time. To MPs he turned over keys and the contents of his safe and the "Top Secret" white badge. He also left with them a letter of resignation to be delivered to Oppenheimer upon his return from Trinity, assuming there would be a return.

By seven he was ready to go. Seated on the sputtering Harley he took a last look around. Customarily there would have been sirens and factory whistles blowing at seven every morning but Sunday. Today everything in the city was quieter than usual; the city, in fact, seemed deserted. A lambent breeze played in the leafed-out trees and deposited slow-moving washes of shadow on the mesa. With a little effort he imagined how Fuller Lodge once had been, full of cheerful boys, and still he seemed to hear Karl playing the bagpipes, to see him marching up and down, his kilt and sporran swinging, chandelier lights glinting in his silver-handled dirk, the sound thrilling, mournful, indomitable. Once, warrior-heroes, following warrior-gods, had rejoiced in the glories of virtuous battle. Once, but no longer, Los Alamos had been part of an Old West where distance from society was considered a virtue and repudiation of the past a ding-dong of freedom bells. It was no Shangri-la now, if indeed it ever had been.

He lowered goggles over his eyes, gunned the Harley, and descended the road to Otowi bridge on the Rio Grande. Once there, instead of heading directly toward Santa Fe, he swerved onto the road to Española. A sudden impulse had blossomed in his mind. From Española it would be only a few miles to the tiny Santuario de Chimayó, sometimes grandiosely called "the Lourdes of America." He had visited it once as a boy, coming with Ma-Betty by wagon through the gulches to the eroded pink granite of ancient Tsi Mayoh, the hills dotted with thick juniper and piñon scrub, the air of the plaza scented by lilac and wild plum bushes, and then to the earthen-floored church that to his then-irreverent eyes resembled a sort of ungainly tugboat with two crooked wooden belfries serving as smokestacks. It had been Holy Week. The church had been packed with pilgrims, many of whom had walked barefooted for dozens of miles. The boy had had little concept of sacrifice expressed through pilgrimage or of salvation earned by suffering. He had nevertheless been fascinated by a side shrine in which supplicants gathered handfuls of soil from a dry well. The faithful believed in the healing power of that dirt, as attested to by the number of abandoned crutches that lined the wall.

Now Aeneas wanted to receive the gift of resignation to painful circumstances present and to come. He was a pilgrim.

Arriving half an hour later at the Santuario, he entered the dark candlelit chapel as Mass was ending with a priest's softly intoned, ". . . *en el nombre del padre, del hijo y del Espíritu Santo.*" Bearded men and bent-over women in their black *rebozos* surged toward the shrine. Aeneas sat on a hand-carved bench and adjusted his eyes to the dim light. Santo Niño and other festively arrayed statues in front of the retable gave off a warm glow that soon dispelled feelings of self-consciousness. He closed eyes and silently prayed as best he could. . .

Startled by a hand laid gently on his shoulder, he glanced up to the kind face of the small priest. "*Pareces preocupado, hijo mío,*" the priest said.

It was true. He was very troubled indeed. "*Sí, padre,*" Aeneas sighed. "*Lo estoy.*"

The priest held out a small paper bag and pressed it into Aeneas's hand. "*Acepta este regalo, por favor.*"

The bag was filled with some of the healing dirt. "*Gracias, padre*," Aeneas nodded. He put the bag in his breast pocket to signify its position over his heart. Although he was ashamed of his lack of traditional faith, he was glad to have a talisman of earth to carry with him on his journey.

IT WAS A JOURNEY OF ALMOST 200 MILES, Española to Santa Fe, Albuquerque, Belen, Socorro and finally to Trinity. The skies were overcast; the air was hot and humid. Several times he stopped at filling stations to pump gas and to wipe insect-goo from his goggles. Having tied his red bandanna over forehead and hair, he looked like a bandit. All he had stolen was the fire of the sun! South of Socorro he crossed the sluggish Rio Grande. Parched river terraces faded behind him as he entered the stretch of desert called Jornada del Muerto—"Dead Man's March"—lying between Socorro and El Paso. Feared by early travelers for its lack of water, the Jornada seemed uninhabitable save for a herd of antelope which he saw apparently glaring at him before it plunged away. Gradually to the east the peaks of the Sierra Oscuro range rose to elevations of over 4,000 feet above the shimmering heat of the high alkaline plain. He stopped at a security checkpoint, received directions. He made his way past earth-sheltered bunkers, reported to Base Camp. After dining in a mess hall he sat in the shade of a barracks building, smoking his pipe, surveying the site with his binoculars and waiting for the temperature to drop below a hundred degrees.

Five miles to the north a Command Center protruded above the plain. About six miles further beyond that was Ground Zero. It was marked by a steel tower in which was cradled the Bomb. About twenty miles northwest of Zero was the hill named Compañia where the VIPs would soon be gathering. If only Japanese and Russian diplomats would be present for a demonstration, then this Ahab-like madness . . ! Wishful thinking clutched him.

In spite of the hum of generators and the groaning of vehicles busily coming and going, he felt detached from the whole scene. Where previously, and to the detriment of his personal and family life, he had been engrossed in his work, now it no longer belonged to him, if it ever had. He had resigned his position and renounced further responsibility for the project. All was in any case beyond his control. The world would wag without him. Anxiety was pointless. He felt free to imagine himself in the sky, looking down from a realm of cosmic silence upon the piled-up centuries of hubristic folly.

High and deep in that sky, coming into focus through binoculars, an eagle was undulating, resting on thermals, wings steady and sure and serene as it was spiraling upward in tight circles, coasting downward only to mount upward again. Could it see with the eyes of its ancestors a continent pristine and inviolable, the shining mountains, the glistening rivers, the shadowed barrancas and the abysmal gorges? In the last millisecond of the Earth's existence would it see the surface shake and sigh a moment, then lie still in an ineluctable light?

HE LAY AWAKE IN A PUP-TENT THAT NIGHT. He remembered, as he often did when he felt an inner need for an anchor, Throstle's Nest in the old days, how Old Joe Shuffle kicked out pots and the family took them by wagon to market in Carthage. The wagon would be piled high with vessels for sale—crocks, churns, telegraph insulators, pickle jars and whiskey jugs, all glazed in tobacco-spit brown. While Calhoun inched the mule over rutted roads, the boy would sit with Ma-Betty on top of the vessels and watch small fields of wheat being harvested.

Some day he would write his memoirs. He would neither immobilize his spirit in the pastoral past nor capitulate to the onrush of technological civilization. He would explore upstream past cities and machines, against the current of time and toward clear waters of an inexhaustible source of life. He would recall his relationship to that source—it was always in nature—and try to clear away the shrubbery of despair that concealed the sanctuary of hope.

He slept.

At midnight a fierce clap of thunder directly overhead woke him up. A torrential downpour with high winds was battering his tent. Cloud-to-cloud lightning illuminated the desert at frequent intervals. The test shot, he reckoned with more wishful thinking, would have to be postponed.

The storm abated. Outside the tent a revival meeting of countless frogs rent the night with a raucous sound of copulation. He reached for his boots and was about to put them on when he tilted them upside-down as a precaution. Out fell a scorpion. Boots on and laced he crawled from the tent and stood up. Occasional stars were visible. The sparkle of lights in the Command Center indicated that the shot was still possible.

He squashed through mud to the mess hall. As he finished a breakfast of powdered eggs, French toast, and coffee, Karl Playfair approached his table, clothes sopping wet and blond hair plastered to forehead.

"Mind if I join you?"

"Sit down, please, mister."

"Talk about English weather." Karl raised eyebrows. "I've been up on Compañia Hill with the big blimps, Conant and Bush and my boss, Chadwick, and everyone's feeling a trifle edgy. What if lightning had exploded our little toy before we were ready? We would probably all be radioactive, thanks to the beastly winds . . . You seem calm enough. How many roentgens can one take before one sloughs off the old mortal coils?" He tapped the film badge on his shirt. The badge measured exposure.

Aeneas shook his head. "Nobody really knows. Five, I'd guess. What's the scoop? The gen, I mean. Any time soon?"

"Five thirty," Karl said. "Zero Hour in—" he paused to look at a wristwatch "—two more hours . . . I don't suppose you bloody Americans serve tea around here?"

"Any VIPs who look like Japanese or Russian diplomats?"

"Blest if I know," Karl replied with a shrug. "Why do you ask?"

"Oh," Aeneas said, "I was hoping we could scare up a Japanese surrender by means of a demonstration that meets a moral condition . . . Given your love of Scotland, you wouldn't happen to have a drink by any chance, mister?"

Karl drew a flask from a pocket and passed it over. "Presto," he said. "And now for my next trick—"

Aeneas tilted the flask, drank until the scotch burned his throat, and returned the flask. He wiped lips with the back of a hand caked with gypsum soil. "Thanks. There's something you should know, Karl. I've resigned from the project."

Karl drew back in surprise. "I hope that doesn't mean you'll be taking Diana away. I'm in love with her, you know."

"She's only eighteen," Aeneas smiled.

"I intend to wait, of course. Hang it, I was wondering if you had objections."

"I wouldn't drink a man's whiskey, mister, if I didn't like him . . . We'll stay in Santa Fe until my job situation is clarified. There's a chance I'll be fired back at my university and blacklisted anywhere else."

"Jolly good," Karl whistled in amazement full of sympathetic irony. "In that case you must come to Cambridge. Dad will do the necessary, a Sir Isaac Newton Fellowship and all that. It won't pay more than a thousand or two quid, but you have to consider the advantages: decent beer, port and cigars at High Table, punting on the Backs, cricket and the royal family. And *tea*!"

"I hadn't considered exile until this moment, Karl, but I shall do so in future. That is, assuming all's lost on this side of the pond."

"What you lose on the roundabouts you gain on the swings." With this philosophical bromide Karl stood up in the puddle of water at his feet. "Time for tea, correction, coffee. I have to toddle on back to Chadwick before he bothers people with his flaming neutrons. See you at the Apocalypse. *Ciao*."

He watched his young friend depart. Cousin Tubby's father, Van Dyke, had disinherited her and driven her to become the mistress of the German psychiatrist Dr. Karl, by whom she had this child. Trinc had given Tubby a loan sufficient not only to support her but also to enable her to make a home for him, Aeneas, in Cambridge. Married to Professor Playfair, the Trinity don, Tubby had raised Karl, seen him graduate from the university with a first-class Honours degree and be retained as a Fellow at St. John's College. And now he was working with Chadwick, discoverer of the neutron in 1932. The roundabouts and the swings.

During the next hour he passed time by consuming three more breakfasts, stuffing his pockets with French toast for later snacks. He decided to cycle down to the Command Center. If today was the time for an apocalypse-crisis, he might as well have a ringside seat only 10,000 yards from Zero.

EMACIATED, PALE, AND APPREHENSIVE, Oppenheimer leaned against a post as a 5:25 siren signaled five minutes to go. He looked like a lost shade waiting for the next ferryboat to Hell. Kenneth Bainbridge and George Kistiakowsky, both of Harvard, had put into operation a timing mechanism. Joe McKibbin and Don Hornig were throwing switches. Sam Allison of the University of Chicago had begun counting over a loudspeaker.

When Kistiakowsky announced that he was leaving in order to observe events from the earth mound that covered the Command Post, Aeneas followed him, taking with him a plank in which dark welder's glass had been inserted. Presently he was lying on the mound with his feet facing in the direction of the blast and with his eyes shielded by the welder's glass.

In the slate-gray dawn Allison counted the final seconds

over the loudspeaker:

"... minus 45 ... minus 40 ... minus 20 ... minus 10 ... 3 ... 2 ... 1."

Dark horizon is streaked with the first faint rays of dawn. In the darkness of dawn, in the absolute silence, suddenly there is light.

A billion searchlights have been turned on simultaneously and directed into your eyes.

A billion oxyacetylene torches have been simultaneously ignited and directed into your eyes.

A billion magnesium flares have been simultaneously exploded.

It is light as it must have been at the beginning of the world.

Twenty suns have been switched on.

Brightlightflash fuses earthsky.

It is light as it must be at the end of the world.

The world stays lighted.

Has the thermal nuclear transformation of the atmosphere actually occurred?

He counted five seconds, dropped the welder's glass, and spun himself around to see Zero.

The sky has turned red.

The Oscura Mountains are bright as day.

There is a ball of fire. It is about a mile in diameter and changes colors from deep purple to orange to greenish chlorine yellow.

The fireball is the snaky head of a luminous Medusa. She swells over the sweep of desert, bathing it in her brilliant glow. A tidal wave of dust erupts from her loins.

Men were cheering jubilantly over the PA system as the detonation wave hit. Kistiakowsky went sprawling in mud.

Blast-thunder growls and reverberates in an awesome roar.

The earth shakes, rumbles.

A cloud like a gigantic mushroom billows upward. It

spreads in a "Z" form.

He had a sensation of heat on his face and realized it had been sunburned in thirty seconds.

"God-a-mighty!" he muttered under his breath.

He used binoculars to pan across the Jornada. A herd of antelope burst from concealment, silently galloped just in front of the dust storm. Dawn was breaking.

It is dark again.

WHEN AT NINE O'CLOCK IN THE MORNING the Command Center was approached by fog, Geiger counters began to click with an ominous rapidity. Aeneas climbed on the Harley and began his journey home. He had not gone more than five miles before he slowed to a stop. A stratum of fog was slowly creeping upon the speckled arroyo in front of him. Was the fog filled with radioactive dust? If he hurried he could still get across the arroyo before the fog smothered it.

A strange sight met his eyes. An eagle, perhaps a thousand feet above his head, suddenly folded its wings and plummeted straight down to earth. Dismounting, Aeneas ran to the spot where the eagle had disappeared from his sight and found the broken, partly eviscerated, bubbling birdflesh, already smelling of death, lying, a fallen star, eyes melted, beak opened wide as if around a silent scream.

It had, he reasoned, been blinded by the first flash of the Bomb. Unable to find its bearings in relation to the earth, it had been gradually and helplessly descending upon thermals.

Kneeling, he removed from his breast pocket the bag of Chimayó soil and sprinkled some of it over the eagle.

By the time he was back on the Harley the fog had rolled in. He started the engine. Just before he released the brake, he remembered the French toast he had crammed in a pocket of his dungarees. Taking out a piece of the toast he clamped it against his nose and breathed through it. With his free hand he settled goggles in place, then roared into and through the fog in less than two minutes. When he stopped in bright sunlight on the other side of it and looked at his film badge, he discovered he had exposed himself to 5.5 R., a dangerous dose of radioactivity. Exposure to gamma radiation was one of the possible causes of leukemia.

His clothes were covered with a white powder as fine—and in its own way as wanton—as a strumpet's cosmetic. As soon as he got home he would burn boots, dungarees, shirt, bandanna, goggles, all.

A CROWD OF INDIANS AND HISPANICS as well as Anglo tourists was gathered in the plaza in front of the Governor's Palace at two in the afternoon. A weird light had been observed by many people that morning. Cristo Rey! It is the end of the world! Sacred Heart of Jesus! It is as you say, Madre. Here is Jesus himself! *¿Quien sabe?*

At the center of the crowd stood a tall, fiercely bearded white man wearing little but a loincloth and bearing on his back a cottonwood cross. Near him another bearded white man— dressed in a white robe, sandals, and Texas hat—was saying, over and over, "My Lord tells me to tell you to repent! My Lord tells me to tell you to repent!" He kept eyes shut tight for a while, then popped them open to look at the heavens and smile. Some weeping women fell down, crawled forward, and kissed the feet of the sudden Jesus.

Observing the scene from the street was a sort of bandit on a motorcycle. His body was covered with mud and dust. From his pocket he drew scraps of bread and tossed them to pigeons. Then he kicked the motorcycle into a roar, accelerated out of the plaza up East Palace, and was lost to sight somewhere on the hill near La Posada. Half a mile from P. O. Box 1663 and abreast of the adobe gate to the driveway in front of Trinc's house, in the quiet, tree-shaded street, Aeneas cut the motor and stared at a sight more alarming to him than the Second Coming had just been: it was an olive-drab truck marked "U. S. Army Corps of Engineers" parked across the street.

Turner's? A tingle of fear and loathing traveled through his heart. *The ten to the tenths are saying things they'll regret. Three men in short-sleeved shirts and panamas. Old grudge. Might try to take it out on you.* The F. B. I. had been snooping around. Suppose the agents reported to Turner. Suppose Turner expected him, Aeneas, to be at Trinity and Trinc off at work. Who was home now? The cook. Diana. Perhaps Diana had taken the Daimler for a drive. Check the garage. Don't track radioactive dust into Trinc's house.

He propped up the Harley, pulled off boots. On an impulse, instead of approaching the house via the gate, he ran crouching along a pebbled lane between Trinc's wall and a neighbor's. The pebbles were smooth. He felt no pain. Close to the garage he scrambled over the wall, squatted behind a lilac bush amongst crushed tiger lilies, paused to steady his breathing. He crawled on his stomach but in one swift motion stood up, peeped through a window of the garage, and crouched. Splinters of sunlight had identified the waxed Daimler.

Had he heard a noise, a muffled noise?

There it was again, a noise like the cry of a bird in a far-away cave. He ran twenty yards to the house. The back door was open. He pushed it, paused, listened, tiptoed into the kitchen, paused, listened.

There! He heard the voice from somewhere in the cool depths of the house, distinct: *Nooo-oo! . . . hands . . . Ai ahg!* A girl's cry.

Diana's.

Gock! Sta! Um!

Sweat rolled down his nose. As he wiped it away his glance was carried to the tile floor of the open pantry to a spreading stain, to a foot. A few moments later he had seen the perpetually staring eyes, slashed throat, blood still bubbling: Aida.

He moved swiftly from the pantry and across the kitchen and

into and across the dining room, thinking *Trinc's gun* even as he plunged toward the living room, thinking *If the man has it* even as he came to the *kiva* fireplace, reached up to the leather holster—and found it empty.

Something knocked over.

Listen.

Master bedroom.

Listen.

"Gock! . . . Fah! . . . Nooo!"

Into the master bedroom he rushed.

He would always see the scene as one of his nightmares frozen in time because he had always met in dreams what he feared to meet in dreams, had seen Calhoun's skull and a headless corporal and a screaming German machine gunner and a starvation-bloated blind boy and a dying wolf and a dead eagle and a cook with her throat so brutally cut the poll was half parted from the neck—and now there was a peerless beauty, his own flesh and blood, his Diana pinned to the floor, Turner's hand over her groaning mouth, Turner's other hand holding a scalpel against her throat, Turner a big balding man in a seersucker suit, pants unzipped, an emblematic machine thrusting tumescence toward her loosening thighs.

If Aeneas had been entirely shaped by some biochemical process, he would have hurled himself in the rage called blind and the wrath called righteous upon a creature less than human, but he was not one of the sick of the world, not one of the violent.

He hesitated before he lunged. In that moment of hesitation Turner scrambled to his feet and met the charge with body empowered to counter it and with the scalpel gripped like a dagger in his right hand, poised to plunge down. Perhaps a splash of sunlight through the window was mirrored in the knife as it came down. Swift it was. Aeneas glimpsed it just in time to shrink back. The knife entered his chest just above the heart— and clattered upon the tile floor.

Turner was screaming obscenities and howling in pain as

blood spurted from his right hand. He clutched it as if he had just pulled it out of a blast furnace. In an instant Aeneas was able to comprehend what had happened: the knife had struck the soil of the Santuario of Chimayó in its bag over his heart. The surgeon's grip had slithered over razor-sharp edges. The fingers were sliced to the bone. And in the next instant Aeneas's fist slammed into Turner's face. Turner tripped over Diana and fell against the wall.

Turner's eyes widened, jaw slackened. He raised a red paw. "Mercy," he whimpered, gaze fixed on someone whom Aeneas didn't see.

A shot rang out.

And what Aeneas now saw was this: behind him had stood a woman in white, her Colt .44-caliber revolver still aimed, and where she still was glaring with lids narrowed over blaze of eyes was the faceless head of a man whose brains were just beginning to drip off the wall.

24

The Voice of the Children

Octavio Nishimoto had been kidnapped to the United States from his native Peru, had been separated from his family, and had had a tumor removed from a lung.

Trinc had scar tissues of her own: a father and a mother who, she believed in childhood, had not wanted her, a grandfather who had wounded her lover and husband-to-be, a society which habitually harassed women. She, like the lost and the marginalized and the oppressed, lived in a kind of internal exile. In her desire to serve them, many of whom humbled her by the sheer magnitude and helplessness of their suffering, she had never been motivated by noblesse oblige but, rather, by a feeling of kinship.

It was that way with Octavio. Even though she could do little to help him except to serve *in loco parentis*, she had for his sake given herself Spanish lessons, the better to express those cultural courtesies which would give his heart a home.

On the night of July 15, when Aeneas was somewhere in southern New Mexico, she received bad news. Octavio's lung had collapsed. He had been rushed to Bruns Hospital for an emergency operation. According to the nurse who telephoned her from the Center, Octavio had begged to see "Susan"—Trinc's professional name. She decided to go to the hospital at once, the hour being midnight, remain there all night, and go from there to the Center at seven o'clock in the morning when her regular twelve-hour duty would begin. After dressing in a clean starched uniform, she woke Diana and instructed her to keep the house locked until Aida came to make breakfast. Just as she was about to leave she took the revolver from its holster and hid it in her purse. A violent electric storm was venting its spleen on the city. To her, because Aeneas was testing the monster instrument, it seemed an augury of disturbances in the human sphere for which she had best be prepared.

Upon arrival at the hospital she found Octavio still unconscious in an intensive-care room. The operation, she was told, had gone well; however, he was running a high temperature that drugs so far had failed to bring down. She received permission to sit by his bedside in the dark. After a while she fell asleep with her forehead resting on his bed.

"*¿Mama?*"

His barely audible voice penetrated consciousness. A hand gently stroked her hair, a sensation during which, for a semicomatose moment, she seemed, herself, to be receiving strokes which Hen had never given her. Her eyes opened upon pale light filtered through curtained windows. She raised her head. Octavio was smiling at her with bright eyes. She returned his smile, rose and placed her hand on his brow. It was cool. She felt his pulse. Normal. "*Amoroso,*" she said.

At once he drifted back to sleep, still smiling.

It was six o'clock. By now the instrument must have been tested. Aeneas would soon be coming home, home for good.

She left Octavio's room and walked down a corridor toward the emergency entrance by means of which she had arrived in the night. The dying wail of an ambulance siren could be heard. The next thing she knew, State troopers were bursting through the entrance followed by orderlies wheeling a gurney out of the ambulance.

"What happened?" she inquired of an officer who wore dark

sun glasses. The patient, she could see, was a woman, only her face visible above sheets.

"Unidentified Caucasian woman," the officer explained. "Her nude body was found in a gulch near the Museum of Anthropology. Evidence of multiple stab wounds. Probably laying in that gulch all night, bleeding. Them ambulance boys think they got a pulse. Ask me, she's D. O. A."

Trinc took a closer look at the patient's face. The death-pallor was a sight she had un-seen. Undeniable, though, was the dimpled chin set at a defiant angle. Trinc drew back.

"I know her slightly," Trinc said. "Her name is Theodosia— Theodosia Bird."

She spent the next half hour telling the officer most of what she knew. Theodosia was or had been a law student at the university in Albuquerque. A week or so ago she had been observed leaving La Fonda Hotel in the company of Dr. Troy Turner of G-2 on the Hill.

"Ah, Chihuahua," said the officer with a tired sigh. "We'll have to call the Governor on this one." He thanked Trinc and said that the local police would probably be asking her more questions.

She had reached the car in the parking lot before she began to doubt her discretion. She had mentioned to the officer neither Theodosia's life-style nor Turner's record of alleged rape. But she hesitated to return to the hospital with the information. An investigation into the murder of a prostitute might prove dilatory. After all, the Turner she had seen recently had been arm in arm with Theodosia, the two of them laughing comfortably with one another. Turner would be interrogated at Los Alamos as soon as the police obtained authorization to enter the secret city.

After arriving at the Center she made an effort to keep herself focused on work. By noon she could no longer resist the temptation to call home for any news. Aida answered that "*el patrón*" was not yet home, that she and Diana were in the kitchen canning chile peppers, and that the radio was reporting that a mysterious and brilliant light had been seen south of

Socorro early that morning. As Trinc replaced the receiver, she could barely restrain her excitement. There was a joke, too: she who had been infuriated with Aeneas for marrying his work was herself allowing work to supersede her personal life. Why should she not just go home and be there to greet with open arms El Patrón?

All morning she performed her duties as usual. Her mind, however, was focused elsewhere and with such an intensity she could no longer doubt its power. Previously when she had leaped to conclusions, first when she questioned Uncle Doc's integrity, then when she mistook Aeneas's obsession with his work as a sign of his lack of love for her and for the family, she had come a cropper. It had all been as if she, as a woman, simply lacked the capacity for penetrative perception. She recalled how Aeneas, at their first encounter, had praised intuition as a mental faculty equal to, even superior to, reason in the struggle for survival. But the Heartwell *No Trust* sign, partially inscribed on her heart, had led her to distrust herself and usually to submit, far more often than she wanted to admit, to the authority, in mentation, of men. Now her mind was refusing to back down from a conclusion that was based on faint clues and indirections, on hearsay and circumstantial evidence, and yet she knew for a certainty she was right: Turner had raped and murdered Theodosia Bird. Of course there had been Uncle Doc's letter, confirming Turner's curiously nonchalant admission of medical malpractice and, more, revealing the fact of a near-trial on the charge of rape. Of course, too, Turner had made ugly threats against Aeneas, had had her house searched, and had tried drunkenly to get himself introduced to Diana.

Uncle Doc had warned of a vendetta against *her*, against the family, so why the savage killing of Theodosia Bird if vendetta were motive? Turner surely had no cause to avenge himself upon Theodosia unless he hated all women and had Jack-the-Ripper fantasies behind the secretive smile. Somehow this picture of Turner did not quite fit itself into the picture of a spineless and sentimental fool she had known. Oh, yes, she realized, now, the picture had been incomplete. Ever since her discovery of Grandpa Deck's wickedness she had learned to accept the possibility of savagery, dark and deep, in anyone. And especially now, as the whole world approached the verge of madness, the permitted violence of nations and races was but the manifestation on a vast scale of what savage individual hearts everywhere might for millions of years have been dreaming.

Throughout the morning Trinc assembled her thoughts as an interrogation, a questioner vaguely resembling Colonel DeRoman, the witness also herself. . .

Q. What did you really know about Turner in the old days, apart from the fact that he was a doctor of surgical nursing?

A. Uncle Doc evidently approved of Turner's credentials and professionalism, at least at first, and I assume he went to college. There was that snapshot of himself as a football player with a leather helmet. He never spoke of his education, though, and I never found out where he was from. He had a New Yorker's accent and used language aggressively. Once he mentioned an uncle whom he admired for an "easy-come-easy-go" attitude to life.

Q. Your first impression of him was favorable?

A. I suppose so. He gave me a chance to sew up a patient, something the doctors never did. He liked music, or he pretended that he did. Above all, he was a wonderful dancer. I became almost breathlessly aware of him the first time we danced, and intimacy seemed to have been achieved at once. This feeling of intimacy faded very quickly, even though he told me he loved me, called me "darling" and tried to portray the two of us as kindred spirits attuned through poetry and alcohol and jazz. That was when I realized he was phony as

a rubber check. He had those Tarzan books by Edgar Rice Burroughs and some Michael Arlen books about pseudo-sophisticated London West Enders. There was, too, that poetry of Tagore, sentimental images passed off as genuine emotion.

Q. But you didn't consider him violent?

A. Well, he tried to seduce me, and when I repulsed him, he was insulting, but, no, he didn't seem violent. On the contrary, he seemed utterly lost, a puppet on a string. He married Dora, who was pregnant with Nicky Nicovich's child, and it was such a farce I was persuaded that Turner would make her a good husband. . . . Now that you push me, I recall something I had completely forgotten until now. Dora's baby was aborted. Nicovich was in her room. Turner was absent. Dr. Van Dine wanted me to cover up the whole affair. I went for a long walk. I sat down on a bench in a small, dimly-lit park by the East River. I must have been there for several hours . . . Then it happened. A man in a surgeon's cap and gown, and wearing a surgeon's mask, came running full-speed out of the darkness. When he passed under a lamppost, I thought I recognized him as Turner. A little while later, mounted policemen went in the direction of the park, and later there were sirens. I see: Turner plus police plus something violent. If I'd bothered to read the *Times* the next day, I might have discovered that a woman had been raped and murdered not far from the park. In other words, Turner has been on the loose from the time I first became acquainted with him. Il rêve d'échafauds en fumant son hooka. That's it, the motive: the modern devil.

Q. "He dreams of scaffolds while smoking his hooka." Do you remember the name of the figure in Baudelaire's poem?

A. *Ennui.* Boredom. Boredom dreams of scaffolds. Boredom has a secretive smile. Boredom has no genuine emotions. Boredom dreams of corpses . . . The more I look at him, the more transparent he becomes. Why did he marry Dora? Why didn't he protest that she was carrying another man's child? Why didn't he hide the fact that he amputated the wrong leg of a patient? He never cared one way or another. He doesn't have reasons for his actions. He is careless. Easy come, easy go.

Q. One more question. Did you endorse Hen's philosophy?

A. The *Meditations* of Marcus Aurelius has splendid things to say about kindness. Marcus Aurelius was a Roman emperor. He didn't reveal anything about the tens of thousands of human beings who were slaughtered, enslaved, and tortured during his rule. At least he had a heart. He cared.

Q. No more questions . . .

At two-fifteen she remained on duty. She was outside the TB ward, sitting on the steps and smoking a cigarette—it would, she promised herself, be her last—when she heard, off in the city in the direction of Cerillos Road, repeated blasts of a car-horn. When she identified the car that was making the noise and saw in it a man who was waving his arm and making the V-for-Victory sign, she, if only she, understood the significance of the sign and rushed to be excused from duty.

In retrospect, from the moment she left the Center to the moment she saw the Harley and the boots, she had been self-contained and self-possessed. She saw Creeping Jesus in the plaza. She saw the olive-drab "U. S. Army Corps of Engineers" truck parked in the shade of the street across from her house. It was the Harley and the boots that really arrested her attention.

Why would Aeneas prop the Harley up in the street outside the gate to the house? He was seldom so careless he would leave an expensive toy, let alone a toy belonging to her, out where it could be stolen. The empty pair of boots meant dead soldiers, did it not?

Her heartbeat quickened. She stopped the car in the gateway and turned off the ignition.

She seemed to be out of her body. She grabbed the revolver from her purse, half ran to the rear of the house, and entered it by the wide-open kitchen door. It was as if an energy had poured into her blood through an umbilical cord connected to an infallible and inexhaustible source. She cocked the hammer of the revolver. A buzzing of flies directed her gaze to Aida's mutilated body. Hearing the howling in the master bedroom, she flew there without pausing to reflect upon her actions. Instinctively, though poised, as soon as she saw Diana rising from the floor and Aeneas touching a blood stain on his shirt, she aimed her revolver at Turner and squeezed the trigger. She returned to her body then without trailing a semblance of either sorrow or righteousness.

UNIDENTIFIED AUTHORITIES ON THE HILL must have known exactly what to do, because after Aeneas telephoned P.O. Box 1683 he advised Trinc and Diana not to call or talk to the police. While they were waiting for agents from Los Alamos to show up, he incinerated his clothes in an oil drum in the back yard, took a hot bath, shaved, and let Trinc bandage his superficial wound before he dressed in t-shirt and Bermuda shorts. By late afternoon the agents had come and were satisfied with the Caldwells' stories, had removed Turner's body, had cleaned up the mess in the bedroom, and had called in the local police to ponder the murder of Aida Martínez. The next morning a local paper printed the story of a woman murdered by an unknown intruder and of another woman murdered by an unknown rapist.

A suspect, it was reported, had been seen in Mesilla, a border town associated with Billy the Kid, but he had disappeared into Mexico. Turner's name was never mentioned.

But he had an afterlife. He had not waited for Aeneas's resignation to circulate lies. A few days after the bombing of Hiroshima the administration of South Atlantic University sent Aeneas a letter advising him his appointment had been terminated on grounds of moral turpitude. He and Trinc, after consulting with an attorney, decided against returning to Poe's Hill to fight an expensive legal battle for reinstatement. Such appeals, especially when a plaintiff had political enemies arrayed against him, were seldom successful. Although Peregrine Pinker, Dean of Divinity, hadn't seen anything at the Bright Leaf Hotel that amounted to more than what Aeneas described as "a shit hill of beans," no one was going to believe that Aeneas and Blevyn had not been caught in flagrante delicto. Moreover, the correlation of total death with eroticism was sure to make an atomic physicist into a subject for endless ridicule. In future, young women were certain to wear a bathing suit in the shape of a mushroom cloud with Ground Zero coyly prophesied in the crease of a dainty diaper.

On the day the Japanese surrendered in mid-August Ma-Betty had arranged for the family to come to Taos for a luncheon party with Blevyn and her grandparents, the Skyes having left Los Angeles on their way back to Throstle's Nest with a stopover in Taos to deliver Blevyn's truck and belongings. Billy had a temporary driving license. He was more than delighted to take the wheel of the Ford and demonstrate to his parents their obsolescence. Diana and Karl followed in the Daimler.

Before taking the road to Taos, Aeneas showed Trinc the letter Blevyn had written him about her cross-country journey with the Skyes and subsequent internment with her mother at Tule Lake.

"The Japanese were our enemies, no doubt about it, my enemies, too," Aeneas remarked, "but I don't think we would have decided to use atomic bombs against them if we hadn't already dehumanized them. In other words, if we had all of us come to know and understand Blevyns, as I did, and Juns, as we and Uncle Doc did, and the Peruvians as you did, that word 'enemies' could have been modified to include images of 'friends'."

So Trinc looked forward to meeting Blevyn at the Blumberg's ranchhouse. When in fact everyone had gathered for cocktails in Ma-Betty's living room and Blevyn arrived in her truck from the *morada*, Trinc took one look at her in her Saks Fifth Avenue suit and had to admit that Aeneas had good taste in women. Blevyn was indeed a beautiful girl—*well, a woman of thirty-five must have beauty from within*—she had a good figure—*well, she starved in that concentration camp*—she had a pretty face—*but that scar on her cheek looks as if it has been sewn with baling wire.* Ma-Betty, Archie, and Flora obviously adored Blevyn. *Well, she's no threat to me.* Trinc liked her.

After Blevyn showed the family what she called her "medieval" accommodations at the *morada*, she asked "Professor Caldwell" to tell of his life there and in New Mexico near the turn of the century. *Socially adroit. Let's him know he's too old for her.* Aeneas, hitherto strangely bashful, began to talk stories which the children had never heard before, of Tiresias the half-blind horse, of trading eggs for chocolate, of lowering food into a well in lieu of a refrigerator, of encountering armed Navajo Indians on the trail to Chaco Canyon where he found the skeletal remains of his father.

"Where was the river where, you know, the hired thugs assaulted you?" Trinc prompted with a wink.

Aeneas took the cue. "Rio Hondo. Turley's Mill. You know, back in the old days, there was a fella named Turley, made a whiskey called Taos Lightning. The trappers and the mountain men and the army deserters from down Mexico way used to come to the mill and drink themselves into a stupor. And so when there was this rebellion—1847 I'm talking about—300 Mexicans and Indians snuck up and surrounded the mill, meaning to scalp everyone in it the way they had just scalped Governor Bent . . ."

"Blevyn?" Trinc beckoned her to the door. When they were in bright sun, she addressed Blevyn with a feeling of intimacy. "How do I get to Turley's Mill from here? Can I walk?"

"I won't hear of it," Blevyn said. "We can take my truck along Hondo rim. It's only a short switchback for us to walk to the river. Shall I take a bottle of wine?"

A few minutes later they were jouncing in the truck along a washboard road. In less than twenty minutes they were following a trail beside the roaring, tree-lined, sparkling white waters of the Hondo. Soon they entered a canyon in the midst of which were strewn the rocky ruins of the abandoned whiskey mill.

A place of stones, Trinc recalled with a tight feeling in her chest. Had the sun been setting in the west, she realized, she would have seen a magenta sky where the river cleft rocks of the canyon walls, would have seen everything as it had been in her dream except silhouetted men and Bruno Rancis with the lance that was an ice-pick. She shuddered not from remembered terror but in awe of the relationship between a dream and reality. How passing strange the timeless bonding of two souls!

Blevyn gave her a paper cup, poured a red wine into it, and gestured for her to follow. "Ma-Betty showed me something magical over there where boulders have tumbled down from the cliffs . . . It's a petroglyph inscribed by the Old Ones over a thousand years ago. It may be all ye need to know on earth . . ." When they came close to the boulder, Trinc saw etched in it a small series of circles with a dot in the center. "Ma-Betty says it signifies the interrelationship of all things."

Trinc ran forward with a cry, so unexpected was the sight of the simple symbol and yet so apt that it evoked in her a feeling of awe and reverence. Whereas she had long avoided the formalized church, its hierarchic and patriarchic pattern of relationship to the creative source seeming to demand obedience to a power "out there" and a willed effort to be assimilated into it, experience had engendered in her another pattern: she was recognizing it as the dot within the circles signifying no blind seeking of her self outside herself, no abject dependence on outer objects and persons. She was related to and reconciled with an eternal order beyond local boundaries of time and space. She and Aeneas, she believed, had been interrelated all along, part of an all-pervading universal drama, each an individual, each a dot, a central spiritual core connected to an always present power of the outer circle, be it family, society, or ultimately the cosmos.

On sudden impulse she held her hand out to Blevyn, who took it. "May I think of you as my sister?" She squeezed Blevyn's hand. Her first "sister," Tubby, had been worth every bit of a similar impulse.

"I'd love it."

The two of them hugged.

"I have some letters," Blevyn was saying as they drank wine, sat on a rock, dangled bare feet in icy mountain water. "Some of them Professor Caldwell addressed to me at the time of Pearl Harbor. They really belong to you . . . I mean, he never intended for me to have them. He was communing with himself."

"I think I know what you mean," Trinc said. "I let him down, oblivious to his need to communicate the hell he was going through. When I read his letter to a 'Lady', I got angry instead of realizing that he feels related to the Mother Goddess of Creation. She is the circle."

"I'll give them to you later, along with an excerpt from my diary," Blevyn went on, "but I want you to know, as my sister, how much they meant to me at a critical moment in my life. My mother, Minnie, died a year after we were interned at Tule Lake, died of cancer. It went undetected for quite some time despite her visits to indifferent camp physicians. She was getting a temperature every morning and having a funny feeling in her chest. She would go to the hospital and tell the doctor, 'There is something wrong with me', and the doctor would tell her, 'It's all in your head' . . . Finally a surgeon from Fresno found a cancer well advanced. It was too late to do anything. Minnie was sent to Klamath Falls Hospital. She had to go alone."

Blevyn blinked away tears, splashed cold water on her face, resumed. "I couldn't get a clearance to go with her. She went to Klamath Falls and died all alone. Before she went she wrapped her wedding ring in a handkerchief and gave it to me. 'I love you', she said. 'I'll never see you again', she said. After word came that she had died, I became depressed. I didn't know whether I could make it through. But I started re-reading Professor Caldwell's letters, over and over, especially the first ones which weren't addressed to me but to a creative power whose love, he said, encompasseth all things . . . He gave me *heart*."

"Speaking of depression," Trinc said after a long pause, "I'm worried about Diana. She had a traumatic experience recently. A man tried to rape her. She doesn't talk to me about it, but I think she has decided not to go to college this fall. Instead, she wants to be near Karl Playfair . . . I was wondering, do you think she could come to live with you in Los Remedios until she has things sorted out? I know you'd do her a world of good."

"She's a lovely girl," Blevyn said. "I'd like nothing better."

When they returned to the *morada* an hour later, Billy came rushing up to the truck. "Mom, can I go with Diana and Karl to the celebration downtown? We can all stay at Ma-Betty's tonight and come home in the Daimler tomorrow. Dad said it would be all right."

"I celebrated the end of the first war by deciding to become a nurse," Trinc said. "You celebrate the end of this war by thanking the stars you didn't have to fight it . . . What is it, Diana?"

Diana had climbed out of the waiting Daimler and come running, face beaming. "Look, Mom! Look at what Karl gave me!" She exhibited an engagement ring on her finger.

ALTHOUGH SHE HAD GIVEN UP CAMPAIGNING as being overly assertive, Trinc still stuck pins in the metaphorical map from time to time. The most difficult pin to move was for Aeneas and herself, from Santa Fe to England. She loved New Mexico, she loved her house even though she could never *un*-remember the crimes there committed. Billy's pin moved between school in Andover and vacation home with Ma-Betty in Taos; if he won a scholarship to Yale, his pin had but to move between New Haven and Taos. As for Diana, her pin, Los Remedios, would soon join Karl's in Princeton. Trinc didn't like the idea of couples living together before marriage—to her surprise, because she had, as a girl, gone to bed with Aeneas with no reservations. It seemed, willy-nilly, Diana and Karl would be sharing an apartment in Princeton until they sailed for England, to be married at Christmas in Cambridge at "the Catholic," as Tubby called it.

The houses in Santa Fe and Poe's Hill were sold profitably, precious belongings either distributed to family or stored away. Diana kept the Daimler; the Ford and the Harley were garaged in Taos until Billy went to college, whereupon they would be his. In May of 1946 Trinc quit her job at the Detention Center. It was being closed anyway to the quiet relief of Santa Feans. She and Aeneas spent the summer as Ma-Betty's guests in order to have the family together one last time. Then in August they took the train from Lamy to New York. Already in New York was Blevyn whose one-person show was opening at a gallery in the Village. The plan was, Blevyn would join them at Uncle Doc's for a luncheon party a week prior to the boat's departure for England.

Aeneas's health had Trinc worried. He was not only anemic, he was also periodically afflicted by diarrhea, hemorrhages, and skin infections. He was subject to moods of crankiness bordering upon despair. "Something I picked up at Trinity," he said. He wouldn't say what it was. Several times he alluded mysteriously to a dying wolf he had seen at Los Alamos. Trinc didn't press him for an explanation. In a way she didn't want one. He was, she believed, dying the death of that wolf.

The obviously dying "wolf," the one who was breaking her heart with his frail and trembling body, his blue eyes without brightness, his failing mind and air of being submerged in another time and place was Uncle Doc. Well could she understand Blevyn's feelings about the most beloved parent who has to go to the last oubliette alone. She hoped that Mallie Devine, martyred in China, was right, that death was not annihilation but a transformation.

There were at Uncle Doc's dining room table in the old brownstone near Central Park just Uncle Doc and his four guests, Trinc, Aeneas, Blevyn and Jun Takamatsu, the latter still in Ike-jacket covered with a fruit salad of ribbons and medals.

Uncle Doc, who had listened to Aeneas's lament about the bombing of Hiroshima and Nagasaki, put a glass of wine down with shaking hand and said, "Leonardo planned a submarine. He feared that man would not apply it to the constructive uses of civilization, but, instead, to its ruin. He did not carry out his plans. Mankind did not think as Leonardo. Still doesn't. But I tell you." He reared back in his wheelchair. For a moment his eyes flared with old fire. "Teddy and I tried to put through a platform for national health insurance way back, Bull Moose days, and the A.M.A. wouldn't hear of it. Recently Senator Wagner tried to introduce a comprehensive national-health-insurance bill that would have covered almost everyone in the country. 0. K., failed again. Now we have the Hill-Burton bill. It provides federal grants to build hospitals all around the country. Get the idea? The bulk of medical practice will be moved out of the doctor's office and into hospitals where our new diagnostic, surgical, and therapeutic techniques developed by research can be put into practice. That means we're winning the battle to have government involved with medicine. Give us another twenty years or so and, by God, we'll have people covered, at least the elderly! . . . Get the idea? The only thing you can count on is change, and sometimes it's change for the better. We might abolish your Bomb and even catch up with Leonardo before we pack in the human race." He sat back, fire going out.

"Changing the subject," Trinc cut in with a glance at Jun, "are you going to Cornell Medical School when you leave the Army?"

"You bet he is," answered Uncle Doc. "He's got so many bullets in him he's going to learn how to take 'em out with his own hands! Reminds me of Teddy . . ."

Jun smiled shyly, rested eyes on Blevyn. It seemed to Trinc that a soldier who listened to nightingales during a bombardment would make Blevyn a fine husband. Blevyn loved him, she could tell.

It was not, then, altogether surprising what happened as the party was breaking up. Jun, who was going to Blevyn's show and had already escorted her downstairs to the front door, limped back upstairs and burst upon the company with face lit by amusement.

"Dr. Knight!" he cried dramatically, hands over heart. "I'm in love!"

Later that evening Trinc and a nurse wheeled Uncle Doc to his bedroom and settled him into bed for the night. He had a high fever and was moving his lips with words Trinc couldn't comprehend until she bent her head near to him. "Teddy, Teddy," he was muttering.

"What is it, Uncle Doc? Do you miss Teddy?" she asked in quiet voice.

"Teddy," he said not to her but to a hallucination, "there's something I've been meaning to tell you for a long time. The Riders and I don't want you to get upset. We're with you all the way. Call us and we're riding in and we're going to put things right, the way they ought to be . . . Teddy, they've fenced us in, Teddy. They've fenced in the whole buzzard-pissin' world . . ."

GARBAGE-JUNKIE SEAGULLS yo-yo'd and *creek-creeked* in the wake of the reconverted troop ship as it sailed down the Hudson. Most of the passengers were top-deck, scanning the New York skyline with its checkerboard pattern of nightlights.

"There must be a million women over there," Aeneas pointed,

"down on their knees scrubbing floors."

Trinc snuggled closer under his arm. "What do you mean by that?"

"Oh," he said, "it means that women are the unacknowledged legislators of the world." Putting hand over mouth, he coughed.

"You're going to catch another cold. Are you feeling all right?"

"Look over there." He pointed. "We are exiles."

The ship was passing the Statue of Liberty.

"Caldwell," she said, "don't be cranky. We're going to Cambridge to write your book and you'll be coming back in two years to your new professorship, Berkeley or Princeton, whatever you decide."

"No," he said, "I let down my science. I let you down, too. You should have married somebody whose head wasn't stuffed with goofy dreams about abolition of nuclear weapons."

She groaned, shook his arm. "Don't talk like that! You're my prince! Listen, love! Listen to the waves! Listen—remember?— 'the stillness between two waves of the sea'."

For more than a year they had been reading aloud to one another from T.S. Eliot's *Four Quartets* and could quote by heart many lines, including the concluding ones. Quoting from them, Trinc had found a sure way to raise Aeneas out of gloom and renew his acceptance of a redemptive vision that lay at the very ground-zero of their souls.

Aeneas gazed out to sea. She heard him quote: "'At the source of the longest river' . . ." He turned to look at her. "The longest river is human time falling into the sea of eternity. . . . 'The voice of the hidden waterfall' . . ."

". . . 'And the children in the apple tree'," Trinc said. "What, Professor, does the voice of the children in the apple tree symbolize?"

"Oh, dear," Aeneas sighed. He had recovered his humor, his tone of self-mockery about inadequacy about himself as poet. "Eliot wrote the last quartet during the London Blitz. Smoking ruins. Purgatorial fire. Out of such images there came to him the simple image of the children's voice half-heard from a regenerated Garden-of-Eden apple tree. The image symbolizes the mystical moments of insight that arrive to save us from ourselves . . . How's that?"

"Haven't we been lucky, dear," Trinc said, "half-hearing the voice of the children in the apple tree?"

"'Deed we have," Aeneas said, "'deed we have."

"And you," she said, "have sacrificed everything in order that children may sing."

NOT FROM THE PERSPECTIVE OF JULY 16, 1945, nor from that of August 6, 1945, when an atomic bomb was dropped on Hiroshima and the secret work of scientists at Los Alamos was disclosed, but from the perspective of autumnal days in 1947 when Aeneas was writing his "Sketches for a Memoir" in his tutorial rooms at St. John's College, Cambridge, England, did certain events of his life come into final focus. Often, then, writing at ocean's length from his beloved country, he paused to listen to the close-by *ting clang ting clang*, like a harbor buoy in fog, of the Trinity College clock. Before him, open, lay Wordsworth's *The Prelude*. As an undergraduate at St. John's in 1787 Wordsworth had heard the same sound at the same distance:

> *Near me was Trinity's loquacious Clock,*
> *Who never let the Quarters, night or day,*
> *Slip by him unproclaim'd, and told the hours*
> *Twice over with a male and female voice . . .*

A few lines further on in the poem, Aeneas often read:

> *And, from my Bedroom, I in moonlight nights*
> *Could see right opposite, a few yards off,*
> *The Antechapel, where the Statue stood*
> *Of Newton, with his Prism and silent face. . .*

And still further on, the great and inspiring lines:

The marble index of a mind for ever
Voyaging through strange seas of Thought, alone.

Aeneas could, like Wordsworth, see right opposite his rooms at St. John's the Trinity antechapel with its statue of Sir Isaac Newton. The sight filled him with awe and reverence and gratitude. Who would have dreamed that he would be ending his life in such close proximity, as it were, to the founder of modern science? Who would have dreamed that here in Cambridge a quarter of a century ago he would be present during the exciting—and humane—early stages of the Age of Atoms? Dying now of leukemia, the likely result of exposure to radiation at another, but unholy, Trinity, he, presumably like a billion others worldwide, could reflect upon the morally unjustified sacrifice of more than 100,000 innocents in the atomic bombing of Hiroshima. But Newton's voyaging through strange seas of Thought, alone, reassured him of the value and necessity of free inquiry unfenced and permitted him to forgive himself: he had upheld the honor of living. When he had stopped to bless the eagle, he had honored life, itself—at the price of his own. Perhaps in his fifty-seven years he could not have done much more. He could certainly not have done any less.

But who would have dreamed he would fall afoul of the Laurentian indictment of the American soul, not that he was altogether hard, isolate, stoic and a killer? Who would have dreamed that his belated repudiation of weapons of mass annihilation—for the sake of science and for the sake of children not yet born—would be compromised? Retaliation he had expected. Support he had believed possible. Already the number of concerned scientists and leaders were increasing. And so when he was fired from South Atlantic University on the spurious grounds as supplied by Turner, he had not been entirely surprised. But who would have dreamed that Turner would be killed and that Oppenheimer would reject Aeneas's letter of resignation? Although universities in California had invited him to join their faculty, he had accepted the Fellowship offered him at St. John's because, in America, he had become a hero and seemed to have the benefit of a free ride, exactly what he didn't want.

Framed on the wall of his tutorial room was the front page of the Late City Edition of the *New York Times* for August 7, 1945. When he took off his reading glasses, he saw the familiar headline plainly enough:

FIRST ATOMIC BOMB DROPPED ON JAPAN; MISSILE IS EQUAL TO 20,000 TONS OF TNT; TRUMAN WARNS FOE OF A "RAIN OF RUIN"

This was the glory he had abdicated. In a cruel irony another newspaper had published photographs of the "heroic" scientists—including one of himself. So how could he then have said, I *abjure*?

From the perspective of autumnal days in 1947, as he was slowly and painfully dying in voluntary exile, he could survey the world he was leaving and find signs of hope. Although Uncle Doc had died the evening of the party, he had been faithful: Trinc was financially secure for the rest of her life. More than that, Uncle Doc's lifetime dream of a national health program for the elderly, though still beset with political difficulties, would assuredly one day become the law of the land. The Playfairs had been faithful: they had secured him his Fellowship at St. John's. Karl, now at Princeton and talking of plans to put a man on the moon, had married Diana; they were expecting their first child by Christmas. Billy had just matriculated on an academic scholarship to Yale. To help him in his determination to become a writer, Aeneas and Trinc had deposited with him a box of family letters and chronicles. Then there was Blevyn. After a successful opening of her one-person show in New York in

1946, her promise as an artist was being fulfilled. Recently, too, there had come the news of her engagement to Jun Takamatsu. He had returned from Italy in time to attend Uncle Doc's last party, had met Blevyn there, and been smitten. Ma-Betty was still alive and well and living in Taos and seeking a recipe for grasshopper molasses.

As for Trinc, what could he think beyond what he already knew and approved, that wherever the International Red Cross in London would ask her to go, she would go, that wherever there were signs of apocalypse, whether in Europe, Africa, Asia or South America, she would be there?

Though he would never finish writing the book of his dreams, "The New Physics and the Coming World of Conscience," his lectures on the subject at Cambridge and at Oxford and over the B.B.C. Third Programme had been received enthusiastically. He was confident that, just over the horizon, as 2,000 years of personal, tribal, and national separations came to a close, there would indeed and at last be a new world.

Afterword

For portions of this novel I am indebted to a number of persons, either for unpublished reminiscences or for anecdotal information. My mother, Elizabeth Cheney Blackburn, was a student nurse in New York in the 1920s, and I have drawn upon her recollection of that experience. My grandfather, Hugh A. Bayne, has provided me with miscellaneous information about World War I, life in France, and New Orleans. The Mrs. Jacques Busbee Collection, North Carolina State Archives, has given me a glimpse into folkways in rural North Carolina a century ago. On the ordeal of the Native American Sun Dance and its healing properties, I have consulted Dr. Steven Wong, a Denver psychiatrist who has twice participated in the ritual. Finally, I am grateful to Bill Hosokawa, who kindly agreed to advise me about Japanese American experiences in the United States during World War II.

The following is a partial bibliography of works consulted during composition of the novel. Whatever the degree of my indebtedness, usually very slight, I remain grateful to the authors. In particular, the book by Professor Gar Alperovitz, listed below, has been an invaluable guide.

Gar Alperovitz, *The Decision to Use the Atomic Bomb and the Architecture of an American Myth*; Lawrence Badesh et al, *Reminiscences of Los Alamos*; Kenneth T. Bainbridge, *Trinity*; Edward Barnhard, "Japanese Internees from Peru," *Pacific Historical Review*, May 1962; Tad Bartimus and Scott

McCartney, *Trinity's Children*; Hans A. Bethe, *The Road from Los Alamos*; Larry Bograd, *Los Alamos Light*; Allen Bosworth, *America's Concentration Camps*; Paul Boyer, *By the Bomb's Early Light*; Bernice Brode, *Tales of Los Alamos*; McGeorge Bundy, *Danger and Survival*; Glyn G. Caldwell et al, "Leukemia Among Participants in Military Maneuvers at a Nuclear Bomb Test," *Journal of the American Medical Association*, 244:14 (3 Oct 1980):1575-78; Fritjof Capra, *The Tao of Physics*; Arthur Compton, *Atomic Quest*; Jean Crawford, *Jugtown Pottery*; Roger Daniels, *Concentration Camps USA*; Nuel P. Davis, *Lawrence and Openheimer*; Alan Donagan, *Theory of Morality*; Larry Dorsey, *Space, Time & Medicine*; John W. Dower, *War Without Mercy*; Sir Arthur Eddington, *Space, Time, and Gravitation*; Walter M. Elasser, *Memoirs of a Physicist in the Atomic Age*; Herbert Feis, *The Atomic Bomb and the End of World War II*; Laura Fermi, *Atoms in the Family*; Phyllis Fisher, *Los Alamos Experiences*; A. P. French and P. J. Kennedy, eds., *Niels Bohr*; David H. Frisch, "Scientists and the Decision to Drop the Bomb," *Bulletin of the Atomic Scientists*, 26:6 (Jun 1970):107-115; Clinton Harvey Gardiner, *Pawns in a Triangle of Hate*; Deborah Gesensway and Mindy Roseman, *Beyond Words*; James Gleck, *Genius*; Peter Goodchild, *J. Robert Oppenheimer*; Stephane Groueff, *Manhatten Project*; Leslie R. Groves, *Now It Can Be Told*; Stephen Harper, *Miracle of Deliverance*; Ann Koto Hayashi, *Face of the Enemy, Heart of a Patriot*; James H. Hershberg, *James B. Conant*; Jameke Highwater, *Ritual of the Wind*; Bill Hosokawa, *Nisei*; Daniel K. Inouye, with Lawrence Elliot, *Journey to Washington*; Sir James Jeans, *The Mysterious Universe*; Eleanor Jette, *Inside Box 1663*; Joseph G. Jorgensen, *The Sun Dance Religion*; Robert Jungk, *Brighter Than a Thousand Suns*; Takeo Kaneshiro, comp., *Internees*; Fred Kaplan, *The Wizards of Armageddon*; David Kevles, *The Physicists*; Daisuke Kitagawa, *Issei and Nisei*; James W. Kunetka,

City of Fire; Douglas P. Lackey, *Moral Principles and Nuclear Weapons*; Lansing Lamont, *Day of Trinity*; William Lanouette, with Bela Silard, *Genius in the Shadows*; Lawrence LeShan, "Physicists and Mystics: Similarities in World View," *Journal of Transpersonal Psychology*, 1:2 (1969):1-20; Los Alamos Historical Society, *Behind Tall Fences*; Los Alamos Scientific Lab, *Los Alamos*; Fern Lyon and Jacob Evans, eds., *Los Alamos*; David McCullough, *Truman*; Frank McNitt, *Richard Wetherill*; Carey McWilliams, *Prejudice*; Jerre Mangione, *An Ethnic at Large*; Katrina R. Mason, *Children of Los Alamos*; Mine Okubo, *Citizen 13660*; Gwen Raverat, *Period Piece*; Richard Rhodes, *The Making of the Atomic Bomb*; Blackwell P. Robinson, *Moore County, North Carolina*, 1747-1847; Santa Fe *New Mexican*, 20 and 21 Mar 1946; Jonathan Schell, *The Abolition* and *The Fate of the Earth*; Claudio G. Segré, *Atoms, Bombs, & Eskimo Kisses*; Martin J. Sherwin, *A World Destroyed*; Alice Kimball Smith, "The Decision to Use the Atomic Bomb, Chicago, 1944-45," *Bulletin of the Atomic Scientists*, 14 (Oct 1958):351-2; Monica Sone, *Nisei Daughter*; Edward H. Spicer et al, *Impounded People*; Arthur Steiner, "Baptism of the Atomic Scientists," *Bulletin of the Atomic Scientists*, 31:2 (Feb 1975):21-28; Henry L. Stimson, "The Decision to Use the Atomic Bomb," *Harper's*, Feb 1947; Ferenc Morton Szasz, *The Day the Sun Rose Twice*; Dorothy Thomas and Richard S. Nishimoto, *The Spoilage*; Michael Uhl and Tod Ensign, *GI Guinea Pigs*; Stanislaw Ulam, *Adventures of a Mathematician*; Renée Weber, *Dialogues with Scientists and Sages*; Michi Weglyn, *Years of Infamy*; Alfred North Whitehead, *Science and the Modern World*; Jane S. Wilson and Charlotte Serber, eds., *Standing By and Making Do*; Peter Wyden, *Day One*.

Have you seen
our other
Rhyolite Press
Publications . . ?

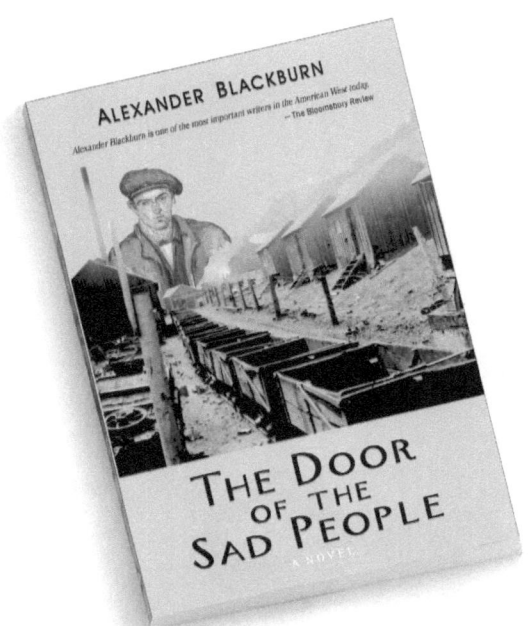

The Door
of the
Sad People
by Alexander Blackburn

The Door of the Sad People is one of the most remarkable books I have read, ever. It caught me pleasurably off guard at almost every turn.

> —Fred Chappell - Recipient of the Bollingen Prize for Poetry, Yale University

$16.95 at bookstores everywhere, or direct from the publisher:
www.rhyolitepress.com

ISBN 978-0-9896763-4-2

THE DOOR OF THE SAD PEOPLE is a coming-of-age story that takes place against the background of the Colorado coalmining wars long-remembered for the Ludlow Massacre of 1914. Visionary, the novel traces the tyrannous countenance of a corporate society to its origins in humankind's "sad" limitations and flaws.

Young Tree Penhallow escapes an abusive father and an attempted murder but finds a surrogate father in "Kill Devil" Dare, a friend in Mother Jones, "the miners' angel," and a home in a loving, once-patrician Hispanic family now eking out a hardscrable life through farming and mining. When his adoptive family is almost entirely exterminated by militia during a strike, a spiritual "door" opens, confirming for Tree the eternal truth of compassion, how it holds humanity together.

Tree Penhallow matures into an artist and hero who confronts the violent and perverse powers of evil, a theme as relevant to today's world as it was to the world of yesterday.

————

Every once in a while a good unknown writer gets anointed, the Pulitzer committee issues a prize, and sales jump. Still, for every winner there are scores of writers who are as good but are virtually unread. To that list of unknown writers, good writers toiling in obscurity, add the name of Alexander Blackburn. —*The Dallas Morning News*

Colorado Noir is a walk on the dark and wild side of America's
most controversial city. Ten stories and one novella.

$16.95 at bookstores everywhere, or direct from the publisher:
www.rhyolitepress.com

ISBN 978-0-9896763-0-4

Colorado Noir by John Dwaine McKenna

2014 Silver Medal Winner for Fiction/Mystery/Noir

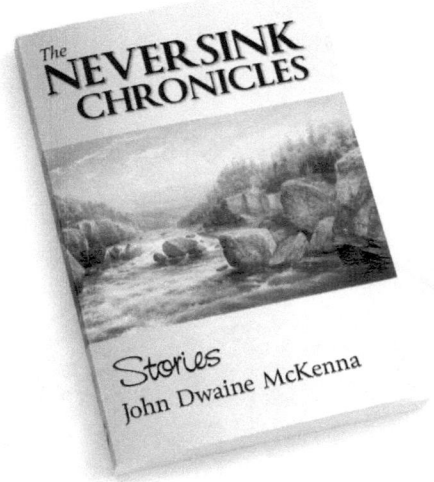

<u>Praise for *The Neversink Chronicles*</u>

"A gifted and natural born story teller with command of dialog and dialect. Congratulations!"
—Clark Secrest, Author, *Hells Bells,* San Diego, CA

"A gifted storyteller. An amazing first book. Keep writing, you have a great future ahead of you."
—Allison Auch, Copy Editor, Durango, CO

"Hated parting with the manuscript, as I knew things were changing quickly in *Neversink.* That's when you know you have a great book in your hands."
—*Leigh Daily,* Paralegal, Boulder, CO

"This is a book to read over and over. The people are real, the life is true and the author has to have been everywhere and met everyone to have captured all of these personalities so well. I'm waiting for more from him."
—Mary Lelia, Austin,Texas

" 'Just Another Day', gave me chills remembering my own Vietnam experience".
—Skip Mooney, Financial Consultant, Manitou Springs, CO

". . . and the winner, First Prize for fiction, 2012 goes to . . .
The Neversink Chronicles"

18th Annual CIPA Awards Ceremony
Denver, CO May 17, 2012

The Whim - Wham Man

A STORY THAT HAS IT ALL . . .
A CRIME YOU CAN'T FORGIVE
A PLOT YOU COULDN'T IMAGINE
AND A CHARACTER . . .
YOU'LL NEVER FORGET!

There's no sanitary way to write about murder.
"The Whim-Wham Man," a gut-punching novel of a teen-aged
boy whose idyllic life in rural Colorado comes crashing down
when reality and adulthood rush in after the brutalization and
savage killing of two young girls . . . **It's a helluva yarn.**

CIPA EVVY Award Winner, 2013
2nd prize, Best Fiction

$15 at bookstores everywhere, or direct from the publisher:
www.rhyolitepress.com

ISBN 978-0-9839952-2-7

Praise for *The Whim-Wham Man*

"It's a helluva yarn."
—Dick Kreck, Author of *Murder at the Brown Palace* and *Smaldone*

"Great Job! It got my blood boiling! Then it got my mind thinking."
—Linda Comando, Publisher and Editor of *The Tri-Valley Townsman*

"It was like eating popcorn . . . I couldn't quit. . Congratulations. I am looking forward to more Jake McKern novels."
—Bill Calls, Scottsdale, AZ

"This short book with the odd title is the hard-to-put-down story of a 15-year-old youth who grows up in a hurry when a grisly tragedy strikes his family."
—Mary Jean Porter, *The Pueblo Chieftain*

"Well-written, so compelling I couldn't stop reading until the last page."
—S.M. Albany, NY

"*The Whim-Wham Man* is the most thought-provoking novel I've read in a long time. Thanks for writing it."
—Kathy Hare, *The New Falcon Herald*

". . . and the silver award winner for fiction 2013 is . . .
The Whim-Wham Man."
19th Annual CIPA EVVY Awards, Denver Co
May 10, 2013

THE BOY WHO SLEPT WITH BEARS

Pulled from the pages of history, a fiction novel that tells the heart wrenching and heartwarming story of Tomas Dequine, or Sak-wa-ma-tu-ta-ci, 'Blue Hummingbird' in his native tongue, a thirteen-year-old Southern Ute boy whose family and way of life are being crushed by the onrush of white European settlers in 1880s Colorado . . . a time when the Utes were being driven off of their ancestral lands to be resettled on reservations. Told in a warm, grandfatherly voice, Douthit's novel is a past winner of a coveted golden CIPA-EVVY award for fiction. It has been read and loved by ages eight to eighty, and contains a reader's guide and bibliography.

One of our hottest novels!

CIPA EVVY Award Winner, 2005
1st prize, Best Fiction

$15 at bookstores everywhere, or direct from the publisher:
www.rhyolitepress.com

ISBN 978-0-9839952-8-9

Praise for *The Boy Who Slept with Bears*

I loved this book. The author, George Douthit, does a beautiful job of taking a young Ute boy and "brother bear" paralleling their lives and trials. This book made me feel like I was right their in the tepee with Tomas and his mother. This book also made me think about the Ute Indians and the many hardships they had after they were forced to move to the reservations. I love how the writer begins to blend history, culture, and symbolism all into one story. Being a Colorado native I really loved the use of historical fact mixed with fiction. I rarely read a book that I want to not end and this was one of these books. I grew to understand Tomas and his relationship with the earth and brother bear. This book is a great book for young and old alike.

—Valorie R. Hornsby, Interior Designer

George Douthit's book *The Boy Who Slept with Bears*, is the moving story of a Southern Ute boy coming of age at a time when the Ute traditional territories were being overrun by non indians during the gold rush and the Utes removal to reservations. The author captures the boy's desire to avenge his father's murder at the hands of white soldiers. He steps from boyhood into a man's world while struggling to hold onto his traditional beliefs. Though fictional, Douthit weaves true historical details of the Southern Utes and a legendary grizzly bear named "Old Mose" into a masterful story that leaves the reader enthralled and captivated.

—Vickie Leigh Krudwig, Author, *Searching for Chipeta*

A terrific read for both young and old! Outstanding! *The Boy Who Slept with Bears* is the best book about native Americans I've ever read. Please send two more copies for my nephews.

—Leonard Foxworth